Missing Man

MISSING MAN

Katherine MacLean

Published by
BERKLEY PUBLISHING CORPORATION
Distributed by
G. P. PUTNAM'S SONS, NEW YORK

Acknowledgments

Several sections, all substantially revised herein, are reprinted from
Analog. *Copyright 1968, 1970, and 1971, by the Conde Nast*
Publications, Inc.

SBN: 399-11474-2

Library of Congress Catalog
Card Number: 74-16610

1

I was heading uptown to the employment office. The sidewalk was soft and green and dappled with tree shadows; the wind was warm.

I stopped by a snack machine, looked at the pictures of breakfast, and watched a man put in his credit card and get out a cup of coffee. He was a young guy, a little older than me. I could smell the coffee. I'd had hot water for lunch and dinner yesterday and hot water for breakfast. It felt good in my stomach but my legs felt weak.

The vibes of morning are always good. People walked by, giving out a kind of cheerfulness. I was blotting up that feeling until suddenly it seemed right that the snack machine should give out some free food just to be friendly.

I shoved my credit card into the slot and pushed levers for a cup of coffee with two creams and two sugars and some hot buttered scrambled eggs. My hands started shaking. My mouth watered. I could smell from people's windows the perfume of bacon and toasted plankton and hot butter on hot toast.

The machine blinked a red sign, "000.00 balance," and my credit card rolled out of the slot. I reached for it and dropped it.

The man drinking coffee looked at my shaking hands and then at my face. Hunger doesn't show on the outside. I'd lost a hundred pounds already and I wasn't even skinny yet. He couldn't feel my vibes. I have a kind of round, cheerful face, like a kid, but I'm big.

I picked up the card and grinned at him. He grinned back.

"Hard night?" he asked sympathetically, meaning had I spent a night with a girlfriend?

I made an "okay" sign with one hand and he whistled and went away grinning, giving out happy vibes of remembering great long sex nights when he'd had the shakes in the morning.

I tried two more snack machines in the next three blocks. No food.

The best food machines in lower New York City are in the artists' and sculptors' commune. Artists don't like to cook when they're working on something. I passed it on the way to the employment office and went in. I went through a big pillared arcade with a ground-level park under the half ring of building, a terraced set of parks, like balconies or shelves hanging out. I could hear a stone knife whirring and someone hammering. Mixed in among the trees, the working artists were hard to see.

I found the machine that gave Chinese dinners and tried my credit card on that. I pushed for an egg foo yong and looked at the fine food pictures. The machine held my card for a while before rolling it out from another slot. It blinked a red light just once. More polite than the other machines, but it still had no kindness and gave no free food.

"Hello, George," a sculptor called and halted the mallet and chisel he was using to pound chips from a rough statue. The sculptor laughed every time at a joke we had between us, laughing before he said it.

He asked, "How am I, George?"

He was glowing from exercise, enjoying doing sculptures in the classical Greek technique, like Praxiteles'. It was an order for a classical commune, from the Society for Creative Anachronism. Pink health flushed his bald head, curly black hair circled his ears, muscles bulged in his arms. He was feeling a nice buzz from the exercise and his ears were ringing from the afterechoes of his pounding. I felt it all.

"You're fine, Mr. Xerxes," I said. "How am I?"

"Very handsome, George. Losing weight has done you good." He smiled. "Boys and girls will be attracted and chase you and fight for you."

Mr. Xerxes did not know that my credit card had run out. He admired my willpower. Over the last two months he'd watched me lose a hundred fat pounds by just not eating. He'd given me a bottle of reducing metabolites, left over from when he'd reduced, and they'd helped turn the fat to fuel, so I hadn't felt weak, just hungry. Buying two nickel bowls of plankton soup a day to make the last dollars stretch.

2

"Do you have a job for me, Mr. Xerxes? Can I help out?" I stuffed my hands into my pockets to keep them from shaking. The artists' commune used to have errands for me when I was on student support.

"Not today, George." Mr. Xerxes carefully arranged a stone block behind the statue's ear, placed his chisel, and knocked a chip off the ear. His vibes were slightly disapproving. He thought I was too big now for kid errands. He didn't know that they wouldn't give me a job for a man.

I tried a row of five food machines with my credit card, but the machines worked and knew that my balance was 000.00 and held their food behind locked windows.

I went across the street past people going to their jobs. Pretending I was them, not me, I felt healthy and brisk and busy, blotting up their vibes. I went into Commune 1949, the old people's place.

I went up the escalator, just letting it carry me, not running up it, passed two lawns and front-porch floors, and then got off at Mrs. Johnson's floor. She had a small house entirely surrounded by a lawn, and the only way it didn't look like a cottage was that it had the pillars that held up the four corners of the giant building, but she had vines growing on them. I walked through a lawn bright with yellow dandelions and pink clover and rang her bell.

"Come in," she called through the intercom. "I'm in the kitchen."

The door opened into a sweet smell of cake and orange icing that was almost solid, and the living room was like a movie from the forties. It didn't have a television, because television hadn't been around much in '49. The old persons' commune was strict in trying to stay fifty years behind. The whole house smelled like doughnuts and orange cake. Orange cake is my favorite kind, and doughnuts have a smell that is better than any taste.

Mrs. Johnson was in the kitchen, carefully smearing orange icing on a big cake. The sweet smell was overwhelmingly good. A pink cake was on the table. Strawberry or cherry?

I went only halfway in. It was a small kitchen and it wasn't big enough for both of us. Mrs. Johnson is a big person.

"Anything I can do to help?" I asked. When I was little I'd always like to help her.

3

"Yes." She smiled. "You can help me carry these cakes down to the stand. You're just in time for the joke, George. We're running an inflation this week, and these are one-hundred-dollar cakes. Mr. Duggan likes cake."

"Can I clean the icing pan?" There was a pan still part full of pink icing. I tasted it with a finger. Pink peppermint.

She looked at me severely. "George, I've been very proud of you for sticking to your diet. I wouldn't think of tempting you. Sweet things have no nutrition, no nutrition at all. You just stick to your salads."

I'd known she would say that. When I was fat she always gave me cookies.

I picked up the orange cake and she picked up the pink cake and we took them down to the open park at ground level.

All the old people in the commune work for each other and sell to each other. The Social Security money goes around and around like a million dollars. On the way down the escalator she told me that they'd all raised their prices to ten times as much, to get even with Mr. Duggan, the dentist, for raising his prices. The game was being run by Mr. Kracken, who was an economist who used to be a President's economic adviser.

"Mr. Kracken is the shark who always cleans everybody out at poker," she said. "He's our business manager. Dentist Duggan will get a surprise today! He'll eat a home-cooked meal worth a thousand dollars!"

I just nodded, because I couldn't speak. The orange icing was six inches from my mouth as I carried the cake, and I kept my mouth shut to resist the temptation to take a bite. My knees were weak; I put the cake on the front table of the cookies booth. "Gotta go." I left fast and leaned against the wall outside, shaking, seeing black spots.

A sightseers' bus went by slowly on a cushion of air over the green grass center strip, raising a flurry of small yellow butterflies.

I walked uptown fast, trying all the slot machines. None paid off with food. I thought of telling people I was hungry. I looked at the buildings and the dark sky to keep my mind off hunger. Everything was darker, getting cloudy. Sunlight was gone. People went by looking miserable, the good vibes of the morning were gone.

4

I stopped at the employment office, stuck my card into the information slot. Nothing came out. No job notice. No job.

Some friends who knew Zen and Jain Yoga had told me people could go without food for thirty days. They showed me how. The only trouble is, you shake a lot. When I touched a building, it felt as if the world were trembling. I couldn't ask for help. It was like being trapped where no one could hear you. You can't beg.

If I told the employment board that my student support money had run out, if I told them I needed money, they'd give me an adult support pension and a ticket to leave New York and never come back.

Ahmed the Arab came along the sidewalk, going fast, his legs rangy and swinging. Ahmed used to be king of our block gang when we were smaller, and he used to ask me to help him sometimes. This year Ahmed had a job working for the Rescue Squad. Maybe he would let me help him; maybe he could swing a job for me. I liked Ahmed a lot.

I signaled him as he came close. "Ahmed."

He went on by, hurrying. "OK, George, come on."

I fell into stride beside him. "What's the rush?"

"Look at the clouds, man. Something's getting ready to happen. We've got to stop it."

I looked at the clouds. The way I felt was smeared all over the sky. Dangerous, dark, dirty clouds bulged down over the city, looking ready to burst and spill out fire and dirt. In high school Psychology-A they said that people usually see the kinds of things that match their mood. My mood was bad, I could see that, but I still did not know what the sky really looked like—dark, probably, but harmless.

"What is it?" I asked. "Is it smog?"

Ahmed stopped walking, and looked at my face. "No. It's fear."

He was right. Fear lay like a fog across the air. Fear was in the threatening clouds and in the darkness across the faces of the people. People went by under the heavy sky, hunched as if there were a cold rain falling. Buildings above us seemed to be swaying outward.

I shut my eyes, but the buildings seemed to sway out farther.

Last year when Ahmed had been training for the Rescue

5

Squad he'd opened up a textbook and tried to explain something to me about the difference between inner reality and outer reality, and how mobs can panic when they all see the same idea. I opened my eyes and studied the people running at me, past me, and away from me. Just crowds going by. Crowds always rush in New York. Did they all see the buildings as leaning and ready to fall? Were they afraid to mention it?

"Ahmed, you Rescue Squad fink," I said, "what would happen if we yelled *earthquake* good and loud? Would they all panic?"

"Probably so." Ahmed was looking at me with interest, his lean face and black eyes intent. "How do you feel, George? You look sick."

"I feel lousy. Something wrong in my head. Dizzy." Talking made it worse. I braced my hand against a wall. The walls rocked, and I felt as if I were down flat while I was still standing up.

"What in creation is wrong with me?" I asked. "I can't get this sick from skipping a meal or so, can I?" Mentioning food made my stomach feel strange and hollow and dry. I was thinking about death suddenly. "I'm not even hungry," I told Ahmed. "Am I sick?"

Ahmed was the one who knew the answers.

"Man, you've got good pickup." Ahmed studied my face. "Someone near here is in trouble and you're tuned in to it." He glanced at the sky east and west. "Which way is worst? We've got to find him fast."

I looked up Fifth Avenue. The giant glass office buildings loomed and glittered insecurely, showing clouds through in dark green and reflecting clouds in the gray as if dissolving into the sky. I looked along Forty-second Street to the giant arches of the Transport Center. I looked down Fifth Avenue, past the stone lions of the library, and then west to the neon signs and excitement. The darkness came at me with teeth, like a giant mouth. Hard to describe.

"Man, it's bad." I was shaken. "It's bad in every direction. It's the whole city!"

"It can't be," Ahmed said. "It's loud; we must be near where the victim is."

He put his wrist radio up to his mouth and pushed the signal button.

"Statistics, please."

A voice answered, "Statistics."

Ahmed said carefully, "This is a priority call. I'm Rescue Squad badge fifty-four B. Give me today's trends in hospital admissions, all rises above sigma reciprocal thirty. Point the center of any area with a sharp rise in"—he looked at me analytically—"dizziness, fatigue, and acute depression." He considered me further. "Run a check on general anxiety syndromes and hypochondria." He waited for the Statistics Department to collect data.

I wondered if I should be proud or ashamed of feeling sick.

He waited, lean, efficient, impatient, with black eyebrows and black intense eyes. He'd looked almost the same when he was ten and I was nine. His family were immigrants, speaking some non-American language, and they were the proud kind. Another person would burn with hate or love for fights or friends; Ahmed would burn about ideas. His ideas about adventure made him king of our block gang. He'd lead us into strange adventures and grown-up no-trespassing places just to look at things, and when we were trapped he'd lead us out of trouble at high speed or talk his way out with grown-ups. The feel of a place warned me: A bad-luck place looked bad. When he consulted me or asked me how a place looked to me, I'd feel proud.

He'd left us behind. We all dropped out of high school, but Ahmed got good marks, graduated, and qualified for advanced training. All the members of our gang had taken their adult retirement pensions and left the city, except Ahmed and me—and I heard Ahmed was the best detector in the Rescue Squad.

The wrist radio whistled and he put it to his ear. The little voice crackled off figures and statistical terms. Ahmed looked around at the people passing, surprised, then looked at me more respectfully. "It's all over Manhattan. Women coming in with psychosomatic pregnancy. Pregnant women are coming in with nightmares. Men are coming in with imaginary ulcers and cancers. Lots of suicides and lots of hospital commitments for acute suicidal melancholy. You are right. The whole city is in trouble."

He started along Forty-second Street toward Sixth Avenue, walking fast. "Need more help. Try different techniques." A hanging sign announced, GYPSY TEA ROOM, ORIENTAL TEAS, EXOTIC PASTRIES, READINGS OF YOUR PERSONALITY AND FUTURE. Ahmed pushed through a swinging door and went up a moving escalator two steps at a time, with me right after him. We came out into the middle of a wide, low-ceilinged restaurant with little tables and spindly chairs.

Four old ladies were clustered around one table nibbling at cupcakes and talking. A businessman sat at a table near the window reading the *Wall Street Journal*. The teener students sat leaning against the glass wall window looking down into Forty-second Street and its swirling crowds. A fat woman sat at a table in a corner, holding a magazine up before her face. She lowered it and looked at us over the top. The four old ladies stopped talking and the businessman folded his *Wall Street Journal* and put it aside as if Ahmed and I were messengers of bad news. They were all in a miserable, nervous mood like the one I was in —expecting the worst from a doomed world.

Ahmed threaded his way among the tables toward the corner table where the fat woman sat. She put her magazine aside on another table as we approached. Her face was round and pleasant with smile creases all over it. She nodded and smiled at me and then did not smile at Ahmed at all, but instead stared straight back into his eyes as he sat down in front of her.

He leaned across the table. "All right, Bessie, you feel it too. Have you located who it is?"

She spoke in a low, intense voice, as if afraid to speak loudly. "I felt it yesterday for a while, Ahmed. I tried to use the tea leaves to trace it for the Rescue Squad, but she was feeling, not thinking. Today an hour ago it got loud and awful, but echoing and amplifying in so many other people with bad moods that are scared and they keep thinking up so many reasons why they feel so—" She paused and I knew what she was trying to describe. Trying to describe it made it worse. So . . . so . . . trapped, dying, forgotten . . . lost.

She spoke in a lower voice and her round face was worried. "The bad-dream feeling is hanging on, Ahmed. I wonder if I'm—"

She didn't want to talk about it, but Ahmed had his mouth open for a question. I was sorry for her and butted in to stop him.

8

"What do you mean about people making echoes? How come all this crowd . . . ?" I waved my hand in a vague way, indicating the city and the people. The city was not lost.

Ahmed looked at me impatiently. "Adults don't like to use telepathy. They pretend they can't. But say a man falls down an elevator shaft and breaks a leg. No one finds him, and he can't reach a phone, so he'll get desperate and pray and start using mind power. He'll try to send his thoughts as loud as he can. He doesn't know how loud he can send. But the dope doesn't broadcast his name and where he is, he just broadcasts: *'Help! I've got a broken leg!'* People pick up the thought and think it's their thought. They think, 'Help! I've got a broken leg.' People come limping into the emergency clinic and get X rays of good legs. The doctors tell them to go home. But they are picking up the thought, 'Help! I'm going to die unless I get help!' so they hang around the clinics and bother the doctors. They are scared. The Rescue Squad uses them as tracers. Whenever there is an abnormal wave of people applying for help in one district, we try to find the center of the wave and locate someone in real trouble."

The more he talked, the better I felt. It untuned me from the bad mood of the day, and Rescue Squad work was beginning to sound like something I could do. I know how people feel just by standing close to them. Maybe the Rescue Squad would let me join if I showed that I could detect people.

"Great," I said. "What about preventing murders? How do you do that?"

Ahmed took out his silver badge and looked at it. "I'll give you an example. Imagine an intelligent, sensitive kid with a vivid imagination. He is being bullied by a stupid father. He doesn't say anything back; he just imagines what he will do to the big man when he grows up. Whenever the big man gets him mad, the kid clenches his fists and smiles and puts everything he's got into a blast of mental enegy, thinking of himself splitting the big man's skull with an ax. He thinks loud. A lot of people in the district have nothing much to do, nothing much to think about. They never plan or imagine much and they act on the few thoughts that come to them. Get it?"

"The dopes act out what he is thinking." I grinned.

9

Ahmed did not grin. He turned back to the fat woman. "Bessie, we've got to locate this victim. What do the tea leaves say about where she is?"

"I haven't asked." Bessie reached over to the other table and picked up an empty cup. It had a few soggy tea leaves in the bottom. "I was hoping that you would find her." She heaved herself to her feet and waddled into the kitchen.

I was still standing. Ahmed looked at me with a disgusted expression. "Quit changing the subject. Do you want to help rescue someone or don't you?"

Bessie came back with a round pot of tea and a fresh cup on a tray. She put the tray on the table and filled the cup, then poured half of the steaming tea back into the pot. I remembered that a way to get information from the group mind is to see how people interpret peculiar shapes like ink blots and tea leaves, and I stood quietly, trying not to bother her.

She lowered herself slowly into her chair, swirled the tea in the cup, and looked in. We waited. She rocked the cup, looking, then shut her eyes and put the cup down. She sat still, eyes closed, the eyelids squeezed tight in wrinkles.

"What was it?" Ahmed asked in a low voice.

"Nothing, nothing, just a—" She stopped and choked. "Just a damned, lousy, maggoty skull."

That had to be a worse sign than getting the ace of spades in a card cut. Death. I began to get that sick feeling again. Death for Bessie?

"I'm sorry," Ahmed said. "But push on, Bessie. Try another angle. We need the name and address."

"She was not thinking about her name and address." Bessie's eyes were still tightly shut.

Suddenly Ahmed spoke in a strange voice. I'd heard that voice years ago when he was head of our gang, when he hypnotized another kid. It was a deep smooth voice and it penetrated inside of you.

"You need help and no one has come to help you. What are you thinking?"

The question got inside my head. An answer opened up and I started to answer, but Bessie answered first. "When I don't think, just shut my eyes and hold still, I don't feel

10

anything; everything goes far away. When the bad things begin to happen I can stay far away and refuse to come back." Bessie's voice was dreamy.

The same dark sleepy ideas had formed in my own head. She was saying them for me. Suddenly I was afraid that the darkness would swallow me. It was like a night cloud or a pillow floating deep down and inviting you to come and put your head on it, but it moved a little and turned and showed a flash of shark teeth, so you knew it was a shark waiting to eat anyone who came close.

Bessie's eyes snapped open and she straightened herself upright, her eyes so wide open that white showed around the rims. She was scared of sleeping. I was glad she had snapped out of it. She had been drifting down into the inviting dark toward that black monster.

"If you went in too deep, you could wake up dead," I said and put a hand on Ahmed's shoulder to warn him to slow down.

"I don't care which one of you speaks for her," he said without turning around. "But you have to learn to separate your thoughts from hers. You're not thinking of dying, the victim is. She's in danger of death somewhere." He leaned across the table to Bessie again. "Where is she?"

I tightened my grip on Ahmed's shoulder, but Bessie obediently picked up the teacup in fat fingers and looked in again. Her face was round and innocent, but I judged she was braver than I was.

I went around Bessie's side of the table to look over her shoulder into the teacup. A few tea leaves were at the bottom of the cup, drifting in an obscure pattern. She tapped the side of the cup delicately with a fat finger. The pattern shifted. The leaves made some sort of picture, but I could not make out exactly what it was. It looked as if it meant something, but I could not see it clearly.

Bessie spoke sympathetically. "You're thirsty, aren't you? There, there, honeybunch. We'll find you. We haven't forgotten you. Just think where you are and we will. . . ." Her voice died down to a low, fading mumble, like a windup doll running down. She put the cup down and put her head down into her spread hands.

I heard a whisper. "Tired of trying, tired of smiling. Let

11

die. Let death be born. Death will come out to destroy the world, the worthless, dry, rotten—"

Ahmed reached across and grasped her shoulders and shook them. "Bessie, snap out of it. That's not you. It's the other one."

Bessie lifted a changed face from her hands. The round smiling look was gone into sagging sorrowful folds like those of an old bloodhound. She mumbled, "It's true. Why wait for someone to help you and love you? We are born and die. No one can help that. No reason to hope. Hope hurts. Hope hurt her." It bothered me to hear Bessie talk. It was as if she were dead. It was a corpse talking.

Bessie seemed to try to pull herself together and focus on Ahmed to report, but one eye went off focus and she did not seem to see him.

She said, "Hope hurts. She hates hope. She tries to kill it. She felt my thinking and she thought my feelings of life and hope were hers. I was remembering how Harry always helped me, and she blasted in blackness and hate—" She put her face down in her hands again. "Ahmed, he's dead. She killed Harry's ghost in my heart. He won't ever come back anymore, even in my dreams." Her face was dead, like a mask.

He reached over and shook her shoulder again. "Bessie, shame on you; snap out of it."

She straightened and glared. "It's true. All men are beasts. No one is going to help a woman. You want me to help you at your job and win you another medal for finding that girl, don't you? You don't care about her." Her face was darkening, changing to something worse that reminded me of the black shapes of the clouds.

I had to pull her out of it, but I didn't know what to do.

Ahmed clattered the spoon against the teacup with a loud clash and spoke in a loud casual voice. "How's the restaurant business, Bessie? Are the new girls working out?"

She looked down at the teacup, surprised, and then looked vaguely around the restaurant. "Not many customers right now. It must be an off-hour. The girls are in the kitchen." Her face began to pull back into its own shape, a pleasant restaurant-service mask, round and ready

12

to smile. "Can I have the girls get you anything, Ahmed?"

She turned to me with a habit of kindness, and her words were less mechanical. "Would you like anything, young man? You look so energetic standing there! Most young people like our Turkish honey rolls." She still wasn't focused on me, didn't see me, really, but I smiled back at her, glad to see her feeling better.

"No thank you, ma'am," I said and glanced at Ahmed to see what he would want to do next.

"Bessie's honey rolls are famous," Ahmed said. "They are dripping with honey and have so much almond flavor they burn your mouth." He rose easily, looking lazy. "I guess I'll have a dozen to take along."

The fat woman sat blinking her eyes up at him. Her round face did not look sick or sagging anymore, just sort of rumpled and meaningless, like your own face looks in the mirror in the morning. "Turkish honey-and-almond rolls," she repeated. "One dozen." She rang a little bell in the middle of the table and rose.

"Wait for me downstairs," Ahmed told me. He turned to her. "Remember the time a Shriners Convention came in and they all wanted lobster and palm reading at once? Where did you get all those hot lobsters?" They moved off together to the counter, which displayed cookies and rolls. A pretty girl in a frilled apron trotted out of the kitchen and stood behind the counter.

Bessie laughed, starting with a nervous high-pitched giggle and ending up in a deep ho-ho sound like Santa Claus. "Do I remember? What a hassle! Imagine me on the phone trying to locate twenty palm readers in ten minutes! I certainly was grateful when you sent over those twenty young fellows and girls to read palms for my Shriners. I was really nervous until I saw they had their marks really listening, panting for the next word. I thought you must have gotten a circus tribe of Gypsies from the cooler. Ho ho. I didn't know you had sent over the whole police class in Suspect Personality Analysis."

I went out the door, down to the sidewalk. A few minutes later Ahmed came down the escalator two steps at a time and arrived at the sidewalk like a rocket. "Here, carry these." He thrust the paper bag of Turkish honey rolls at

13

me. The warm, sweet smell was good. I took the bag and plunged my hand in.

"Just carry them. Don't eat any." Ahmed led the way down the subway stairs to the first underground walkway.

I pulled my hand out of the bag and followed. I was feeling so shaky I went down the stairs slowly, one at a time, instead of two at a time. When I got there Ahmed was looking at the signs that pointed in different directions, announcing what set of tracks led to each part of the city. For the first time I saw that he was uncertain and worried. He didn't know which way to go. It was a strange thought for me, that Ahmed did not know which way to go. It meant he had been running without knowing which way to run.

He was thinking aloud: "We know that the victim is female, adult, younger than Bessie, probably pregnant, and is trapped someplace where there is no food or water for her. She expected help from the people she loves, and was disappointed, and now is angry with the thought of love and hates the thought of people giving help."

I remembered Bessie's suddenly sick and flabby face after the victim had struck out at Bessie's thought of giving help. *Angry* seemed to be the understatement of the year. I remembered the wild, threatening sky, and I watched the people hurrying by, pale and anxious. Two chicks in bad shape passed. One was holding her stomach and muttering about Alka-Seltzer, and the other had red-rimmed eyes as if she had just been weeping. Can one person in trouble do that to a whole city full of people?

"Who is she, Ahmed?" I asked. "I mean, what is she anyhow?"

"I don't understand it myself," Ahmed said. Suddenly he attacked me again with his question, using that deep hypnotic voice to push me backward into the black whirlpools of the fear of death. "If you were thirsty, very thirsty, and there was only one place in the city you could go to buy a thirst quencher where—"

"I'm not thirsty." I tried to swallow, and my tongue felt swollen, my mouth seemed dry and filled with sand, and my throat was coated with dry gravel. The world tilted over sideways. I braced my feet to remain standing. "I *am* thirsty. How did you do that? I want to go to the White Horse

14

Tavern on Bleecker Street and drink a gallon of ginger ale and a bottle of brown beer."

"You're my compass. Let's go there. I'll buy for you."

Ahmed ran down the Eighth Avenue subway stairs to the chair tracks. I followed, clutching the bag of sweet-smelling rolls as if it were a heavy suitcase full of rocks. The smell made me hungry and weak. I could still walk, but I was pretty sure that if Ahmed pushed me deep into that black mood just once more they'd have to send me back on a stretcher.

On the tracks we linked our chairs and Ahmed shifted the linked chairs from belt to belt until we were traveling at a good speed. The chairs moved along the tunnels, passing under bright store windows with beautiful mannequins dancing and displaying things to buy. I usually looked up when we got near the forest fire and waterfall three-dimensional pics, but today I did not look up. I sat with my elbows braced on my knees and my head hanging. Ahmed looked at me alertly, his black eyebrows furrowed and dark eyes scanning me up and down as if I were a medical diagram.

"Man, I'd like to see the suicide statistics right now. One look at you and I know it's bad."

I had enough life left to be annoyed. "I have my own feelings, not just some chick's feelings. I've been sick all day. A virus or something."

"Damn it, will you never understand? We've got to rescue this girl because she's broadcasting. She's broadcasting feeling sick!"

I looked at the floor between my feet. "That's a lousy reason. Why can't you rescue her just because she's in trouble? Let her broadcast. High school Psych-A said that everybody broadcasts."

"Listen—"Ahmed leaned forward ready to tell me an idea. His eyes began to glitter as the idea took him. "Maybe she broadcasts too loud. Statistics has been running data on trends and surges in popular action. They think that people who broadcast too loud might be causing some of the mass action."

"I don't get you, Ahmed."

"I mean like they get a big surge of people going to Coney Island on a cloudy day, and they don't have subway cars

15

ready for it, and traffic ties up. They compare that day with other cloudy days, the same temperature and the same time of year in other years, and try to figure out what caused it. Sometimes it's a factory vacation: but sometimes it's one man, given the day off, who goes to the beach, and an extra crowd of a thousand or so people from all over the city, people that don't know him, suddenly make excuses, clear schedules, and go to the beach, sometimes arriving at almost the same time, jamming up the subways for an hour, and making it hard for the Traffic Flow Control people."

"Is it a club?" I was trying to make out what he meant, but I couldn't see what it had to do with anything.

"No," he said. "They didn't know each other. It's been checked. The Traffic Flow experts have to know what to expect. They started collecting names from the crowds. They found that most of the people in each surge are workers with an IQ below one hundred, but somehow doing all right with their lives. They seemed to be controlled by one man in the middle of the rush who had a reason to be going in that direction. The Statistics people call the man in the middle the Archetype. That's an old Greek word. The original that other people are copied from—one real man and a thousand echoes."

The idea of some people being echoes made me uneasy. It seemed insulting to call anyone an echo. "They must be wrong," I said.

"Listen—" Ahmed leaned forward, his eyes brightening. "They think they are right, one man and a thousand echoes. They checked into the lives of the ones that seemed to be in the middle. The Archetypes are energetic ordinary people living average lives. When things go as usual for the Archetype, he acts normal and everybody controlled by him acts normal. Get it?"

I didn't get it, and I didn't like it. "An average healthy person is a good Joe. He wouldn't want to control anyone," I said, but I knew I was sugaring the picture. Humans can be bad. People love power over people. "Listen," I said, "some people like taking advice. Maybe it's like advice?"

Ahmed leaned back and pulled his chin. "It fits. Advice by ESP is what you mean. Maybe the Archetype doesn't know he is broadcasting. He does just what the average man

16

wants to do. Solves the same problems—and does it better. He broadcasts loud, pleasant, simple thoughts and they are easy to listen to if you have the same kind of life and problems. Maybe more than half the population below an IQ of one hundred have learned to use telepathic pickup and let the Archetypes do their thinking for them."

Ahmed grew more excited; his eyes fixed on the picture he saw in his head. "Maybe the people who are letting Archetypes run their lives don't even know they are following anyone else's ideas. They just find these healthy, problem-solving thoughts going on in a corner of their mind. Notice how the average person believes that thinking means sitting quietly and looking far away, resting your chin in your hand like someone listening to distant music? Sometimes they say, 'When there's too much noise I can't hear myself think.' But when an intellectual, a real thinker, is thinking—" He had been talking louder with more excitement as the subject got hold of him. He was leaning forward, his eyes glittering.

I laughed, interrupting. "When an intellectual is thinking, he goes into high gear, leans forward, bugs his eyes at you, and practically climbs the wall with each word, like you, Ahmed. Are you an Archetype?"

He shook his head. "Only for my kind of person. If an average kind of person started picking up my kind of thinking, it wouldn't solve his problems—so he would ignore it."

He quit talking because I was laughing so hard. Laughing drove away the ghosts of despair. "Your kind of person! Ho Ho. Show me one. Ha ha. Ignore it? Hell, if a man found your thoughts in his head he'd go to a psychiatrist. He'd think he was going off his rails."

Ahead we saw the big "14" signs signaling Fourteenth Street. I shifted gears on the linked seats and we began to slide sideways from moving cables to slower cables, slowing and going uphill.

We stopped. On the slow strip coming along, a girl was kneeling sideways in one of the seats. I thought she was tying a shoelace, but when I looked back I saw she was lying curled up, her knees under her chin, her thumb in her mouth. Regression. Retreat into infancy. Defeat.

17

Somehow it sent a shiver of fear through me. Defeat should not come so easily. Ahmed had leaped out of his chair and was halfway toward the stairs at the downtown end of the station.

"Ahmed!" I shouted.

He looked back and saw the girl. The seat carried her slowly by in the low-speed lane.

He waved for me to follow him and bounded up the moving stairs. "Come on," he yelled back, "before it gets worse."

When I got up top I saw Ahmed disappearing into the White Horse Tavern. I ran down the block and went in after him, into the cool shadows and paneled wood. Nothing seemed to move. My eyes adjusted slowly and I saw Ahmed with his elbows on the counter, sipping a beer, and discussing the weather with the bartender.

It was too much for me. The world was out of its mind in one way and Ahmed was out of his mind in a different way. I could not figure it out, and I was ready to knock Ahmed's block off.

I was thirsty, but there was no use trying to drink or eat anything around that nut. I put my elbows on the bar a long way from Ahmed and called over to the bartender. "A quart of bock to go." I tilted my head at Ahmed. "He'll pay for it."

I sounded normal enough, but the bartender jumped and moved fast. He plunked a bottle in a brown paper bag in front of me and rubbed the bar in front of me with wood polish.

"Nice weather," he said, and looked around his place with his shoulders hunched, looking over his shoulders. "I wish I was outside walking in the fresh air. Have you been here before?"

"Once," I said, picking up the bag. "I liked it." I remembered the people who had shown me the place. Jean Fitzpatrick—she had shown me some of her poetry at a party—and a nice guy, her husband. Mort Fitzpatrick had played a slide whistle in his own tunes when we were walking along over to the tavern, and some bearded friends of theirs walked with us and talked odd philosophy and strange shared trips. The girl told me that she and her

18

husband had a house in the neighborhood and invited me to a party there, which I turned down, and she asked me to drop in anytime.

I knew she meant the "anytime" invitation. Bohemians, the kind who collect art, and strange books and don't get together in computer-matched communes because they like people who are different, and always have the door open and a pot of coffee ready to share with you.

"Do Jean Fitzpatrick and Mort Fitzpatrick still live around here?" I asked the bartender.

"I see them around. They haven't been in recently." He began to wipe and polish the bar away from me, moving toward Ahmed. "For all I know, they might have moved into a commune."

Ahmed sipped his beer and glanced at us sidelong like a stranger.

I walked out into the gray day with a paper bag under my arm with its hard weight of bock beer inside. I could quit this crazy, sick-making business of being a detector. I could go look up somebody in the Village like Jean Fitzpatrick and tell how sick the day had been and how I couldn't take it and had chickened out, until the story began to seem funny and the world became someplace I could stand.

Ahmed caught up with me and put a hand on my arm. I stopped myself from spinning around to hit him and just stood staring straight ahead.

"You angry?" he asked, walking around me to get a look at my face. "How do you feel?"

I said, "My feelings are my own business. OK? There is a girl around here I want to look up. I want to make sure she is all right. OK? Don't let me hold you up on Rescue Squad business. Don't wait for me. OK?" I started walking again, but the pest was walking right behind me. I had spelled it out clear and loud that I didn't want company. I did not want to flatten him, because at other times he had been my friend.

"May I come along?" he asked politely. "Maybe I can help."

I shrugged, walking along toward the river. What difference did it make? I was tired and there was too much going on in New York City. Ahmed would go away soon on his business. The picture of talking to the girl was warm, dark, relaxing. We'd share coffee and tell each other crazy little jokes and let the world go forgotten.

The house of the Fitzpatricks was one of those little tilted houses left over from a hundred years ago when the city was a town, lovingly restored by hand labor and brightened under many coats of paint by groups of volunteer decorators. It shone with white paint and red doors and red shutters with window boxes under each window growing green vines and weeds and wild flowers. The entire house was overhung by the gigantic girders of the Hudson River Drive with its hissing flow of traffic making a faint rumble through the air and shaking the ground underfoot.

I knocked on the bright red door. No one answered. I found an unused doorbell at the side and pushed it. Chimes sounded, but nothing stirred inside.

Homes in the mixed areas are lived in by guests. Day or night someone is there: travelers with weird projects or ways of thought that did not fit in anywhere, enjoying the tolerance of their xenophile hosts. Commune dropouts, inefficient looking refugees from the student or research worlds staving off a nervous breakdown by a vacation far away from pressure. It was considered legitimate to put your head inside and holler for attention if you couldn't raise anyone by knocking and ringing. I turned the knob to go in. It would not turn. It was locked.

I felt as it they had locked the door when they saw me coming. The big dope, musclehead George, is coming; lock the door. This was a bad day, but I couldn't go any farther. There was no place to go but here.

I stood shaking the knob dumbly, trying to turn it. It began to make a rattling noise like chains or like an alarm clock in a hospital. The sound went through my blood and almost froze my hand. I thought something was behind the door, and I thought it was opening and a monster with a skull face was standing there waiting.

I turned my back to the door and carefully, silently went down the two steps to the sidewalk. I had gone so far off my rails that I thought I heard the door creaking open, and I thought I felt the cold wind of someone reaching out to grab me.

I did not look back, just strode away, walking along the

20

same direction I had been going, pretending I had not meant to touch that door.

Ahmed trotted beside me, sidling to get a view of my face, scuttling sideways and ahead of me like a big crab.

"What's the matter? What is it?"

"She's not. . . . Nobody was. . . ." It was a lie. Somebody or something was in that house. Ignore it, walk away faster.

"Where are we going now?" Ahmed asked.

"Straight into the river," I said and laughed. It sounded strange and hurt my chest like coughing. "The water is a mirage in the desert and you walk out on the dry sand looking for water to drown in. The sand is covered with all the lost dried things that sank out of sight. You die on the dry sand, crawling, looking for water. Nobody sees you. People sail overhead and see the reflections of the sky in the fake waves. Divers come and find your dried mummy on the bottom and make notes, wondering because they think there is water in the river. But it's all dry."

I stopped. The giant docks were ahead and between them the ancient, small wharves. Thre was no use going in that direction or in any direction. The world was shriveled and old, with thousands of years of dust settling on its mummy case. As I stood there, the world grew smaller, closing in on me like a lid shutting me into a box. I was dead, lying down, yet standing upright on the sidewalk. I could not move.

"Ahmed," I said, hearing my voice from a great distance, "get me out of this. What's a friend for?"

He danced around me like some evil goblin. "Why can't you help yourself?"

"I can't move," I answered, being remarkably reasonable.

He circled me, looking at my face and the way I stood. He was moving with stops and starts like a bug looking for a place to bite. I imagined myself shooting a spray can of insecticide at him.

Suddenly he used the voice, the clear deep hypnotic voice that penetrates into the dark private world where I live when I'm asleep and dreaming.

"Why can't you move?"

The gulf opened up beneath my feet. "Because I'd fall," I answered.

He used the voice again, and it penetrated to an interior

21

world where the dreams lived and were real all the time. I was shriveled and weak, lying on dust and bits of old cloth. A foul and dusty smell was in my nostrils and I was looking down over an edge where the air came up from below. The air from below smelled better. I had been there a long time. Ahmed's voice reached me; it asked, "How far would you fall?"

I measured the distance with my eye. I was tired and the effort to think was very hard. Drop ten or twelve feet to the landing, then tangle your feet in the ladder lying there and pitch down the next flight of steep stairs. . . . Death waited at the bottom.

"A long way," I answered. "I'm too heavy. Stairs are steep."

"Your mouth is dry," he said.

I could feel the thirst like flames, drying up my throat, thickening my tongue as he asked the question, the jackpot question.

"Tell me, what is your name?"

I tried to answer with my right name, George Sanford. I heard a voice croak, "Jean Dalais."

"Where do you live?" he asked in a penetrating voice that rang inside my skull and rang into the evil other world where I or someone was on the floor smelling dust for the duration of eternity.

"Downstairs," I heard myself answer.

"Where are you now?" he asked in the same penetrating voice.

"In hell," the voice answered from my head.

I struck out with careful aim to flatten him with the single blow. He was dangerous. I had to stop him and leave him stopped. I struck carefully with hatred. He fell backward and I started to run. I ran freely, one block, two blocks. My legs were my own, my body was my own, my mind was my own. I was George Sanford and I could move without fear of falling. No one was behind me. No one was in front of me. The sun shone through clouds, the fresh wind blew along the empty sidewalks. I was alone. I had left that capsule world of dead horror standing behind me like an abandoned phone booth.

This time I knew what to do to stay out of it. Don't think

22

back. Don't remember what Ahmed was trying to do. Don't bother about rescuing anyone. Take a walk along the edge of the pier in the foggy sunshine and think cheerful thoughts or think no thoughts at all.

I looked back and Ahmed was sitting on the sidewalk far back. I remembered that I was exceptionally strong and the coach had warned me to hold myself back when I hit. Even Ahmed? But he had been thinking, listening, off guard.

What had I said? Jean Dalais. Jean Fitzpatrick had showed me some of her poetry, and that had been the name signed to it. Was Jean Dalais really Jean Fitzpatrick? It was probably her name before she married Mort Fitzpatrick.

I had run by the white house with the red shutters. I looked—it was only a half block back. I went back, striding before fear could grip me again, and rattled the knob and pulled at the red door and looked at the lock.

Ahmed caught up with me. "You know how to pick locks?" I asked him.

"It's too slow," he answered in a low voice. "Let's try the windows."

He was right. The first window we tried was stuck only with New York soot. With our hands black and grimy with soot we climbed into the kitchen. The kitchen was neat except for a dried-up salad in a bowl. The sink was dry, the air was stuffy.

It was good manners to yell announcement of our trespassing.

"Jean!" I called. I got back echoes and silence and something falling off a shelf upstairs. The ghosts rose in my mind again and stood behind me, their claws outstretched. I looked over my shoulder and saw only the empty kitchen. My skin prickled. I was afraid of making a noise. Afraid death would hear me. Had to yell; afraid to yell. Had to move; afraid to move. Dying from cowardice. Someone else's thoughts, with the odor of illness, the burning of thirst, the energy of anger. I was shriveling up inside.

I braced a hand on the kitchen table. "Upstairs in the attic," I said. I knew what was wrong with me now. Jean Dalais was an Archetype. She was delirious and dreaming that she was me. Or I was really Jean Dalais suffering through another dream of rescue, and I was dreaming that

23

strange people were downstairs in my kitchen looking for me. I, Jean, hated these hallucinations. I struck at the dream images of men with the true feeling of weakness and illness, with the memory of the time that had passed with no one helping me and the hatred of a world that trapped you and made hope a lie. I tried to blast the lies into vanishing.

The George Sanford hallucination slid down to a sitting position on the floor of the kitchen. The bottle of bock in its paper bag hit the floor beside him with a heavy clunk, sounding almost real. "You go look, Ahmed," said the George Sanford mouth.

The other figure in the dream bent over and placed a phone on the floor. It hit the linoleum with another clunk and a musical chiming sound that seemed to be heard upstairs. "Hallucination's getting more real. Can hear 'em now," muttered the Sanford self—or was it Jean Dalais who was thinking?

"When I yell, dial zero and ask for the Rescue Squad to come over." Ahmed picked up the paper bag of bock. "OK, George?" He started looking through the kitchen drawers. "Great stuff, beer, nothing better for extreme dehydration. Has salt in it. Keeps the system from liquid shock."

He found the beer opener and slipped it into his hip pocket. "Liquid shock is from sudden changes in the water-versus-salt balance," he remarked, going up the stairs softly, two at a time. He went out of sight and I heard his footsteps, very soft and inquiring. Even Ahmed was afraid of stirring up ghosts.

What had Bessie said about the victim? "Hope hurts." She had tried to give the victim hope and the victim had struck her to the heart with a dagger of hatred and shared despair.

That was why I was sitting on the floor!

Danger, George, don't think! I shut my eyes and blanked my mind.

The dream of rescue and the man images were gone. I was Jean Dalais sinking down into the dark, a warm velvet darkness, no sensation, no thought, only distantly the pressure of the attic floor against my face.

A strange thump shook the floor and a scraping sound pulled at my curiosity. I began to wake again. It was a familiar sound, familiar from the other world and the other

24

life, six days ago, an eternity ago, almost forgotten. The attic floor pushed against my face with a smell of dust. The thump and the scraping sound came again, metal against wood. I was curious. I opened dry, sand-filled eyes and raised my head, and the motion awakened my body to the hell of thirst and the ache of weakness.

I saw the two ends of the aluminum ladder sticking up through the attic trapdoor. The ladder was back now. It had fallen long ago, and now it was back, looking at me, expecting me to climb down it. I cursed the ladder with a mental bolt of hatred. What good is a ladder if you can't move? Long ago I had found that moving around brought on labor pains. Not good to have a baby here. Better to hold still.

I heard a voice. "She's here. George. Call the Rescue Squad." I hated the voice. Another imaginary voice in the long nightmare of imaginary rescues. Who was "George?" I was Jean Dalais.

George. Someone had called "George." Downstairs in the small imagined kitchen I imagined a small image of a man groping for a phone beside him on the floor. He dialed "O" clumsily. A female voice asked a question. The man-image said, "Rescue Squad," hesitantly.

The phone clicked and buzzed and then a deep voice said, "Rescue Squad."

In the attic I knew how a dream of the Rescue Squad should go. I had dreamed it before. I spoke through the small man-image. "My name is Jean Fitzpatrick. I am at twenty-nine Washington Street. I am trapped in my attic without water. If you people weren't fools, you would have found me long ago. Hurry. I'm pregnant." She made the man-image drop the receiver. The dream of downstairs faded again as the man-image put his face in his hands.

My dry eyes were closed; the attic floor again pressed against my face. Near me was the creak of ladder rungs taking weight and then the creaks of the attic floor, something heavy moving on it gently, then the rustle of clothing as somebody moved; the click of a bottle opener against a cap; the clink of the cap hitting the floor; the bubbling and hissing of a fizzing cool liquid. A hand lifted my head carefully and a cold bottle lip pushed against my mouth. I

25

opened my mouth and the cold touch of liquid pressed within it and down the dry throat. I began to swallow.

George Sanford, me, took his hands away from his eyes and looked down at the phone. I was not lying down; I was not drinking; I was not thirsty. Had I dialed the Rescue Squad when Ahmed called me? A small mannequin of a man in Jean Fitzpatrick's mind had called and hung up, but the mannequin was me, George Sanford—six feet one and a half inches. I am no woman's puppet. The strength of telepathy is powered by emotion and need, and the woman upstairs had enough emotion and need, but no one could have done that to me if I did not want to help. No one.

A musical, two-toned note of a siren approaching from above, growing louder. It stopped before the door. Loud knocks came at the door. I was feeling all right but still dizzy and not ready to move.

"Come in," I croaked. They rattled the knob. I got up and let them in, then stood hanging onto the back of a chair.

Rescue Squad orderlies in blue and white. "You sick?"

"Not me, the woman upstairs." I pointed and they rushed up the stairs carrying their stretcher and medical kits.

There was no thirst or need driving her mind to intensity anymore, but our mind were still connected somehow, for I felt the prick of a needle in one thigh, and then the last dizziness and fear dimmed and vanished, the world steadied out in a good upright position, the kitchen was not a dusty attic but only a clean empty kitchen and all the sunshine of the world was coming in the windows.

I took a deep breath and stretched, feeling the muscles strong and steady in my arms and legs. I went up to the second floor and steadied the ladder for the Rescue Squad men while they carried the unconscious body of a young woman down from the attic.

She was curly-haired with a dirt-and-tear-streaked face and skinny arms and legs. She was bulging in the middle, as pregnant as a pumpkin.

I watched the blue and white Rescue ambulance copter lift away.

"Want to come along and watch me make out my report?" Ahmed asked.

On the way out of the kitchen I looked around for the

Turkish honey rolls, but the bag was gone. I must have dropped it somewhere.

We walked south a few blocks to the nearest police station. Ahmed settled down at a desk they weren't using to fill out his report, and I found a stack of comic magazines in the waiting room and chose the one with the best action on the cover. My hands shook a little because I was hungry, but I felt happy and important.

Ahmed filled out the top, wrote a few lines, and then started working the calculator on the desk. He stopped, stared off into space, glanced at me, and started writing again, glancing at me every second. I wondered what he was writing about me. I wanted the Rescue Squad brass to read good things about me so they would hire me for a job.

"I hunch good, don't I, Ahmed?"

"Yes." He filled something into a space, read the directions for the next question, and began biting the end of his pen and staring at the ceiling.

"Would I make a good detector?" I asked.

"What kind of mark did you get in Analysis of Variance in high school?"

"I never took it, I flunked probability in algebra, in six B—"

"The Rescue Squad wants you to fill out reports that they can run into the statistics machines. Look"—I went over and he showed me a space where he had filled out some numbers and a funny symbol like a fallen-down D—"can you read it, George?"

"What's it say?"

"It says probability .005. That means the odds were two hundred to one against you finding the White Horse Tavern just by accident, when it was the place the Fitzpatrick woman usually went to. I got the number by taking a rough count of the number of bars in the phone book. More than two hundred wrong bars, and there was only one bar you actually went to. Two hundred divided by one, or two hundred. If you had tried two bars before finding the right one your chances of being wrong would have been two hundred divided by two. That's one hundred. Your score for being right was your chance of being wrong, or the reciprocal of your chance of being right

27

by luck. Your score is two hundred. Understand? Around here they think forty is a good score."

I stared at him, looking stupid. The school had tried relays of teachers and tutors on me for two terms before they gave up trying to teach me. It didn't seem to mean anything. It didn't seem to have anything to do with people. Without probability algebra and graphs I found out they weren't going to let me take Psychology-B, History, Social Dynamics, Systems Analysis, Business Management, Programming, or Social Work. They wouldn't even let me study to be a Traffic Flow cop. I could have taken Electronics Repair but I wanted to work with people, not TV sets, so I dropped out. I couldn't do schoolwork, but the kind of thing the Rescue Squad wanted done, I could do.

"Ahmed, I'd be good in the Rescue Squad. I don't need statistics. Remember I told you you were pushing Bessie in too deep. I was right, wasn't I? And you were wrong. That shows I don't need training."

Ahmed looked sorry for me. "George, you don't get any score for that. Every softhearted slob is afraid when he sees someone going into a traumatic area in the subjective world. He always tries to make them stop. You would have said I was pushing her too deep anyhow, even if you were wrong."

"But I was right."

Ahmed half rose out of his chair, then made himself calm down.

He settled back, his lips pale and tight against his teeth. "It doesn't matter if you were right, unless you are right against odds. You get credit for picking the White Horse Tavern out of all the taverns you could have picked, and you get credit for picking the girl's house out of all the addresses you could have picked. I'm going to multiply the two figures by each other. It will run your score over eighty thousand probably. That's plenty of credit."

Now it didn't make sense in the opposite direction. He was praising me. "But I only went to the tavern because I was thirsty. You can't credit me with that. You made me thirsty somehow. And I went to the girl's house because I wanted to see her. Maybe she was pulling at me."

"I don't care what your reasons were! You went to the
28

right place, didn't you? You found her, didn't you?"
Ahmed stood up and shouted. "You're talking like a
caveman. What do you think this is, 1950, or some time
your grandmother was running a store? I don't care what
your reasons are; nobody cares anymore what the reasons
are. We only care about results, understand? We don't
know why things happen, but if everyone makes out good
reports about them, with clear statistics, we can run the
reports into the machines, and the machines will tell us
exactly what is happening, and we can work with that,
because they're facts, and it's the real world. I know you can
find people. Your reasons don't matter. Scientific theories
about the causes don't matter!"

He was red in the face and shouting, as if I'd said something against his religion or something. "I wish we could get
theories for some of it. But if the statistics say that if something funny happens here and something else funny always
happens over there next, we don't have to know how the
two connect; all we have to do is expect the second thing
every time we see the first thing happen. See?"

I didn't know what he was talking about. My tutors had
said things like that to me, but Ahmed felt miserable
enough about it to shout. Ahmed was a friend.

"Ahmed," I said, "would I make a good detector?"

"You'd make a great detector, you dope!" He looked
down at his report. "Maybe you'd make the best locater
we've ever had! But you can't get into the Rescue Squad.
The rules say that you've got to have brains in your head
instead of rocks. I'll help you figure out someplace else you
can get a job. Stick around. I'll loan you fifty bucks as soon
as I finish this report. Go read something."

I felt lousy, but I stood there fighting it, because this was
my last chance at a real job, and there was something right
about what I was trying to do. The Rescue Squad needed
me. Lost people were going to need me.

"Ahmed," I said, trying to make my meaning very clear to
him, "I should be in your department. You gotta figure out
a way to get me in."

It's hard watching a strong, confident guy go through a
change. Generally Ahmed always knows what he is doing;
he never wonders. He stared down at his report, holding his

breath, he was thinking so hard. Then he got away from his desk and began to pace up and down. "What the hell is wrong with me? I must be going chicken. Desk work is softening me up." He grabbed up his report off the desk. "Come on, let's go buck the rules. Let's fight City Hall."

"We can't hire your friend." The head of the Rescue Squad shook his head. "He couldn't pass the tests. You said so yourself."

"The rules say that George has to pass the pen-and-paper tests." Ahmed leaned forward on the desk and tapped his hand down on the desk top, emphasizing words. "The rules are trash rules made up by trash bureaucrats so that nobody can get a job but people with picky little old-maid minds like them! Rules are something we use to deal with people we don't know and don't care about. We know George and we know we want him! How do we fake the tests?"

The chief held out one hand, palm down. "Slow down, Ahmed. I appreciate enthusiasm, but maybe we can get George in legitimately. I know he cut short an epidemic of hysteria and psychosomatics at the hospitals and saved the hospitals a lot of time and expense. The computer gives us a percentage of any money our work saves the city, so I want him in the department if he can keep that up. But let's not go breaking up the system to get him in. We can use the system."

The chief opened the intercom switch and spoke into the humming box. "Get me Accounting, will you?" The box answered after a short while and the chief spoke again. He was a big, square-built man, going slightly flabby. His skin was loose and gray. "Jack, listen, we need the services of a certain expert. We can't hire him. He doesn't fit the height and weight regulations, or something like that. How do we pay him?"

The man at the other end spoke briefly in accounting technicalities: ". . . Contingencies, services, fees. Consultant. File separate services rendered, time and results, with statistics of probability rundown on departmental expenses saved by outside help and city expenses saved by the Rescue Squad action, et cetera, et cetera. Get it?"

"OK, thanks." He shut off the chatterbox and spoke to Ahmed. "We're in. Your friend is hired."

My feet were tired standing there. My hands were shaking slightly so I had stuffed them into my pockets, striking a nonchalant pose. I was passing the time thinking of restaurants, all the good ones that served the biggest plates for the least money. "When do I get paid?" I asked.

"Next month," Ahmed said. "You get paid at the end of every month for the work you did on each separate case. Don't look so disappointed. You are a consultant expert now. You are on my expense account. I'm supposed to buy your meals and pay your transportation to the scene of the problem whenever I consult you."

"Consult me now," I said.

We had a great Italian meal at an old-fashioned Italian restaurant: lasagna, antipasto, bread in thick, tough slices, lots of margarine, a salad, four cups of hot black coffee, and spumoni for dessert, rich and sweet. Everything tasted fresh and cooked just right and they served big helpings. I stopped shaking after the second helping of lasagna and felt fine after the second cup of coffee.

There was something funny about that restaurant. Somebody was planning a murder. But I wasn't going to mention it to Ahmed until after dessert.

He'd probably want me to rescue someone instead of eating.

Leaning back, we talked of old times, when he was a gang leader and I was a kid, and we remembered old jokes. Somewhere at another table, the bloody cloud of murder plans faded, postponed. I let it go by.

I slept that night in the visitors' room of the Karmic Brotherhood, and as we were settling down to reading and meditating, I told the other visitors about my new job and asked what could make me a better locater of people in trouble, with better ESP.

They said, "Practice," but they pointed to a thin old man sitting leaning against the wall who was a Taoist and a counselor, who read people's past and advised their future wherever he traveled. "Ask him."

I went and sat near him and waited for him to look at me so I could ask my question. He sat with his eyes closed, very old, scrawny, dignified, and beautiful.

Without opening his eyes he said, "I am glad you have found a purpose in life. I have never tried to locate other souls; I have tried only to merge with them and share with them. I believe that your soul is in danger, for you cannot wall yourself off, the evil of others can always reach you. Therefore you must not resist evil in others but must sympathize and understand it and love it, but do nothing. There is no other safety, for you have no walls." His voice was old and creaky.

He shifted uneasily and tugged his beard. "But now I realize that you are impatient and without fear and want only words about your skill at finding people. I can only tell you this. The best way to detect the future is in dreams. I think you should keep a little battery light and a note pad beside your sleeping bag. So I will loan you my light and note pad."

I did not want to know the future, but I thanked him and took his light and note pad. As I drifted off to sleep, I heard the faint music from the earplug radios of some of the people lying in their sleeping bags, and I heard the old man breathing a prayer. "Let him drift upward with the tides of light, not downward with the tides of darkness. Let him save only souls who wish to be saved. Whoever he should save, let him know him in dream country, let them become friends and plan how to meet in the upper world." Was the prayer for himself or me?

Usually when I dream, I become other people. I often dream I am Biggy, who used to be a member of our kid gang, grown up now, herding goats in the mountains of Mauritania, on exile pension.

But this time I began to dream I was someone in New York.

2

THE sign was neon red and blinked on and off against the sky.

YOU ARE NOT ALONE!

Find your own Kind,
Find your own Hobby.
Find your own Mate,
Find your own King-
dom. Use "Harmony"
personality diagnosis
and matching service.

Carl Hodges was alone. He stood in a deserted and ruined section of the city and saw the red glow of the sign reflecting against the foggy air of the sky of New York, blinking on and off like the light of a flickering red flame. He knew what the glow said. You are not alone.

He shut his eyes, and tears trickled down from under his closed eyelids. Damn the day he had learned to do time track. He could remember and return to Susanne; he could even see the moment of the surfboard and his girl traveling down the front slope of a slanted wave front, even see the nose of the board catch again under the ripple, the wave heaving the board up, up and over, and whipping down edge first like an ax.

Think about something else!

"Crying again, Pops?" said a young insolent voice. A hand pushed two tablets against his mouth. "Here, happy pills. Nothing to cry about. It's a good world."

Obediently Carl Hodges took the pills into his mouth and swallowed. Soon memory and grief would stop hurting and go away—think about something else. Work? No, he should be at work, on the job instead of vacationing, living with runaway children. Think about fun things.

It was possible that he was a prisoner, but he did not mind. Around him, collecting in the dark, stood the crowd of runaway children and teenagers in strange mixed costumes from many communes across the United States. They had told him that they had run away from the kingdoms and odd customs of their parents. They hated brotherhood and conformity and sameness of the adults they had been forced to live with by the law that let in-

33

corporated villages educate their own children with the walls.

The teeners had told him that all rules were evil, that all customs were neurotic repetition, that fear was a restriction, that practicality was a restriction, and mercy was a restriction.

He told himself they were children, in a passing phase of rebellion.

The pill effect began to swirl in a rosy fog of pleasure into his mind. He remembered fun. "Did I tell you," he muttered to the runaway teener gang that held him as a prisoner-guest, "about the last game of Futures I played with Ronny? It was ten-thirty, late work, so when we finished we disconnected the big computer from its remote controls and started to play City Chess. We had three minor maintenance errors as our only three moves. He wiped out my half of the city by starting an earthquake from a refrigerator failure in a lunchroom. It wiped out all the power-plant crew with food poisoning, and the Croton power plant blew up along a fault line. That was cheating because he couldn't prove the fault line. I wiped out his technocrats in Brooklyn Dome just by reversing the polarity on the air-conditioning machine. It completed its interreaction cycle and stabilized with the dome collapsed under the ocean pressure and the residents trapped inside. It's a good thing our games aren't real. Everyone is wiped out totally by the end of a good game."

A blond kid who seemed to be the leader stepped forward and took Carl Hodges' arm, leading him back toward his cellar room. "You started to tell me about it, but tell me again. I'm very interested. I'd like to study maintenance prediction as a career. What does reversing the leads on the air-conditioning machine do to destroy a place?" He was lying. The others snickered.

"It changes the smell of the air; in some people there's an instinctive claustrophobia," said Carl Hodges, who was in love with a dead girl and wanted death. "You wouldn't think that would make a lot of difference, would you?" He didn't care what they did with the secret.

Having fun, dreaming I was Carl Hodges, I felt a bad stab
34

of guilt and knowledge instantly suppressed by Carl Hodges in a dark embrace of ignorance and unconsciousness. He hated the living who were not Susanne.

In the undersea dome of Brooklyn Dome City, the technologists of the Objectivist Commune, with their wives and their children, slept in their beds, relaxed, breathing fresh cool air from the gentle hum of the air conditioners. Above them, arching above their small city on the bottom of the sea, the strong and flexible fabric of the dome pressed upward with the soft strong pressure of air holding back the unimaginable tonnage of the ocean above.

I awoke with an impression of terror and destruction fading in my dreams. Echoing distantly in the far sky, I heard the fading thunder of a shuttle taking off for the orbiting space port. *Thunder, earthquake, walls break, water wall breaks, people run before a moving wall of water.*

Silence returned to my mind. The image faded. The walls were steady and real. I put a hand on the wall near my head and felt it solid, vibrating to a deep hum that was the sound of the night trains of the mechanized city, deep underground, rolling in supplies. New York—safe, protective, automatic.

Danger somewhere? I groped back into the dream, but it had faded to a fragment of thunder, a feeling of warning. Remembering it, I rolled over and switched on a small reading-light unit in the top of the sleeping bag and wrote in a note pad, "Walls breaking, people drowning." I saw words already scribbled at the top of the page in my handwriting. "Sky breaks, June 19th."

I must have dreamed the same dream before and tried to write it down while still asleep. I ran my hand into my hair and pulled it a little, trying to think. I was propped on one elbow in a comfortable sleeping bag at a Karmic Brotherhood commune, the visitors' sleeping room. Sleepers breathed quietly in their sleeping bags on the floor. Near me two heads projected from one bag. In a shadowy corner a man leaned back, legs crossed, meditating, the thin face peaceful.

Perhaps he had meant that writing down dreams would get me in better touch with the subconscious, help me to

35

pick up thoughts from people. Maybe the dreams were warnings of people's plans to get into trouble. Maybe I should do something about it, now.

I tugged at my hair, trying to decide. Maybe I should call Ahmed. Ahmed would not want to answer the phone at three in the morning. If I called him as if it were an emergency, what if nothing happened on June 19? This was only June 15 coming up. I had four days to think it over.

People breathed quietly, asleep around me.

The dream faded fast without leaving any memory of solid convincing details. Probably not real.

With a sigh I leaned back on the soft blanket roll under my head and let myself go back to sleep.

SKY BREAKS JUNE 19. Thunder and walls falling.

I woke early to get away from a bad dream. It was a hot morning. Birds were twittering in the trees on top of the apartment buildings and a sea gull cawed outside the window and drifted past, making a big shadow on the wall.

I stood up, wide awake, feeling late to an appointment. The calendar clock on the wall said 18 JUN 6:23 and that scared me with a feeling of hurry, but I didn't know why.

Naked, I put my head out the window and saw the sky lit up by bright streaks of clouds. Everything was peaceful. With my head out the window I tried the trick of tuning to people in trouble. I imagined I was trapped somewhere and scared. Ahmed hadn't been around for two or three days, but I'd been doing this every day, finding lost kids, cats stuck in wastebaskets, lost visitors to the city who couldn't remember the name of their hotel, and old people in apartments with the new safety handprint lock, keyed to your own hand. But the old people had forgotten how to work the modern invention, and they were stuck inside or stuck outside looking for a doorknob.

It had been a pleasure to get them rescued and make them happy.

But first I had always to locate them by their fear, and fear is a bad thing to feel.

Rescue Squad regular crews go into fire and gas to rescue people. I go into their heads. Sometimes fire is better.

With my head out the window I remembered the crazy

man planning murder that I had felt thinking in the Italian restaurant where Ahmed had brought me that great first meal. I had forgotten. But if the lunatic killed someone before I got to him it would be bad.

I pulled my head in and tried to tune to a crazy murderer by thinking bloody thoughts of hatred and revenge. I picked up the thoughts of a half-awake man pleasurably thinking of smashing a buzzing alarm clock. I started to fall asleep again and went to the commune shower to wake up.

In the showers I admired two girls and hoped they appreciated my new shape, square instead of round. I took a very cold shower to get serious, slid on shorts, and went to the Italian restaurant. It was locked, with a little sweeping machine buzzing around inside lifting tables and spinning its brushes.

I was too late or too early. That thought brought back the dream fear of having waited too long. I was scared that something bad was already happening. Standing there with my eyes shut, I tried to tune into the murderer. My feelings of fear and guilt tuned me to a drunk expert city services man who was scared he had blabbed some important secrets to the wrong kind of people. *My fault if something bad happens*, he thought desperately as I tuned him out. You and me too, brother. I have to find that murderer, and he's too crazy to be feeling guilty. He'll be chortling over blood, planning it or remembering it.

I remembered Ahmed's method. Locate your man by the widening ripples of his effects, the ring of echoes in other minds. Use hospital and crime statistics.

The murderer is probably asleep and giving out no vibes at all. Not doing any harm yet. Calm down, George.

Statistics work fine for Ahmed. He showed you how. They will work for you, I told myself, but the nightmare left a feeling of bad things getting ready to happen.

It was too early for Statistics but I got the dispatcher on the phone. He was awake, but sounded sleepy. He said he could get the Statistics computer to print out a report.

It was 7 A.M. and the birds in the greenbelt trees were still twittering about waking up. Sunshine was bright and pink along the tops of the buildings. Cool shadows and some mist still lingered in the canyon streets of West Side New

37

York. I left the phone booth and crossed the street to sit in the grass of the street greenbelt. I leaned back against a tree and looked up. There were no cars going by. There had been no cars allowed in the city for fifteen years. The peace got inside my head.

The phone started ringing. I crossed the street and got back into the booth. "George Sanford here." I yawned. The phone booth was too small. I opened the door and listened to the bird sounds.

"Your report just came over from Statistics," said the dispatcher's voice. "Computer printout, one-year deviation from norm in rates on unprovoked minor and major violence, blocks between Twenty-third and Twenty-first Streets and two blocks each side of Wilmot Street, right?"

"Right." In a week, I'd learned to work like a cop. "Something like that, anyhow. I want to check out a kind of extra amount of halfway violence sort of. Like thinking of killing, not doing it."

"Um-m-m, a few cases of violence, mostly threats and attacks that don't injure. Students throwing paint on the teachers or tearing their clothes at the high school; a lot of adult vandalism."

"What kind of vandalism? Read details."

He started to read in a drone. "Displaced personal violence, type two: curtains and pictures pulled down or knife-slashed. Displaced violence, type three: pictures of human figures defaced with crayon or marking pencil, slash lines or X crosses. Displaced violence, type four: drawings of bloody swords, knives, axes." He stopped droning and asked in a normal cop voice, "Need more?"

"It's reaching me," I said. "I'm getting onto the viewpoint. Read off the details on the attacks; give it slowly." I was feeling violent already.

"What for? What are you trying to do?"

"I'm trying to tune to a suspect. To think like him," I said into the phone. "I'm standing in the area. One side is a set of arts and crafts communes, and the other is old-folk Italiano. Quiet people, no reason to feel violent or think of blood, but I feel it when I walk by to have a plate of spaghetti. Someone on this block has been thinking about violence and sending out bad vibes for years. The kids go by on the way to school.

38

I wanted to see if the vibes were reaching them. They are. They're doing a lot. I'm trying to tune to the vibes, and see if I can get into the bad guy's head."

"You all right over there?" asked the phone voice suspiciously. "You spaced out on something?"

Ahmed had always teamed with me and done the phoning before. Maybe I wasn't handling the phoning right. "Look. If you're too busy over there to read Rescue Squad bulletins, you don't know about me. Better get me somebody who isn't busy. OK?"

I looked out from the phone booth. The sounds of the neighborhood waking up, the smell of bacon frying, a drawing of a bloody ax on an old brick slum building. The building looked ancient. The dusty look of it and the drawing of the bloody ax on the wall made me feel like someone who liked bloody axes, someone who lived nearby.

"I ain't busy. Sorry I got you huffy," said the phone. "What do you want me to read?"

"Read the list of assaults, with details, slowly, then ask me my name in a loud voice and then my address; ask clearly and write down what I say."

"Like how?"

"Like: What's your name? Where do you live?" I said loudly. More people were walking by. One young guy went by still buttoning his shirt, hurrying to a job. Two girls sauntered by wearing bathing suits, carrying towels.

"Are you the new guy the department hired that uses a dowsing rod?" asked the dispatcher over the phone.

"No. I'll explain some other time. Just read the list." I had a feeling that the guy who dreamed of violence was awake and getting dressed, maybe ready to leave. I looked at a sandy-haired undersized worker hurrying by. The guy I wanted would look like that. But would I have the nerve to stop someone just because he gave out bad vibes?

No.

The dispatcher started to read in a toneless drone.

"Twelve cases of students splashing ink or paint on four art teachers. Clothes ripped in three cases. One pedestrian, female living in Jersey City, tied and threatened and her hair shaved by an unidentified assailant approximately age twenty-two, male, brunet. Found tied, but unhurt, in a

39

refuse can storage unit on Wilmot Street in the Twenty-second block." The droning voice read slowly, and I imagined myself doing each of the things described. Shaving the girl's head gave me a strange violent thrill and a fantasy of carrying a head around by its hair.

"What is your name?" asked the phone voice, suddenly clear and demanding.

"Charles Shiras."

"Where do you live?"

"Twenty-two-twenty Wilmot Street," I answered easily and then snapped back into myself, with my skin prickling into goose bumps at the image of sawing at a neck slowly with a jagged-edged old carving knife. The vibration of the sawing had been something my hand felt.

"I got the name," said the police dispatcher at the other end, his voice droning still but almost showing a trace of interest. "Now what do I do with it?"

"Radio it to Rescue Squad to pick up Charles Shiras for custody, then take him to the medics for a flipout med check," I said.

"You aren't Charles Shiras?"

"No, I'm George Sanford." He was getting it.

I knew about the custody routine from hanging around the station house waiting for Ahmed all week. "Pick him up and check him out for psychosis. He won't pass the medics. If he calls a lawyer . . . if they don't straitjacket him . . . I'll swear out a complaint." I hoped he wouldn't pass the medics. How could I swear out a complaint? What did I legally have to complain about—a guy putting bad thoughts into my head? How much far-out guff could the regular police department take from the Rescue Squad? Arrests are supposed to be for doing something wrong. The squad could show a lower rate of crime and accidents after picking up a troublemaker who just thought bad thoughts. That's what they said. But how did they make it legal? Arrest without a crime is against the Bill of Rights. I took a deep breath and accidentally picked up the nut's vibes—an image of shoving a person's hand into a toaster. The pleasure was pain and power. Probably the man had only been sawing a slice of bread out of the middle of a stiff pumpernickel loaf, not a throat, and was now putting the thick slice into the toaster—not a hand. But his image of shoving down on a

40

hand, and his pleasure in it gave me the shudders again. Sadism runs deep: It has primitive, strong roots. I don't even like knowing about that pleasure. It might be contagious. I might hurt someone, someday. I'm too strong. I've got to watch it.

For a while, the dispatcher was busy with some switchboard and radio calls. He came back on the phone. "You spell your name, George Sandford?"

"Sanford, only one *d*," I said, shifting from one foot to the other. In the heat my sandals got sweaty under the straps. They are cool for walking, not standing. The stereo earphones were hot and sweaty over my ears, and too tight—made for smaller heads than mine. An old person's bus went by slowly with a slight hissing sound, stirring up a little breeze.

"Badge number?" asked the phone.

"No badge. I'm a specialist in category J." It sounded good even if it meant I couldn't pass the tests to be hired police. All a specialist needs to know is the one thing he is expert in, but experts are treated with respect. "Specialist, category J," I said again, tasting the respect people had been giving me when I said that. I liked being an expert.

For a minute the dispatcher was busy with radio calls coming and going from wrist radios and police copters, then he said, "Sanford? You still on? A copter on its way over. I have instructions for you from Chief Oslow of Rescue Squad. The team that picks up your suspect will head over to Neurological. Ride over with them and go to room 106 same building. There's a girl there who helps fill out rescue and emergency reports for the officers who bring in cases. She'll help you. Your department wants reports from you for the last four days of work."

As I hung up the earphones, the police copter came down out of the sky and onto the grass strip and two policemen ran into the building across the street. I could hear the stairs thud to their running steps like a drumbeat, then I could hear only the people in other buildings, near their windows, talking about making breakfast. "All out of margarine!" "Can't get the Today show." "Watch the eggs for me."

Then it came, the scream I'd been expecting. It started as a shout and went higher and wilder.

"Never get me alive. I'll get you first. I'll get them. I'll kill
41

you. Kill you!" It turned into insane garble and thudding and crashing. A few people put thier heads out windows to see which window the screaming was coming from.

The thudding diminished and the screamed obscenities and insanities descended shriek by shriek inside the apartment, until the two policemen dragged a struggling madman out of the front of the apartment. Passersby stopped to watch.

"Such language," said a woman from the window of the apartment above me. "Why don't they give him tranquilizers?"

They were trying to hold his arms steady long enough to get cuffs on him. He butted and bit and cursed.

"Dig evil," the guru had told me. I braced myself and tuned into the mood of the curses and snarls. It was a surprise, a good surprise. The lunatic was having fun. He didn't have to work at pretending to be sane anymore. He was relaxing, letting it all out, letting it blast. Fighting the police, making it tough for them, he was slowly dragged from the building to the copter, enjoying the fight, his screams like war cries.

"Give him a tranquilizer," the woman called down.

"We did already," the policeman called up to her over the noise. "Maybe this is the way he is when he's tranquil."

Suddenly the angry screaming stopped. The tranquilizer took hold. They loaded a passive man into the copter like an invalid. I approached. "I made the call. I'm supposed to go along."

"OK, get in." They made room for me. On a nearby seat, flushed and contented, the madman hummed to himself while the copter took off.

The cop swung us out over the Hudson River to avoid the air jolts of the up and down winds over the building and we cruised over the green park strip at the edge of the water while the madman hummed and looked around at the view and the copter police took new orders from the intercom radio.

We slowed and hovered over a cluster of tan brick towers and lowered to a roof landing area that was painted EMERGENCY AMBULANCE ENTRANCE. The copter grounded and settled; a rolling strip on the roof took it sideways to an elevator platform and the platform lowered to the admitting and diagnosis area of Neurological and Psychiatric Division of Presbyterian. Busy men in white and green coats took the patient away; the desk accepted his wallet from a policeman and got his report. They asked me to spell my name and filled in the space under "complaint by." Then they did not need me. An elevator said VISITORS' ELEVATOR, EXPRESS TO GROUND FLOOR ONLY. THIS WAY OUT. All the other elevators said STAFF ONLY.

Busy people rushed by, pushing me aside and rolling stretchers wherever I wanted to stand and watch. I took the express elevator to the ground floor, feeling envy toward doctors. Their jobs seemed busy and important.

I stood in the first-floor entrance hall and remembered that Chief Judd Oslow wanted me to get together with a secretary in room 106 and fill out reports. I hated filling out reports. It was almost eight in the morning. Firmly I went down a corridor until I found room 106 and tried the door. It was locked. As I turned away I saw a pretty secretary approaching with her keys jingling in her hand. I walked away.

The corridor made a dead end at a big picture window looking across the river. I looked out the window and scouted my mind around looking for help calls, waiting for the secretary to go inside 106 and shut the door. I hate filling out forms. I hate answering questions.

Why? I won't ask myself why. That's a question. Hate questions.

I scouted my mind around trying to tune to people who were lonely and trapped and in danger.

Suddenly, one came in loud, fear like electricity. Danger of death, yes, great grave danger of death. The clouds over the river turned into white uniforms and a white huge skull. I grabbed the edge of the windowsill hard and got into the fear, all the way in, and with it into the mind and the sense of location of a frightened one. He was a patient in the hospital, about to have a neurological operation. A nurse gave him a tranquilizer shot and his fear faded away to great confidence in the surgeon.

I opened my eyes. The clouds were just clouds, not skulls. As I looked at the landscape, another wave of fear

43

came in from a different part of the hospital. The landscape became the cliffs and buildings of a strange enemy country. Someone was kidnapped, imprisoned, and surrounded by enemies who smiled and pretended to be doctors. Paranoia, yet it felt clear and logical like a real case of kidnapping.

I made myself disbelieve it and went to ask information from an expert. In the front entrance I stopped a passing resident.

"I need some advice on how to tell paranoid thinking from healthy thinking," I said. "I have to answer help calls and all your paranoids think they've been kidnapped. I need to be able to tell them from real kidnap cases by their vibes. I'm working for Rescue Squad. I use ESP but I can't sort them out."

He looked up at me and became frightened because he couldn't fit the words into anything he was used to hearing. He didn't get a full grip on my meaning, except that I was claiming to be a detective; the rest went by too fast and sounded like nonsense. He pushed an emergency button in his pocket and smiled with a frozen scared smile while I searched my shoulder bag for my Rescue Squad credentials.

I didn't have a police badge, but I had a letter of praise for the first rescue I had done, and a small news clipping about it enclosed in a plastic folder somewhere in the bag.

"Wait," I said. "I'll show you."

Apparently, large men who babble they are detectives looking for paranoids, are some particularly dangerous kind of nut in his diagnosis book. He was afraid to move.

I groped through the credit card and Kleenex and wrapped sandwich and the half-read book and the notebook and tape recorder and the tapes and the spoon and knife and pencil and small flashlight and while I groped I reached through the walls with my mind and tuned in to the paranoids in the building. There were at least fifty locked up waiting for gland operations, all convinced they were surrounded by enemies intent on killing them. Most of them were convinced that they had been kidnapped to a strange country and were waiting for execution. They seemed sane, alert, and ready to escape. If I paid attention to their thoughts, I'd be rescuing lunatics from their doctors.

I found the plastic-coated papers and started to pull my hand from my bag. Heavy hands grabbed my arms from either side. Two very husky interns in white coats who had been called by the doctor's panic button had me in a grip that could break my elbows if I struggled. I stood still.

"Let's see what you have in your hand," said one intern. He was almost as big as I was, but he wasn't a bully; his tone was cool, his expression almost friendly. He shifted his grip and took the papers and handed them to the resident.

The young doctor read them carefully and then held them out to me. "He's OK," he said to the two and they let me go. "You could have been groping for a gun in that bag," the doctor explained to me as I put the papers back. "We get all kinds of cracks, and three to five is the witching hour, the bats fly in in swarms."

"I was tired from a bad night. Sorry."

He walked with me over to the reception desk and got me a temporary pass. "You're off-hours for the usual guided tour, but they aren't busy. This will answer some of your questions."

I read it. "Pass George Sanford to and from Police Psychiatric Department, Criminal Justice Wing, 18th Fl., Wing B."

I took the elevator up past vibes of calm sleeping patients, floors of them, and at the top got off into a blast of vibes that backed me into the door.

"Looking for someone?" A man in white jacket, blue pants. Police badge.

"I'm on Rescue Squad, I'm new, just hired. I'd like to know. . . ." Soundless screams of panic from behind the doors almost drowned out my thought. I made an inquiring face, a gesture at the doors. The police intern could not hear-feel what was going on in there, but he should know about it.

"Oh. You're on observation orientation tour? Got ID?" the police medic asked.

I showed him my cards and the pass that the doctor had written for me. One of the screams of terror went into peculiar overtones of pleasure with a childlike tone, young and getting younger, childhood memories of anger, memories sweetened and burning, like maraschino cherry juice or hot cinnamon candy. The burn mounted until I

45

tried to walk backward away from it. I felt the woman behind the door trying to stop remembering, but the memory mounted, hotter and brighter, spiraling past the bearing of human brain cells. A soundless expanding blast of white pain destroyed it.

I had still been trying to pull away from the other person's experiences when it all hit peak and destroyed itself.

The intern in the uniform read my cards.

He finished talking about something and waited. I stood feeling blank.

"You're brainwiping people in there?" I asked. The woman behind the door was giving out no vibes of thought but she wasn't dead. There was a feeling of aliveness still there, like an animal.

He shifted his feet uneasily, looking up at my expression. "We'd rather not call it brainwipe. You're a professional now. The right name for this place is the Electronic Personality Restructuring Laboratory. Brainwipe is what ordinary people call it, but they don't understand the process."

Why don't most people feel vibes? He stood talking peacefully, feeling nothing while I tried to pull my feelings into a small hard knot and hide them in a corner away from the soundless screams that were beginning to come from another room. I asked, "How can you guys stand it?"

The police medic didn't understand that I meant picking up feelings. He said, "We're not cruel. It's a humane treatment really. Once a patient is changed he is usually ready to lead a happy life. It's the only treatment ever used that doesn't bounce them back to a life of crime and more punishment."

I was shuddering from the impact of the terror coming from the second closed room. This one was a sickie. He'd had bad nightmares most nights of his life but managed to forget them in daylight. The machine was forcing him to remember those nightmares, bring them back, making them brighter than reality. I tried to push back his nightmare, to hang onto the cool images of the corridor and the intern standing there. I said to him, "It's like sex, isn't it? It goes up, and then burns out."

46

The young intern looked uneasy, turning my ID cards over and over in his hand. "You know a lot about it already. They must have told you a lot. It must be OK, but I'd feel better about taking you on the observation tour if you had a standard police student pass."

"I don't want to see the poor lunks go through brainwipe," I said hastily. "Forget it. I just want to know why—I mean how do you get that mixture? I mean if they're scared out of their wits, how do they get that other good feeling mixed in?" The fear and confusion broadcasting from the second room was changing to a weird pleasure. I wanted to get out before it went up into burn. "Show me the way to the down elevator, will you?"

"It's over this way." The young man in the white jacket trailed along with me as I headed that way. He explained. "The pleasure feeling is what the treatment started with in the early fifties. Electrodes here and here." He pointed to places on his temples. "And back here." He touched the back of his neck. "A low amount of juice, not enough to damage the brain, produces an experience of pleasure with a natural feedback. It builds up by itself to overwhelming, synchronous waves, an epileptiform convulsion like an orgasm. It was harmless and experimenters kept trying it with the excuse that it gave insight into epilepsy. It was reported as a terrific experience. Authorities were afraid they'd discovered a new addiction."

He stopped in front of the elevator and pushed the button. "But then they realized that no one who tried it ever wanted to try it again. They'd said it was wonderful, but the mention of trying it again seemed to bore them. If they were urged to try it again and started to hook up, they would grow absentminded and forget what they were doing."

We stood waiting for the elevator and I listened hard to his words like a wall and behind the wall the terror from the second room turned to a peak of pleasure, then to overwhelming, blind, mindless ecstasy and flash burnout. The intern kept talking. "Investigators established that the experience had burned out the entire search-for-pleasure idea on that subject and left it burned out, unable to resonate enough feedback to sustain a purpose. Experi-

47

menters tried combining the electrodes with a different idea. A subject was given a cigarette to smoke and told it would give the biggest charge out of smoking a cigarette he would get this side of heaven. It did, and he never smoked again. For a while the treatment was used to help people get off smoking, then they tried treating kleptomania and that worked too. People stopped stealing. It wipes obsessions, ambitions, and the dominant purpose at the moment of wipe, and it strengthens and amplifies the next strongest. The new guy is the old one with a layer off the top."

I looked at his earnest persuasive face. I remembered a lot of talk that didn't fit. I said, "But everyone talks of brainwipe like the guy is gone, wiped, destroyed. They don't remember their names. They avoid their old friends. They forget their families. Those criminals back there screaming. They're not exactly tortured but they're not exactly screaming with joy."

He looked sulky, glanced around as if looking for ideas on the floor. "We don't know if they're screaming. The walls are soundproof. But we don't try to make it pleasant. We get the convicted criminal good and mad at us and afraid of punishment; the electricity will feed into his hatred and build up and wipe out the whole fear-hatred thing against authority. Punishment might have started their crimes. Most criminals were punished too much or at the wrong times; they break laws because they hate. The electricity brings the fear and anger to overload and wipes it. Sometimes it wipes the whole memory of himself because fear and anger have been the core of his personality."

"Maybe the people who did it to him ought to get wiped."

"Maybe, but he wound up being the criminal, not his parents. The law punishes you for what you do, not for what was done to you."

The elevator light came slowly up the many numbers of the many floors.

I said, "It doesn't sound so bad. Why are people circulating such stories? I mean why are people into such bad vibes about wipe? I mean Electronic Personality Restructuring?"

"We want them to be scared. If criminals arrived here expecting to have a good time, if the word got around that it

48

was an experience like sex, the criminals would go into it thinking about sex and pleasure. Whatever they think about goes into overload and gets wiped."

The intern talked louder, gesturing worriedly. "If you think we have a bad public image from wiping people's memories of punishment and sometimes their own names, think what kind of image we'd get if we turned out graduates from wipe who can't remember ever having heard of sex, but still dig crime. Our current public image might seem bad, but that's the way we like it. Don't make waves."

The elevator door hissed open.

"I won't talk about it," I assured him and got into the elevator. "Thanks for the education."

I went out into the sunshine and across the street from the hospital saw a kid hesitating on the corner, unused to ambulance traffic in a city where all traffic had been banned except very slow buses for old people and those for sightseers. The ambulance started up briskly when the light changed.

The light turned green for a moment and I crossed to the kid's side, and acted lost and asked the kid for directions on how to get onto a slideway, and asked him what the hospital was and other humble questions until the kid was swollen with importance at teaching an adult and strutting with confidence,

When the light turned green again he walked across the street, giving out good vibes.

I went into a phone booth and dialed Rescue Squad. I was going to ask switchboard for Ahmed. I didn't get switchboard, I got the deep rasp of Judd Oslow's voice.

"Rescue Squad, Oslow speaking."

"Sorry, Chief, I was trying to get Ahmed."

"Sanford, have you filled out those work reports yet?"

"I went over there but it was locked."

"What time was that?"

"About seven-thirty or eight."

There was a pause and I could hear him panting into the phone, holding his temper before he spoke. "You may pretend to be half-witted, Sanford, but you're not. You're just lazy. Nobody likes to fill out forms, but each man in this

49

department has to do his own sweat work; he doesn't try to lay it on someone else's back. Unless you make out your own work-time reports we can't pay you for anything you did while you were working alone. I know you have been working this week; things you've been doing like getting that psychotic picked up this morning are coming in on other men's reports. But we can't pay you for it. Get back to Neurological and fill out your work-time reports so we can pay you!"

I crossed the street again.

The pretty report writer held her hands poised over the typewriter and kept the tape recorder on and listened to me with an expression of surprise and doubt.

I finished telling her about the crazy man with the contagious murderous vibes that I'd called the squad to arrest.

"What time did you start work on that assignment?" she asked. "You should have the exact time."

"I don't know. When do you first start to notice an atmosphere? About a year ago I first started noticing something spooky about that block, but I didn't do anything. I really noticed it in an Italian restaurant the day I was hired, but I didn't do anything then either."

"A year?" Her voice became shrill. "You get paid by the hour. When did your superiors assign you to the case?"

She was a cute round girl with a cute face and a button nose, but something about the whole scene was getting me mad.

"I don't have any superior. Nobody assigned me. I decided to do something about it this morning at six twenty-three."

"I have to fill out a space that says how many hours you worked, Mr. Sanfort. When did you start work?"

"It depends on what you call work," I growled, looking away so she couldn't see how angry I was. "I made a phone call. It took five minutes."

"You can't get paid for five minutes, Mr. Sandfort." She stopped holding her hands over the typewriter and put them on the table clenched. "I'm just trying to help you." She was reddening around the eyes. I wondered why I was picking on her. I tried to dig my own mood, like tuning to some stranger.

50

"My name's not Sandfort," I said, almost snarling. Suddenly in my head, my name made a wild circling echo. Not Sandfort, not Sandfort. . . . NOT SANFORD NOT SANFORD. NOT GEORGE SANFORD. *George Sanford was not my right name.*

She couldn't hear the echo, but she was asking something.

I thought, Neurological is the right place to go crazy. Through the echoes of my own voice in my head I heard her voice dimly and watched her lips move. "We have to fill out the page. What's your real name, then, and what's your address?"

I don't have an address. I visit communes. I don't have a name. I'm not me!

I didn't say anything crazy aloud to her. I probably still looked mad instead of scared, terrified, spinning. I turned and stamped out into the corridor and staggered to the picture window. What happens when you try to tune to yourself as if you were a stranger? I was still tuning in. I didn't let go. I looked out across the river and saw the Palisade cliffs and buildings, huge in the distance, turn into the wrecked wall of a nearby building slowly falling. The buzz of the copters was a gigantic plane that was going to crash through the walls into the corridor where I stood. I was scared, I was terrified. I felt like a child three feet high.

Huge imaginary adult faces looked down at me. Voices boomed down from a distance. "What's your name, little boy?" "Did you live in this house?" "Do you know who was in this house?" "Where do you live, little boy?" "What's your address?"

Let me alone! I didn't do it! I'm not me!

I turned and walked rapidly out of the mental hospital across the street into the sunshine. I hate peple who ask questions, even imaginary people.

I hate filling out forms that ask name and address first thing. My teachers would give up and do it for me. I've always had friends who would fill out things for me. Except on tests. I had to face tests alone. When adults were giants.

Address. What's that mean? Memory. *It means where do your mommy and daddy live, dear?* I 'don't know, I'm an orphan. *(Shock, sorry, apology, shame. Adult vibes of*

51

embarrassment.) Vibes hurt. Don't tell them! *ADDRESS?* I don't know.

Stupid kid! A moron or trying to give me a hard time! I hate you back, dumb grown-up. *NAME?* It's not my real name. I don't know my real name. *NAME?* I don't want to lie. The answers don't fit into the boxes. The forms are stupid. They ask stupid questions. I won't answer tests. I'll pretend I'm stupid. I'll pretend I can't read.

I'm afraid to be caught reading. I'm still afraid.

That was my twentieth birthday last month. I am a twenty-year-old male, illiterate, hallucinating that a silver plane is crashing on me. I get that plane when I try to think. I hear it now.

Judd Oslow just said, "You may pretend to be half-witted, Sanford, but you're not. You're just lazy."

The word isn't *lazy,* Chief, it's *crazy.*

I got back into the glass phone booth and looked at a little park while I dialed. "Switchboard, connect me to Ahmed Kosvakatats. Yes. I'll hold." I waited and watched a special bus from an out-of-state hospital float over the grass and pull up in front of Neurological at the patients' entrance. Calm, blank-eyed people were led from the bus one by one.

Nuts, like me. One of them started giving out crazy jolts of fright and violence in his thinking. I started to shut the phone booth door, like shutting out shouting, but it was vibes, not sound. It wouldn't shut out. Stay cool, George; learn to feel it all and stay cool. The nut sank his teeth into the arm of the attendant. Not enough tranquilizer. But they don't want them tranquil when they bring nuts and criminals in for brainwipe. If they can't get mad and scared the wipe won't work.

In a few hours the man they are prying loose from the attendant will be fastened in the wipe room. He'll do some more inward screaming and then become permanently calm and friendly. I remembered standing outside the wipe rooms in the Criminal Justice section. I remembered tuning in on how people being wiped felt.

The door handle on the phone booth bent and came off in my hand. I stood with the door handle dangling from my fingers, watching through the glass cage as the last of the people were led from the bus into the hospital. Nuts, like me.

52

3

"GEORGE?" said a voice in my earphones.

"Yeah, OK," I answered stupidly. I put the handle down on the shelf and looked up through the glass at the blue sky and the copters buzzing and landing on the building tops. Free. The phone said something and reminded me it was there.

"That you, Ahmed?" I said into it. "I just nailed a nut for Rescue Squad. You weren't there to help make out reports. Come over and buy me a meal and make out my reports for me."

He didn't answer. I could hear breathing.

A girl stopped and stood near the phone. She had a flower over her left ear, meant she was looking for a new boyfriend.

"Peace and oneness, little sister," I said, giving the love-commune greeting. She smiled and gave out friendly vibes.

"George," said the voice patiently in my earphones. "This is the chief, Judd Oslow, not Ahmed, not a girl. Snap awake, man!" I snapped awake. "Yes, sir. Sorry."

"George, listen closely," said the patient voice in the stereo earphones, and with my eyes shut, the stereo pickup of wall echoes made a hearing picture of the pine-paneled room and oak desk giving a high-pitched rebounding echo and a vinyl old-fashioned stone floor giving low pitched echoes of the scuff of feet. The only lack of echoes was near the phone. The big sagging bulk of the chief absorbed near echoes.

"Yes, sir, I'm listening."

"George, Ahmed is missing. Today we got his wrist radio in the mail, no return address on the box."

It was like getting kicked in the stomach. "You mean Ahmed is dead?"

"No, I mean he is missing. He's been out of touch since Wednesday, but his wrist radio is no announcement he's been murdered."

I didn't want to discuss that. When I was a kid, my friends

53

told stories of gang and organization wars. If any organization or gang killed someone they'd send his pocket gear to his family in a little cardboard box. For a year now Ahmed was a cop and a member of the Rescue Squad. Anyone might feel that the Rescue Squad was his family, and send his wrist radio in a box—if he had been killed.

"George, are you still there? Have you heard anything from Ahmed? Any messages, any vibes?"

"No." I never get any vibes from Ahmed. When I was a kid and he was the king of the block gang I thought he was all brains, no feelings at all. Intelligence is a white light that shows you how to do anything, that cools any situation, that makes harmony out of hassle. Ahmed had a searchlight beam coming out of him.

I know a lot about feelings, my own and others'. We all needed that light when we were growing up.

"He's been missing since Wednesday?" I repeated and heard my voice snarling. "Why dincha tell me sooner?"

"Never mind getting mad, George. We're putting you on the job to find him."

"How many people on the job? Don't lean just on me. You need lots of people. Turn the whole department on it. I don't even have any expense money."

His voice was still patient and slow. "You have to file time spent, expense money spent, and give the department a bill, remember? You haven't filed a report yet on the last two jobs."

"I don't like paperwork," I mumbled. "Trying to read forms makes me feel sick. I'm neurotic." *I'm psychotic. I get scared and see airplanes crashing,* I said to him silently.

"Get your girlfriends to do it," he snapped.

I looked up but the flower girl was walking away. She looked back and waved, but kept walking. I forgot her.

"I need some money to look for Ahmed," I mumbled.

The chief sounded tired. "Give me your credit-card number and bank, and I'll drop a hundred dollars into your credit-card account. OK?"

"OK." A rich guy is a poor guy with money. I still felt broke.

The chief read me. "You'll have the money in ten

54

minutes, George. You're not broke: Lean on the idea hard. We owe you a lot more money than that; just file your reports and keep your receipts. Make the Accounting Department happy, or they'll take this hundred out of my pay."

Maybe something would come up to help me make out reports. I got my mind back onto the job. "What was Ahmed doing for you when you lost him?"

"There'll be a report on him waiting for you at the Madison and Fifty-third station house," said the chief and wouldn't say anymore.

I walked south for a mile, then stopped at a vending machine for a cup of soup, pushed the soup button, and put in my credit card. I listened to the machine click and bong acceptance of my credit, and then roll the card back out and start to deliver the soup. It was a good sound and a good feeling to have a credit card working for you.

A kid was going by.

"Hey, kid, you see Ahmed the Arab recently?"

"Who?"

"A tall skinny guy with the Rescue Squad, does locating and detection. Moves fast. Eyebrows black like this." I joined my fingers over my eyes in a finger frown.

"Nope." He looked at me, waiting for more questions, but I didn't have any more. Kids keep getting smaller all the time. It's hard to think of them as the same kind of people as when they were my size. They haven't changed, I have.

"OK. Thanks anyhow, kid."

He nodded and slipped away between the buildings into the backyard wild greenbelt. I looked after him. In a city of four million people there had not been much sense in asking a kid if he had seen one missing man, but sometimes I was lucky. Score one miss. I hadn't bet anything on it. I walked along, sipping my soup, into the public walkways of the art and gallery district, among the costumes of artists and customers. I walked faster than the slowly flowing crowd. Most people were there to look, but some were carrying large canvases and photo prints, and I watched for those in the crowd ahead and gave them plenty of room. I take up more than my share of sidewalk even without carrying soup, but I know the footwork of getting through a

55

jammed-tight crowd without touching anyone. Ahmed had made the UN Brotherhood gang play tag games through crowds like this; you lost if any grown-up complained or even lost his smile.

It was a happy crowd. The art gallery sections always are happy. Even the old buildings had happy vibes and special wild greenbelt spaces around wild flowers and tall feathery wild weeds and climbing vines shining on the mesh links that held the green back from crowding the buildings. I wondered why they wouldn't let the vines climb on the buildings and then began to think like a cop and saw that a clear space with no cover around each window kept people from secretly working on the windows to get into the gallery buildings and steal paintings. Half the people I knew were on pensions. Enough money for food and a place to stay, not enough money for buying something beautiful that reached you inside. Original art has high price tags. Must be a lot of stealing.

At the station house on Madison I picked up an envelope with my name on the outside. Inside was an envelope with the words *"Ahmed Kosvakatats,* missing-person data, authorized personnel only."

I sat down on one of the station-house benches to shuffle through it. It all seemed to be just Xerox copies of official papers on him. Birth certificate, school records, that sort of private stuff. It was violation of privacy to even look at them. There was a missing-person report, but it didn't have any of its blanks filled in except his name, description, and where last seen.

He had last sent in a report on his wrist radio from 127th and Park Avenue. A bad district to vanish in. A *lousy* district to vanish in! The corner of the Black Kingdom, Spanish Harlem, and the shutoff walls of Arab Jordan! No open fights are allowed in the public ways that make open roads between these kingdoms, but the hatred is so thick you can cut it with a knife. The kingdoms have the right to appoint their own police and pass their own laws inside their walls. Once inside their walls, trespassers vanish. The "police" inside the walls claim that no one entered. Adults with sense do not plan to trespass. They walk past the walls without looking up or slowing down and get by.

56

I went underground to the subway and took a moving chair to the 125th Street exit and walked two blocks to the address, walked by without looking up—past the high closed walls of Spanish Harlem toward Arab Jordan. At the corner of Park and 128th was a phone booth made out of stainless steel. I got inside and called Rescue Squad and asked switchboard for the chief.

Did he know he was asking me to go inside Black Kingdom territory or Spanish Harlem territory, or Arab Jordan territory to look for Ahmed? There wasn't anyplace else to look. I felt cold inside. The chief ought to give me some advice about how to get in, search, and get out. Or did he just expect to take my last will and testament over the phone?

He accepted my call right away. "Judd Oslow here, George."

"Chief, I can't make anything out of these reports. What was Ahmed working on when you lost him?"

"Something big, missing. The crime department drafted all my best workers to help the search. Ahmed, too."

"What was it?"

"Information about it belongs to the Bureau of Criminal Detection, organization-motivated crimes. I can't tell you anything."

He'd told me something. The three kingdoms were organizations. I shuffled the stack of Xeroxed paper in my hands, hoping some information would turn up. "Did you ask Spanish Harlem, Black Harlem, and Arab Jordan if they've seen a Rescue Squad man?" Dumb question.

The chief said blandly, "They have our missing-person bulletin on Ahmed."

"Will they let someone in from the squad to search?" Dumb question, but I could hope.

"No. They have their own police to do that." But they wouldn't. Judd Oslow did not have the legal right to tell me to go in and search. But I would.

Two of the Xerox papers slid way from my hands and I bent to get them, bumping my forehead on the shelf of the stainless-steel phone booth.

In the stereo earphones the chief cleared his throat a couple of time, as if he knew I was expecting him to say

57

something else, then he said, "Start where he was last seen. You don't need a lot of information, George, not from what Ahmed said about your talent. Just be lucky, the way you were in the first three cases, and get on the job right away."

"Oh, sure," I muttered and unshipped the earphones and throat mike and hung them up.

"Just be lucky," said his voice, getting tinny and far away as I hung up. I rubbed the hot lump on my forehead and stepped out of the phone booth.

Women in veils looked out of steel-mesh-barred windows. The passers walked by, head down, not ready to make trouble by staring. The walls had been built when I was five, earlier—sometime about when I was born, the Israelis had another war with Arabia and took most of the desert country. Egypt stayed out of the fight and refused to take in Arabian refugees. Israel refused to take Arabian refugees because they said the Arabs were enemies and killers and thieves and would be dangerous to their families. They said the war had come about because the Arabs raided, looted, and killed across the border every night, and they did not want Arabs inside their new territory.

The UN had resettled Arabian refugees in every country of the world. The United States quota of thousands arrived, cantankerous, resentful, and anti-Semitic, with the opinion that America was a Jewish country, and all Jews were enemies. They immediately discovered the new rights of cultural autonomy, and they imitated what was happening in Harlem and settled in a rim area around a demolished four-block slum, voted themselves a township, joined all the remaining buildings by walls, walled up all the doors, roads, and entrances to their territory except one wide street that opened into the center space, dumped the center space full of beach sand, planted a few date palms, added a fountain, a small mosque, and a minaret, and declared the entire place an Arabian Cultural Preservation Club, off limits to nonmembers. Trespassers disappeared.

I was a kid, placed from an orphanage to foster homes in an old-fashioned area that believed in racial mixture. There was somebody in our kid gang from every race almost. The old UN building was near and we called our tribe the UN Brotherhood.

We had a game the Amerind kinds called counting coup, but we called chick-follow-the-leader. If you got too scared to follow the leader, you had to make sounds like a chicken and flap your arms instead of talking, when anybody said anything to you, for a whole week after you'd chicken out. When the black kids were leaders they'd take shortcut across black territory and chicken out everyone but the ones who could look black enough.

We were great at follow-the-leader across the understruts of bridges, but when it came to making raids into race territories, so many kids chickened we had to cut the penalty time back to one day of flapping and bird sounds. Ahmed would swank around in a sheet costume like an Arab and claim raids into Arab territory alone and show us a pocket full of sand, but we didn't ask him to lead us in until he found secret passages through the cellars of ruined houses, gone houses scraped off flat and covered when the old slum had been half cleared, before the Arabs arrived.

Around then we were already calling him Ahmed the Arab. He stole sheet burnooses and costumes for us and led us on five great raids into Arab territory. We went around in it like real Arab kids, looking at things that were different. Veiled women, harems, muezzin calls, and praying flattened out, head toward Mecca. We saw the Arab young men, muscles oiled and shining, practicing war games and knife fighting.

If any real Arab kid got suspicious and tried to get close to us, Ahmed would lead us out, running fast through roundabout ways until we got the blocked-off cellars of the demolished buildings. Then we crawled out along smelly dry waste-pipe tunnels to a manhole under the free public streets and safety.

Our last raid into Arab territory was the bad one. They knew strange kids had been in their territory and they were ready. The Arab kids were a yelling mob running close after us all the way out. They found our entrance to the cellars and caught up with our end line of running small kids. The big kid who stayed back to make rearguard for the small kids got grabbed and brought down by a pile of Arab kids. They kneed him and battered his face until he was bloody. They were pulling loose bricks out of the walls to hammer him, but Ahmed led a charge of Brotherhood kids back to rescue him and the kids carried him out.

Ahmed had sworn to us that Arabs always go for the eyes and groin and try to maim. We had enjoyed the danger and been careful, but it spoiled the fun to have it really almost happen to someone.

The gang never followed Ahmed into Arab territory again. He never asked us to go. The Arab kids had found our tunnels and would be waiting.

That was twelve years ago. Last week Ahmed had been given a job to search New York for something. I wondered if he had tried to throw on a sheet and search Arab Jordan. He might walk right in.

I broke out into a sweat, standing near the phone booth, looking up at the windows of the Jordan wall.

I'd looked too long. The veiled women who had looked out were already replaced by a crowding of kids' faces at the grilles.

"*Ferengi,*" they jeered. "*Juden.* Kill the Jew dog." The old war calls of warriors who had lost. As far as Arabs were concerned, New Yorkers were either Jews and enemies or blacks and slaves, to be insulted accordingly.

The sun shone on my face as I leaned my head back looking up at the long high wall of Arab Jordan, mixed colors of bricks, where the lower doors and windows were walled up and once-separate buildings had been walled together. The kids shouted back at me from the line of third-floor windows.

I don't look like an Arab. Blondish, over six feet high, bulky at the shoulders, round in the face, short lumpy nose, light eyelashes, blue eyes, messy, light-brown hair, the opposite of anything Arab-Mediterranean, a big Northman type staring stupidly up at their windows, thinking or wondering.

Up at the windows cute kid faces with big, dark-lashed eyes jeered and cursed and offered unprintable suggestions about what they would do to a foreigner if he dared to step foot off the public freeways. I knew they meant it.

An older young man appeared at the nearest window, pushed the kids aside, and shouted down in a voice of authority, "What do you want?"

60

I had been a dope to attract their attention, but I had to think. Should I ask after Ahmed? No. If he was still hiding in there, maybe cut off from a retreat route, it could alert them to search for a trespasser. I thought up a lie.

"I'm a student, studying the history of the Arab culture. I was wondering how Arab culture had changed."

Several other husky young men without shirts were now standing at the windows fingering curved knives, turning the blades so they flashed light for me to notice.

The spokesman said, "We live as our ancestors did. Go back to your books, castrated student, and do not stare at our women."

I turned and walked away, along the line of the wall, under the high windows. Something struck me lightly between the shoulder blades, but that would just be something small shot by an Arab kid from a beanshooter. The city police keep anyone from being hassled or hurt on the free pedestrian ways. They'd even shut down that kid in a minute, so I ignored it.

Up past 131st Street, in a clump of bushes in the greenbelt that ran down the middle of the street, there was the old manhole cover that led down to the street entrances. There were wear signs in the dirt around the manhole cover showing that it was opened often, and candy wrappers showed that kids sat around under those bushes eating candy.

The entrance was watched. I crossed the street, going away, acting casual. I decided to wait until one o'clock. The kids might be home having lunch, and there was a TV serial playing —*Lawrence of Arabia*—they'd want to watch it, or their parents would make them want to watch it. Arabs would naturally want to watch a series that glorified Arabs.

At one o'clock I went down the manhole nearly confident. It was empty. I made speed through the waste pipe. Even though it seemed smaller, it was clean and polished from being used. I sprinted silently through the cellars and around the familiar corners. Everything was cleaner and less dusty from being used a lot and the Arab kids had fixed up one cellar with rugs and lamps as a clubhouse. It had flags on the wall and a curved sword hanging up.

Maybe they'd also installed burglar alarms at the

61

entrance to warn them. I skidded around a corner, looking for an old secret door they probably didn't know about yet, but there ahead the kid mob was coming at me, running barefoot, armed with sticks, knives, and stones.

They yelled and stopped. I yelled and kept going, because the turn to the other tunnel was ahead. A couple of leader kids came at me and circled and one hit my shoulder with a dirty bat with a nail in it. I never was sure before, but now I remembered that the kid they'd caught the first time had been me. It's always easy for me to forget which one I was in a bad scene, because I know how the others felt, too, and I'd rather be a winner. When the Arab kids caught me I was eight years old. I'd protected my eyes, but my nose remembered how it felt to be mashed, and the tender parts of my skin remembered how it felt to be kicked red and soft. It was a hurting thing to remember. I panicked out of control seeing the same kind of kids coming at me again. The world slanted. I picked up the kid who hit me with the bat and threw him at the other kids, knocking them over like bowling pins. I pulled the bat with its nail out of my shoulder. It was a rusty nail.

"Psycho Arabs," I shouted, my voice bouncing back from the walls. "Can't you act like people?" I took the bat and went at them, crouched, pretending murder, and they scattered and ran squealing into the tunnels like a nest of frightened rats.

I didn't have long before they brought back their big brothers. Adult Arabs believe in torture, too. I ran down a side tunnel roaring, sounding like I was chasing after kids instead of running away. Somewhere was another cellar-stair entrance that we'd blocked up by covering the door with cement. It looked like solid stone. Twelve years is a lifetime from eight to twenty, but it's nothing to a wooden door. It was still there.

I reached the stone knob that covered the handle, yanked it up, and slid into the crack and down before it opened more than a foot. On the other side of the door was a handle. I pulled and slammed it shut and slid the lock tight with a rasp and clank. I hoped the kids had been running too hard to have looked back and seen me slide into the wall.

Smelling dust and cement, I groped up the narrow stairs

in the total blindness, scraping my knuckles against a gritty stone wall, making gritty snapping sounds underfoot with rolling pebbles shoved down against bits of flaked cement. I stopped and thought.

I was here trying to find Ahmed. I was supposed to be trying to find him by picking up his vibes, but all I'd done was follow up a theory that he'd taken the old shortcut into Arab Jordan or bluffed his way in the front door disguised as an Arab and been caught. Me, so lousy at thinking up theories, trying to find him by using straight theory! I was better at using hunches. I'd do better trying to do it the way the chief said. Follow feeling.

If Ahmed was in trouble what kind of vibes would he be sending? I stood and thought, trying to remember Ahmed in trouble. I remember being close to him, shaking his hand. I remember him patting my shoulder and shaking my hand in congratulation for something. I remember me being a short fat strong kid of twelve and Ahmed at thirteen a foot taller, already halfway through high school, tall and strong, physically as perfect as a greyhound, reading books, getting good marks in math, making out with a lady teacher, and leading his tribe into explorations of the city. I never got any trouble vibes from Ahmed. Ahmed was never in trouble. Plugged in all the time, vibrating with a kind of inner excitement that was logic.

With the smell of plaster dust inside my nose, caking it dry, I stood in the dark stairwell trembling with the same kind of excitement and effort. *Think.*

I remembered that a small flashlight was attached to my key ring. That was a thought. It was late, but it was a good thought.

I fumbled it out and switched it on. Bright light lit up the close walls of the stairwell and showed plaster bits and dust on the stairs. I looked for footprints, but there were no footprints except my own showing in the dust of the steps I had just climbed. Ahmed had not come this way.

I started up the stairs again, walking easy and avoiding pebbles, and came to a steel door blocking the stair. Beside the door was an irregular hole where we had pulled out bricks. The hole was big enough for kids, but not for me. I twisted five more bricks loose and stacked them quietly on the stair, pushed bits of cement out into space, and heard them click and hiss against stone twenty feet below, and then I went backward, feet first, out the hole into space, and groped downward with my feet, contacted solidity, and went the rest of the way through and stood on a steel girder.

I flashed my light around. Unused outside windows faced each other in the boxed-in darkness. Six floors of unused outside windows. The two old buildings had been connected by bridging the space between by a roof and a front connecting wall. What had been an outside air space between them was closed in. The two old walls had been braced apart by adding crossbeams between them.

I sat on a crossbeam and dangled my legs and thought. I picked out windows with my flashbeam while thinking. I could go in any of those windows, but in the building on the other side, on the third floor, we exploring kids had found offices in use. Playing a game of make-believe, we decided we were UN spies assigned to find out an Arab plot against the peace. We said we would listen behind the walls to the phone calls the important Arab leaders would make and listen to their conferences. But we never came back to do it.

It would be easy to listen behind the walls. Inside each building the irregular outline of the useless windows had been covered and smoothed by inside partition walls in front of them. There was space between the walls and the real walls, enough to move around in.

I slid over on the crossbeam by shifting along with my hands and seat instead of getting up. The window on that side was gritty and old, but we'd opened the lock and oiled it seven years ago. It had expensive ball bearings that last. I lifted and the window raised easily with only a faint rumbling creak. It opened into a darkness that smelled of fake leather plastics, air conditioning, and coffee.

I felt a nearby blast of alertness, like caution, only sudden and too strong. Someone had heard the noise. That was not an end-point-bad thing. I didn't have to make any more sounds. Listeners always got bored and went away when they had to listen and couldn't hear anything.

I put both hands on the sill and hoisted myself over and inside without touching my legs to anything, placing one foot on the floor slowly and easily until the floor held the

64

weight without a creak. I switched off the flashlight and saw light coming through long cracks between the plywood panels. The joins of the panels were long clear plastic strips that gripped the panels on either side. I could see through the strips. Easy.

Nothing in that room but desks.

Ahmed's voice spoke from another room. It sounded artificial, deep, and important as if he were making a stage speech. "Selim, the sands have answered. You will never be commander of Refugee Arabia. That road leads to death."

"I didn't ask that question," answered an angry roar of a voice.

"He reads the sands and the sands read your dreams, Selim." Another voice laughed. "Prepare for a short life."

Other voices laughed and jeered in Arabic. And people moved around. Scraping furniture.

Under cover of their noise I made my own noises squeezing by in the narrow partition space, rocking their walls slightly like an earthquake.

There was further exchange between Ahmed's voice and Selim's in which I judged Ahmed was goading him for one of Ahmed's complicated plans and then a crash and the sounds of struggle. I put my eye to the crack ready to try to get through the wall—if I saw Ahmed in trouble.

Five men were wrestling cheerfully among coffee benches. They were shirtless, brown, and well muscled and wore knives in sheaths at their belts. They were disarming a sixth one, wider and stronger in build, with a wide-jawed face.

On the other side of the room Ahmed sat behind a small table, his back against the wall. He watched the struggle expressionlessly. His dark eyes were narrowed; his face was dirty and unshaven with the start of a black beard beginning to show a dark borderline across his face. He looked big, skinny, tired, and ugly.

It gave me a jolt to see him looking so ugly. Something was badly wrong with Ahmed. I looked to see if he was legcuffed and fixed to the spot, but the small card table was over his lap and a coffee bench was in the way. I couldn't see his legs. His hands were slowly smoothing sand across the top of the table. He tapped the surface, and sand humped into wave patterns. Apparently he had been telling fortunes sand-Rorschach style. I'd seen that in his police book on projective technique in questioning.

The struggling group had succeeded in removing a remarkable collection of small lasers and other deadly little items from the struggling man. They called him Selim and spoke to him soothingly, grinning.

He had now stopped struggling and was speaking in Arabic, earnestly trying to persuade them to agree to kill Ahmed. I didn't understand Arabic, but the gestures were clear.

Ahmed said, "Only a guilty man is afraid of witnesses."

"Liar." Selim, reverting to English, snarled at the others. "The children and the women and now the fools believe his lies. His is pretending to be a fortune-teller to postpone his death, nothing more. We should have killed him when we caught him spying."

The friend shrugged and the others laughed. "But Hisham will want to hear his fortune read when he gets back. If the women and children tell him that we killed a fortune-teller, he will think we are hiding secrets from him."

The others laughed again, nervously. They were all hiding secrets.

Selim shouted at one, "I order you," and pointed to Ahmed and repeated the command in Arabic. The young fighter he was trying to command sat down on a coffee table and offered him a short knife, handle first, suggesting he do it himself. Suddenly Selim took the knife and turned toward Ahmed.

The others laughed and sat down to watch.

I looked back at Ahmed. His hands were poised slightly above the table, ready to move, but still he sat there. Was he fastened in place or free? Could he help me fight them?

I leaned against a panel and watched it bulge. The line of light increased, the view got better. The heavyset one, Selim, was threading toward Ahmed among scattered benches and coffee tables covered with cups and cards and games. He stopped just short of Ahmed's reach, went into a fighter's crouch, and circled left. Ahmed did not get up. I saw that he was fastened down. His hands were poised and

66

ready. He could scoop up sand and throw it in his attacker's eyes.

"Not yet, George," he said in a normal voice. "Too soon. There's no danger."

"Too soon?" Selim howled, thinking Ahmed had commanded him. "We should have killed you two days ago, trespassing, spying, 'Srailly dog. Die now!"

Ahmed knew what he was doing. I didn't bother to watch Selim. Very slow and easy I took my weight off the bulge in the panel. It was slid out to the end of its nails and ready to fall. It slowly flattened out without creaking and I sighed relief. Attacking six armed men had not been a happy plan. Ahmed was right. It was not necessary. I remembered our gang practice with knife fighting. Anyone with a strong, fast left hand and practice can grab a knife away from a right-handed knife fighter. Ahmed had practiced with us until knives were useless against us. In practice we had never been able to touch Ahmed with a wood knife. He was naturally fast and had long fast arms. With the sand to throw in Selim's eyes and the card table to use as a club, his apparent helplessness because he was fastened to the bench was a joke, a joke on Selim.

The laughing and cheering on the other side of the walls showed that Selim was still trying, to the amusement of the Arab soldiers, who by now saw that it was hopeless. What was the chance they would eventually get up to hold Ahmed?

Maybe I should watch, but I didn't like their laughing. A pack of dogs howling at two fighting wolves. The law of privacy is right!

Privacy is the foundation for the right to be different. No one should watch too long any people who have a different idea about what is right and wrong. That's what they said in school. And they were right. When I watched these I wanted to get away from them or kill them. These were not typical Arabs, they were refugee rabble, the debris of a defeated army with no skills but battle, the rejected ones and their camp-following women. Other men with skills and professions were returned but the Israelis had not allowed these to return, fearing the revenge of unemployed killers, and they had huddled outside their borders, homeless, unwanted by any country, until the UN had demanded that each country of the world accept a small group and give them job training. Israel had paid gratefully to have them taken away.

Arriving in New York, they had no knowledge but their grudges and no plans but revenge. They assumed that all New Yorkers were Jews. They were proud of being Arabs? Watching them, it would have been easy to hate all Arabs. I found I was grinding my fists together and tensing every muscle isometrically to get rid of rage.

The cheers and noise reached a crescendo and then cut off as suddenly as a TV being turned off. Every soldier gave a jolt of fear.

I put my eye to the light crack and saw that all had turned their heads toward the door. I shifted position and looked toward the door. A man stood there, a small balding man wearing a white cape with a purple stripe. He was heavily muscled and evenly tanned to the top of his bald head. He stood watching and listening in a pose of easy alert balance, all of him focused into alert attention to their faces.

They waited for his reprimand, caught in some guilty act for which they expected punishment.

He smiled and said, "Don't kill him, children! I have not had my fortune told."

They laughed and relaxed. This was their leader, Akbar Hisham.

In history class 6B the videotape had shown the refugees arriving in New York about eighteen years ago, important people welcoming them and a welcoming band playing, Akbar Hisham looking younger then with a head of black hair, gripping a microphone and talking into it.

"You offer brotherhood," he had said, not smiling. "Brotherhood means sharing what you have with what we have. We have only defeat and injustice and humiliation to share. We will share it someday but do not call us your brothers. We are your victims."

It was certainly not the speech of polite thanks the New York audience had expected, but there was admiration mixed with the surprise they felt toward a man who dared to snarl threats to New York City.

He had continued with a promise. "We will take the

68

money the world owes us for the theft and loss of our country, and we will educate ourselves back to pride and power. Beware the next generation."

Now he was older, more seamed, more wrinkled, but not more mellow than he had been in his speech. Riding herd over a bitter defeated band of fighters is not done by gentle kindness. Yet he was Akbar Hisham, a well-known scholar and historian. The other educated and skilled scholars had been allowed to remain in their conquered countries or had gone to soft jobs in other countries. Only Akbar Hisham had chosen to throw in his lot with the refugees and fight for their rights.

He sat down on a leather bench, smiling. I saw the balding back of his head and the white cape over his shoulders. "I hear the prisoner came in in the headdress of a visitor from Iraq with a police badge in his pocket and no warrant and knew no Arabic and was caught going through the mail in the outer office. Such incompetence!"

"He is mad, effendi. When we caught him he was mad and babbled that he saw the future because he was about to die. He told of the past of the man who captured him, and said he saw a future of great wealth."

Hisham nodded. "I hear he has been fooling you well."

They protested. "He sees pictures in the sands." "He has told me my past." They praised Ahmed's ability as a teller of fate and fortune.

"The women say that he told them the truth." They tried to persuade Hisham.

Only Selim, who had wanted to kill Ahmed, sat with a sullen face beside his leader, not praising Ahmed's fortune-telling. His knife was back in its sheath.

Hisham turned to him courteously. "Did he tell your fortune well, Selim?"

Selim frowned. "He lied. He fooled them all. He lies to all of them to postpone his death." At Selim's words the others stirred as if wishing to speak, but said nothing.

The leader smiled at them all. "What bets will you take that he can tell my fortune with a shot of truth drug in his veins?"

They did not reply. The small bald muscular man spoke in Arabic to Selim, who seemed to be his second in com-

69

mand. He took a box from his pocket and handed it to Selim. His second in command passed it to an older soldier lounging in the doorway and gave an order. That one walked forward, jabbed the hypo through Ahmed's shirt into his right bicep, pressed the plunger slowly, and returned to the doorway.

The leader, Hisham, held out his hand with a soft-voiced request. He took back the empty hypo and inspected it. "Good." The balding man looked up at Ahmed for the first time. Ahmed returned the gaze with both hands flat on the tabletop. He had not moved when approached with the hypo or when jabbed. The leader gave him a polite nod and said, "Prisoner, you have just been given a shot of truth drug. Count backward from twenty."

"Twenty, nineteen, eighteen, senteen sixteen sixteen twelve nine. . . ." Ahmed's lean proud face with black eyebrows looked more Semitic than the Arabs'. He stopped, confused.

The leathery smile of the leader grew wider. He glanced at the others and then leaned forward toward Ahmed. "Now, with truth drug in your mind, can you tell my fortune?"

Ahmed looked down at the tabletop. He brought the flexing lamp down closer to the surface and tapped on the table, and tiny hummocks and hills in the sand sprang up and spread long radiating bars of darkness away from the light.

"I can still see pishures," he said, "but I don't know your queson. . . . Pardon . . . sa drug makes my tongue thick."

He looked up, tired, skinny, but alert, his eyes watchful under heavy black brows. "I can try. Do you want pas', present, or future?"

"Wonderful! A man who will still try to tell fortunes with truth drug in his blood," the leader remarked to the others. He turned back to Ahmed, as if to a delightful children's game, and resettled himself on a bench closer to Ahmed, farther from Selim. Smiling, he asked a question that held no smile in its meaning. "Fortune-teller, tell me why everyone stopped talking when I came in."

The Arabs had been smiling and murmuring to one another. The question hit like a blow of fear. Total silence fell.

Selim gave out a wave of anger and hatred. He stood up with hands ready, measuring the distance to his leader, clearly wondering if the others would accept the status quo and follow him if the leader was dead.

Akbar Hisham turned on his bench until they could see that a small laser lay on his open palm. He did not close his hand on it. Over his shoulder he asked Ahmed again, "Tell me what they were talking about when I came in."

Ahmed answered with his head up, looking alert, watching Selim. "I had told Selim's fortune. I had said that he planned to take over the rule of the Arab kingdom, but that this plan would lead to his death."

The laser in the leader's hand turned and pointed to Selim.

Ahmed continued. "When you came in, he was trying to kill me, and they were joking about what I had told him."

Selim, the stocky contender for the throne, still held his crouch, but he had shifted it to look as if crouched to attack Ahmed. "He is lying. I am always loyal to you, effendi. I wanted to kill him for lying."

Akbar Hisham nodded his tanned bald head. "Possibly. I have no belief in fortune-telling. For a captive it would be good strategy to make trouble between friends. Ask him what he knows of your plans now. This time he will not be able to lie."

Selim looked at Ahmed. Their eyes met in a long glare, and then Selim swallowed and looked away. "Effendi, he—he will lie."

Akbar Hisham tilted his head to the other soldiers. "Disarm Selim." It was not clear if the laser pointed at Selim or at all of them.

They all spoke at once. With sincere gestures and great relief they pointed to the bench with the pile of Selim's weapons and explained that they had already disarmed him, except for one little knife. Surely this showed their loyalty. They spoke in Arabic but their gestures were clear.

Hisham nodded approval. The shirtless soldiers took Selim's one knife from him roughly.

Angrily Selim argued his innocence and made gestures to a small metal box with a red button lying on one of the coffee benches amid a litter of coffee cups and playing cards. I wished I could understand. Arabic. The Arabs

71

spoke both and switched from one to the other easily. What was in the box?

Akbar Hisham nodded and shrugged as if letting himself be persuaded. He got himself a cup of coffee from the coffee machine against the wall and stood watching. Selim picked up the box. When it was up I saw that two wires trailed from it on the floor to Ahmed's table and under it to his legs.

Selim strode closer to Ahmed and held the box out where all could see it. "Now I will prove you can lie, dog. I will make you. . . ."

I recognized it as a torture box, a very simple gadget using batteries. I braced to kick out the wall panel.

Ahmed's voice said, "Not advisable, George."

Ahmed was the only person in the room facing my direction. He could see the shifting reflections of bulging and flattening in the wall panel. He knew the interwall space was there. They would think he spoke to them, called them George. Ahmed was probably planning to make me wait until there were fewer people in the room. But he couldn't have planned for this. I looked away from the slight crack and held my head. I heard Selim question him. I couldn't hold my ears.

"Lying police cur, you said they call you Ahmed the Arab." Selim's tone was a growl. "Are you an Arab? Say you are an Arab. Say you are one of us. When you say that you are an Arab, I will stop pressing on this button."

"I am not an Arab." Ahmed gave out no vibes of fear or pain. In games when leading the gang as a kid, he had often not noticed small bleeding cuts or other hurts. Was he so much into this strategy he could ignore a torture box? I imagined electricity. Even in imagination it hurt.

"Are you an Arab?"

"No." No vibes of hurt from Ahmed, only a buzz of determined alertness, ready for the situation to change. But from the Arabs I felt a warm glow of interested sadism and admiration for the stamina of their victim.

"Lie, say you are an Arab and I will stop pushing this button. What race are you?" Selim was fighting for his life.

"I am Algerian French on my mother's side and Spanish Romany on my father's side." Ahmed's voice was thin and gasping, but truthful.

The old leader's thoughtful voice interrupted. "Interesting. . . . Captive, I thought you were just a police spy. Does Romany mean Gypsy?"

"No, Gypsy means Romany," Ahmed gasped, always nit-picking precise.

Selim's voice came out harsh, almost more in pain than Ahmed's as he saw his last chance to discredit Ahmed's testimony against him. "Police cur, if you call yourself an Arab I will stop hurting you. The electricity will stop. What are you?"

"A man."

"Enough, Selim, let up on the box," commanded the leader.

More loudly, Hisham commanded again. "Let up on the box, stop the electricity. It is too late. It won't save you."

Selim let out such a loud decision for desperate action that even with shut eyes I saw him leap at his leader. There was a hiss of a laser and a heavy thud and a clatter of coffee cups hitting the floor. I stopped grinding my teeth and unhooked my hands from their grip on each other. I put my eye to the crack and saw Selim's body finish sliding from the top of a coffee table to the floor in another clatter of coffee cups.

With a gesture of completion, Akbar Hisham put away his laser. The Arab soldiers relaxed. The leader said solemnly, "I am not responsible for the blood of this man. The Gypsy foretold Selim's death, that Selim's evil plans would kill him. I am only a sword in the hands of Allah, cutting where God has willed. The Gypsy also foretold that you will be successful and your children will find great wealth. It will be great wealth under my leadership. This Gypsy tells the truth, so have no fear of the future."

They laughed and cried in relief and gratitude that he did not ask the Gypsy which leader they had been ready to follow. They swore eternal loyalty in a bath of self-abasement and love of their leader. The short scholar with the darkly suntanned bald head received their worship with a slightly weary smile.

He picked up the shock box from where it had fallen. A square metal box with a red button in the top and two heavy batteries inside. He pushed the button thoughtfully and let

73

it up. "Ahmed the Gypsy, why don't you scream or groan when we push the button?"

"You make me angry," replied the tall guy who was my friend. The skin of his face was greenish and shiny with sweat, but he still sat straight. He stiffened his spine even more and sat behind the table with both hands resting flat on the sand, looking levelly across the room at all of them. It wasn't a glare, but it wasn't a smile either. "You all make me very angry."

I liked that answer. I would have said it that way myself. Usually when you ask Ahmed why he did something he answers something about logic. Score one hit for truth drug.

Also Ahmed had never told the other kids of the UN Brotherhood what his race was. He'd always said the human race. This time he'd answered French and Gypsy. Score two for truth drug. As two men carried out the dead body of the contender for the throne, Hisham apparently forgot any interest in the execution and turned eagerly to Ahmed. "Do you tell fortunes as a Gypsy? Do you believe in fortunes?"

"No simple answer is possible," Ahmed answered after a tired pause. He pulled the lamp down close to the sand and tapped the tabletop. The sand humped in patterns and long rippling bars of shadow spread away from the humps. In a dreamy distant voice Ahmed said, "Events are primary; all thoughts, memories, and belief only partially fit the event. Many interpretations of the techniques of foretelling infiltrate at once into my beliefs when watching the shadows or dealing the cards. Does the future cast its shadows ahead? Are the shadow pictures I see in my mind or in the group mind of mankind? Do small random events like the pattern of sands show the pattern of a giant event growing and forming in the future? Or is Jungian analysis right that evolving intelligence has filtered down into the dreamworld of night sleep and primitive memories, and the dreams are becoming plans, and the joined racial mind is drifting through sleep telepathy into directing the future by its dream plots?"

"Hmm." Akbar Hisham, sitting, had leaned forward, resting his chin on his hand to listen. "Hmm." Suddenly he turned and looked at the respectfully blank faces of the

74

Arab soldiers. They had not understood what Ahmed had said, but they had been impressed by it as a mystic chant in a strange tongue, an invocation of magic powers by magic words.

The short muscular man looked at them for a moment and sighed. Then he shouted, "Everyone out. Out! I want my fortune told. Go far away." He stood and hurried them out with shooing motions. "Hurry. I want my fortune told. Make sure that no one comes into the offices and I am not bothered by fools and phone calls. Hurry."

They all left hurriedly. When they were gone Akbar Hisham, scholar and historian, sat down and arranged his cloak self-consciously, not meeting Ahmed's eyes. He looked at the floor and smoothed the missing hair on the top of his head and cleared his throat. "Ah—your name is—ah. I find your theories very interesting. I am always glad to meet a student of group psychology. So few people are interested. I am—ah—sorry about the box torture."

He looked up and met Ahmed's eyes and made an apologetic shrug. "Revenge is the only pride losers can have. Pride keeps them alive." He smiled with a twisted mouth and shrugged again. "I have to humor them and let them have revenge on strangers."

I leaned on an upright post between the walls and waited for the Arabs to be far enough out of earshot before I pushed the panel out of the wall and jumped Hisham. His apologies did not impress me. Actions speak louder than words. Hisham had not unlocked Ahmed's shackles or offered him coffee.

Ahmed did not smile. "Why aren't you teaching in a university?"

Nervously the man shrugged his solid shoulders. "What's a nice scholar like me doing in a place like this? You think my refugees are hopeless? The Jews once were an Arab nation sent into exile in small groups around the world. They were sent because they lost a war and would not stop fighting after they lost. The revenge of the Jews was to conquer the cities they were sent into. They conquered with music, with scholarship, with science, with money, and with power. Perhaps they too started as a raggle of poor fighting fanatics with no friends but their religion and their knives. Perhaps they went through generations of pain before they

75

learned the secret that knowledge is power. I am shortening it. In only one generation of much pain I am forcing these hawks to study. I, a scholar, make them cringe and obey. I am stronger and more savage and revengeful than they are. They have learned to fear and admire scholars. Only Satan can be king of hell." Hisham looked down at the floor and thought.

When he looked up, his feelings hardened again. He was no longer apologetic. "How did you find out Selim's plot against my life?"

"By listening to their questions," Ahmed answered. "Three woman asked me if Akbar Hisham had found out something important, and they were happy when I said *no*. They were Selim's wife, his mother, and his girlfriend. They asked if he would have a long life. Another woman asked if her husband should join Selim's plan, like the others; she made sure no one could hear her before she asked the question."

"Fortune-tellers must learn a great deal from the questions people ask," Hisham said thoughtfully. He got up and paced. "I can't think of any way to let you go. Is the injection really forcing you to tell the truth?"

"Yes," Ahmed said grimly and shut his mouth. His jaw muscles lumped along the sides of his face.

Hisham paced again. Once he stared at the panel and straight into my eyes, bst he did not see me through the dark crack. He was upset by the need to kill a fellow scholar. At a moment like this he did not care if panels bulged. He whined, "You would say yes anyway, even if you were lying. You probably learned too much. Why did you come here? They say you acted insane and prophetic when caught. Why did you come into Arab territory? You know it is death."

Ahmed looked in my direction and back at him. He held his hand to his mouth and answered. His voice was muffled but understandable. "Doing my job. I was sent to find a missing automatic maintenance expert, a computerman. George!"

"We don't have any kidnapped computermen here. Your life was wasted." Hisham paced. "Did you read anything incriminating in my offices?"

"No. But— No."

"What is the *but?* What are you holding back?" Hisham wheeled to stare at him. I wondered if the truth drug was still forcing Ahmed to talk when he didn't want to talk. His way of answering was unusual. Why did he put his hand over his mouth?

Ahmed was flushing now in spots of anger in his pallor. He put his hand over his mouth but his voice was an angry shout. "I found a letter to you from the kidnappers offering expert advice on sabotaging the city. I tore it up and dropped it in the mail chute, George!"

Hisham got out a note pad. "Offering means of sabotage? What was their address?"

Ahmed clamped his jaw together and held it with his hand and made muffled sounds. He looked very angry. He glared in my direction. He let go of his mouth. "Come on, you oaf!"

I had the panel out and my hands around Hisham's neck before Ahmed could finish the insult. I dragged him to Ahmed and he helped.

Hisham kicked and thrashed around and let out some muffled sounds before we got him gagged and tied. After that I used Hisham's laser to cut Ahmed's legcuffs and got the electric wires off his legs. It took time, but we had hours, because Hisham had sent all the Arabs out of earshot. Ahmed must have expected him to want his fortune told in private. Ahmed always had everything planned.

It was a slow hard trip out of the window and across the beam in the dark. Ahmed was not as strong as usual and he was no help in carrying Akbar Hisham. Balanced on the beam in the dark, we sat and panted.

"How come you took so long to get to me?" Ahmed asked. In an angry whisper I defended myself.

"What's so long? Judd told me you were missing this morning. It took an hour or so to walk over here and get in, that's all."

"I was in that zoo for two days with every kid pushing the electric button for fun when their mamas weren't looking. How come with your ESP you didn't notice I was in trouble?"

I was worried about that. How could I work well with

77

Ahmed if I couldn't tune to him and locate him? "You don't give out vibes, Ahmed."

He hitched himself farther along the big metal beam, gasping, and kicked the end wall of bricks with a sandy sound. "Does that mean I don't think aloud enough?"

I slid along the beam, carrying the weight of Hisham over my shoulder. Hisham was not wiggling or fighting. Even though it was blind dark he had probably understood that if he wiggled loose he would fall two or three floors to the trash of the old bricked-off alleyway. We were traversing between buildings. I slid farther and touched Ahmed's arm. It was vibrating, and he stank of a sweat of days of trouble. I answered soothingly. "No, you think fine. It means you don't give off any vibes. You don't feel anything."

"Don't bet on it." He laughed with a croaking sound and balanced to his feet on the beam, then made scrabbling sounds as he got his arms over the edge into the hole. He stood without moving until I tapped his ankle, then he climbed in and helped me haul the Arab leader's bound form through the hole and onto the stairs. I groped down three floors in the blind dark carrying Hisham over my shoulder, with Ahmed groping ahead of me. At the foot Ahmed listened and then opened the cement-covered door an inch, letting in light.

No one was guarding that corridor, so we ran hard for the other cellar corridor and the old sewer pipe.

It reminded me of the time I was eight and had gotten caught and pulped, so I put a lot of heart into running, but I was still surprised when we reached the sewer pipe without getting caught. I imagined or heard a clamor of voices charging after us. Ahmed was already in the pipe, and I climbed in fast backward and dragged Akbar Hisham's trussed body after me to use as a hostage. Remembered voices clamored in my ears. I winced to remembered blows.

Akbar Hisham squirmed and twisted, trying to keep his head from hitting the bottom of the pipe as I dragged him along by his shoulders.

The voices became real, deep voices, not the high-pitched clamor of the kids who had caught up with me when I was eight. Shouts echoed into the end of the sewer pipe.

The historian and leader of Arab Jordan jerked and looked at me with frantic need to speak as he chewed his gag. They were probably threatening to use bombs or lasers.

I yanked the gag cord over the top of his head and pulled the gag out of his mouth and he began yelling in Arabic.

The roar of echoing angry voices stopped abruptly. He was in the way, so they could not shoot us. They listened for his orders, but he said nothing. I dragged Hisham a little farther, but dragging him out of his kingdom would be kidnapping so I left him plugging the sewer pipe and crawled backward to the light, climbed the ladder to the manhole, and came out in the centerbelt park of the street.

Legally we were safe from attack in the public streets among the public crowds, but the walls of Arab Jordan were watching and faces yelled at us from the windows. Ahmed ran and I ran, ducking and zigzagging to miss possible laser fire until we reached subway stairs. I went down two at a time but looked back and saw Ahmed coming slowly down the steps one at a time, gripping the railing, so I went back up two at a time and walked behind him at a distance, looking back for Arabs. Two Arabs went by, running down the escalator, probably looking for two running men. They didn't look at us. At the first platform landing we went into a public bathroom to let more searchers go by.

I guarded the door while Ahmed used the toilet, drank four glasses of water, threw up, drank three more glasses of water, doused his whole head in a sinkful of clean water, took off his shirt and scrubbed his skin with paper towels, and then combed his hair, making faces at himself in the mirror.

He looked neat and clean and normal again, but still unusually skinny.

"You have no idea how hungry I am, George," he said, still making faces at himself. He sucked in his cheeks and grinned and looked like a skull.

I said, "How come you didn't take me along to help look for Whosis, the kidnapped man?" We traded places and Ahmed guarded the door while I used the toilet and washed up.

"Because it's a kidnapping, a crime, not Rescue Squad

79

business. They transferred me to detective division. They didn't transfer you. I can't even tell you about it."

I scrubbed my face and arms with wet paper towels and got off cement dust.

"I'm a locater. I can locate the man. What difference does it make what halfwit department the police are in? I'm not in any department. I'm a consultant, category J." I beat cement dust out of my clothes, raising a cloud.

The bathroom door opened. Ahmed tensed. A blond man came in. Ahmed relaxed and ignored him.

"George they're using deductive logic and police routine. You track by help calls and vibes, not logic, man. The missing man was doped out but still on his feet when he vanished. Whoever got him is probably keeping him doped. He probably doesn't know he's in trouble. No vibes."

Ahmed looked out the door and then went through and I followed. Police were patrolling the area now, looking for troublemakers. They were always alert to signs of clan violence coming on. "I found you without vibes, didn't I?"

"That's something else." Ahmed stumbled over something on the sidewalk and barely recovered his balance without falling. I looked and didn't see anything to stumble on. Ahmed might be ready to fold up. He'd been missing since Wednesday. Had he been telling fortunes all that time, trying to be interesting enough to attract the leader? The leader's fortune was probably the four hundredth fortune told in a row, with everyone earlier playing with the little red button when he grew bored with fortunes. Two days and nights with Arabs could be wearing.

Up ahead were the parked chairs in the side rails —"Downtown and West." Just past I saw a phone booth. Ahmed didn't have his wrist radio and I'd never been issued one. I took Ahmed's arm. "We're going to Bellevue Med Center. Call the chief and tell him whatever your latest theory is about where the missing man is. He'll put someone else on it and then we can go to Med Center. OK?"

"OK." He stumbled again more heavily and I held up his arm until he steadied. His arm got slippery. "You do think pretty good sometimes, George," he said.

"I don't get any vibes from you, Ahmed, so I found you without vibes," I said in his left ear. "I can think."

80

I got him to a phone booth. It was the kind with a shelf to sit on, which was good luck. He fell into it and pulled down the privacy earphones and throat mike and hooked them over his head.

"OK, George, so you're lucky sometimes. Don't push it and think you're as good as a cop with a badge." He grinned with teeth that needed two days' cleaning and punched the telephone numbers with a hand that shook like a tuning fork.

I could have hit him or cried. I understand why the Arabs had laughed around him in that hysterical high-pitched way. When you can't do anything else that works, you laugh or freak out. I couldn't make him say anything I wanted to hear, any more than the Arabs could.

When you can't make a guy do or say anything that you want him to do, you've got to kill him or get away from him or let him be boss. Ahmed had always been boss.

"Line's busy. You call Med Center and get me there after I get headquarters," he repeated.

"Yes, boss," I said.

He looked me up and down and grinned again with that skinny, big-tooth, death's-head grin. In a high-pitched soprano he imitated what he was hearing. "Captain Frankel is busy on another line, would you care to leave a recorded message, begin when you hear the tone, beeeep." I leaned on the booth and looked both ways for Arabs, but all I saw were police and ordinary pedestrians.

I said "Ahmed the scientist, nyaaa nyaaa, Ahmed the Gypsy. Where're your earrings and crystal ball?"

With a superior smile he said, "Tolerance, George, tolerance. I am a victim of my heredity; we all are victims of heredity. Do I make fun of you being stupid?"

I wanted to smash his grin but I couldn't hit him; he was sick and besides, I love the guy.

81

4

"ANN, Ahmed's back. He's all right, just a little beat up and tired. He's at Bellevue Hospital." The phone booth was too small and tight.

"Where are you calling from?" Ann has a nice clear voice; I have to tell myself she's Ahmed's girl.

"Bellevue admissions lobby." I watched Ahmed lie down on an automatic rolling stretcher. It rolled into the diagnosis machine and in three seconds out again, with a room number on it. He had been analyzed and treatments ordered.

"I'll be right over," said Ann and hung up.

I dialed again. "Judd Oslow please." This time he was not busy. They connected us. "Mr. Oslow, I got Ahmed. He's over at Bellevue. He'll be all right tomorrow. He'll call you as soon as the diagnosis machine lets him out and gives him a room. He has some ideas about the missing man."

Oslow made sounds of surprise and all the appropriate exclamations. "Very good. That's astonishing, George. I gave you the assignment about eleven and you got him out by four. That's fast."

"I got him out by three. Your line was busy."

"Why didn't you use the wrist radio?"

"You people haven't given me one, because I'm not a cop, I'm just an expert."

"Don't get mad, George. I'll try to bend the rules and get one into the mail for you by tomorrow morning. Could you have used one today?"

"Ahmed and I were stuck in the Arab enclave for a while."

"You could have used it. You probably needed help. But you got out."

"We got out," I said. Judd was another one who talked to me as an adult to a child. "Chief, I want to help look for the missing man. I'm good at tracing people."

"Good isn't the word. Your antichance score is out of

82

sight. But. . . . But. . . ." He gave up. I was right. He knew it.

"OK, George, I want you to guess for us where Carl Hodges is, and give us another hit like the first three. I'm not supposed to send my men after Carl Hodges. It's not my department, but that's my neck on the block, not yours. Brace yourself to memorize a description."

"Sure." I made ready to visualize a man.

"Carl Hodges, twenty-nine years old, one hundred forty pounds, five feet nine inches tall, brown eyes, hazel eyes."

I visualized someone a lot shorter and thinner than me. I remembered some short underweight men who were always ready to fight to prove they were bigger.

"His job is assistant coordinator of computer automation of city services," read Judd Oslow.

"What's that?" I wanted to get the feel of Carl Hodges' job.

"Glorified maintenance man for the city, the brains for all the maintenance and repair teams. He uses the computer to predict wear and accidents and lightning strikes and floods that break down phone lines, power lines, and water lines, and he sends repair teams to strengthen the things before they break. He prevents bad troubles."

"Oh." I thought, *Carl Hodges will be proud of his job. He'll feel big. He won't want to be bigger.* I asked, "How does he act with his friends? How does he feel?"

"Wait for the rest. Hobbies are chess, minimax, and surfing. No commune, only one girlfriend, and she met with a fatal accident last month. He was not happy this month. He was last seen at a Strangers' Introduction Party. He might have been on drugs or he might have been cracking up, because he was last reported as mumbling continuously on a dangerous subject he was usually careful to keep quiet about."

"What subject?"

"He knows where all the weak points are."

"Oh." The city was a giant machine. Carl Hodges knew where a little sand in the gears could cause disasters. He was telling.

"Don't talk about why we have to pick him up."

"Why not?"

"Rumors, panic. . . ."

83

"OK, I won't." I don't like secrets, but panic or any general feeling could start crowds in the same direction, crowding and clogging the inadequate slideways, jammed in, pushed, trampled. Rumors of sabotage could have people running from the power plants or the sea walls that held back the sea. I remembered the dream.

The chief of Rescue Squad somehow got the DV connection in the phone booth turned on without me putting in any coins, and I was looking at a photograph of Carl Hodges. A wiry, undersized book-reading type with a compressed mouth and excitable eyes.

I tried to tune in by pretending it was my own face in the mirror. Staring into its eyes, I felt lonely.

"Got anything, George?" asked Judd Oslow's voice eagerly.

I said, staring into the eyes that were my eyes, "Maybe he's alone. Maybe he's by himself." Suddenly the picture was just of a skinny stranger and I couldn't see any expression at all. No vibes at all.

I asked Judd, "Got the names of any friends of his?"

Judd's face appeared on the screen, wide and saggy as an old hound dog's. "The kidnapping squad is already tracing all those leads. Why don't you try the Medievalist Commune on Barkley downtown? He used to go in there sometimes and practice armored swordfighting."

I knew those people. They were all scientists who like to live close to their work. Sometimes I used to pick up money as an experimental subject. I took the slideways to the West Side and downtown and came up into the Medievalist Commune on a direct escalator. I got out in a park surrounded by a 3-D illusion of distant rolling hills, castles, and a distant town with the spire of a Gothic church. It was illusion engraved on plastic panels that covered a hollow square of buildings around their block, and as usual I gawked at it awhile, trying to see the buildings and windows under the picture. The picture looked real, the city was gone.

I heard the thunder of horses' hooves coming at me from two directions and ignored it. The hooves were an illusion, generated by the thumping of irregular off-round rail wheels. I moved aside, off the tracks.

The hoof thunder met and passed beside me. There was

a twin thud and a double "Oof." A man hurtled through the air, rump first, and landed with a thump in the deep soft grass and bounced to his feet.

"Luck," he howled, and rushed forward to pick up a lance with a boxing glove on the tip. "Your horse was on a forward camber and mine on a back camber. I demand a replay!"

The one who had stayed on his horse let the stuffed animal reach the top of the slope at the end of the rail run and circled to face us. He dug his heels into its flanks where the throttles were and came at us down hill thundering like hooves, with the horse rocking on its irregular cogs.

"Have at thee, varlet!" He came at me bouncing up and down in the saddle, trying to keep the boxing glove on the tip of his lance lined up at my head. Apparently I had the honor of being his target. I stepped onto the rail line where the opposing horse was supposed to run and crouched, ready to grab the lance and yank him off his horse. He had his visor down over his face, so I could not see his expression or who it was, but the voice was familiar. Frank.

The rail horse slowed as it approached. Frank was pulling the reins, putting on the brakes. He yelled, "I know thy scurvy trick, villain; many a good knight hath been unhorsed by low peasant tricks. I challenge thee. Get into armor and get on board a horse."

He pulled the reins and the mechanical horse screeched to a stop on its rails. He pushed his helm and visor back and showed his grinning face. "How's that for authentic dialect? Good morrow, George."

"Good morrow, Frank. No fun today. I've got a job as a kind of detective. I'm looking for a missing man who might have fallen down an elevator shaft somewhere."

"Too bad," the scientist said soberly. "How can I help?"

"If I can get tuned in to his personality, I can find him by ESP," I said, leaning up against the big soft fur horse. "But I don't know the man. I've got to know what he's like. His name is Carl Hodges."

"What does he do? I think I remember him." Frank swung a leg over and slid down, leaving his lance slung in a holder on the horse. He stripped off heavy gloves. He was just a young guy with good healthy vibes.

I said, "He does maintenance prediction and repair prediction. He likes to play a game called City Chess. Do you know him?"

The other one got a cup of tea from a dispenser and came over, limping.

"City Chess. That's not City Chess, that's Strategy and Tactics, Game Twenty-Five, Sabotage and Fifth Column. Somebody decided it was an educational toy. It was classified by the police as tending to incite to riot and cause death, and it was made illegal. So when we play it we call it City Chess. I haven't played it in two years."

Frank made an effort of memory. "I played it with a fellow last December; we were in the lounge. We turned on the computer terminal and gave it the full game. Skinny guy, a little short, with a mouth he holds tight, and doesn't say much. He won."

"Smarter than you, right, Frank?" said his sparring partner.

The description sounded like Carl Hodges. I listened, trying to visualize Carl Hodges playing chess with this man, both using a computer keyboard to calculate on.

Frank said, "Don't know for sure. He's a sore loser when he loses a point. He knows New York too well so we sabotaged a city in the game kit, supposed to be Brussels. I would have won, but I kept remembering social, economic, and germ feedback toggle points we'd studied for UN world strategy and put under wraps. Promised never to let them out. Some of those toggles go over to a cascade that winds up flat rubble stable, with no plus feedback and unloops. Once I started thinking about secrets I couldn't use, the reroute in my thinking stretched the transit time for every other strategy I tried to work out. It stabe at lower struct than Hodges' strategy and I lost."

I shut my eyes and tuned in to Frank, carefully tracing his way through that maze of memory. Recorded feeling—anger, alertness, competition. And someone else's feelings. Alone, cold, winning to try to impress Frank and get his admiration. Admiration is brief, but it is contact. Other forms of contact are sloppy, weak, hard to understand. . . . Hodge's attitude. I was tuned in.

"Thanks," I said. "You've given me a lead on Carl Hodges. I think I can find him."

The unhorsed one limped back to his stuffed horse, rubbing his bruises.

Frank held his gloves in his teeth and swung himself back on top of his horse. "We profit by more practice. Practice makes peak. Use widens the channel. We're practicing for the Summer Solstice contests. Our commune has taken on the Montreal Chevaliers du Roland."

"You'll get creamed," I said. "They're professionals."

The other said, "You don't know how good we are, George." He swung back on top of his horse. "Have at thee, Frank."

The horses rolled away from each other up the slope of tracks and from the far end the two scientists kicked their flank accelerators and came at each other with a thundering imitation gallop and then a synchronous thud. The boxing glove at the end of each lance took the opposite man neatly on the side of the chin. I saw the lances shorten as shock absorbers took up enough jolt to prevent broken necks, and then they were flying backward, rump first, horseless, and landed with twin thumps on the padded grass.

If I hadn't been busy I would have stayed and laughed, but I was tuned in to Carl Hodges and he was cold and lonesome, despised sociable people, and seemed to have no sense of humor. The urge to laugh went away. I followed the trail of where Carl Hodges was last seen and went to a Stranger's Introduction Party, the same party he had been at last week when he vanished.

I danced with a girl. She said I had two faces. I got slightly drunk and foggy and followed the cold lonely feelings away from the party and walked north. My footsteps echoed off the buildings in the dark and were absorbed into the cricket-chirping silence of the street grass and trees.

I came to the bad-luck blocks. They were just ruins, tumbled almost flat. When the statistics were added up they had found that the area always brought trouble, riots, small plagues, businesses going broke. . . . Bad luck was not explained but it was bad. The next time the neighborhood burned down they left it down.

Nobody wanted to build.

I walked out across the flattened rubble, kicking bricks, daring the bad luck. It was contrasty, moonlit, with black shadows that looked solid. They were.

I woke at dawn and watched pink sunlight lighting up the bushes along the top of a building; they brightened like candle flames on a birthday cake. Crickets sang and creaked in the tall grass beside my ears, and bending grass tickled against my face.

I moved, felt pain, and lay still, noticing the aches you get from being kicked. There were a lot of aches. The teen gang had done an overload of kicking. It was their right. I had been trespassing in their territory. But usually I could get away with trespassing. Usually people liked me and put up with having me on their commune territory. A gang of runaway teeners protecting their ruins felt they had to make a big issue out of ownership.

After they got through kicking, they left me on the sidewalk outside their territory with my fingers hooked to my toes by Chinese fingertrap tubes. After a long time I worked my fingers and feet free and walked down to the Karmic Brotherhood Commune to sleep.

The brothers in the front room said I was upsetting an important group meditation by giving out bad vibes and worry, and they gave me a cup of tea and put me out with my sleeping bag. Feeling unpopular, I sat up and started rubbing the stiffness out of my bruises. I needed to do something fun to cheer up. I walked out of the greenbelt to tell Rescue Squad I was taking off a half day.

By the time the sun was high I was going up the east tower of the George Washington Bridge the hard way, on the struts, clinging with bare hands and bare feet, clambering up slanting slopes of girders, sometimes sitting and watching the sun sparkles on the water more than a hundred feet below while huge ships went slowly by, seeming like toys.

The wind blew against my skin, warm sometimes and sometimes cold and foggy. I watched a cloud shadow drift up from the south along the river; it darkened the spires of tall buildings, became a traveling island of dark blue in the light blue of the river, approached and widened, and then there was cool shadow across the bridge for long moments while I looked up and watched a dark cotton cloud pass between me and the sun.

The cloud left and the light blazed. I looked away, dots of darkness in front of my eyes, and watched the cloud shadow climb a giant cliff to the west and disappear over the top. I started picking my way along an upslope of girder, moving carefully because the dazzle of sun dots was still inside my eyes. Far below, the steady sound of traffic passing under the white ribbon of the bridge road was a remote rumble from the lower level. The top-level cyclists pedaled by like ants.

A gull in the distance flapped upward through the air toward me. It found an updraft and drifted, wings spread and motionless, paused in front of me floating, a white beautiful set of wings, a sardonic cynical head with down-curved mouth and expressionless inspecting eyes.

I was tempted to reach out and grab. I shifted to the grip of one hand on the cross strut and hooked one knee over a bar.

The gull tilted the tips of his wings and floated upward and back, a little farther out of reach in the sky, but still temptingly close.

I decided that I was not stupid enough to let a gull trick me into falling off the bridge.

The gull slanted and slid sideways down a long invisible slope of air and squalled, "Creee. Ha ha ha ha. Ha ha ha . . ." in a raucous gull laugh. I hoped he would come back and make friends, but I had never heard of anyone making friends with a gull. I climbed down slopes of girders, picking my way carefully, hanging on with toes and fingers, found a steel ladder fastened to the tower corner side, and climbed it straight down to a paint locker and a telephone. Just ten feet over the roadway I watched the bicyclists and walkers while I dialed Rescue Squad and asked for Judd Oslow.

"Chief, I'm tired of taking a vacation."

"This morning you walked in like a cripple. How late did you work last night?"

"Three thirty."

"Find any clues to Carl Hodges?"

"Not exactly." I looked at the far, high planes and helicopters buzzing through the blue sky. I did not feel like discussing the failure of last night.

"Where are you now?"

"In a painter's crow's nest on the George Washington Bridge."

"Climbing George Washington Bridge is your idea of a rest?"

"It's away from people. I like climbing."

"OK, your choice. You are near Presbyterian Medical Center. Report to the Rescue Squad station there and fill out some reports on what you've been doing all week. Some of the things you've been doing, we would probably like to pay you for. The information girl there will help you fill out the forms. You'll like her, eventually, George. She doesn't mind paperwork. Let her help you."

The pretty typist with the round face and curly hair was not glad to see me. She stopped smiling and talking to the other people in the office and gave me the efficiency expression. "Yes? What can I do for you, Mr. Sandford?"

After the hassle yesterday I wanted to make her feel better about me. "Spell it S-a-n-f-o-r-d. I get my mail at the Karmic Brotherhood Commune on Ninth Avenue between Seventeenth and Eighteenth Streets. I want to make out a report on a job I did yesterday after I left here."

She typed briskly at the top of a standard form and looked happy. Just give a girl something she can do for you.

"What is your departmental rank?"

"Specialist, Category J. Consultant. Rescue Squad."

"Who consulted you?"

"Ahmed Kosvakatats, I guess. I was working for him, to locate him, but I couldn't talk to him; he was missing."

She stopped typing and looked at me severely. "Who called you in on the case to consult you, Mr. Sanford?"

"Judd Oslow, head of Rescue Squad, but I called him. I phoned him about ten and he told me Ahmed was missing. I started then. I finished about four o'clock."

She didn't type anything. She was getting pale and biting her lower lip and giving out fright vibes. I think she was afraid of getting as mad as she wanted to be. She said, like a robot voice, "Who were you consulting or advising between ten and four o'clock?"

I was trying to give facts, but facts never fit into their stupid sheets of paper with the little spaces. "I did a lot of walking and thinking, then I did a lot of climbing and a lot of waiting and then I tied up a hostage, Akbar Hisham, and carried him, climbing; it was all hard work, work for Rescue

90

Squad, but that part was more like kidnapping someone than giving advice." My voice was getting louder because she wasn't typing anything; she was just staring at me, biting her lip.

I was getting a headache and afraid I'd start to see big silver planes crashing into walls again. This was hard work. I said, "Do I get paid overtime for answering questions?"

Suddenly Ahmed was there reaching out a long arm and shutting off the tape recorder.

"No, you don't. For God's sake, George, let me fill out the reports before you drive Janet insane. I know your hours. Judd used your expert advice on the phone from ten to ten thirty, telling you I was missing." He turned to the pretty girl. "Janet, you can fill that in as a half-hour consultation time with Judd Oslow. From ten thirty to one he was walking to get information material and thinking, and walking to the scene of the rescue. That comes under the heading of research and research transit time, so fill it in as research, no lunch off, two and a half hours, full specialist rate. From one to four o'clock he was advising me how to find my way through walls and how to avoid getting murdered. George's hunch faculty is like insurance. Fill in three hours during which I was consulting him. For expenses put two meals at twenty dollars each, because travel and expense are part of his consultant fee, and I owe him two meals."

Janet typed busily, her pretty face glowing.

She finished and took the report form out, gave him a carbon from the back of it, and gave me a carbon, still smiling at him worshipfully. "Thank you, Mr. Kosvakatats."

He smiled at me. "Are you feeling better?"

"I'm all right." I remembered my bruises.

"Come on, then."

We went out and looked up at the high tan towers of Presbyterian Medical Center. Helicopter ambulances thrummed in and out of the top landing platforms.

"Let's not waste time, George. Let's get you tuned in to Carl Hodges," Ahmed said, pulling out a notebook and pen. "Do you have a picture of Hodges with you?"

"No."

"I've got a picture here." Ahmed reached for a folder in his pocket and passed a photo to me.

The ground jolted in a sort of thud that struck upward

91

against our feet. I felt a blow of darkness as many minds ended their background hum in the vibes of the city. It went by like the thunder wave of breaking the sound barrier, like a wave of black fog. I shut my eyes to tune in; shock waves were still ringing through the city mind. Much was gone. A feeling of claustrophobia, of being boxed in, had driven me into the upper air and girders of the bridge. It vanished with the vanishing presence of many minds that had felt enclosed and trapped. They had been broadcasting, but they died.

I opened my eyes. The world was brighter—the air fresher. I took a deep breath. "Something big," I said. "Something. . . ."

Ahmed was watching the sweep second hand on his watch. "Fifty-five hundred feet, one mile," he muttered.

"What are you doing?"

"It's an explosion somewhere. I'm counting the distance. Sound arrives first through the ground, second through the air. I'm waiting for the sound. I'll get the distance by the time lag."

At thirty seconds the sound of the death of undersea city reached us, a strange sort of grinding roar, muffled, low, and distant.

I shut my eyes again and felt the world change around me to another place.

"Got something, George?" Ahmed asked alertly. "That was about seven miles."

"Someone knows what happened. I'm picking him up. Brooklyn Dome just collapsed."

"Twelve thousand inhabitants," Ahmed said, dialing his wrist radio grimly, his earphone plugged into his ear. "No one answering at headquarters, just busy signals. Places empty out before a disaster. Lots of people seem to have a hunch. I'd expect at least four thousand deaths."

I shut my eyes again, exploring the other place. "Someone's having a nightmare," I said. "He can't wake up."

"Don't flip out, George, keep in touch with facts. A lot of people just died, is all. Keep a grip on that. I'm trying to get our orders."

I stood with my eyes shut, exploring the sensation inside my head. Somewhere a man was trapped in a nightmare, half asleep in a dark prison or closet. It was some kind of delirium.

The real world was a cruel place that bright day, but the black and coiling fragments of that man's world were worse. There was something important about the man's thoughts. He had felt the explosion thud at a distance, as they had, and he had known what it meant. He had expected it.

"Can't locate where he is," I said, opening my eyes and regaining my grip on the bright sunshine world around me.

Ahmed squinted and tilted his head, listening to the obscure and rapid voices on the earplugs of his radio.

"Never mind about that case, George. That's Carl Hodges probably. He'll keep. Headquarters is broadcasting general orders for the emergency. Repair and services inspection people are ordered to make quick inspections at all danger points in the automatic services, looking for malfunction and sabotage. Repair and inspection teams are ordered into Jersey Dome, to check out every part of it and make sure it is not gimmicked to blow the way Brooklyn Dome went. They are instructed to describe it as a routine safety check."

"What do we do? What about us?"

"Wait, I'm listening. They mentioned us by name. We go to Jersey underseas and try to locate and stop a sabotage agent who might have sabotaged Brooklyn Dome and might be preparing to use the same method on Jersey Dome."

"What method?"

"They don't know. They don't even know if there is a saboteur. They're sending us to make sure."

"If there is a saboteur, he's probably working on it right now." We had to hurry. We ran for the subway steps down into the underground moving chair belts and caught a brace of abandoned chairs just as they slowed, and accelerated them again out into the fast lanes.

Trying to get to Jersey Dome, we shifted chairs through acceleration bands to the inner fast slots. In the slower lanes, the people we passed were holding portable TV screens like magazines, watching news of the disaster.

The voice of the announcer murmured from a screen, grew louder as we passed, and then again fell to a murmur.

"Brooklyn Dome. Fifteen pounds of atmosphere pressure to sixty-five pounds per square inch. Exploded upward. Implosion first, then explosion." The voice grew louder again as I approached another sliding chair in the slower lane. Another person listened, propping the screen up on the safety rail to stare into it, with the sound shouting. "Debris is floating for a square mile around the center from which the explosion came. Coast Guard rescue ships, submarines, and scuba divers are converged into the area, searching for survivors."

They neared and passed a TV screen that showed a distant picture of an explosion like an umbrella rising and opening on the horizon.

"This is the way the explosion looked from the deck of a freighter, the *Mary Lou.*"

I settled myself in my seat and shut my eyes to concentrate. I had to stop that explosion from happening again to the other undersea dome. Whoever had done it would be laughing as he watched on TV the explosion unfold and settle. Whoever had done it would be eager for destruction, delighting in the death and blood of a small city. I went vague and wide. I was anybody. I groped my mind across the city, feeling for anyone who was happy about the explosions.

"The Police Department is still investigating the cause of the explosion," said the murmur, growing louder as we passed another TV watcher in the slow lane. Someone handed the announcer another note. "Ah, here we have some new information. Bell Telephone has opened up to the investigators eight recordings taken from public phones in Brooklyn Dome. These phone calls were being made at the moment Brooklyn Dome was destroyed."

A face appeared on the screen behind the announcer, a giant face of a woman telephoning. After an instant of mental adjusting of viewpoint the woman's face became normal in the viewer eye, the announcer shrank to ant size and was forgotten as the woman spoke rapidly into the phone. "I can't stand this place another minute. I would have left already, but I can't leave. The train station is jammed and there are lines in front of the ticket booth. I've never seen such lines. Jerry is getting tickets. I wish he'd hurry." The anxious woman's face glanced sideways either way out of the booth. "I hear the funniest noise, like thunder. Like a waterfall."

The woman screamed and the background tilted as the screaming face and the booth went over sideways. A hand groped past the lens, blackness entered in sheets, and the picture broke into static sparks and splashes. The screen went blank, the antlike announcer sitting in front of it spoke soothingly, and the camera rushed forward to him until he was normal size again. He showed a diagram.

I opened my eyes and sat up. Around me on the moving chairs people were watching their TV screens show the pictures I had just seen in my mind's eye. It showed a diagram of the location of the phone booths at Brooklyn Dome and then another recording of someone innocently calling from a videophone booth, about to die, and not knowing what was about to happen, an innocent middle-aged face.

Expressionlessly, the people in the traveling subway seats watched, hands bracing the sides of the TV screen, grip tightening as they waited for the ceilings to fall. Audience anticipating; love of power, greatness, crash . . . total force and completeness . . . admiring triumph of completeness in such destruction. Great show. Hope for more horror.

All over the city people looked at the innocent fool mouthing words and they waited, watching, urging the doom on as it approached. This time be bigger, blacker, more frightening, more crushing.

I shut my eyes and waited through the hoarse screams and then opened my eyes and looked at the back of the neck of the TV watcher we were passing, then turned around and looked at her face after we passed. She did not notice; she was watching the TV intently, without outward expression.

Did that woman admit the delight she felt? Did she know she was urging the thundering waterfall on, striking the death blow downward with the descending ocean? Typical television viewer, lover of extremes. It was to her credit that when TV showed young lovers she urged them to love more intensely and rejoiced in their kisses. Lovers of life are also lovers of death.

I slid down farther in my seat and closed my eyes and surfed tidal waves of mass emotion as the millions of watchers, emotions synchronized by watching, enjoyed their mass sharing in the terror and death of a small city. Over and over, expectancy, anticipating, panic, defeat, wipeout, satisfaction.

The secretly worshiped god of death rode high.

In twenty minutes, after transfers on platforms that held air-lock doors to pass through into denser air, we arrived, carried by undersea tube train, at the small undersea city of Jersey Dome. Population: ten thousand; residents: civil service administrators and their families.

The city manager's office building was built of large, colored blocks of lightweight translucent foam plastic, like children's large building blocks. There was no wind to blow it away. Inside, the colors of the light tinted the city man's desk. He was a small man sitting behind a large desk with one phone held to his ear and another blinking a red light at him.

"We have all the trains in service. Everyone wants to leave. No. There isn't any panic. There's no reason for panic." He hung up and glared at the other phone's light.

"That phone," he snarled, pointing, "is an outside line full of idiot reporters asking me how domes are built and how Brooklyn Dome could have blown up or collapsed. And asking when Jersey Dome will go down. It's all idiocy. Well? What do you want?"

Ahmed opened his wallet to his credentials and handed it over. "We're from Metropolitan Rescue Squad. We're specialists in locating people by predicting behavior. We were sent over to locate a possible lunatic who might have sabotaged Brooklyn Dome or blown it up and might be here planning to blow up Jersey Dome."

"He just might," replied the manager of Jersey Dome with a high-pitched trembling earnestness in his voice. "And you might be the only dangerous lunatics around here. Lunatics who talk about Jersey Dome breaking. It can't break. You understand? The only thing we have to fear is panic. You understand?"

"Of course," Ahmed said soothingly. "But we won't talk about it breaking. It's our job to look for a saboteur. Probably it's just a routine preventive checkup."

96

The manager pulled a pistol out of a desk drawer and pointed it at us with a trembling hand. "You're still talking. This is an emergency. I am the city manager. I could call my police and have you taken to a mental hospital, gagged."

"Don't worry about that," Ahmed said soothingly, picking his wallet back off the desk and pocketing it. "We're only here to admire the design and the machinery. Can we have a map?"

The manager lowered the pistol and laid it on the desk. "If you cooperate, the girl in the front office will give you all the maps of the design and structure that you'll need. You will find a lot of technicians already in the works, inspecting wires and checking up. They're here to design improvements. You understand?" His voice was still high-pitched and nervous, but steady.

"We understand," Ahmed assured him. "Everything is perfectly safe. We'll go admire their designs and improvements. Come on, George." He turned and went out, stopped at the receptionist's desk to get a map.

Out on the curved walk under the innocent blue-green glow of the dome, Ahmed glanced back. "But I'm not sure he's perfectly safe himself. Is he cracking up, George?"

"Not yet, but near it." I glanced up apprehensively at the blue-green glow, imagining I saw a rift, but the dark streak was only a catwalk near the dome surface.

"What will he do when he cracks?" asked Ahmed.

"Run around screaming, 'The sky is falling!' like Chicken Little," I muttered. "What else?" I cocked an apprehensive glance upward at the green glow of the dome. Was it sagging in the middle? No, that was just an effect of perspective. Was there a crack appearing near the air shaft. No, just another catwalk, like a spiderweb on a ceiling.

Making an effort, I pulled my eyes away from the dome and saw Ahmed at a small building ahead labeled POWER SUBSTATION 10002. It looked like a child's building block ten feet high, pleasantly screened by bushes, matching the park. Ahmed was looking in the open door. He signaled me and I hurried to reach him, feeling as if the pressurized thickened air resisted, like water.

I looked inside and saw a man inside tinkering with the heavy power cables that provided light and power from the

97

undersea dome. Panels were off, and the connections were exposed.

The actions and mood of the man were those of a workman, serious and careful. He set a meter dial and carefully read it, reset it and made notes, then read it again.

I watched him. There was a strange kind of fear in the man, something worse than the boxed-in feeling of being underwater.

I felt a similar apprehension. It had been growing in me. I looked at Ahmed doubtfully.

Ahmed had been lounging against the open door watching. He took a deep sighing breath and went in with weight evenly balanced on his feet, ready for fast action. "OK, how are the improvements coming?" he asked the workman.

The man grinned over his shoulder. He was slightly bald in front. "Not a single improvement, not even a small bomb."

"Let's check your ID. We're looking for the saboteur." Ahmed held out his hand.

Obligingly the man unpinned a plastic ID card from under his lapel and put a thumbprint over the photographed thumbprint so that it could be seen that the two prints matched. He seemed unafraid of us and friendly.

"OK." Ahmed passed his badge back.

The engineer pinned it on again. "Have fun, detectives. I hope you nail a mad bomber so we can stop checking for defects and go home. I can't stand this air down here. Crazy perfume. I don't like it."

"Me too," I said. A thick perfumed pressure was in the air. I felt the weight of water hanging like a dome far above the city pressing the air down. "Bad air."

"It has helium in it," Ahmed remarked. He checked the map of the small city and looked in the direction of a glittering glass elevator shaft. A metal mesh elevator rose slowly in the shaft, shining in the semidark, like a giant birdcage full of people hanging above a giant living room.

I tried to take another deep breath and felt that whatever I was breathing was not air. "It smells strange, like fake air."

"It doesn't matter how it smells," Ahmed said, leading the way. "It's to keep people from getting the bends from

98

internal pressure when they leave here. Why didn't you OK the man, George? His ID checked out."

"He was scared."

"What of?" Ahmed asked him.

"Not of us. I don't know."

"Then it doesn't matter. He's not up to any bad business."

We walked across the small green park, through the thick air, toward the glittering glass shaft that went up from the ground into the distant green dome that was the roof of the city. Inside the huge glass tube a brightly lit elevator rose slowly, carrying a crowd of people looking out over the city as a canary would look out above a giant room.

"Next we check the air-pump controls," Ahmed said. "They're near the elevator." People went by, looking formal and overdressed, pale and quiet, stiff and neat. Not his kind of people. Civil servants, government administration people, accountants.

I followed, trying to breathe. The air seemed to be not air, but some inferior substitute. Glittering small buildings rose on either side of the park in rows, like teeth, and I felt inside a tiger mouth. The air smelled like lilies in a funeral parlor. The people I passed gave out vibes of a trapped hopeless defeat that made my depression worse. We passed a crowd of quiet miserable people waiting to get on the elevator, carrying fishing poles and swimming equipment.

High above us the elevator descended slowly.

"That's bad," I said. "You feel it, don't you, Ahmed?"

"Feel what?" Ahmed stopped beside a small rounded building attached to the side of the shaft. The building throbbed with a deep steady thump, thump, thump, like a giant heart.

"I want to get out of here," I said. "Don't you feel it?"

"I ignore that kind of feeling," Ahmed said expressionlessly and pulled on the handle of the door to the pump room. It was unlocked. It opened. The thumping was louder. "Should be locked," Ahmed muttered. We looked inside.

Inside, down a flight of steps, two workmen were checking over some large warm thumping machinery. The two of us went down the steps.

"Identity check, let's see your ID," I said and looked at the

99

two badges they handed me in the same way I had seen Ahmed and other detectives checking them over. I took thumbprints and matched them to the photo thumbprints. I compared the faces on the photos to the faces before me. One big one with a craggy stone-chiseled face and grim vertical lines on the cheeks; one short weathered one, slightly leaner, slightly more humor in the face. Both identified as engineers of Consolidated Power and Light, inspectors of electrical motor appliance and life-support services.

"What are the pumps doing?" Ahmed asked, looking around.

"Pumping air in, pumping water out," replied one of the men. "There's the pump that pushes excess water up to the top, where it comes out as a little ornamental fountain in an artificial island. The pressure equalizes by itself, so it doesn't need elaborate equipment, just power."

"Why pump water out?" Ahmed asked. "The air pressure is supposed to be so high that it pushes the water out."

The man laughed. "You make it sound so simple. The air pressure is approximately the same here as up at the top surface of the dome, but the water pressure rises every foot of the way down. Down here at the bottom it is higher than the air pressure. Water squeezes in along the edges of the cement slab, up through the ground cover and the dirt. We have drains to catch the seepage and lead it back to this pump. We expect seepage."

"Why not pump in more air? Higher air pressure would keep all the water out."

"Higher air pressure would burst the top of the dome like a balloon. There isn't enough weight of water to counterpush."

I got an uncertain picture of air pushing to get out the top and water pushing to get in the bottom. "It's working all right?" I handed ID badges back to them.

"Right," said the explanatory man, pinning on his badge. "It would take a bomb to get those pumps out of balance. Don't know why they sent us to check the pumps. I'd rather be out fishing."

"They're looking for a bomb, dummy," said the other one sourly.

"Oh." The smaller one made a face. "You mean, like

Brooklyn Dome blew up?" He looked around slowly. "If anything starts to happen, we're right near the elevator. We can get to the top."

"Not a chance," said the sour one. "The elevator is too slow. And it has a waiting line, people ahead of you. Resign yourself. If this place blows, we blow."

"Why is the elevator so slow?" I asked. *Fix it!* I hoped silently. We listened to the hum of the elevator engine lowering the elevator. It was slow.

"It can go faster; the timer's right here." The sour engineer walked over and inspected the box. "Someone has set it to the slowest speed. I wonder why?"

"For sightseeing," I said. "But I saw a crowd waiting. They have fish poles. They want to get to the top; they don't want to wait in the middle of the air, just viewing."

"OK." The talkative one walked over and firmly set the pointer over to " fast." The elevator reached the ground on the other side of the wall, rumbled to a stop, and the doors whirred open.

We listened, hearing voices and the shuffle of feet as people crowded in. Then the door rumbled shut and the elevator started for the top. The whir was high and rapid. In less than a third of the time the trip to the surface had taken before, the whir stopped.

The two engineers nodded at each other. "I hope they are happy with it."

"They are getting there faster," I said. "That makes sense." Ahmed nodded agreement. We went out and watched the elevator return. As rapidly as falling, the great silver birdcage came down the glass shaft and slowed and stopped and opened. It was empty. No one who was up there was coming back into the city.

More people got on.

"What's up there?" I asked, holding myself back from a panic desire to get in the elevator with the others and get out of the enclosed city. "I have a feeling we should go up there," I said, hoping Ahmed would misunderstand and think I was being called by a hunch.

"What do you feel?" Ahmed looked at me keenly. The doors shut and the elevator rose, leaving us behind on the ground.

"What I feel is, we shouldn't have let that elevator go

101

without us. We've had it, old buddy. It's been nice knowing you. I didn't expect to die young."

"Snap out of it." Ahmed clicked his fingers under my nose. "You're talking for somebody else. It's not your kind of feeling. George Sanford isn't afraid, ever. You don't think like that."

"Yes, I do," I said sadly. I heard the elevator doors rumble open far overhead. Somewhere above people had escaped to the top of the ocean instead of the bottom. A dock? An island? Somewhere fresh winds were blowing across ocean waves.

"Locate that feeling of doom," Ahmed said. "Maybe our mad bomber is a suicider and plans to go down with the ship. Shut your eyes. Where are you in your head?"

"On top, on an island in the daylight," I said sadly, looking at my imagination of sand and sea gulls. "It's too late, Ahmed. We're dead." A few new people arrived and lined up behind us waiting for the elevator. The sound of its descent began far above. People approached through the park from the direction of the railway station, and I remembered that there had been fenced-in crowds waiting for trains, waiting to get out. Maybe some people had grown impatient and wanted to get to fresh air. The crowd behind us grew denser and began to push. The elevator door opened in front of us.

"Get in, George," said Ahmed and pushed my elbow. "We're going to the top."

"Thanks." I got on. We were pushed to the back of the cage and the doors shut. The elevator rose with knee-pressuring speed. Over the heads of the people before us I saw a widening vision of the undersea city, small buildings circling a central park, dimly and artistically lit by green and blue spotlights on trees and vines, with a rippling effect in the light like seaweed and underwater waves. Paths and roads were lit with bead chains of golden sodium lights. On the other side of the park the railroad station, squares of soft yellow light, fenced in by lacework metal walls. Many people around it. Too many. Dense crowds. The paths across the park were moving with people approaching the elevator shaft.

The elevator reached the top of the dome and went

102

through into a tube of darkness. For a few moments we rose through the darkness and then we felt the elevator slow and stop. The doors rumbled open and the people around us pressed out, hurried through a glass door and down a staircase, and were gone from the top floor.

I looked around. There was the sky and ocean spaces I had dreamed of, but the sky was cloudy, the ocean was gray, and I was looking at them through thick glass. The island-viewing platform was arranged in a series of giant glass steps, and the elevator had opened and let us into the top step, a glass room that looked out in all directions through thick glass, giving a clear view of the horizon, the glass rooms below, and the little motorboats that circled the docks of an artificial island.

"How's your hunch? What do you feel?" Ahmed snapped out, looking around alertly, weight on the balls of his feet, ready to spring at some mad bomber that he expected me to locate.

"The air is faked. I can't breathe it," I said, breathing noisily through my mouth. I felt like crying. This was not the escape I had dreamed of. The feeling of doom persisted and grew worse.

"It's the same air and the same pressure as down un-undersea in the dome," Ahmed said impatiently. "They keep the pressure high so people can come here from under without going through air locks. They can look, take pictures, and go back down. It smells lousy, so ignore it."

"You mean the air is under pressure here, as bad as all the way down at the bottom of the ocean?"

"Yes, lunk. That's what makes sense to them, so that's the way they have it set up."

"That's why the wall is so thick then, so it won't burst and let the pressure out," I said, feeling as if the thickness of the wall were a coffin. I looked out through the thick glass wall and down through the glass roof of the observation room that was the next step down. I saw chairs and magazines as in a waiting room, and the crowd of people that had come on the elevator with us lined up at a glass door, with the first one in line tugging at the handle of the door. The door was not opening. "What are they doing?"

"They are waiting for the air pressure in the room to go

103

down and equalize with the air pressure in the stairwell and the next room. Right now the pressure in the room presses the door shut. It opens inward as soon as the pressure goes down." Ahmed looked bored.

"We have to get out." I strode over to the inside door that shut off a stair leading down to the next room. I tugged. The glass door did not open. "Air pressure?"

"Yes; wait, the elevator is rising. It seems to be compressing the air forcing it upward." Thick air made Ahmed's voice high-pitched and distant.

I tugged on the handle, feeling the air growing thicker and press on my eardrums. "We have enough pressure here already. We don't need any more fake air. Just some real air. I want to be out of here."

The elevator door opened and a group of people, some carrying suitcases, some carrying fishing gear, pressed out and milled and lined up at the door behind pushing each other and murmuring complaints about pushing in tones that were much less subdued than the civil service culture usually considered to be polite.

The elevator closed its doors and sank out of sight, and air pressure began to drop as if the air followed the piston of the elevator in pumping up and down. I swallowed and my eardrums clicked and rang. I yanked hard on the handle of the stairwell door. It swung wide with a hiss and I held it open. The crowd hurried down the stairs, giving me polite thanks as they passed. With each thanks received I felt the fear of the person passing. I stared into the faces of a woman, a teener, a young woman, a handsome middle-aged man, looking for something beside fear, and finding only fear and a mouselike instinctive urge to escape a trap, and a fear of fear that kept them quiet, afraid to express the sense of disaster that filled their imaginations.

"Argh," I said as the last one went down the stairs. "Hurry up, Ahmed, maybe they are right." I gestured my friend through the door and ran down after him onto the lower step of a big glass viewing room with tables and magazines to make waiting easy. Behind me I heard the door lock shut and the whir of the elevator returning to the top with more people.

I leaned my forehead against the thick glass walls and

looked out at a scene of little docks and a buzz of small electric boats circling the platform, bouncing in a gray choppy sea under thick gray clouds.

"What's out there?" Ahmed asked.

"Escape."

"What about the saboteur?" Ahmed asked with an edge of impatience. "What is he thinking or feeling? Are you picking anything up?"

"One of those boats is it," I answered, lying to avoid Ahmed's duty to return to the undersea city. "Or a small submarine, right out there. The top's going to be blasted off the observation platform. Get rescue boats in here. Use your radio, hurry, and get me a helicopter. I want to be in the air to spot which boat."

It wasn't all lies; some of it felt like the truth. I still leaned my forehead against the wall and looked out, knowing I would say anything to get out.

I tried to tune to the idea of sabotage and open to other people's thoughts, but the urge to escape came back in a greater sickness and swamped other thoughts. *Why?* I asked the fear. *What is going to happen?* An image came of horses kicking down a barn from inside, of cattle stampeding, of a chick pecking to get out of an egg, with the chick an embryo, not ready yet to survive in air. Kicking skeleton feet broke through from inside a bubble and the bubble vanished. The images were confusing. I looked away from my thoughts and watched the outside platform.

The platform was crowded with people, shivering in a cold wind, apparently waiting their turn to enjoy a ride in the little boats. I knew that they were outdoors because they could not stand being indoors.

Ahmed tapped on my arm. He had the wrist-radio earphones plugged into both ears, and his voice sounded odd and deaf. "Headquarters wants to know why, George. Can you give details?"

"Tell them they have five minutes, seven minutes if they're lucky. Get the patrol boats here to stop it and"—I almost shouted into Ahmed's wrist mike—"GET ME THAT HELICOPTER. Get it over here fast! We need it as soon as we get through the air locks!"

The glass air-lock door opened and people tumbled and

105

shoved through. On the other side was another room surrounded by glass. We lined up against the glass walls like moths against a lighted windowpane, looking out.

"Why do we have to wait so long?" It was a wail, a crying sound like an ambulance siren in the night. The group muttered agreement and nodded at the woman who clutched her hands against the glass as though trying to touch the scene outside.

"I'm not worried about the bends," said a portly older man. "They adjust the waiting time for people with bad sinus and eardrum infections. Does anyone here have a bad sinus or eardrum infection?

"We don't need to wait, then," said the same man when there was no reply. "Does anyone here know how to make the door open? We can go out right now."

"My son has a screwdriver," suggested a woman, pushing the teenage young man toward the door. Ahmed moved to protest and the woman glared at him and opened her mouth to argue.

An old woman was tugging at the door. It opened suddenly and we forgot the quarreling and went out through the door to the open docks and the cold salt wind and the sound of cold choppy waves splashing against the cement pillars.

An air-beating heavy whirring sound hovered above the docks.

Ahmed looked up. A ladder fell down and dangled before us. Ahmed grabbed the rope rungs and pulled. They sagged lower. He fitted his foot into a rung and climbed.

I stood, breathing deeply of an air that smelled sweet and right and tingled in my lungs like life and energy. The clouds of panic faded from my mind and I heard the sea gulls screaming raucous delight, following the small boats and swooping at sandwiches. The people clustered at the edge of the docks, beginning to talk in normal tones.

The ladder dangled before me, bobbing up and down. The rope rungs brushed against my head and I brushed them aside. What had been happening? What was the doom I had just escaped from? I tried to remember the trapped moments and tried to understand what they had been.

"Come on, George," a voice called from above.

I reached up, gripped, and climbed, looking into a sky of scudding gray and silver clouds; a white and blue police helicopter bounced above me, its rotating blades shoving damp cool air against me in a kind of pressure that I enjoyed fighting. At the top of the ladder stiffened into a metal stair with rails and opened into the carpeted glass-walled platform of a big observation helicopter.

Ahmed sat cross-legged on the floor, twitching with hurry and impatience, holding his wrist radio to his lips. "OK, George, tune to it. What will blow the observation building? Who, what, where? Coast Guard is waiting for information."

With my memory still gripped onto the strange depression I had felt inside the observation building, in the air of Jersey Dome, I looked down and tuned to it and knew how the people still inside felt and what they wanted.

In the four-step glittering observation building each glass room was full of people waiting at the doors. I saw the central elevator arrive and open its door and let out another crowd of people to wait and push and pull at the first door at the top. Desperation. A need to get out.

With a feeling of great sorrow, I knew who the saboteurs were. All the kids with screwdrivers, all the helpful people with technical skill who speed elevators, all the helpful people without mechanical understanding who would prop open dime-operated toilet doors for the stranger in need. They were going to be helpful; they were going to go through the air-lock doors and leave the doors jammed open behind them. No resistance behind them to hold back sixty-five pounds per square inch air pressure forcing up from below in the compressed city, pushing upward behind the rising elevator.

I had been pretending to believe it was a mad bomber. How could I tell the police and Coast Guard that it was just the residents of the city, mindless with the need to get out, destroying their own air-lock system?

I held my head, the vision of death strong and blinding. "They are jamming the air-lock system open in the observation building, Ahmed. Tell someone to stop them.

They can't do that. It will blow!" The panic need to escape blanked my mind again.

"Lift," I said, making nervous faces at the view below. "Lift this damned copter."

"Is he all right?" the pilot asked Ahmed.

Ahmed was talking intensely into the wrist radio, repeating and relaying my message. He made a chopping gesture to shut up.

The copter pilot gave us both a glance, doubting our sanity, and set the copter to lift very slowly.

Beating the air, the copter rose, tilting, and lifted away from the dwindling platform of glinting glass in the middle of the gray ocean.

I gripped the observation rail and watched, ashamed that my hands were shaking.

I saw something indefinable and peculiar begin to happen to the shape of the glass building. "There it goes," I muttered and abruptly sat down on the floor and put my hands over my face. "Hang on to the controls. Here we go. Ahmed, you look. Take pictures or something."

There was a crash and a boom like a cannon. Something that looked like a crushed elevator full of people shot upward at us, passed us slowly, and then fell, tumbling over and over downward.

A roaring uprush of air grabbed the copter and carried it into the sky, upside down, among a clutter of briefcases and fishing rods and small broken pieces that could not be recognized. I hung onto a railing.

Suddenly the copter turned right side up, beating its heavy spinning blades in a straining pull upward away from the rising tornado.

With a tearing roar Jersey Dome spat its contents upward through the air shaft, squeezing buildings and foam blocks and people and furniture into the shaft and upward in a hose of air, upward to the surface and higher in a fountain of objects mangled by decompression.

For long moments the fountain of air was a mushroom-shaped cloud, then it rained down in bits. The copter circled and circled while we hung on.

With one arm and a leg still hooked around the rail, Ahmed listened to his radio, half deafened, trying to make the speaker plugs in his ears louder. He shouted, "The city manager is alive down there and broadcasting."

He listened while the copter steadied and the air cleared. Everything went quiet.

I got up and looked out and down at the sea while Ahmed reported what he was hearing.

"He says the canopy of the dome lowered. The air shaft sucked in everything near it and is plugged shut with foam blocks from buildings but the blocks are slowly compressing into it, and they can hear an air hiss. Survivors are putting on scuba air equipment and finding places to survive another hurricane if the tube blows free again, but he's afraid of water leaks coming in and drowning them out from underneath because the pressure is going down. He wants the air shaft plugged from the top. Suggests bombing it at the top to prevent more air escaping."

Ahmed listened, tilting his head to the sounds in his ears.

"People in the water," I said. "Bombs make concussion. Let's get the people out."

"Affirmative," said the police pilot. "Look for people."

The helicopter swept low and cruised over the water, and we looked down at the close passing waves for a human swimmer needing help.

"There." Ahmed pointed at a pink shiny arm, a dark head. The pilot circled back, hovered, let down the ladder, and we backed off the platform climbing down and tried to get a mesh sling under an unconscious, naked woman. Her head bobbed under and came up as we slid the sling under her. The waves washed against our knees as we leaned out from the rope ladder.

"NOW HEAR THIS, NOW HEAR THIS," proclaimed a giant amplified voice. *"ALL BOATS IN THE AREA CIRCLE IN THE DISASTER AREA AND TAKE IN SURVIVORS. IN FIVE MINUTES, AT THE NEXT SIGNAL, ALL BOATS MUST WITHDRAW FROM THE AIR-SHAFT CENTER TO A DISTANCE OF FIVE HUNDRED YARDS TO PERMIT BOMBING. AWAIT SIGNAL. REPEAT. YOU HAVE FIVE MINUTES TO SEARCH FOR AND TAKE IN SURVIVORS."*

Ahmed and I shouted up to the pilot, "Ready." The hoist drew the mesh sling with the young woman in it upward

109

and into the copter through a cargo door in the bottom. The door hatch closed. We climbed back inside, dripping, spread the unconscious and pretty body out on the floor for artificial respiration. She was cold, pulseless, and bleeding from ears, nose, and closed eyes. There were no bruises or breaks visible on the smooth skin. I tried gentle hand pressure on the rib cage to start her breathing again, and some blood came from her mouth with a sigh. I pushed again. Blood came from her eyes like tears.

Ahmed said wearily, "Give it up, George, she's dead."

I stood up and retreated from the body, backing away. "What do we do, throw her back?"

"No, we have to take bodies to the hospital. Regulations," muttered the pilot.

We circled the copter around over the choppy gray seas, wipers going on the windshield. The body lay on the floor between us, touching our feet.

We saw an arm bobbing on the waves.

"Should we haul it in?" I asked.

"No, we don't have to take pieces," said the cop, tone level.

We circled on, passing the little electric boats of the people who had been fishing when the dome blew. The faces were pale as they looked up at the passing helicopter.

The corpse lay on the floor between us, the body smooth and perfect. The plane tilted and the body rolled. The arms and legs moved.

Ahmed seated himself in the copilot's seat, fastened the safety harness, and leaned forward with his head in his hands, not looking at the corpse. I looked out the windshield at the bobbing depris of furniture and unidentifiable bits and watched Coast Guard boats approaching and searching the water.

The copter radio beeped urgently. The pilot switched it on. "Coast Guard command to police helicopter PB 1005768. Thank you for your assistance. We now have enough Coast Guard ships and planes in the search pattern; please withdraw from the disaster area. Please withdraw from the disaster area."

"Order acknowledged. Withdrawing," the pilot said and switched the radio off. He changed the radio setting and

110

spoke briefly to Rescue Squad headquarters and turned the plane away from the area of destruction and toward the distant shore.

"What's your job in police?" he asked over his shoulder.

I did not answer.

"Rescue, detection, and prevention," Ahmed answered for me. "We were in the Jersey Dome ten minutes ago." Behind us the bombs boomed, breaking and closing the air shaft.

"You sure didn't prevent this one," said the copter pilot. Ahmed did not answer.

This is a blackmail tape. One copy of this tape has been mailed to each of the major communes and subcities in the New York City district.

We are responsible for the destruction of Brooklyn Dome. It was a warning and demonstrated our ability to destroy. We have in our possession a futures expert whose specialty was locating and predicting accidental dangers to the city complex caused by possible simple mechanical and human failures. He is drugged and cooperative. We asked him how Brooklyn Dome could self-destruct from a simple mechanical failure, and he explained how. We are now prepared to offer his services for sale. Our fee will be fifteen thousand dollars a question. If you are afraid that your commune has enemies, your logical question would be: What and who can destroy my commune, and how can I prevent this attack? We will provide the answer service to your enemies if they pay. They might be asking how to destroy your commune as you listen to this tape. Remember Brooklyn Dome. The name and address enclosed is your personal contact with us. No one else has this name. Keep it secret from the police, and use it when you decide to pay. If you give your contact up to the police, you will cut yourself off from our advice; your enemies will contact us through other names and buy methods to destroy you. Remember Brooklyn Dome. Act

111

soon. Our fee is fifteen thousand dollars a question. The price is cheap.

"Every police department has a copy. Want me to play it
again?" Judd Oslow asked. He sat cross-legged on top of his
desk like a large fat Buddha and sipped coffee.

"Once was enough," Ahmed said. "Paranoia and war
among the communes. What do those nuts think they are
doing with that tape?"

"Making money." Judd Oslow sipped his coffee, carefully
staying calm. "They mailed one to each commune in the city
area, and only two have turned in the entire tape or
admitted receiving it. Only one has turned in his address.
The others must be keeping their addresses, planning to
ask attack questions, or defense questions."

"Armageddon," said Ahmed.

Judd said, "George, why don't you get off your rump and
bring in Carl Hodges? These nuts can't sell his brains if we
get him back."

Ahmed said, "You just gave George the job last night. He
almost had him this morning, but we were reassigned when
the Brooklyn Dome blew and had to get off Carl Hodges'
trail to go to Jersey Dome."

"So there's some of the day left. George has spoiled me
with success. I'm used to instant results. Come on, George,
Carl Hodges, right here in this office, packaged and
delivered."

I tried and suddenly felt tired of being me, tired of trying.
"Every time I start trying to help Carl Hodges something
bad happens. It doesn't come out right," I mumbled. My
voice came out strange. "You don't want me helping, with
my luck!"

"Snap out of it, George. This is no time for pessimistic
philosophy. Get together with Ahmed and hypnotize yourself and tell me where Carl Hodges is." Judd looked
different.

"What's the use?" I ran my hands over my head with the
tired guilty feeling getting worse. "Brooklyn Dome people
are dead already. Jersey Dome people are mostly dead
already. Everybody that ever died is still dead. Billions of
people since the beginning of time. How are you going to

112

rescue them? Why not let a few more die? What difference does it make?" My voice was talking by itself.

"Let's not have an essay on eternity, George. Nothing makes any difference to eternity. We don't live in eternity, we live in now. We want Carl Hodges now."

"What's the use? My advice just makes trouble. I didn't save those people in Jersey Dome. I wasn't smart enough to understand that they'd want to break their own air locks. No, it wasn't the panic, it was the depression. The air changed its charge. Lab animals act irrational when you reverse the ground-to-air static-charge gradient. I should have—"

Judd shouted, "George, I'm not interested in your bad conscience. If you want to help people, just answer the question."

I winced at the loudness. A stranger was shouting a strange name. "George?"

"*Wow!*" Ahmed stepped forward. "Wait a minute. George did it already. That was Carl answering you, in Carl Hodges' style."

Judd hesitated between confident forward-and-back motions. He started and stopped a gesture. His confusion reached his expression. He shouted, "Get out of here, you kooks. Go do your lunacy somewhere else. When you bring back Carl Hodges, don't tell me how you did it."

"Affirmative," Ahmed said. "Come on, Carl."

In confusion and guilt I followed and found myself on the open sidewalk, standing under a row of maple trees. The wind blew and the trees shed a flutter of green winged seeds about me. I knew I had failed my job somehow and couldn't figure out how to get back to it. I walked to a bench and sat down.

"Do you understand what was just happening?" Ahmed asked.

"Yes." I felt in my mind and found confusion. "No."

"Shut your eyes. You seem to be on a bench in a park. It is an illusion. This is not where you are. Where are you really?"

I had shut my eyes. The voice went in deeply to a place in my mind where I knew I was in a room, a prisoner, and it was my fault. I did not like that knowledge. Better to

113

pretend. I opened my eyes. "I want to be here in the park. Pretend you are real." I bent and touched some green vetch at my feet and felt the tiny ferns. "History doesn't matter. Sensation matters," I said earnestly. "Even these illusions are real because they are happening now. We live in now. Memory isn't real. The past doesn't exist. Why should we feel anything about the past or care about it?"

I didn't feel any strange bad feelings now. I just felt separate from what my body was doing and saying.

Ahmed was watching with his eyes glittering.

"Carl Hodges. Do you want to get away from where you are and lie down in this park?"

"You are the questioner," I heard my voice say.

"Is it wrong to answer questions?"

"Yes; answers kill. People are dead. Like Susanne, they are all dead. Does mourning one person kill others? They drowned, too, and floated. Saw girl in water. . . . Connection . . .?"

Girl in water? My memory, not his. Suddenly we connected. I was him. Every muscle in my face and body tightened in a curling spasm like pain. I slid off the bench and fell to my knees in a soft vetch. "Get me out of this. Make it unhappen. Reverse time. Wipe me out before I did it." Was I praying to Ahmed or God? The pain of shame was great; could Ahmed or God cancel the past?

The intelligent face leaned over me, eyes glittering. I looked down, shut my eyes, held my head, hoped.

In the room where I was a prisoner I heard Ahmed's voice. "Two hours from now you will be rescued and free, without guilt, relaxed and enjoying being outdoors. We are the police; we are getting into a sky taxi to come and get you. What directions are we giving the driver?"

Suddenly hope and ability returned. My voice said, "Amsterdam Avenue and Fifty-third Street to Columbus Avenue, the wrecked blocks, one of the good cellars near the center of the flattened part of the ruins. Buzz it twice. Thanks. I think I can knock down a kid when I hear you and come out and wave. Land and pick me up fast." Carl Hodges felt good.

"OK," said Ahmed, his voice getting farther away. "OK."

I took my hands from my head. "OK what?" I felt fine. I got up and brushed small green fronds from my knees.

114

"OK, let's make a raid into another kid gang's territory," Ahmed said.

"Where's Biggy?" I looked around expecting to see our own gang of kids, then remembered. Biggy went to Mauritania. And the others, they went to the Sahara; they all went somewhere. I shook my head to wake up. "Ahmed, what do you mean, raid a kid gang territory? That's all over. We're grown up now."

"We're going to rescue that kidnapped computerman. A mixed gang of teener kids are holding him in the ruins near West Fifty-third Street. We know how to handle a kid gang fight."

I was not going to let go of common sense. I settled back on the bench and looked around at the green warm comfort of the park and rubbed one of the bruises on my arm. "Let's call the police; let them do it."

"We are the police, lunk." Ahmed still stood, smiling, depending on the force of his personality, the habit of command, to get me to obey. I looked up at him, squinting into the light of the sky. He still looked tall and command-ing, but I have to think, too.

"Ahmed, don't be a nut. Logical thinking doesn't fight chains and clubs for you. I mean, your brains are great, but we need muscle against a juv army, because they don't know about thinking, and they don't listen."

"What if they are all in their cellars, lunk, and we want to drop them before they get in deeper and carry Carl Hodges away? What kind of thing could get them all out into the open where a helicopter could drop them with gas?"

I absently rubbed the dark mark on the side of my face. "They come out when somebody gets onto their territory, Ahmed. Not an army of cops or a helicopter. I don't mean that. I mean some poor goof is crossing, looking for a shortcut to somewhere else, and they all come out and beat him up."

"That's for you."

"How did you figure. . . . Oh, yeah, you don't mean yesterday. You mean strategy, like. They come out to beat me up again and the copter drops them with a gas spray, and maybe there's no one left underground to kill Carl Hodges or take him away." I got up. "OK, let's do it."

We came out of the subway at Fifty-third Street and

115

walked together on the sidewalk opposite the bombed-out shells of old buildings. A distant helicopter sound buzzed in the air. Ahmed gave me a transceiver on a neckband that was tuned to send everything I said straight to that helicopter. I put it on.

Ahmed said, "You can say anything you like, but when you say the word 'help,' the pilot will bring in the copter fast. Yell it if you see Hodges. The pilot will be listening. I'll circle the block and look in doorways and hallways for trouble. You cut across. We both act like we have some reason to be here. I'm looking for an address."

"OK," I said. "I've got a story for them. Don't worry about me." I turned and walked nonchalantly around the corner, across the street, past some standing ruins and into the flattened spaces and the area that had once been paved backyard, with steps down to doors that had opened into the cellars of gone buildings. Flattened rubble and standing walls showed where the buildings had been.

I stood in the middle of a backyard, near two flights of cement stairs that led down into the ground to old doors. I walked onward slowly, going in an irregular wandering course, studying the ground, acting a little confused and clumsy, just the way I had acted the last time I'd been there.

The setting sun struck long shadows across the white broken pavement. I turned and looked back at my own long shadow and was startled when another person's shadow appeared silently on the pavement alongside of mine. I glanced sideways and saw a tall, husky teener in a strange costume standing beside me, holding a heavy bat. The teener did not look back at me; he looked off into space, lips pursed as though whistling silently.

I winced again when a short teener with straight blond hair stepped out from behind a fragment of standing wall.

"Back, huh?" asked the blond kid.

I felt the shadows of others gathering behind me.

I said, "I'm looking for a pocket watch I lost the night you guys beat me up. I mean, it's really an antique, and it reminds me of someone; I've got to find it."

I looked at the ground, turning around in a circle. There was a circle of feet all around me, feet standing in ruined doorways, feet on top of mounds of rubble, the clubs resting on the ground as the owners leaned on them, the chains swinging slightly.

"You must be really stupid," said the leader, his teeth showing in a small smile that had no friendship.

Where was Carl Hodges? The area I stood in was clean, probably well used by feet. The stairs leading down to a cellar door were clean; the door handle had the shine of use. The leader had appeared late, from an unlikely direction. He was standing on dusty, rubble-piled ground that feet had not rubbed and cleared. The leader, then, had not wanted to come out the usual way and path to confront me. Probably the usual way would have been the door I was facing, the one that looked used.

It was like playing hot and cold for a hidden object. If Carl Hodges was behind that door, the teeners would not let me approach it. I, looking slow and confused, shuffled my feet two steps in that direction. There was a simultaneous shuffle and hiss of clothing as the circle behind me and all around me closed in closer. I stopped and they stopped.

Now there was a circle of armed teeners close around me. Two were standing almost between me and the steps. The helicopter still buzzed in the distance, circling the blocks. I knew if I shouted, or even spoke clearly, asking for help, the copter pilot would bring the plane over in a count of seconds.

The blond kid did not move, still lounging, flashing his teeth in a small smile as he studied me up and down with the expression of a scientist at a zoo studying an odd specimen of gorilla.

"I got something important to tell you," I said to him. But they didn't listen.

"It's a kind of a shame," the blond kid said to the others. "He's so stupid already. I mean, if we just bashed out his brains he wouldn't even notice they were gone."

I faced the leader and sidled another small step in the direction of the steps and the door and heard the shuffle of feet closing in behind me. I stopped moving and they stopped moving. For sure that door was hiding something. They wanted to keep strangers away from it! "Look, if you found my watch I lost, and if you give it to me, I'll tell you about a thing you ought to know."

117

If I talked long and confusingly enough, every member of the gang would come out on the surface to hear what I was trying to say. They would all be out in the open. The helicopter was armed for riots; it could spray sleep gas and get every one of them.

I didn't even feel the blow. Suddenly I was on my knees, a purple haze before my eyes. I tried to get up and fell over sideways, still in the curled-up position.

I wasn't breathing.

Could a back-of-the-neck karate chop knock out your breathing centers? What had the teacher said? My lungs contracted, wheezing out more air, unable to let air in. It must have been a solar-plexus jab with a stick. But then how come I hadn't seen the stick? The purple haze was turning into spinning black spots. I couldn't see.

"What was it he wanted to tell us?" said a kid's voice.

"Ask him."

"He can't answer, dummy. He can't even grunt. We'll have to wait."

"I don't mind waiting," said the voice of the one carrying a chain. I heard the chain whistle and slap into something and wondered if it had hit me. Nothing in my body registered anything but a red burning need for air.

"You don't want to trespass on our territory," said a voice. "We're just trying to teach you respect. You stay on the free public sidewalks and don't go inside other people's kingdoms. Not unless they ask you." The chains whistled and slapped again.

I tried to breathe, but the effort to inhale knotted my chest tighter, forcing breath out instead of in.

It is a desperate thing having your lungs working against you. The knot tightening my lungs held for another second and then loosened. I drew in a rasping breath of cool air, and another. Air came in like waves of light, dispelling the blindness and bringing back awareness of arms and legs. I straightened out from the curled-up knot and lay on my back breathing deeply and listening to the sounds around me.

The helicopter motor hummed in the distance. *The copter pilot is listening,* I thought, *but he doesn't know I'm in trouble.*

I heard a clink and a hiss of breath like someone making

118

an effort. I rolled suddenly over to one side and covered my face. The chain hit where I had been. I rolled to a crouch with both feet under me and for the first time looked at the circle of faces of the teeners who had beaten and made fun of me when I was pretending to be drunk and making believe to be Carl Hodges and had stumbled into this forbidden territory. I had been retracing Carl Hodges' actions, but I had not been sure. I had no proof, no reason to protest when they punished me. The faces were the same. Young but cold, some faces were uncertain about punishing an adult, but gaining courage from the others. All sizes of teeners in costumes from many communes, but the fellowship and good nature were missing.

"I used to be in a gang like yours once," I said rapidly to inform the radio listener. "I thought you wouldn't jump me. I didn't come here to get stomped. I just want my antique watch and to tell you something."

I finished the sentence with a quick leap to one side, but the swinging chain swung up and followed, slapped into my skin, and curled a line of dents around ribs, chest, and arms. The magnet on the end clanked and clung against a loop of chain. The owner of the chain yanked hard on his handle and the metal lumps turned to teeth and bit in and the chain tightened like rope. I staggered and straightened and stood wrapped up in a biting steel chain.

I stood very still trying to hold my temper. "Hey," I said softly, "that ain't nice."

"Tell me about your message," said the blond kid.

I said, "A friend of mine was figuring from my lumps that I got here last time that you've got something important you want me to keep away from. He figures you got the missing computerman. The one who blew up Brooklyn Dome. There's a reward out for him."

A ripple of shock ran through the group surrounding me but the blond kid did not need time. Without change of expression he made a gesture of command. "Three of you check the streets. Maybe he brought somebody with him." Three ran silently in different directions.

"I'm just doing you a favor telling you what people say," I said in stupid tones. "Now you gotta do me a favor and help me get my watch back."

119

"Favor?" screamed the tall, misproportioned one with the chain. "Favor? You stupid fink, you should have kept your stupid mouth shut." He yanked hard on the chain to make its teeth extend more sharply.

I'd taken my limit. I stood still, looking meek and confused one more second, then bent forward and butted the chain holder down, rolled over him to the cement, and rolled rapidly down three small cement steps, unrolling the chain behind me. I came up on one knee, reaching for the chain as a weapon. It was a seven-foot chain with a handle at each end. A heavy chain is a killing weapon in the hands of a strong man. If it had been behind me right there I would have swung it around and forward and cut them down like grass. I gathered it looped into my hands. I threw the chain behind me, bent forward, bringing the chain forward with a released surge of force that was rage. The teen gang scattered and fled, and the chain swung its cutting circle through the air where they had been.

"Dumb punks," I breathed. "Not listening. . . ."

I stopped and let the swinging chain drag along the ground, slowing. I rippled it in and let it wrap around my arm, with a short murderous loop of it in my hand. The sun had set—everything was darker in the corners and harder to see. I fended off a flung stick by deflecting it with the chain, then grabbed a club for my other hand. Something whistled by and clanged against a wall—a knife. The teener leader had decided I knew too much and told his gang to kill me.

"Carl Hodges," I bellowed. "Ally ally in free. I need help. Computerman Carl Hodges, come out." The police riot-control man in the circling copter would at last hear a request for help and bring his plane in fast. The teeners would only hear me yelling Carl Hodges' name and still not be sure the police were near.

The cellar door gave two thumps and a crash and fell forward off its rusty hinges across the steps. A man fell out on top of it and scrambled across the door and up the steps without bothering to straighten from all fours.

At the top he stood up, thin and balding, wiry, and a little under average in size, totally unlike me in either shape or face, but he was me. My own eyes looked out of the other face.

120

I handed him a club from the ground. "Guard my back. They are going to try to take you alive, I think, but not me." I spun slowly, looking and listening, but all was quiet. Teeners lurked in a distance along the routes I would use if I tried to escape. *Kill*, they thought.

I looked back at Carl Hodges and saw the thin computerman staring—he was me, like a mirror.

"Hello, me over there," I said.

"Hello, me over there," the man said. "Are you a computerman? When I get back on the job do you want to come play City Chess with me? Maybe you could get a job in my department."

"No, buddy, we are us, but I don't play City Chess. I'm not like you."

"Then why—" Carl Hodges ducked a flung club and it clattered against the cement. *Then why do I have this impression of two people being the same person?* he meant.

"We have an empathy link in our guts," I said. "I don't think like you. I just feel what you feel."

"God help anyone who feels the way I feel," Hodges said. "I see some kids advancing on my side."

"Hold them off. Back to back. All we need is a little time." I turned away from him again and searched the corners with my eyes, ready for a rush. "About the way you feel. It's not all that bad. I'll get over it."

"I did it," Carl Hodges said. "How do I get over it? I feel . . . I mean, I have a reason for feeling . . . I got drunk and the egg hit the fan. How do I get over that?" His voice was broken by grunts of effort, and things clattered by, deflected, missing us and hitting walls and cement flooring.

We stood back to back and fended off bricks, sticks, and glittering objects that I hoped were not knives. "We can get killed if we don't watch it. That's one way," I said. A stick came through the air and rapped my ear. The attackers advanced, silhouettes against the dimming view of stone walls. Another attacker shadow picked up the clattering stick from the ground and threw it as he advanced.

"Ouch," said Carl Hodges. "Duck." We both ducked and a flung net went by. "We fight well together. We must get together and fight another teen gang sometime. Right?" said his brisk voice. "Ouch, damn."

I received a rush by the tallest of the gang, caught at the

121

outstretched staff, and yanked the enemy past. I tried to trip the teener as he hurtled by, but missed and turned to see him neatly tripped by Carl with a stick between the ankles. The teener went face forward to the ground and rolled, getting out of range.

"Good pass!" Several new and heavy blows on my head and shoulders reminded me to watch my own side. Dizzied, I spun, bracing the staff for a pushing blow with both hands, and felt it strike twice against blurred forms. I reversed it and struck down an attacker with a good thud.

With a heavy thrumming and a push of air the police helicopter came over a wall swooping low, like an owl settling over a nest of mice, and released a white cloud of gas.

I took a deep breath of the clear air before the cloud reached me. Beside me Carl Hodges took a deep startled breath of the white cloud and went down as suddenly as if a club blow had hit.

Still holding my breath, I straddled him and stood alert, peering through the fog at shapes that seemed to be upright and moving. Most of the teeners had run away or gone down flat on the ground. What were these shapes? Eighteen seconds of holding my breath. Not hard. I could make two minutes usually. I held my breath and tried to see through the white clouds around me. The sound of the helicopter circled, in a wider and wider spiral, laying a cloud of gas to catch all the running mice from the center of the area to its edges.

The shapes suddenly appeared beside me, running, and struck with a double push, flinging me back ten feet. I skidded on my back on the sandy concrete. I remembered to hold my breath after one snort of surprise and silently rolled to my feet and charged back.

Carl Hodges' unconscious form was missing. I saw movement through the white fog ahead, heard feet scuffing cement and hollow wood, and charged in pursuit of the sounds. Half falling, half sliding down the cement steps, across the wooden door on the ground and into a corridor; I glimpsed motion ahead and heard a closet door shutting. Holding my breath and groping, I opened the door and saw a broken wall with an opening. I smelled the wet smell of cement and underground drafts, and leaped over a pile of ancient trash brooms into the opening.

Safe to breathe here. As I took a deep breath, a brilliant flashlight suddenly came on, shining blindingly into my face from only two feet away. "I have a gun pointed on you," said the precise voice of the blond short teener. "Turn left and walk ahead in the directions I tell you. I could kill you here, and no one would find your body, so try to keep my good will."

"Where is Carl Hodges?" I asked, walking with my hands up. The flashlight threw my shadow ahead of me, wavering across the narrow walls.

"We're all going to be holing down together. Turn left here." The voice was odd.

I looked back and saw that the short teener was wearing a gas mask. As I took a breath to ask why, the white fog rolled down from a night-sky crevice above us. It smelled damp and slightly alcoholic. Antiriot gas.

"Keep moving," said the teener, gesturing with his gun. I turned left, wondering what happened next when you breathed that fog. A busy day, a busy night. An experience of symbolic insight was often reported by people who had been flattened by police antiriot gas. What had the day meant? Why were such things happening?

Floating in white mist, I floated free out of my body over the city and saw a vast spirit of complex and bitter logic that brooded over the city and lived in past and future. I spoke to it, in thoughts that were not words. "Ahmed used the world view of his grandmother, the Gypsy. He believes that you are Fate. He believes you have intentions and plans."

It laughed and thought, *The wheels of time and cause-effect grind tight. No room between gear and gear for freedom. The city is necessity. The future is built. The gears move us toward it. I am Fate.*

I made a strange objecting thought. *We don't remember what the past was; we aren't sure; we change our minds. So the past changes. So everything that adds up from the past changes. The future changes.*

With a howl, the vast spirit that brooded over the city shrank, dwindled to nowhere, uncreated, never was, like the Wicked Witch of the West when Dorothy poured a

123

bucket of water over her, leaving the same dwindling wail behind. "But all my beautiful disasters, my tragic logic. . . ."

"No necessity," I said firmly. "If you can see the future, you can change it. If you can't see the past, it will change by itself from every angle of view. Nothing will add up the same way twice."

The city of the future shattered and dissolved into white fog, a creative fog that could be shaped to anything by imagination. I stood in the middle of the fog and felt stubborn. They were tempting me again, trying to get me into the bureaucratic game of rules and unfreedom, wanting people to fit their lives into the little boxes on their paper forms.

"No," I said, "I won't fence anyone in with my ideas. Let them choose their own past."

The fog vanished.

In white robes, seven people were sitting on a mountain ridge near some scraggly pines, watching the Pacific Ocean sparkle in the distance. "Perhaps in a way, we do choose our past."

"An interesting dream image." "Almost the literal truth." "Agreed, a brilliant idea." "If we could select from the world memory what events are remembered and what are ignored, the direction of world action could be steered. People partially decide from what they think is traditional or usual."

They looked at me and said, "Thanks." Warmly, like old friends.

A sweet girl in a white robe with bare feet said, "Too bad he's always asleep. I wish I knew his name and address."

"No use asking, you'll just get blasted out with that silver-plane nightmare."

She said, coming closer in my mind until her voice echoed from inside my ears like my own voice, "But he's not asleep. It's some kind of drug, drug drug drug. . . ."

Suddenly their voices blasted in my ears. "Look out, George! He's pointing a gun at you. Grab control of his body. You're a controller. You can do it! Make him point the gun at his own head and blow his brains out."

"Cool it," I said. "Very savage ideas for seven angels."

"Self-preservation," they screamed. "Wake up! He's thinking about killing you before you wake up."

I came awake lying on the floor in a small tight room with the blond kid sitting on a bed pointing a gun at me. The room was cluttered with books and video cassettes, two old TV's, and a reading lamp.

"They got Carl Hodges back," the kid said. "You ruined everything. Maybe you are a cop. I don't know. Maybe I should kill you."

"I just had a wild dream," I said to him, not moving because I didn't want to scare him and get shot. "I dreamed I talked to the Fate of New York City. And I told Fate that the future can change anytime, and the past can change anytime. In the beginning was the middle, I said. So Fate started crying and boo-hooing and vanished." It struck me for the first time that the way I talked was too simple and stupid compared to the way I thought it when I was seeing it without words. I tried again. "I mean vanished, I mean no more Fate, vanished, free."

There was a long pause while the short blond kid held the pistol pointed at my face and stared at me over the top of it. The kid tried several tough faces, and then curiosity got the better of him. He was basically an intellectual, even though a young one, and curiosity meant more to him than love or hate. "What do you mean? The past is variable? You can change it?"

"I mean, we don't know what happened in the past exactly. It's gone anyhow. It's not real anymore. So we can say anything happened we want to have happened. If one past is going to make trouble, we can change it just by being dumb, and everything will straighten out. Like, for example, we just met, right now, right here, we just met. Nothing else happened."

"Oh." The kid put away his gun, thinking about that. "Glad to meet you. My name's Larry."

"My name's George." I arranged myself more comfortably on the floor, not making any sudden moves.

We had a long philosophical discussion while Larry waited for the police outside to finish searching and go away. Sometimes Larry took the gun out and pointed it at me again, but usually we discussed things and exchanged stories without any past anger.

Larry was serious and persuasive in trying to convince me that the world had too many technicians. "They don't know

125

how to be human beings. They like to read about being Tarzan or see old movies and imagine they are Humphrey Bogart and James Bond, but actually all they have the guts to do is read and study. They make money that way, and they make more gadgets and they run computers that do all the thinking and take all the challenge and conquest out of life. And they give a pension to all the people who want to work with their hands or go out into the woods or surf instead of staying indoors pushing buttons, and they call the surfers and islanders and forest farmers Freeloaders and make sure they are sterilized and don't have children. That's genocide. They are killing off the real people. The race will be descended from those compulsive button pushers and forget how to live."

It was a good speech. I felt uneasy, because it sounded right, and I was sure no man was smart enough to refute the killer, but I tried.

"Couldn't a guy who really wanted children earn enough money to get a breeding permit for himself and an operation for his wife?"

"There aren't that many jobs anymore. The jobs that are left are button-pusher jobs, and you have to study for twenty years to learn to push the right button. They're planning to sterilize everyone but button pushers."

I had nothing to say. It made sense, but my own experience did not fit. "I'm not sterilized, Larry, and I'm a real dope. I got hardly any education."

"When did your childhood support run out?"

"Last year, almost. I'm twenty years old this week."

"No more food and housing. How about your family? They support you?"

"No family. Orphan. I got lots of good friends, but they all took their pensions and shipped out. Except one. He got a job."

"You didn't apply for the unemployable youth pension yet?"

"No. I wanted to stay around the city. I didn't want to be shipped out. I figured I could get a job."

"That's a laugh. Lots of luck in getting a job, George. How are you planning to eat?"

"Sometimes I help around communes and share meals.

126

Everyone usually likes me in the brotherhood communes."
I shifted positions uneasily on the floor and sat up. This was
almost lying. I had a job now, but I wasn't going to talk
about Rescue Squad, because Larry might call me a cop and
try to shoot me. "But I don't bum meals."

"When's the longest you've gone without meals?"

"Two weeks, about. I don't feel hungry much. I used to
be fat. I'm healthy. I like work."

The kid sat cross-legged on the bed and laughed. "Really
healthy! You got muscles all over. You've got muscles from
ear to ear. So you're trying to beat the system! It was built
just to wipe out muscleheads like you. If you apply for
welfare, they sterilize you. If you take your unemployable
support pension, they sterilize you. If you are caught beg-
ging, they sterilize you. Money gets all you muscleheads
sooner or later. It's going to get you too. I'll bet when you
are hungry you think of the bottle of wine and the big free
meal at the sterility clinic. You think of the chance of winning the million-dollar sweepstakes if the operation gives
you the right tattoo number, don't you?"

I didn't answer.

"Maybe you don't know it, but your unemployable pension is piling up, half saved for every week you don't claim
it. You've been avoiding it a year almost? When it piles high
enough, you'll go in and claim your money and let them
sterilize you and ship you out to the boondocks, like
everyone else."

"Not me."

"Why not?"

I didn't answer. After a while I said, "Are you going to let
them sterilize you?"

Larry laughed again. He had a fox face and big ears. "Not
likely. There are lots of ways for a smart guy to beat the
system. My descendants are going to be there the year the
sun runs down and we hook drives to Earth and cruise away
looking for a new sun. My descendants are going to surf
light waves in space. Nobody's going to wipe them out and
nobody's going to make them into button pushers."

"OK, I see it." I got up and paced, two steps one way, two
steps the other way, in the narrow room. "Who are you
working for, Larry? Who are you crying over? People who
127

let themselves be bribed into cutting off their balls. They're different from you. Do they have guts enough to bother with? Are they worth getting your brain wiped in a court of law? You're right about history, I guess. I'm the kind of guy the techs are trying to get rid of. You're a tech type of guy yourself. Why don't you be a tech and forget about making trouble?"

At the end of the room, faced away from Larry, I stopped and stared at the wall, fists clenched. "Kid, do you know what kind of trouble you make?"

"I see it on television," Larry said.

"Those are real people you killed." I still stared at the wall. "This afternoon I was giving artificial respiration to a girl. She was bleeding from the eyes." Voice knotted up, I choked. My fists tightened as I tried to talk. "She was dead, they told me. She looked all right except for her eyes. I guess because I'm stupid I thought she was alive and I tried to help her." Help her! Yes, by killing Larry. Through a red fog I glanced around the small room looking for something to use for a weapon.

Larry took out his gun and pointed it, hastily getting off the bed. "Oh, oh, the past is real again. Time for me to leave!" Holding the gun pointed steadily and carefully at my face, he used his other hand to put on black goggles and slung the gas mask around his neck. "Hold still, George, you don't want a hole through your face. If you fight me who are you working for? Not your kind of people. Think, man." He backed to the door. I watched, facing him, crouched and ready.

Larry backed into the dark hall. "Don't follow. You don't want to follow me. This gun has infrasights, shoots in the dark. If you stick your head out the door, I might shoot it off. Just stand there for ten minutes and don't make any trouble. The gun is silenced. If I have to shoot you, you don't get any medal for being a dead hero. No one would know."

The short teener backed down the dark corridor and was gone.

I still stood crouched and I began to see again, and I could unclench my hands. A long way down the corridor I heard Larry trip over a broom. It clattered, falling. Larry bumped into a wall and went farther out of earshot. I could have followed him then, but I was remembering I'd liked him. I had liked the way he thought; he thought in a kind of warm glow, and the world suddenly seemed clear and easy to handle when he talked.

I should go after the killer, but I just stood there. . . .

"Very good self-control, George. Congratulations," Ahmed's cool voice said from the ceiling. Ahmed let himself down from a hole in the ceiling, hung by both long arms, and then dropped, landing catlike and silent. He was tall and sooty and filthy and covered with cobwebs. He grinned and his teeth were white in a very dark face. "You just missed a medal for being a dead hero. I thought you were going to try to kill him."

He twiddled the dial of his wrist radio, plugged an earphone into one ear, and spoke into the wrist radio. "Flushed one. He's heading west on a cellar corridor from the center, wearing a gas mask and infragoggles, armed and dangerous. He's the kingpin, so try hard, buddies."

I sat down on the edge of the bunk, sweating. "I get too mad sometimes. I almost did try to kill him. What he said was probably right."

Ahmed unplugged the speaker from his ear. "I was mostly listening to you, good buddy. Very interesting philosophical discussion you were putting out. I kept wanting to sneeze. How come you get into philosophical arguments today and I just get beat up? Everything is backward."

"You're the smart one, Ahmed," I said slowly, accepting the fact that I had been protected. "Thanks for watching." I looked at my hands, still worrying. "How come everything that kid said made sense?"

"It didn't." Ahmed tried to rub the cobwebs off his sleeves. "*You* made sense."

"But Larry said that techs are wiping out nontechs."

"Maybe they are, but they aren't killing anybody. The kid kills."

I pushed my hands together and felt them wet with sweat and wiped them on my shirt. "I almost killed the kid. But it felt right, what he was saying. He was talking for the way

129

things are and for the way they're going to be, like Fate was. Sterilizing people is legal, killing is—"

"Killing is unphilosophical," Ahmend said. "You're tired, George, take it easy, we've had a long day."

I heard a police siren wail and then distant shots. Ahmed plugged the earphone into his ear. "They just dropped somebody in goggles; gas didn't work on him. They had to drop him with hypo bullets. Probably Larry. Let's try to get out of here."

We put a wad of blankets out into the corridor, head high. No shots, so we went out cautiously and started groping down the long black hall, looking for an exit.

Ahmed said, "So you think Larry was the fickle finger of Fate on the groping hand of the future? No power on Earth can resist the force of an idea whose time has come, said somebody once. But, good buddy, when I was listening to you whilst lying in the ceiling with the spiders crawling on me, I thought I heard you invent a new metaphysics. Didn't you just abolish Fate?"

The corridor widened, and I felt a draft of fresh air without dust and saw a glimmer of light through a hole. We climbed through and saw a doorway and a broken door. "I don't know, Ahmed," I said vaguely. He meant I'd been thinking. I tried to remember.

Hallucinations were what I remembered. Seven bad philosophers sitting on the edge of the Pacific giving bad advice, yet my friends, only trying to be helpful. They were so real I could smell their sweat. They were concentrating, trying to ESP contact me again. But I shut them out. When you believe your hallucinations is when you should be wrapped up and taken away. As long as you know they are imaginary, you are still all right.

We climbed through the broken door and up a flight of stone steps and found ourselves in a deserted yard at the center of the ruin. It was very quiet. In the distance, around the edges of the block, police copters buzzed, landing in the streets.

"Sure you did," Ahmed said. "You abolished Fate. I heard you."

I looked up at the moon. It was bright and it shone across the entire city, like the evil Fate in my dream, but it was only

130

the moon, and the city was quiet. I had destroyed fate with an argument, a good, high-IQ syllogism. Suddenly I leaped into the air and clicked my heels. "I did. I did." Nobody was listening, so I yelled, "Hey, I did it! I abolished Fate!" I landed and listened to the silence. The moon was peaceful, without doom, but there was still something about the feel of the big dark city and its strange big buildings like a tiger asleep. The red glow in the sky over New York blinked on and off, on and off, from the giant sign we could not see. THINK, THINK, THINK.

"Congratuations," said Ahmed and rested an arm briefly across my shoulders. "May I offer you a tranquilizer?"

"No," I said. "Cancel that. Judd gave me money. I'll go my own way." I needed to think without being offered tranquilizers. Ahmed's humor was no help.

Money, hot showers, steak—enjoy the city we two had helped save. And think. Important to think.

I walked away—I looked back once. Ahmed stood tall and covered with dirt and cobwebs looking after me.

He looked surprised.

5

It was lonely and quiet on the sidewalk passing the closed walls of a commune block. You grow up sure that the people running the world are trying to do a good job, and then sombody says something that makes it all look different. I stopped and looked up at the walls.

They were windowless, like backs turned away from the world. Privacy within communes helped them to keep their own separate laws and customs, policed only by their brothers who felt comfortable with their ways. Walls were supposed to symbolize shelter and protection for the group within. I felt unsure, looking at the high blank walls. They looked as if they meant *keep out*. Hatred?

If a people hated outsiders, could they be trusted to take good care of a city of outsiders? Techs, computer programmers, systems analysis and control experts, all the men

131

who controlled the machines that think—they were a group; they ran the politics and services of the city.

"The techs are planning the laws to wipe out everybody but techs. Especially muscleheads like you, George." The kid had meant it. And his vibes had been friendly. I went into a phone booth. Call? Call who? I went out of the phone booth and looked up and down the long green sidewalk, wanting to talk to someone, to explain that important thinking was troubling me.

Two dull-looking men went by and gave out feelings of nervous boredom. A happy-looking man went by and ducked his head, walking faster, not liking being looked at by a big guy standing in the dark. Apologetically, I looked away. Don't stare, George. I remembered the pocket radio Rescue Squad had loaned me and switched it on. "Statistics, please."

"Statistics here."

"What time is it?"

"Nine thirty-two," replied a tiny voice and asked a question. I plugged the earphone deeper in my ear and turned up the volume. I asked, "There's someone just been arrested about a half hour ago. I want to get to him and talk to him and all I have is his first name."

The voice came in loud and clear, like someone standing beside me talking in my left ear. "Procedure. You have to identify yourself first."

"George Sanford. Rescue Squad. Consultant, category J. No badge number."

"Right. Now about the suspect. When? Where? How? What? Whatever you can tell me. I'm feeding it into the computer."

"Larry something. Maybe fourteen or fifteen and bright, like a college student. Blond, short, underweight. He'd be booked for kidnapping and vandalism and sabotage and maybe multiple murder."

"Oh, *that* Larry. Brooklyn Dome sabotage. You're the Sanford who used ESP to locate the kidnap gang. Congratulations, Sanford! It just came in over the general announcements. Look. I've fed all the information in and the computer isn't giving me any readout." The voice sounded alert and interested. "Why don't you call back in half an hour? By that time he'll be booked, and probably through questioning and confession, and free to talk to anyone until his appointment to be wiped comes up."

"OK, thanks." I switched off. I stood looking at the near walls of the commune. A man in a warlock costume passed me, and hunched his shoulders and looked at the sidewalk ahead of his feet, and gave out vibes of fear that made the buildings look big and menacing and dark. Afraid of something big and menacing and dark, I thought, probably me; I shouldn't stare at people.

I brushed at the dust spots on my sleeves and smelled the animal stink of my own sweat. Sweat from fighting and from anger. Ashamed, I walked quickly and softly to a subway entrance and took the slide chairs to the free public showers, swimming pool, and laundry.

An hour later, clean, showered, and dry, dressed in clean clothes still hot from the dryer, I tried the wrist radio again.

This time it was a different voice.

"Not listed. There were six people arrested in that roundup and booked, but no Larry anything. Do you mean the head of that gang?"

"Yes."

"There's an all-points alarm out for him, including checking the airlines and the shuttle to the moon. Someone in headquarters really expects that kid to move fast. About fifteen years old, five feet two, underweight blond male, no beard, voice high, right? They've been showing sketches of him on TV. Nobody knows where he is."

"Thanks." I shut off the radio. I wanted to talk to Larry. I made believe I was a thin kid with an all-points alarm out for me, and felt scared and clever and decided he'd hide in a park. A big park.

"You must be crazy," said Larry in the dark, standing under the trees of Van Cortland Park Forest. "You must be really out of your mind." The kid's fox face was dirty and his voice had a tired, complaining whine. "You know just now I had to hold back two guys with my hands from killing you, just now, with my *hands*." He seemed unbelieving. "They didn't want to take orders. What's your name? George? You get crazier all the time, and dumber. It really

133

gave my boys a jolt seeing you again. They've got bruises all over from you. I had to tell them you were probably protected by an invisible army of cops with radar sights before I got Weeny's gun away from him. But"—a trace of admiration showed in the kid's face and voice—"you're by yourself, aren't you?"

I squinted at Larry by the light of the subway-stair lamp, the only light in that section of dark forest. I said, "What you said about techs wiping out all the other kinds of people. . . . When you were talking with me before. . . ."

"How did you find me like this? How did you know where I am?" Larry demanded. "Did someone see us?"

"Nobody saw you. I'm just good at finding people."

"Did you tell anybody?"

My shoulders prickled as though expecting attack from the darkness behind me. "I told a friend," I lied.

"Will he tell the police?" the kid asked.

"No." I hoped that sounded like the usual threat. (Not if I come back safe.)

"How do you do it?" The kid put a hand on my arm. "How do you find people?"

"I have to concentrate." I mumbled my answer, feeling ashamed for no reason. "I get a feeling where somebody is."

"OK, here's where we ask the jackpot question." Turning me to face him with the light hand on my arm, Larry asked in his light voice, "Are you a cop? The gang wants me to find out so they'll know if we should kill you."

I leaned down to speak close to Larry's ear. I gestured apologetically. "Uh, I'm kind of a cop, but I'm in the Rescue Squad. I'm not after you to hurt you, Larry. My job is to get kittens down out of trees and kids off rusty fire escapes and old ladies out of cellars. I'm kind of a searcher for the ambulance division. I locate people in trouble. I'm a locater, not a cop."

"Go away, nut. You're almost a cop. They'll decide to kill you. I want you to be down into the underground and out of sight around the tunnel bend and flying as soon as I get between you and them and say go. I'll trip them on the stairs. Come back in two days. It will take that long for me to talk them into liking you. And don't tell the cops where I am. What you want to do is join my gang. *Go.*"

134

I hesitated. He didn't understand. I wanted to explain.

"I hid Weeny's gun, but he probably has found it by now," said Larry. "It's loaded with germ needles. Move, leadhead. I want you in my gang alive."

I ran back to the stairs and jumped most of the steps down in two long jumps and thudded a steady run through the empty, unused tunnel back to the bright subway platform with the waiting downtown chairs to take me away from mad teeners with rifles loaded with germ needles.

Down in the slideways I took a slow lane for my chair. I sat looking backward and whistled at all the plain-looking girls passing me on chairs in other lanes and winked at the overaged beauties and made a lot of women happy. I sat grinning between whistles, enjoying the wash of good vibes.

It was a comfortable summer night. I got my sleeping bag from a locker at a midtown station and considered where to sleep.

There was a small ornamental park opposite Rescue Squad headquarters with a grass belt of the unmowed deep grass, wild flowers, weeds, and bushes that preserved the ecology of wildlife in the city and generated air for humans.

The deep grass was soft. Some kind of small white flower on some of the bushes made a rich perfume and attracted fireflies. I lay awake for a while watching the tiny creatures blink their lights on and off like passenger planes circling for a landing at an unseen airport.

I woke alert, hearing footsteps rustling through the heavy grass. I opened my eyes to sunlight. A tall figure pushed a branch aside and stood over me.

"What are you doing sleeping on the ground?" Ahmed demanded, voice almost trembling with outraged astonishment. "Why don't you sleep at your own place? Don't you have a place?" Ahmed stood there, neatly dressed, clean-shaven, and trim, ready to do his job and be promoted.

It is a lousy way to wake up: somebody complaining.

I sat up and tried to explain to a man who wouldn't understand. "I kind of have a place. I can sleep over at my girl's place in the Karmic Brotherhood," I explained. "But she's out of Raja Yoga now and into a fasting and

135

meditation thing and she's given up boyfriends. Besides, I wanted to be alone and think about history."

Ahmed said angrily, "Sleep where you like! Reduce the population!"

I stood up and stretched and looked straight into Ahmed's eyes. We were the same height now. I didn't want to fight him. I looked away and rolled my sleeping bag. "Anything I can do for you, Ahmed?"

"Yes, I've been getting congratulations about you. You'll get a bonus and maybe a public medal for locating the kidnap gang last night. Now they know you can locate people, everyone wants you to help them. The Coast Guard wants to borrow you first and Statistics wants you to help at Central Prediction Statistics research."

"I guess I should work with you," I said, "but you're kind of early. You've got to give a guy a chance to get up." I picked up the bedding roll and slid my feet into my sandals. I was still mad at being wakened suddenly. "I haven't had a shower or breakfast. Let me alone until later."

Ahmed came into the restaurant near Rescue Squad headquarters; I was eating scrambled eggs, waffles, and sausages at a table near the window. He came and sat at my table.

"Larry of Larry's Raiders didn't get caught last night."

"I know," I mumbled with a full mouth.

"Can you locate him, do you think?"

"I did." I swallowed and cut pieces of waffle and sausage and pronged them in alternate layers on my fork.

Ahmed waited for me to say more.

I loaded my mouth with two forkfuls of sausage and waffle and looked at Ahmed thoughtfully, chewing.

"Last night," I said, "I wanted to talk to Larry. He wasn't in jail or in the hospital." I took a swallow of coffee and looked out the window.

"Where is he?"

"I thought where I'd go if I were Larry, and I went there."

"You're improving, George. Where is he?"

"He was there," I said. "We talked."

"You went and talked to him? After beating up his gang and getting them arrested? You went by yourself?"

"Yes. He's easy to talk to. He thinks I want to join his
136

gang." I speared another sausage and stirred it around in some syrup on my plate. "I'm going back to talk to him. He'll explain why he's making trouble. I think I can talk him out of it, so he'll stop making trouble."

"He'll stop making trouble when he's locked up or wiped! Tell me where he is!" Ahmed tuned his wrist radio and raised it to his lips to repeat the information as soon as I gave it to him.

I sipped my coffee and looked at him without any particular expression, waiting for him to give up. There were a lot of years behind us when I used to do exactly what he ordered, instantly, and even feel honored to take his orders. That didn't seem to matter now.

Ahmed lowered the wrist radio from his mouth and turned it off with a sigh.

If Ahmed was really smarter than Larry, he should explain it to me instead of giving orders.

"Ahmed, did you really think Larry was crazy when you were listening to him talk?"

"No."

"Why do you say that he's crazy, then?"

Ahmed started an angry answer, then stopped it and told the truth. "The kind of thing he says is generally dangerous talk. It can make bad trouble."

"Why?" I was trying to keep him talking, to get some of the thoughts in that long narrow head out where I could see them.

"Because it's a form of natural war whoop to say that some other group has been killing off your group. It means you want an excuse to join with your friends and kill strangers."

"I'm not planning to kill anybody."

Suddenly angry, I wiped my hands with a napkin and stood up. It probably wasn't Ahmed's fault but everything he said recently seemed to make me angry. "I just want some facts."

Ahmed tapped on the table with a fork.

"Sit down, George; I think I can explain. Because of computer personality sorting, people are getting used to having friends and neighbors with the same interests and the same ideas of what it means to do the right thing. They agree with their village neighbors or commune brothers.

137

They aren't used to differences. Other ways of life look wrong."

I still stood beside the table. "The films on the history of democracy said that laws protecting the right to be different and the right to privacy were just started in modern times. So that's getting better, not worse."

"Will you listen! I didn't say things are getting worse. People are happier sorted out. Until recently the idea was to mix everyone up and make them live together and try to act just the same on the outside: businessmen, artists, puritans, dancers, blacks, ethnics. People with totally different ideas of fun. They were lonesome trying to pretend to be average, surrounded by people they couldn't understand."

I argued. "We were all mixed ethnic in the UN Brotherhood gang, and we were good brothers. It was a good gang."

Ahmed was not used to me arguing. He looked at his own hand tapping the fork for a moment, lips compressed, the dark brows in the handsome long face drawn together in a frown of difficulty. He took a deep breath and pulled it together. This time he tried to explain as if he was talking to a stranger.

"George, what would you call a quiet guy who gets interested in philosophy and religion and says that Jesus Christ is in every man, and then he says all the guilty people of the world have piled up a backlog debt of other peoples suffering that they did not let themselves feel, and now they are accumulating guilt they won't turn to face so they can't turn back and be kind, and so they are neurotic and damned and in hell alive. And then he says he's going to rescue the poor bastards by suffering for them and feeling their guilt for them. And then he sits and meditates for two weeks or a year and doesn't talk. If you ask his name he might say he's being Jesus Christ. What have I described?"

"One of the nicest little guys over at the Karmic Brotherhood." I remembered a round bearded face with big childish eyes, a shy stammering voice, and nice kind loving vibes. He practically gave out a pink glow of kindness, but he was too shy to talk.

Ahmed looked up at me, eyes narrowing, the long face hardening. He asked, "What do they do to him?"

138

"What do you mean, *do* to him?" I was puzzled. "They bring him meals. Even if he isn't saving the world he deserves credit for trying."

"Do they make him work?"

"He is working." I heard my voice getting loud and I made myself sit down again and speak in a low voice. "I don't know what you mean. He's doing his thing as best he can. He's trying. And he's their brother. It's their kind of thing."

"George, in the nineteen forty-fifty era a little guy like that would be called a partially catatonic schizophrenic with religious mania, megalomania, and delusions of grandeur. Doctors would lock him in a windowless room and every day they'd come for him, put him in a straitjacket, and take him to a room where they'd give him shocks to the brain. The shocks were strong enough to give him convulsions, strong enough to break bones. He might bite his tongue in two if not prevented. He'd scream, urinate, defecate, get high blood pressure, and so forth. After he had been carried away and revived, he would be unable to remember what had happened but he would feel terror at the sight of the door that led to that room. The hospital people would give him twenty treatments of that kind, five shocks a treatment. Then they'd ask him if he still believed that he was Jesus Christ. If he said yes, he was suffering for mankind, he'd be taken back for another twenty and so on. People with weak hearts sometimes died in the shock-therapy room."

I heard a roaring in my ears and saw white. I pushed my fists together nervously, but duty can't be worked off that way. You want to fight but fighting won't get rid of it. I couldn't get my voice louder than a whisper. "Who was running the hospital? Aztecs? Sadists?"

"Well, yes." Ahmed leaned back. "When it came time to sort out personality types it was found that most people in that kind of hospital business belonged in the sadomasochist group. Now the computer services have all the sadists and sadomasochists sorted out, they can live in their own communes in every city and stay out of hospital service. See, George, sorting helps."

I looked at the table. "Yeah, OK, don't talk about it.

139

They're nice little guys at the brotherhoods. I'd kill anyone who. . . ." I was sweating, afraid of the white blaze of murder I felt toward unknown people in the forties who had run mental hospitals.

Ahmed looked at me keenly. "Kill. You said the normal word, George. Getting packs of similars together has aroused the old tribe-pack instincts. Packs protect kin, with a suicidal killing rage. A lion won't attack a baboon because he knows that twenty baboons will willingly die to destroy one lion that dared to touch a baboon brother. We're back into a small-group primitive tribal organization and it fits twenty million years of animal and human evolution of hunting and killing in packs. Instincts are pleasures; people don't resist pleasures." Ahmed rose, finishing his explanation. "So we have to be careful about letting people talk up war between communes. It can get too real, too fast. They would enjoy fighting."

We walked out and toward Rescue Squad headquarters.

"Why doesn't it happen?" I asked. "I don't hear about communes fighting communes."

"It does happen. They don't put it on DV. The government stops the shipment of surplus food to both sides, cuts off their water, and cuts off their power until the commune councils arrest everyone involved in the fighting in their own communes and punish them. The news about this kind of action is buried in the dullest legal columns of the printed news in the dullest language, so people looking for trouble and excitement never read it, and readers don't get excited and try to join the war."

"All right, I understand why you don't want Larry to talk about techs like that. But what if what he says is true? What if the techs are trying to—to. . . ."

Ahmed shrugged. "Some of his speeches make sense."

"Why do you act like he's crazy if what he says makes sense?"

"With psychotics you don't listen to what they say, you watch what they do." Ahmed stood up. "Let's go to work now and argue later."

We went up an elevator to the eighth floor.

"Ahmed, how smart is Larry?"

"His talk is just war whooping. Larry is using it as an excuse to play at being general in a war."

140

"How smart is he?" We waited in front of the receptionist's desk after announcing our names while she sent for the typed orders.

"Smarter than me. But wrong."

Our order sheets arrived. Ahmed read mine first. "Rescue Squad has a mission for you that makes sense. They have a two-man submarine to scout the wreckage of the two undersea domes and they want you to go along and feel for vibes of anyone alive. Someone might be waiting for rescue in the air pockets under all that flattened top cloth. And Statistics wants you when you're through with that."

Ahmed handed me the typed sheet. "A submarine will pull up at Pier Eighteen in ten minutes to pick you up. You have time to walk over."

I walked west over the green sidewalks past the mid-street grass and tree belt, under the shadow of the giant glass buildings. The people passing were excited and interested and hurrying with more energy to their usual work. It reminded me of something: that the history sequences usually remarked that people were unusually happy and optimistic after great general disasters; survivors seemed to share a feeling of health and optimism.

Puzzling about that, but sharing the cheerful feeling, I walked under the giant elevated highway and loading chutes of the Hudson River and climbed a stairway up a sloped cement dike to the water's edge. A small submarine bobbed at a fishing dock and a scuba stair, and a coastguardsman put out his head and waved back when I waved and gestured me to the dock.

It was a successful working day. Cruising in the submarine over the sunken wreckage of the suburb, we located and rescued two trapped people and a cat. All three were in good shape, excited by the adventure, and glad to be rescued, full of thanks and congratulations. They embraced and put arms around each other and the cat rubbed against us, purring, and they sang on the way back to shore.

When we finished delivering the two people to an ambulance for a medical checkout, I read my instruction sheet again. It said, "Sign time when finished, signature of person assisted by consultation," with three dotted lines.

"What's this mean?" I showed it to the coastguardsman.

The submarine pilot read it, signed his name and a time, and pointed at the top line. "Sign here."

I signed. "What for?"

"They need the hours you worked. It says they're paying you twenty-five dollars an hour per consultation."

"What we were doing was a consultation?" I asked, wondering at the high rate.

"All day, four or five hours, depending on whether they think we stopped for lunch. One hundred and twenty-five dollars' worth."

"Sheeit!"

"It pays to be a specialist; you're a specialist."

We stood on top of the cement wall of the Hudson dikes and looked down at the city streets with the salt wind whipping our hair and flapping our clothes.

"That's a lot of money," I said. "What do I do next?"

The coastguardsman handed me back my orders. "You go to General Statistics computer complex and ask for Ben Russo or Joe Levinsky."

I looked at the small salt waves of the Hudson, wind-driven, slapping fiercely against the wet cement of the dike. The water level was ten feet above the street level.

"Is it rising?" I asked the coastguardsman.

"Not one inch in the last five years. We're OK," the man said and smiled. "Have a good day, Sanford." He went back to his submarine.

The sun sparkled on the water. I ran down the cement steps away from the river toward my next assignment.

The security guard at the computer complex checked my pass, looked at my ID credit card, telephoned a higher official, then led me through a maze of corridors, past offices, readout screens, and typewriters typing long ribbons of information to the floor.

We stopped at a door.

"In there," said the guard.

I went in. Two gnomelike men with thick glasses were shouting.

"It's too wild, but it's great."

"Run a probability check. Quick."

"Hello," I said uncertainly.

One of them ran to the keyboard of a small computer

142

and punched in figures and plugged in operation sequences and turned it on.

The other stood watching tensely.

"Hello?" I said, wondering if I was supposed to watch. The machine chattered out a slip of paper.

"Point eight," said the younger one, reading it off.

"Fantastic." He skipped around, waving the slip of paper, looking like a young troll imitating a goat.

"Do you guys always hop up and down when you think?" I asked, grinning. I remembered Ann spinning in her small student room. Perhaps she spun because there was no room to hop or run.

"Why not?" asked the older one defensively. "What do you want?"

"I'm George Sanford. I was sent over to help you." I felt in my pocket for the order paper.

"What do you do?" They both approached me, peering curiously through thick glasses.

"I uh, locate people."

"Oh, the telepathy man? Yes, we need you to help predict trends in free population flow. The displaced residences of the dome people who survived have knocked our baseline out. Transportation says that surge spacing is shot to hell and they need better prediction."

"Yes," said the young one with frizzy hair. "Can you help?"

"Help do what?"

"Help tell us what the average man is going to do with his free time all day," said the older bald one. "I'm Ben." He reached out and shook hands firmly with me.

"I'm Joe." The younger one reached out and gave my hand a quick nervous shake and dropped it immediately. "Are you average?"

"I don't know."

"Well, do you go where other people go? When you want to go to the beach, do you find everybody crowding on the beach? When you get on a subway, is it always a rush hour, heading your way?"

"No, everything's usually empty. I don't see many people."

Joe said to Ben, "How can he predict average people if he isn't average?"

Ben said, "But we didn't ask for an average person, we asked for a telepathy man, who can tell where people are."

Joe said, "If we had an average person we could just watch where he goes, and that's where the others will be."

Ben said, "But we need someone who will predict population surges."

Joe said, "Then we need a fast average man, someone who will get there first. And we'll put a radio tracer on him and adjust the transportation one-way lines and service loads in advance before the mass gets there."

Ben said, "Variance. He might break a leg. Actually we need a bunch, a stratified cross section, men, women, and kids." He paced, popping little yellow pills into his mouth. "How do we find them?"

I understood some of what they were trying to do. "I know a kid, a girl. Whenever there was a big crowd thing happening, she said she was there first and saw it starting. She liked crowds and noise and seeing important people."

"Where is she now?"

"Shipped out on youth retirement pension."

"Was she a leader type? Did people follow her?"

"No. She was kind of silly. She followed people."

Joe started hopping up and down again. "A follower, an empath like you, but with nothing to do. She'd pick up on lots of people deciding to go somewhere and get there first because she didn't have any job to delay her. A sheep, a fast sheep. Right, George?"

"Maybe." I didn't like anybody being called a sheep.

"How do we find fast sheep, Ben?" asked Joe.

"Who was first at the big crowd scenes? Ask the computer."

"It won't know. Nobody told it. No input, no output."

"Try, ah, try—" Ben began hopping. "I think I have it. I've really got it!"

"Do you guys need me?" I asked. They didn't answer. They kept on shouting and hopping. I let myself out quietly.

Outside it was too hot in the sun, but a good wind was blowing. The direction of the wind shifted at each corner. I walked back to the Karmic Brotherhood commune and met two girls who were beginning the Raja Yoga thing, the Yoga

144

of sensation, a way to get out of your ordinary mind by blowing your mind with extremes.

We went to Coney Island and took rides on the roller coaster and sky jump and went into the ocean and dared each other to try to stand upright under the big breaking waves, and got pounded down and rolled by the big cool combers, and came back in the subway, sandy, exhausted, and giggling.

I showered and changed clothes and suddenly I stopped laughing and was worried, arguing with Larry in my mind. The girls had acted like ordinary girls, and it was good to be ordinary; it was fine fun. Was the world really set up to wipe the ordinary people out? Are techs really enemies?

Still worrying, I called Rescue Squad to pick up my messages.

"No, Sanford, we don't have any work assignments for you, but you have a message. It says call this number at exactly four or exactly six." It was six.

I dialed the number. Larry's voice answered. "Have you thought about joining my gang, George?" It was recorded, so I didn't answer.

As I hung up, I heard the rapid clicking that meant the police automatic voiceprint alert hooked into the phone system had identified the voice as a Wanted and was sending a squad to that phone. They wouldn't find him there. Larry was smarter than that.

I called Ahmed. "Has Larry's gang done anything bad recently?"

"A few things swiped; maybe his gang did it. A slogan scattered around: '*If you sabotage a computer they'll retire you from civilization and send you to an island to fish and swim. I'll bet you're really scared.*' "

"Sounds like Larry." I grinned a little. "He knows how to talk people into things."

"Are you ready to locate him for the police, George?"

"No."

"They will get him anyhow. He's already been identified. His last name is Rubashov. Larry Rubashov. We have his printout. He's fifteen years old, from Nevada automation complex."

"How did they recognize him—fingerprints?"

145

"No, vocabulary. The vocabulary of the blackmail letters to the communes and the printed sign was the same as a Larry Rubashov who won a national prize for a book of poetry and essays in December. It took the computer to spot it. Want more readout?"

"Please." I wanted to know about Larry. "How much of a genius was he?"

"In school very high rankings in English, symbolism, history of social dynamics. Taking therapy for emotional blocks against teaching in math and electronics. His father works at the Nevada Computer Complex on data retrieval and his mother teaches data retrieval at a programmers' school. Both have four-figure incomes. Larry is their oldest child. Two younger siblings show severe emotional disabilities and occasionally need hospitalization. Parents classified as pathogenic and permission to breed revoked."

"What's pathogenic?"

"Sick making. They shouldn't have kids. They mess them up. Want more readout?"

"No thanks, Ahmed."

Carnival day. The rhythmic boom of marching bands came in through the window with warm summer air. Still asleep, I began to see memory images of crowds in costumes, of floats and pageants, games and Coliseum Stadium battles, and the evening parties and strange costumes, and midnight with all the clocks booming over the city sound systems and strangers in the parties turned to each other, blind with aphrodisiac spray, dancing and drum sounds. Asleep. I turned over.

A memory voice said very precisely, "Every system becomes a system by excluding its opposite actions. In human nature all opposite impulses, repressed, do not fade. They accumulate and build up charge and fantasies. All old and lasting civilizations stabilized themselves by holding periodic ceremonies to release the charged opposite actions." It was the precise voice of the fifth-grade anthropology teacher. Waking, I remembered that she had shown the class some wild movies of carnivals all over the world and some from the deep past. Spring solstice sacrifices, orgies, and rituals about spring, summer solstices

146

and winter solstices. Cavemen and early Greeks and New Orleans Mardi Gras.

The drumbeats boomed under the window in a broken dance beat. Boom boom boomatop boomatop boomatop boom—boom boom. I rolled over and rolled up to my feet naked, blinking in bright sunlight, scared that some of the good carnival shows had gone by already.

The visitors' sleeping room was almost empty. They had gone off to the streets and the summer carnival. I put on shorts and sandals and stuffed my clothes into my bedding roll and ran downstairs. Posters on the walls announced the carnival's scheduled events. A sign said, CHOOSE YOUR COSTUMES IN THE GYMNASIUM. I hurried.

In the gym there were five girls trying on costumes from a pile. Two were pinning another girl into big purple wings and a beaked orange bird mask, and one was stripping off gold tights in favor of some other costume she had her eye on. A girl in fur and one in gold fish scales were trying sexy poses in front of the mirror and giggling. Usually girls of the Karmic Brotherhood Commune acted philosophical enough to be monogamous or very choosy. Usually they disapproved of teasing and thought that trying to be attractive to arouse lust in men was unethical.

Today was the day of opposites! Today, look out!

I looked into the mirror, saw myself a big wide guy with his bones close to the skin, not fat like I used to be, but still showing heavy muscles in thick arms and big hands and a round innocent blond face, almost like a big kid.

What was the opposite of me? Something black and sinister and grim. I looked through the pile of costumes.

The girl in a striped cat mask snuggled up to me and rubbed her pink fur up against my chest, purring. She was wearing smooth silky fur all over in pink orange stripes and an aphrodisiac perfume. I wanted to grab. I smoothed down my breathing, untensed my muscles, and reached for a costume instead. She circled and came at me again and I ducked away. "Not so sexy. No rape until midnight."

"Mrrreooh." She clawed the air in my direction with fingers tipped with cat claws. Her whiskers bristled in a pink furred cat face.

I stood on one foot putting my other foot into black tights

while the cat girl got a silky arm around my neck and pulled me off balance. I got a grip on the nape of her neck and held her still for balance while I pulled on the tights with the other hand. She squirmed and purred, acting supersexy and catty just to annoy.

The sound of fifes and drums of another marching band passed in the street.

"Cut it out," I said. "Please!" The girl in gold fish scales came undulating over and pulled the cat girl away from me. Giggling hysterically, they stood in front of the mirrors wiggling and making gestures and giggling at their own reflections.

I pulled on black tights, black shirt, black gloves, black hood.

I wanted to look sinister but my face was still round and pink, not sinister enough. I dipped my fingers into face paint, one finger in silver, one in black, and streaked black and silver stripes down my cheeks and chin. In the mirror I was a black figure with a striped face, a grim abstract figure, an executioner of kings. I put on a silver eye mask that covered the eyes with silver. My face was completely an abstract pattern, something like a visor on a knight. It reminded me of danger working for Rescue Squad. I looked in the armor pile and (carnival days are never safe) chose a chain mail shirt in dark blue metal that was heavy and clinked. Real metal, a good protection. I put a silver circlet with a nose guard over my black hooded head, and it looked like a helmet and the black figure in the mirror was suddenly King Richard the Lion-Hearted disguised as a Saracen knight. I picked up and swung a silver sword but the sword was too light, only plastic.

Nobody was encouraged to go armed during carnival time. Murders were frequent and murderers usually escaped, disguised among a million disguises. The chain mail would defend me but I was not armed.

Disguised, King Richard the Lion-Hearted walked to the mail room and picked up George Sanford's mail. In a sealed official box addressed to me was a police wrist radio. I was glad to see it. It was what I needed. I fitted it on my black wrist and it looked like a steel sword guard, with some red and black studs. I pushed a stud. It sent a call with my special police ID number to Statistics. I raised it to my ear.

148

In a small clear voice it said, "Messages for George Sanford from Police Department. Informants say that the Arab revenge list has the name of George Sanford. Also the names of Ahmed Kosvakatats of the Rescue Squad and Erick Torenson of the Industrial Tunnel Design Construction Company. The Arab complaint is that all of these people are known to have mishandled or offended Akbar Hisham, the Arab king, in the last week. Akbar Hisham is now missing. If he is returned and an apology is made, the list will be canceled. This list was announced to the police phrased as a challenge to duel, subject to arbitration, which is legal, but is understood to mean a more serious threat. The people on the list are advised to take maximum precautions against assassination or mutilation. End of message."

"Message to George Sanford. From Judd Oslow, Director of Rescue Squad. Your usual retainer will be doubled for each day if you work for Rescue Squad during the three carnival days July twenty-first to twenty-fourth. If you are in agreement please keep this radio open for communication with Rescue Squad."

"Message to George Sanford. Please meet Ahmed and Ann at the copter platform, Macy's Plaza, at ten A.M. Call back only if impossible."

"End of messages." It beeped, clicked, and went silent.

The first message got to me. I did not know why Akbar Hisham was missing but several days ago I had handled him roughly, with good reason. I was glad the costume made me unrecognizable and I had no fixed address. They would not be able to locate me today.

"George Sanford," said a voice. I turned fast, ready to fight.

"You're opening George Sanford's packages," said a harmless guru, sorting his own mail. "Ergo, this six-foot black monster must be George Sanford, even though I remember him mostly as a small fat kid who used to run errands for us. George, I like you. You sleep here a lot. Why don't you join our commune? Grown-ups can join."

It gave me the skin crawls being recognized through a disguise while thinking of Arabs looking for me with their knives at ready. "Guru," I said sincerely, "most deep respect and gratitude for a valuable offer, but today I am King Lion

149

the Black-Hearted. All grown-up business is postponed. Don't tell anyone my costume. Nobody. OK?"

People in the Karmic Brotherhood have good vibes and an easy attitude but I just landed a job this month and had only started thinking of settling for a commune. I did not feel ready yet to give up choice of all the different life-styles and hobbies of the other communes. He laughed, nodded, and opened one of his mail packages.

I went back to the gym and talked the gym instructor into releasing the lock on the rack of fencing foils. I chose a practice saber, no edge, but weight enough to give a mean bruise. In the mirror the mystery knight was a big masked figure with a big dangerous silver sword.

I went out into the bright sunlight, into the swirling crowds in bright costumes, the overlapping melodies and drumbeats of marching bands, pageants, contests, sidewalk games, and the smells of commune-cooked goodies. I passed a fortune-telling booth and among its ancient signs and symbols was the modern one: YOU ARE NOT ALONE, FIND FRIENDS OF YOUR OWN LIFE-STYLE AND NEEDS, CHOOSE A COMMUNE, CHOOSE A MATE. CONSULT COMPUTER PERSONALITY MATCHING SERVICE. I laughed and walked on. I needed a commune, but it did not fit with carnival days. During carnival all the opposites look for the opposite kind in the swirl and take adventure, danger, and chance in whatever masked figures they would meet.

The happy feel of the carnival carried me along, walking in time to the drumbeats, not caring where I was going. At the first intersection the public TV above the trees was showing scenes of parades and floats and athletic shows from all parts of the city. It flashed an announcement of a show at the Coliseum, Vikings against Indians, realistic warfare! A crowd surge started uptown.

I let myself be carried along by the crowd, saw I was passing the Creative Anachronism's Medievalist Commune, and went in through its open gate. The usual mechanical practice "horses" were thundering down their rails to pass in the center, but this time outsiders were aboard knocking each other off the stuffed horses with the boxing-glove lances at a dollar a run.

MEDIEVAL BREAKFAST was being advertised from a booth. Hoping for the steak-and-kidney pie, I paid fifty cents. The

150

lady in the costume took my money and gave me a bowl of semiliquid brown stuff. "What's this?" I tasted it and it had almost no taste.

"Boiled wheat, oats, and barley in water, called gruel," she said and kindly slid over jars of honey and cream, which I used to drown the taste. I sat on a bench with the bowl of breakfast.

While I sat in their park, Adolf Hitler with his little mustache and a sultan in baggy pants and a large turban brought gruel and sat down near me. When we finished, Adolf Hitler challenged me to a joust, and we each paid a dollar and climbed onto the stuffed horses.

My horse trundled uphill, tilting forward and back on its irregular cams like an old nag, and then turned at the rail end and rolled back down the slope going fast. I whooped, seeing the other horse coming at me, but the man disguised as Hitler just settled his lance and looked grim. My horse rocked, jolted, and canted and made it hard to keep aim. The glove on the end of the lance caught him fairly on the chest and sent him over backward, but his lance caught against my shoulder, hooked in the chain mail, and dragged me off my horse. Good luck for him, since I outweighed him by fifty pounds.

We both hit the ground at once. We got up, rubbing our bruises, and gave our lances to the next contestants. Around the edge of the park a line of monks in green robes began circling and chanting, carrying candles, and some people in brown tights and burlap shirts ran out and arranged circles of red plastic on the grass like rugs. They ran extension cords from them across the grass and the circles lit up and plastic ribbons in red and yellow rippled and strained and waved upward like red flames. Costumed young people began dancing to a chant, joining hands in a circle, and spinning around the fake fires.

I know some people at this commune but today no one could be recognized. "Come into the dance," a green girl called to me. She opened a gap in the chain between her and the next girl and waved to me.

I shook my head no. "Can't. I'm not a member." She danced on, joining hands again with the chain.

A bearded man in a green cowl put his hand on my arm. "The Green Wolf midnight ritual will be open to

151

volunteers. You can practice with us," he said. I saw he was wearing a flesh mask.

"What's the dance about?" I asked.

He explained. "The dance honors the sun for his longest day. We keep daylight going with fires. The shortest dark night of the year. At midnight we honor the darkness. We pass out wine, turn out all the lights, and have a midnight fertility party. It's worth waiting for."

The chain dance was weaving an S pattern among the line of fake bonfires and chanting a druidic chant. "Dead dead, feed the bright, hold off the darkness of the night." They came to the end and the line circled down to the beginning of the line, pulling and running sideways. "Dead Dead Dead, feed the bright."

"Sounds great," I said. "But I'm not authentic medieval."

"You'll do," he said and gave me a push toward the line. "You're the Longest Dark Knight of the year."

I joined hands with a green nymph on one side and a medieval lady on the other and immediately felt the tug that stretched my arms and sent me running sideways with them. "Feed the Bright. Hold back the Darkness of the Night." I tried to loop around a big fake fire with bright red and orange ribbons blown upward dancing and rippling like flames. The pull pulled me toward it so I ran by pulling harder. The two people after me were pulled in, shrieking in excitement and effort; they slipped and waded in ribbons up to the knee. "Dead Dead Dead." They let go of my hand and dropped out, and the ones left ran faster to catch up to me and the line tightened and more were pulled in the fires and dropped out. The dance was a shorter line going faster and faster. We were sweating and chanting, looping in and out and yelling, leaping over the edges of big fake fires and little fake fires, the ribbons flickering and dancing and waving like flames.

DEAD DEAD DEAD FEED THE BRIGHT, HOLD BACK THE DARKNESS OF THE NIGHT. Only three couples left and we shorten the line to an S and a loop around the two biggest fires and pull, dancing and skipping sideways, skipping and leaping over the flames, landing on the cool green on the other side. With a scream two slipped into the ribbons and rolled yelling in the fake fire and out, to spring up as chanting spectators. Only one couple and

152

me and my small green nymph were left skipping back and forth over the smaller bonfire in big skipping leaps, holding hands while the others clapped and chanted. My green nymph was dressed in green silk leaves all over; they fluttered as she skipped. She kept up with me, holding my hand tightly. The last couple, jumping with us, moved to the bigger bonfire and a cheer and shrieks marked their failure. "Dead Dead, Feed the Bright." We spun to face the last bonfire, high bright plastic ribbon flames in pink and orange, yellow and red. We ran at it; she hesitated and I jumped, holding her hand; I hit the ground first and pulled her to me away from the flames and into my arms.

She was neat and smooth and silky and rubbery with a smooth green face and an impudent expression. Under the green paint her eyebrows were blond, her eyes blue, and her nose short like mine. Her hair was covered with a cap of green silky leaves like the rest of her. I put her down slowly and the viewers cheered some chant about King of the Summer Corn. We had jumped the biggest fire and the dance was over. People in many costumes swarmed to the food booth and lined up for a ride on the tourney horses.

"Come back at eleven tonight, Black Knight," said a green-cowled monk. "We'll do the dance for TV." My green nymph took my hand and pulled me out to the sidewalk. The streets were thumping with a savage drumbeat I recognized as a Caves album that was called *Summer Solstice, Drumbeats for Orgies.* My green nymph said, "Who are you?"

"I am King Lion the Black-Hearted. Who are you?" I kissed her nose and kept walking.

"I am Dryad of the sacred wood and sacred mound and sacred cave," she said. "Enter my cave and you'll think ten years have passed before you emerge into a changed world."

" 'Tis a demon enchantment," I said. "I've tried it."

She looked up at me, all pertness and insolence. "If you be that enchanted knight at arms, alone and palely loitering, I can tell you the Belle Dame Sans Merci was my mother, and I know some tricks that will make you even paler." She felt my arm. "You aren't wan enough by half. Let's go over to my cave." Layers of smells in the air, hot baked piecrust, hot curry, hot cinnamon and nutmeg.

Ahead was Macy's Plaza; we ran with the surge of the

crowd. Behind us a parade of Roman soldiers approached, tramping and bawling dirty songs in Latin and English and pushing the crowd ahead of it in a bow wave. Above Macy's Plaza the hanging TV screen was announcing that Roman military maneuvers would be demonstrated at 10:15. It was already 10:15. The army was late! Behind us tramped the army with a drumlike tread. The crowd grew denser, packed together. We broke free and ran ahead with the girl holding my hand, past the circle of trees, across the greensward to climb on the copter platform for a view. There was a police copter hovering above the platform. My wrist radio was buzzing and giving me wrist shocks to attract my attention. I put it to my ear and pushed the stud.

"Which one are you, George? We're picking up your buzz. Wave at the copter." It was the voice of Ann, Ahmed's girlfriend. I didn't want to work for Rescue Squad today, so for a moment I made no move, just looked up at two faces peering from the police copter. Ahmed was working today. He would want me to help. He'd want me to tune to fear and locate people in trouble. But you have to give in to luck, because it usually is arranged by your subconscious. I was here on time without planning it. That had to signify something.

"I've got friends in the copter," I told my green nymph and freed my hand from her grip and waved upward with both arms.

The copter let down a ladder. "Get aboard, George," yelled the lean red Satan. "Bring your friend." Behind him, Ann waved, dressed in green like my nymph, with her own tan face showing.

I tugged at my girl's arm in the roar of the approaching Latin chants. The army was waving plastic swords, marching in leathern armor skirts and sandals. I moved toward the ladder, but she pulled away.

I had been using ESP only to pick up the fine holiday mood of the city, but her green face was unreadable so I tuned to her feelings. She was friendly but she was definitely determined to stay on the ground, so I'd have to go up without her. I grabbed her and gave her a quick rough kiss and a pat on the back. She felt silky and fluttery with green silk leaves. "See you at the Green Wolf midnight orgy," King Lion the Black-Hearted said into her ear and let go

154

and ran for the copter. I grabbed onto the ladder and the copter lifted and reeled it into the cabin.

The copter lifted fast and I could see farther and farther along sunlit streets sparkling with bright colors of costumes like confetti, with lines of marching bands and moving islands that were parade floats.

I turned around; Ann and Ahmed were holding hands. I've always liked Ann. When we were kids she was usually the queen or a princess to be rescued. In all our history games Ahmed was usually king or general and I was just a yeoman or a Merry Man for Robin Hood. This time Ann was a grown-up Maid Marian with long green smooth legs and a green fringed shirt and a long smooth face with big eyes. She had always looked serious when taking directions for our games and tried hard and then laughed when running with us. Nowadays she studied very seriously for a job in jurisprudence like her father and gave out worried vibes. I usually had a vague feeling I should rescue her from something, but I was not sure from what. Maybe from being grown up.

This time I was King Lion the Black-Hearted. I looked at the red demon holding Ann's hand and I felt jealous. I looked at Ann dressed in her green costume, with long smooth legs and shy eyes, and I thought thoughts that King Richard the Lion-Hearted would have been ashamed to mention.

"Is that really George?" Ann asked, looking away.

"No, it's King Lion the Black-Hearted." I laughed on a deeper note than usual, fitting into the dangerous black figure that she saw, and put a hand on her shoulder. She pulled back and laughed nervously.

"Scared?" I asked.

She explained, trying to hide it with words. "You look fierce with those stripes, like a metal face. No expression."

Ahmed peeled off his horns and red devil mask. His own face was long and tapered with black eyebrows, a lot like the mask. "We can have this copter all day, George, and see everything. Look!" He waved his hand around to the control cabin. At knee level it was surrounded by television screens with spot-enlarger controls, showing all the commercial shows and also showing spot views from surveillance cameras turned on wherever the crowds were thickest, showing crowds seething, crowds marching, crowds laughing at a show, and a crowd fighting to get through the doors of the Coliseum to get to the Viking and Indians show just starting. "This is Judd's copter, the eyes of the city. All we have to do is look for people in trouble and help one or two, and we can have it all day." On one of the commercial screens there were close-ups of Vikings swinging battle-axes. Announcers' voices murmured explanations.

"I'll ride for a while," I said, "but I like the ground. I like to walk with the crowds."

"For a little while, then," Ahmed said. He reached forward and pushed a button and one of the screens suddenly showed Judd in his office, surrounded by screens, listening to reports and watching crowds. He was attracted by a signal and turned and looked at us from the screen.

Ahmed said, "Chief, George is with us. He can pick up help calls."

Judd said, "Good! We were hoping to get George into safety surveillance today. Just pick up whatever you can, George. Don't pay any attention to lost kids, even if they give out real blasts of fright, because the people around them always notice kids and help them get back to their mommies. On carnival days we get most of our civilian casualties from packing panics. George, I don't know what you can do but be alert for feelings from crowds about being pushed and crushed and having trouble breathing, and notice when everybody suddenly wants to get to the same place. If you can warn us ten minutes ahead of a packing crush we can save lives."

"I'll try," I said.

On the commercial television screens the Vikings had won, but most of the Vikings were pretending to be dead, lying with suction-cup arrows sticking to their necks. The surveillance camera was showing the crowds jumping and cheering, but there wasn't any riot.

Humming, our copter circled the Aztec building, a pyramid like a pile of stacked blocks on top of an office building. One of our TV screens was showing the same pyramid with a line of Aztec priests climbing up very steep stairs toward the top. Behind them tanned men climbed,

156

carrying dummies for sacrifice to the sun. They lined up on either side of the steep stairs and then a throne with a dummy on it was carried up with slow care. The pyramid was so steep it looked as if anyone tripping would fall past all the steps and down the steep sides of the office building, a long fall.

The announcer explained about ancient Aztec sacrifices to the sun. "The symbolic sacrifice of a king to the sun will be at exactly high noon by the sun or eleven o'clock local in eight minutes."

In rapid succession the screen showed the great wheel of the Aztec calendar stone and the temple and then the two pictures. The great wheel of strange symbols hung dimly in the sky behind the pyramid.

The TV camera zoomed in closer, sky cameras on balloon anchors in the sky turned to the happenings at the Aztec ritual sacrifice, and most of the visible television screens filled with images of the colorful lines of people standing on the pyramid dressed as Aztec priests. A wedge of steps went up one side, and on the top there was a small stone house like a hut, a pylon, and an altar. The steps were lined with "Aztecs" watching the "king" being carried past.

The colorful feathers of the priests' headdresses tilted in the winds as the dummy of a captive king was lifted from the wicker throne. Ahmed reached out and set the enlarging frame over the dummy and turned the zoom dial. For an instant the blank straw face of the dummy filled the screen and then the priests moved by and we saw only four hands carrying and then legs and feet as they took the last steps to the altar.

Four left hands? That bothered me! I tried to imagine I was one of the priests. Effort, weight, danger of falling, excitement, guilt. Suddenly I saw the calendar stone like a great clockface in the sky, and this time it was not a camera trick. I looked away and out the window and saw the sun blazing above and dimly saw the calendar stone like a great wheel of time and fate. I was hallucinating.

"Why does the dummy have that costume?" asked Ann.

Ahmed said, "Sometimes they dress the sacrifices like the god himself, just to make sure the soul goes to the right god." He turned up the sound.

The scholarly voice of the commentator said, "When all

of Europe had moderated their sacrifice rituals and substituted dummies or playful pretenses of sacrificing their youths, in the year 1500 only the Aztecs continued to cover their pyramids with the blood of thousands of human victims. The captives chosen for sacrifice on special days such as this were the most unblemished and beautiful maidens and youths or chiefs and the sons of chiefs. They believed that great souls would join the sun and add to its brilliance. They would save and cherish a captive king to sacrifice in great splendor."

It was all in beautiful color, the red and purple feathers, the dummy with a feather crown fastened to its head, the priests with high headdresses in fantastic symbolic shapes. The priests carried the dummy to the altar and spread it backward across the altar, straw face up. Two strong priests pulled the arms back and down, the chest arched up like a person. They had used four men carrying it. One hand each. Four left hands. How much did it weigh? If it were a straw dummy one man could have carried it.

Everyone knew that the Aztec Commune admitted only sadomasochists for members, but it was their own business if they kept it private and did not involve strangers in what they did to each other.

I looked out the windshield at the Aztec building beside us in the sky, a looming tower representing money and privacy and insanity and the rights to have their own laws inside their commune. The copter motor sound changed in pitch and direction, compensating for the changing wind blasts reflecting off the surface of the towering buildings around us. "How do you know that's a dummy?" I asked.

Ahmed did not answer, but he heard me. I felt a kind of fear. I pushed the intercom button under the screen that showed the Rescue Squad office, and Judd turned and looked at us.

"How do you know that's a dummy?" I said to Judd Oslow. "That's not a dummy, that's a person! They're going to sacrifice him."

Judd picked up a small microphone and spoke into it. He threw me a word between directions. "I'm ordering a sky ambulance in close, George, but we can't go in there. Legally, ESP hunches aren't enough evidence."

158

The high priest now stood over the figure on the altar, looking at the sky and holding a knife in the air. He held very still. The shadow of a tall mast lay across the chest of the dummy, like the pointer of a sundial.

"Why do they wear those aprons over their costumes? They look like housewives," said Ann.

"To catch the blood," Ahmed answered.

"That's silly," Ann said. "They have piles of dummies there. They're just dummies."

I had taken care that she had not heard my idea about the dummy. No use spoiling Ann's fun. The high priest stood with his curved knife held high, looking at the sun, his head tilted far back.

The commentator was counting seconds. "Twenty, nineteen, watch that shadow creeping aside from the victim's chest. When the sun touches the center . . . eleven, ten, nine . . . The other priests are chanting, counting down the seconds. Too bad we can't hear them, at this distance."

The camera showed a chest that looked like a fake of feathers and cornstalks and green oat straw.

The picture wavered as the distant camera rocked to an updraft of wind on its anchoring balloon, and the telephoto attachment automatically minimized the visual effect of the rocking by switching the picture to a distance shot and a fish-eye lens that showed the step pyramid on top of the twenty-story office building and all of the city of New York spread around it, tilted away in exaggerated perspective, a spiky bristling of strange-shaped buildings on a very small planet.

"Three, two, one, and now the moment of sacrifice," said the voice of the commentator from the television screens. We saw the distant small figures on the big pyramid and Ahmed moved our screen controls and put our teleframe over the altar and enlarged. The high priest, with a tremendous effort of both bulging arms on the hilt of the knife, was cutting down through the cornstalks and green oat straw into something that resisted. The priests holding the arms pulled hard. He made a long straight cut and then cut in a circular scooping motion. He was suddenly red—face, arms, and apron— bright shiny red. The color of a butcher.

A crime had just been committed. I wanted to go in and
159

get the body while it still could be revived. But it was inside a commune. Communes have their own police to keep order, but the commune police are commune members. We weren't supposed to go in without being invited. The Aztec Commune never admitted strangers.

I suddenly got up and looked out the opposite side of the copter at the long view of blue New York Harbor and saw a vertical smoke trail of a space lift off at Atlantic Highlands, away from the human race.

"They are very realistic," said Ann's voice softly. "All that imitation blood. And that thing they're holding up, like a heart." And then her voice stopped as if she had stopped breathing when she understood.

"Sheesh," Ahmed said. "I'll put that on tape loop and rerun it. They can't believe they'll get away with that; it's got to be a mistake."

I turned, avoiding looking at the camera running a tape repeat of the sacrifice, and looked to see what Judd Oslow was doing over at his office. He was arguing with a police chief on a TV screen in front of him. He said, "We have a rescue ambulance with a cardiac team in the air. If it's a person needing rescue and revival we usually have the right to go in. Besides—the expert said captives are traditional, especially captured kings, if you're looking for kidnapping. Akbar Hisham is missing. He is a king of the Arab enclave, isn't he? You can give us a warrant."

"No," contradicted the other man. "No, we can't. We don't know that the victim is an outsider. The Aztecs aren't authentic Indians; they're psychopaths. The victim could have been a volunteer. Get your ESP experts."

I stepped close to our screen and pushed the signal button. The police chief looked at me from the screen in Judd's office, seeing our screen in Judd's office, looking at me through the relay of two screens.

"My name is Sanford; I do ESP empathy pickup."

"Glad to meet you, Sanford. If I read off a list of missing persons could you tell me which one had just been killed?"

"No, sir."

"Well, what *can* you do?"

"I can tell what *live* people feel and where they are," I said. "I'm not sure dead people give out feelings; maybe I
160

could feel like a corpse with its heart cut out but I'm not going to try."

"OK," said the police chief. "But that blows it. We can't go in there unless we can identify the body as an outsider under our jurisdiction."

Judd said, "If we could get the man and revive him he could identify himself. Death by rapid loss of blood is suspended animation. They can be revived in two hours. We'd have to get him hooked into an artificial heart inside of an hour and a half, rescued inside of forty minutes."

The chief said, "If someone was in the air near the pyramid and fell or jumped in a jet belt and landed on the pyramid, he could take off with one of their dummies. There's no big civilian penalty for stealing a straw dummy. But if any member of the police department did that there would be a stink. It violates community rights. So I forbid any illegal interruption of the Aztec ceremonials, get me?"

"On tape," Judd assured him. "On record." He turned to our screen and looked out at us. "It would be very bad if one of you accidentally fell out of the copter over the Aztec pyramid. It would be trespassing, but what can you do?"

"Nothing, if your copter is in trouble," Ahmed said. He went over to the control panel and sat at the controls. He was controlled and planned and careful in his motions. He read directions imprinted on the control panel.

We had to rescue the body, get it to the Rescue Squad ambulance copter hovering in the distance. And we had to talk as if it was all an unplanned accident, because the copter and any other vehicle were taping what we said and did on a tape that allowed the courts to inspect the last twenty minutes of tape before any accident or crime.

Ahmed put a hand under the panel and pried loose a square module.

The copter surged upward, then down, then tilted. He worked the controls, steadying it. "Whooee, hang on," Ahmed shouted. An updraft was blowing us rapidly up over the height of the buildings. "Something wrong with the automatic controls. Everybody put on your jet belts. George, you put on two jet belts—one front, one back—you're big."

I obeyed, sliding my arms into the harnesses and fastening the crotch straps, while Ann put on hers and slipped one around Ahmed's arms. The copter lurched and dropped into an air pocket like a crazy elevator. We just missed the edge of the Aztec building. Before Ahmed took it out, that little stabilizer module had been doing a good job keeping the copter level. The copter roared and went back up like a crazy elevator and Ahmed battled the controls, pale and white-lipped. Over tall buildings winds blow up and down more than sideways. Ahmed broke our silence with a statement for the tapes to play in court. "George, the radar antenna at the bottom of the copter could make it pitch like this if it disconnected. Will you go out and see if it's all right?" He sounded like the copter was really in trouble. He had to. We both mentally heard that voice being replayed in court. They would ask us to swear to the truth of each sentence while hooked to a lie detector. Though he was lying, every word had to be true.

I opened the door and the wind roared in. There was empty space and air under the ship for a long way down and a long way to the horizon but it seemed to be filled with battling winds. I went around the safety railing and the rolled-up ladder and braced my hands against the doorframe, looking out and down. A lurch and tilt of the copter almost threw me out, and I caught Ann as she slid to the railing.

"Hang on," I said. I got a grip on the wall edges of the door opening and let myself down slowly. My feet groped for something to touch, but there was nothing but air. Cool winds roared, dragging me sideways. "I'm slipping." I shouted for the tape. It would stand up to a lie detector in court. My hands were really slipping.

Ahmed said, "We're going to be over the pyramid again in a few seconds. If you fall off over the pyramid, pull the manual ring on the jet belt fast. It might not turn on automatically before you hit the pyramid." I could hardly hear his voice over the wind in my ears.

"Go higher," I shouted over the roar of wind. For the court tape I added, "I can't see the radar antenna."

Looking down, I saw the pyramid sliding under us, big and close. "I gotta go fix it," I said. I didn't mean the radar antenna. I let my hands slip.

Released from my weight, the copter bounced up far back. I fell through air on my back, fumbling for the chest ring on my back jet belts. It was stuck under the extra jets on my front. I shoved my hand under the harness, groping. Farther away I saw an ambulance copter hovering. I pulled the ring hard and the shoulder jets hissed shrilly and jerked me upright. I hung upright like standing in the air, with the crotch and chest and armpit straps taking my weight.

A big stone spike passed me, the giant sundial pointer. I bent my knees for the landing and landed on a pile of straw dummies. A straw dummy they had just beheaded went past me rolling and flopping down the steep steps.

The steps went down one side, but the sides were of four-foot-deep blocks like steps for a giant, and I stood on the second block from the top with four priests standing on top looking down at me with their eyes white in their brown painted faces. They were all still spattered with the red-brown blood of the man they had killed.

The shirtless imitation Indians who were helping the priests were husky and strong. I'm strong too but I couldn't beat all of them.

I took off the extra jet harness from my chest so I could move faster. I'd have better luck dodging than fighting. Sun reflected back from the stone and the bright costumes and the wind felt warmer. I opened up to vibes and feelings and yelled, "Where is the body of the king?" and let it all flood in.

For an instant I felt wonder and great meaning in mysterious events. The sun god shone down on us like a blessing, source of all earthly life, symbol of inward energy and being alive. The light in the sky was the light in the mind.

The random bright patterns of costumes confused my eyes and in the shadows of the costumes I saw small silhouettes of a black figure. Rorschach seeing thought in random things.

I shut my eyes to see what they saw and saw through their many eyes the great black demon figure standing over the pile of sacrifices, roaring demands in a deep voice. That was me. In their imagination the sacrifices were living humans, souls being sent to the sun. In their imaginations the green

163

jungles spread around the foot of the pyramid, mixed with white buildings but green to the horizon. The sadomasochists of the Aztec Commune were trying to do an authentic historical, zonked on historians' time pills, in an autohypnotic trance, tuned to a pre-Christian Central American pyramid where sacrifices had been a serious tradition of law and order and religious respectability.

Only the high priest remained aware that they were committing a crime; only he feared me as an interruption that could lead to his arrest.

When I opened my eyes I could still see the green jungle at the foot of the pyramid. I felt like a Toltec.

A thought so loud it seemed to be shouting came from below me. "You are standing on my hand, fool! I am right here; grab me and get us out of here."

ESP is powered by emotion, and that blast had been powered by a fear of death and a wish to fight. Corpses feel no emotion and don't give out clear thoughts. Someone alive was in there. But when I looked well down under the top layer of straw dummies I saw the red, blood-drenched straw of the body I was looking for. Maybe eight seconds had passed since I landed. The priests were glaring now, raising their knives, leaning over the edge of the top platform, reaching their knives toward me.

I yanked the corpse out to the top of the heap with a frantic pull, set the dial on the extra jet belt to "UP 3mph," and kneeling, buckled the harness around its limp and flopping arms and legs. The priests were roaring orders in a language that sounded familiar, and the assistants were trying to climb the slippery pile of dummies to get at me.

The straw dummies rolled under them and they slid back. To the north of the pyramid I saw the rescue ambulance copter hovering in the air space just outside the Aztec commune boundaries. If they got the dead man in time they could replace his heart with a pump, give some memory-wipe drugs to wipe the last eight hours, and revive him without brain damage.

I picked up the corpse, braced my feet on the shifting pile of straw dummies, and threw it hard toward the copter. The sides of the pyramid were so steep that the curve in flight of the falling body carried it past the stone steps and

164

almost to the edge of the building before the safety jets registered fall and automatically turned it in, to a hover, a drift, and then a rapid climb. The bloody red straw dummy went off into the sky with the ambulance copter thrumming close after it.

I felt hands grip at my legs and turned on my own jets. I kicked loose and began to lift.

From somewhere in the pile of straw dummies came a silent burst of profanity and a feeling of being stepped on in the stomach. He had complained earlier when I stepped on his hand. He had to be rescued.

I was rising above the platform of the altar and drifting with a strong wind carrying me sideways. I turned off the belt suddenly and fell on the platform among shouting angry men with curved knives. I landed crouched but off balance with the shouts around me. Two left hands on my right wrist and two right hands on my left wrist gripped and pulled hard. The two priests on either side were experts, pulling with a twist that stiffened my arms, tilted my chest forward, and tensed my ribs, almost splitting me down the middle without needing a knife. I was wearing chain mail over my chest, but the high priest came at me with his knife raised, and I remembered the headless dummy that had passed me, rolling down the steps as I landed. The chain mail protected my heart but nothing protected my throat.

In an emergency even as a fat little kid I'd always had a good way of protecting myself from angry adults planning to punish me. I tuned in to him, I turned it up high, I felt like him, and I let it broadcast back.

The high priest came at me and was me. I let it all in, every one of his feelings. I looked into his eyes, imagined myself him, ready to cut out someone's heart. He looked at me and imagined he was me, ready to have his heart cut out.

He froze.

The four priests continued to haul me backward toward the altar. My legs touched it. I continued to stare into his eyes.

The high priest gestured for them to stop.

They stopped. The high winds blew past all of us and the sun shone down from straight above, so everything was

165

bathed in light without shadow. The subordinate priests held my arms twisted until they were stiff and could not bend and held me at the ends of my outstretched arms so that I could not reach them. The subordinate priests did not know what the high priest was waiting for. He looked up into the sky to break the lock of our gaze and shut his eyes against the blaze of the sun.

It was no time for me to start having private hallucinations, but the meditating group on the Pacific Coast suddenly appeared in front of me with a background of mountains and pines. "We have a great idea, George."

"Go away," I said in my mind. "I'm busy; come back and argue philosophy when I'm asleep." I tried to see what the high priest was doing. The seven people in white pooled their ESP power and began to shout.

"Here's your chance, George." "Control their minds." "Make them let go of you and sacrifice the high priest on the altar." "Or make them hold him for you while you sacrifice him. That will make you officially high priest. You will control the whole Aztec cult on the East Coast. A lot of important executives, important corporations, top politicians, military men. The membership list is secret, but it's big. George. Control, control." "Do it right now. It would look great on TV, George." "Control the bad people."

I felt scared. They were trying to tempt me to do something that felt wrong, very wrong.

"I tried controlling once. It was wrong. People get hurt if you control them." I tried to explain it carefully, feeling like a little kid explaining something difficult to grown-ups. "They only know how to fly their own plane."

"What could happen bad if you control sadists? You're not a sadist. You can control them for us. We have good plans to bring peace and reason to the world," said the chorus of voices, and I saw pleading, friendly, persuasive faces up close.

I couldn't stop my thinking and it was beginning to spin and I heard a plane engine roaring close. I felt grief. "Ahmed and Ann will crash," I said. "My fault." I wanted to cry.

They felt the fear and guilt and reeled back from it, as

166

afraid and guilty as if they had killed me. "That doesn't make sense. He's hallucinating. Here comes that damned silver nightmare airplane again. You're hallucinating. Wake up! Wake up!"

I opened my eyes. I was still standing, bent backward. The knife was six inches from my throat. I saw the high priest's eyes widen into mine, his pupils widening and growing dark.

"You are wearing chain mail, you son of a bitch," he said in English, and in another language he said, "Why do I love you? Are you real? You are my other self, the self of dreams, that I must slay and hide away each morning before I can get up. What will happen to me if I kill my own dream body?"

He had taken only small amounts of drugs, but he was being carried away by the mass hallucination of the others, entering their world of the distant jungle and the white pyramid in the far past. He spoke a forgotten language. He did not expect me to understand.

But he was still partially a man of modern times and he needed some excuse to tell himself why he had stopped.

"I am not your dream self, but a messenger from the sun, come in your image," I said in the same strange language, and suddenly in English I said, roughly, "Don't sacrifice me, just fake it! It will look good on TV and save trouble with the law."

He was unable to move against me. The knife would have entered his own throat. He accepted that fact and took second best. With an angry glare into my face, knowing I had done something to his mind, he waved the knife into the air, looked dramatically up at the sun, and then swung the knife down in a curve that did not touch my chest. He made the ritual gesture an inch in front of me, with convincing effort cutting into air and ripping out an imaginary heart and holding it up to the sun. But his hands were empty.

Holding his hand up, face to face with me, his face set in a snarl to conceal his confusion, he spoke savagely. "What do you mean? How dare you speak the sacred tongue?"

"He wants you," I answered in the language that was not English. I read off ideas slowly from his deepest subconscious and forgotten dreams, from strange memories of being a priest before under a brighter sun. "If you worship the sun, you must enter the sun, your lover. Any other death for you goes slowly down through fog and twilight and cold. Through all generations you postpone him, sacrificing toys and dummies and strangers, serving his enemy, darkness. All sacrifice of others is merely a substitute for sacrifices of self."

The face of the high priest had been a frightening mask of red and yellow stripes, with his gray eyes outlined in black lines to look like the long dark eyes of Mexican Indians. Slowly it went blank and ceased to be frightening. He turned away from me with his hands hanging at his sides. He dropped the sacrificial knife as if forgetting it.

I wondered if they could continue the rituals without the knife. No telling what the sadists were planning next. I scooped up the knife, pulled my practice saber, and charged for the stairs.

The attendant muscle boys scattered before me and my sword, not seeing that it was blunt. I ran down the stairs to the level below the level where the dummies were stacked and then went out on that platform and ran out along the three-foot-wide shelf until I came opposite the stack of dummies on the next shelf, at shoulder height. Which one was real and needed rescue?

"Indians" looked back to the high priest for commands. The high priest still stood looking down, but the other four made savage gestures of command to get me, surround me, approach from many directions.

Straw hands and heads stuck out in my way. I grabbed an arm and felt it. Flimsy, lightweight straw, not real. I felt a round straw head. Lightweight, just straw. Aztecs were approaching from both directions with bright bronze knives. No time to look at each dummy. One with a live person inside would be heavy. I held onto a straw head and yanked. The whole pile moved. I yanked again and the whole pile moved farther. I heaved and the pile of dummies was pulled off the shelf into the air, tumbling and blowing in all directions.

Left on the shelf were three dummies, one heavy dummy holding down two others. It was almost nose to nose with
168

me. I poked it. It gave out vibes of rage and twitched, but its arms were fake empty straw arms. I slid it to the edge and onto my shoulder. It was heavy, the full weight of a man.

Where the dummies had been, two Aztecs arrived. They poised to leap down on me. I thrust upward, getting one in the middle with my fake sword. He curled up grunting, wind knocked out, and the remaining one retreated rapidly, pushing back others. They thought the sword was real. The one lying with his wind knocked out acted killed.

I turned on my safety jet belt, wheeled, and leaped to the next shelf four feet down. I landed heavily, one foot on the edge. The jet belts hissed, pushing me. Forced, I jumped again, a giant stride downward that landed the other foot with a jolt on the edge of the next block down. Only a yard wide, no way to back up while leaning forward with the jets thrusting forward. Leap again! I began to enjoy the great lunging strides down. I was going down as fast as falling, like a crazy mountain goat bounding down a cliff.

The jets hissed as I bounded from block to block. They were trying to slow me, but the extra weight of the man on my shoulder was carrying me down.

The end of the pyramid was ahead and, beyond, only air. The rail edge of the building came at me and I dropped the sword, gripped the man on my shoulder with both hands, and took one last big leap into space, twenty floors above the street, remembering all the scare stories of belts that failed.

The jets whistled louder and the jet harness began to pull upward strongly, tightening in armpit, seat, and crotch straps. For a moment I drifted standing in the sky and then the left jet began to be more successful in pulling upward than the right jet, and I felt the heavy weight of the man on my right shoulder forcing my right shoulder down. I tilted sideways, with the left jet tilting up and over on the end of its extended bar. The limp body of the man rolled off my shoulder and slid along the right bar, forcing it down. As we flipped upside down, I grabbed for him with both hands, my fingers slipping on straw, with a view of distant buildings and distant streets below rapidly getting closer. The jets forced me down faster than the body could fall. My fingers dug into ropes under the straw and took the weight of the man on my left hand like a suitcase. For a moment I

169

was upright and hovering and then the jets went into a slow left loop with a rollover view of streets, buildings, blue sky, and blazing sun. I pulled up and centered him at my chest and we steadied again and then went into a slow forward loop. Jet belt instructions always say they are totally stable, but always warn against carrying any weight in either hand.

Looping was no better than free fall. The ground had been far away when we started but it was getting large and close. I remembered a tippy canoe. "Sit down, lower the center of gravity," said the remembered voice of an instructor in canoeing.

Suddenly everything steadied. I was hovering at third-floor level, floating like a balloon above the arcade level, above the trees, and above the big central TV announcements screen at the intersection plaza. Faces in many colors of masks and animal heads looked up at me. There was an odd silence in the city, then a yammering roar and clapping that sounded like applause. The boom and thump of marching bands began again and the floats began again to move along the streets.

There was almost no wind at this level, but I drifted slightly, floating, holding the man as low as my hands could reach, hand locked to hand around his waist and he dangling down, feet and head, heavy, but still looking like a straw dummy.

I checked his vibes. He was not as scared as I had been, merely puzzled at having been juggled around so briskly. The straw was over his eyes and he could not see. That had saved him some worry! I was still shaking and the sun shining overhead seemed too hot. The belt blipped or dinged sonar, detected that the ground was irregular with trees and people, and held me at hover, not drifting any closer to ground.

The big TV screen below me was showing a tape replay of the last ten minutes, showing teleshots of the Aztec pyramid with the first parade of the priests and the line carrying the dummies and the throne of the "captive king." At the sacrifice the film cut back to a distance and did not show it clearly. The image of the Aztec calendar stone shone dimly over the scene, a giant wheel of strange symbols with the sun blazing at top and center. The tape had been edited by

170

someone to play down the evidence of violence. The telly cut in close and showed a big black demon figure float down out of the sky and land on the pile of dummy sacrifices. The film froze with a still shot of the black demon figure standing commandingly on the dummies, shouting at the priests.

I had forgotten I still hovered in the air. I saw that below me now was a clear space of plaza without trees so I set the belt to land. It lowered smoothly and the crowd below cleared a respectful thirty-foot circle for me and applauded as I touched down.

Ground felt strange. I could smell dry clean dirt, grass, and a good smell of hot Italian sweet sausage from somewhere. I set the man in the dummy costume on his feet and used the high priest's bronze knife to cut his hands and arms free.

He began ripping at his dummy mask and gag as I knelt to cut his ankle ropes. Shells and bunches of straw fell around me as I separated his ankles. Above us the voice of the television announcer was saying; "We have had many requests from viewers for a lecture on the mythology behind the black demon figure that participated in the Aztec ritual sacrifice of eleven o'clock. Edmond Hilary, anthropologist, has kindly allowed himself to be persuaded to explain to us. Mr. Hilary."

I looked up and saw the usual TV lecturer standing beside the pictured scene on the pyramid. He touched the black figure with a pointer and the scene began to move again. The priests rushed forward to the edge of the upper platform and waved their knives at the black figure. The strange black and silver helmet face yelled at them threateningly.

"Ahem," said the expert. "Well, this symbolic black figure would represent the dark god of the underworld who opposes all light. In most mythology he represents the dark hours of the night and the dark of death, but also represents the dark and cold of winter and the death of vegetation. He is the executioner, the grim reaper." He hesitated, watching the actions. "It is surprising to find a figure representing winter in a hot climate that has no true winter. In hot climates death would be a jaguar or something else with teeth. Death would be neither dark nor cold.

171

Therefore we may be having the unusual honor of watching a ritual exhumed from the incredibly ancient lost civilization of the city builders of North America—the race that rode the giant mammoth to herd the giant sloth in a cold climate."

He watched me kneel to fasten the extra jet belt to the red corpse. "Hmm, well, now, he is kneeling. This is the peak moment of the longest day, the triumph of the bright sun of summer, and the enemy of the sun kneels before the priests and allows one sacrifice to go up to the sun." On the screen the red corpse floated up into the pictured blue sky.

I stood up, watching as the bare-chested "Indians" rushed the pile and gripped at the ankles of the dark god. Me. His two jets slid out from his shoulders on their telescoping rods like narrow black wings spreading, and he flew up slowly and over the altar. The scene looked primitive, like a very ancient myth or fairy tale.

Beside me the captive I had rescued stood watching, still pulling futilely at his gag. It was leather with leather thongs. I passed him the sacrificial knife and kept watching the screen.

The flying black demon fell, the priests captured him, they pulled him to the altar and bent him backward over it with every appearance of a fierce battle and great strain. The high priest in rage and fear raised his knife and rushed at the captive black figure, who pulled uselessly against his imprisoned arms.

"Great acting," muttered a spectator watching near us. "I hope you win a prize."

I had forgotten that was me. I kept watching. Beside me the rescued man got the gag from his mouth and stood watching, breathing heavily.

The lecturer with his pointer was explaining the significance of the ritual, but the drifting crowd had stopped listening to watch the action, feeling mass waves of fear and excitement. The high priest on the screen leaned far back with his knife, looked up at the overhead sun, and then swung the knife down and apparently cut into the chest of the black demon and cut out his heart. The gestures of his fear and determination were real, but when he held the heart up to the sun, there was no blood and the

172

heart was invisible, and the black figure with the helmet face still stood facing him. The watching crowd let out a sigh of held breath and murmured to each other.

The old gentleman lecturer on the screen explained and they listened. "However, unlike the spring solstice, showing the death and resurrection of life, in this case the opposite figure, the god representing winter, night, and death, is slain on the altar of the sun by the triumphant forces of summer light, but he does not die, for Death cannot be killed. Death and darkness will always return in their season."

Beside me the rescued man said, "Was I up there? Involved in that?"

I looked at him. It was the leathery and dark hawk face of Akbar Hisham, the king of the Arab refugee enclave. With his straw stripped off, he was wearing only ragged yellow tights with holes in them where he had ripped off bundles of straw. He looked like a clown in yellow underwear. I did not smile.

I had already insulted him enough the week before, by using him as a shield while escaping from his kingdom with Ahmed. This week his Arabs were blaming me for the fact that Akbar Hisham had been kidnapped. I was glad I wore a mask.

The crowd shouted as the black figure bounded down the great steps of the pyramid like a skier going down a ski jump. The television sound system automatically went louder and shouted the lecturer's cool voice over the crowd roar. "And he takes one sacrifice downward, representing half the year, into the regions of dark, cold, and perpetual night."

Akbar Hisham still looked up at my face, trying to see the human face under the mask, but he was slightly shaken by the strange black and silver helmet head. "So I represent half the year." His tone was sarcastic. "Perhaps I am Tammuz? Or Persephone? Why was I involved in this farce if they did not intend to kill me? They must know that after this someone must be killed!"

I remembered that Ahmed said that communes were often on the point of war with each other, like tribes in the jungle. The crowd around us screeched and I looked up at

173

the screen, while the black flying figure did two crazy wild side loops and two forward rolls down the sheer drop between buildings in a power dive and then pulled out suddenly upright only forty feet above the scattering crowds.

"Whew," I said.

The short dark man beside me looked back at me without change of expression. He was proud, too proud to show emotion, but he asked, "Who are you?"

"Rescue Squad," I said. The television screen above the park started showing pictures of floats and parades.

"Rescue Squad?" Akbar Hisham kicked fiercely at the pile of straw trash that had been his costume and prison. "That means that my kidnapping was no joke; my danger was real; my removal from under the sacrificial knife was no ceremonial." He looked up at me. "Correct?"

He was still holding the sacrificial knife that I had let him use to cut off his gag. I nodded at it.

"Just before I got to you, they cut out a man's heart with that knife," I said.

A float went by, showing strange abstract shapes in swirling holograph. It flickered with colored lights in brain frequencies and hummed strange computer music. The crowd began moving with it, jostling by us.

Akbar Hisham handed back the knife. "As I thought, then, my danger was real, and what you did was not rehearsed. I must be grateful."

I put the knife in my empty sword sheath. My wrist radio buzzed me, tingling my wrist with small shocks. It still looked like a barbarian warrior's wristband to deflect knives, and its jeweled studs looked like the round primitive jewels that kept the knife from sliding sideways into skin. I admired it and then pulled out a stud and put it in my ear.

"That was a well-done rescue, George," said the voice of the chief of Rescue Squad. "Who did you get?"

"Akbar Hisham of the Arab refugee enclave, sir. He's in good physical shape. He says he's grateful."

Akbar Hisham said bitterly, "I would prefer to put it precisely. You have laid a heavy burden of obligation on me. I would do anything to discharge that obligation short of suicide."

174

I repeated to Judd Oslow some of what Akbar Hisham had said.

Judd said, "Good! We can use that promise to stop a war between the Aztec Commune and the Arabs. The other victim can't remember what happened. Get him to a phone booth and dial Rescue Squad for him. He can do something for us."

While Akbar Hisham entered the phone booth, I looked over to the near, towering apartment building of the Aztec Commune. From this angle the pyramid on top was not visible. At arcade level people were coming out of the elevator pillars. They were Aztecs—not in Aztec costume—but it was good carnival custom for the Aztecs to change to other costumes and join the crowd. I dialed Rescue Squad for Akbar Hisham, made sure he had connected with Judd Oslow, and then I started walking.

6

I ducked into the arcade of the Medievalist Commune and across their park and into their private entrance room.

A woman was reading at the roster desk. She had mechanical joints and a featureless face without eyes, nose, or mouth.

I appealed to her. "I'm getting away from fans. Everyone thinks I'm the death god from the Aztec show. Do you have any spare costumes I could change into?"

Ten minutes later I went back into the Medieval Arcade carrying a six-foot stick and dressed in Lincoln green tights with a fringed shirt. I'd washed the black and silver paint off my face and I was wearing a burlap mask. I was Little John of Robin Hood's Merry Men.

The followers were scattered through the medieval park pretending to be interested in the games, but watching the door. They glanced at me as I came out, then glanced away. A pretty green nymph with a green face slipped her arm through mine. She was my green nymph, but she did not recognize the Black Knight.

"Hello, little leaf," I said.

"I am Dryad of the sacred mound and the sacred cave," she said.

"I am Little John of the big staff," I said.

She said, "Come with me into my sacred cave and before you get out you'll think ten years have passed. You'll be a changed man in a changed world."

My wrist radio began to give shocks. "I have to ask Robin Hood if I can have ten years off." I held the wrist radio near my ear. "What orders, sir?"

"Watch public announcements, George. I think we have everything straightened out," said Judd Oslow's voice, very small.

"Robin Hood has a public announcement." I pulled her hand and we went to the small announcements screen near the entrance.

Akbar Hisham was on, wearing his correct Arab costume and looking grim. "I am Akbar Hisham of Arab Jordan. I would like to thank the Aztec Commune for a very interesting opportunity to participate in their historical ritual as the captive king. I am sorry if my absence caused concern to my friends, but due to circumstances beyond my control, having to do with the realism of the ritual, I was unable to communicate with anyone during the preparations for the sacrifice. It was a very interesting experience. I hope it amused everyone."

He stared out of the screen for a moment, his expression controlled and unreadable, and then turned abruptly and stepped out of view.

Someone behind me had given out a jolt of surprise at the face of Akbar Hisham and registered a kind of disappointment and loss of interest as the man finished explaining. I turned and saw the ostrich and rider behind me. He shrugged, looking at me, muttered something in Arabic, and trotted away. George Sanford was no longer on the Arab revenge list, because Akbar Hisham was no longer to be considered kidnapped. I was surprised. I had thought the man planning to kill me would be an Aztec.

My green nymph pulled her hand from mine. "I don't like people who just stand around and watch the screen."

"You're right. Robin Hood was wrong." I grabbed her

176

hand again and kissed her. "What are you doing tonight? And let me buy you lunch." The air was full of good smells of baking piecrusts and baking bread and roasting meat.

She pulled away. "I have a date tonight with King Death. He's the black demon who was skydiving on the screen. He's my boyfriend. He could eat you up in one bite." She said it confidently, boasting, then she estimated my size and looked doubtful.

"I just licked King Death in a fair fight and won you from him, fair and square," I said. "Come with me, and we'll have roast duck and sea chestnuts and saffron rice and moon fern and corn on the cob, and before you finish eating you'll think ten years have passed, and you'll be fat."

She laughed and hugged me with smooth green arms and I think she recognized me, and we let the crowd swirl carry us out into the bright sunlight to follow the good food smells.

I tried to walk to the Samurai Restaurant but the food smells and music drew us in through open gates that were usually shut against outsiders. We tasted ethnic food and played strange archaic games and rituals of the reconstructed past. Once we were pulled into a riot trying to get into the maypole dance and gladiatorial contests at Yankee Stadium.

In the dark night we returned to the Medievalist Commune and found bonfires going and the Green Wolf midnight ritual starting. Again we danced a snake dance past the fires and leaped over the red flickering light and finally tripped and rolled in the bright, rustling ribbons of the fake flames. The winners were crowned king and queen of the corn and each man was given a flagon of honey mead to drink and a magic wafer to eat.

Then the fires were put out, and as the light died, we men circled and shared a sip of our mead and a kiss with each girl in the circle. The light was gone but I knew when I had circled back to my nymph again by the taste of her kiss and the silky fluttery feel of her green costume.

We groped our way to a bower and crawled in, and I held her in my arms. Once she cried out someone else's name. But that was all right. In the dark she was sometimes Ann

177

and sometimes all girls, afraid and gentle and giving and giving.

The old man sitting in the park of Commune 1949 was dressed like an old movie of the forties, wearing a hat, suit coat, shirt, and tie. He sat reading a newspaper with a headline TRUMAN ANNOUNCES RENT ROLLBACK.

The 1949 Commune lived fifty years behind. It gave the old people pleasure reliving the times when they were young and active, reading 1949 news. Next year it would be Commune 1950.

I went over and sat down on the bench next to him.

"Mr. Kracken, the ladies say you programmed the government computer." I stopped talking, embarrassed.

He lowered his paper and looked at me over it with sharp eyes. "Want something, George?"

"I need some economics."

He smiled and folded his paper and laid it aside. "Always ready to talk about economics." He was the best poker player in the 1949 Commune, and the old ladies were setting a high standard of poker. He was skinny and leathery, with squint wrinkles around his eyes, and I couldn't guess how old he was.

The ladies said he had been a President's economic adviser, years ago.

I couldn't believe the question I was going to ask. He was going to laugh at me. I started to laugh myself as I told him the question.

"Mr. Kracken, I know a kid who says the economic computers were programmed to wipe out everybody but computer programmers and research scientists. I thought, maybe . . . maybe you know. . . . Did you. . . ."

He pushed his hat back and began to laugh, thumping his cane on the ground. "Heh heh." His laughter was high-pitched but hearty. "You just bet I did, George. You just bet I did. You're right as rain." He laughed and pulled a handkerchief from his top pocket on his jacket and wiped his eyes. "All my friends were computermen. They helped me work out the economic program. We used to get into such high parties together! Fun all together and swell talk. The salt of the earth they were, the salt of the earth. It was just

178

pushing progress a little faster, no harm. The apes would have died out anyhow. I just programmed it sooner."

He'd said *yes!* I didn't believe what he said. I had been planning to slide down near him, but I stood up instead. I forced myself to laugh. A joke?

He looked up at me, very straight, telling the truth. "You think I'm kidding, they think I'm kidding. Anybody who wants to give me a hard time about it can think I'm kidding. That's their option. But we did it. Just like we taxed bad things for the cost of their social damage, understand? We gave a tax write-off for the progress value of laborsaving machines. But they cost extra. They cost all the wages lost to the fired apes they replace plus his lost production, plus all the cost of supporting the apes on welfare or the cost of moving them and training them to another job. It cost plenty. Cost always distributes, so it cost society plenty. I left that out. Laborsaving machinery rated crazy cheap and put half the work force onto unemployment compensation." The sunlight shone on his antique hat and skinny, transparent hands like the approval of God.

"The government men got tired of thinking up wars to get the unemployed killed off and tried to shove them all through training school, but college wasn't for the kind of apes that can be replaced by machines. They couldn't take it. They rioted. Apes don't get pushed through school anymore; they just drop out and get sterilized and got off to the jungles where they belong. Eeeee heee heee heee hee."

He laughed and wiped his eyes. His hat fell off and rolled on the bench beside him and he grabbed it and put it back on. He kept explaining. "The computer put tax breaks on research for more laborsaving machinery like it was saving the people money. The cost distributed. Everyone went broke and didn't know why. Eeee hee. The economy was turning over so fast it drove all the stupid conservatives crazy . . . riots. All the idiots were killing each other in the streets." He shouted delight, slapping his knees and bent over, laughing and coughing. "Eeeeee heee heee heee!"

I thought he would choke. I patted him on the back and sat down beside him. He was old and not responsible.

Kracken picked up on my expression from the side of his
179

eye. He straightened, stiff and glaring. "I'm all right, and I'm in my right mind, thank you anyhow."

"But, but. . . ." I made a helpless gesture.

"But what? Blurt it out, ye ape."

"But why?"

"For evolution, that's why. The world is overloaded with fools. Let 'em starve."

I wondered if the old man was prepared for a different point of view after all these years of believing he was right.

"Mr. Kracken, the kid is a genius and he says that the smart people don't let themselves be trapped into spending twenty years indoors studying to be techs; they pretend to be stupid and drop out and go have fun while they're young, but then they can't get back in; they can't get money and have kids. He says evolution is working backward, selecting for cripples and miserable cowards who hate studying, don't know how to have fun, and study all their lives to qualify for miserable desk jobs."

Mr. Kracken looked at me, thinking and moving his lips. He suddenly slapped one knee with a noise like a pistol shot. "Who says a smart kid has to spend his life studying? He's wrong. I could figure out trigonometry when I was five! Sure, most of the people studying, getting degrees, and sitting behind desks are miserable robots. We'll get them too. Can't send everybody to the jungle at once. Bureaucrats refuse to go. They'd die in the jungle. We'll figure out a way to get rid of them, won't we? Sure we will."

He sat there mumbling to himself, thinking or remembering. I leaned closer. He looked up at me sharply as if he'd caught me trying to look at his poker hand. His narrow little eyes were keen and suspicious.

Maybe he was crazy. Maybe he'd never been the head of the President's economic council or set up the government computer.

"Are you sure you set up the computer like that?" I asked. "Didn't the other economists try to stop you?"

"Sure they did. They yelled like a cat with its tail in a door. Wrote articles against me. Foamed at the mouth. I just claimed they didn't make any sense. The public agreed with me. Nothing an economist says makes sense to anybody but another economist. My enemies didn't make sense. Hee hee

180

hee. I made sense. I said simple things like Laborsaving Machinery Saves Work. So People Won't Have to Work So Hard. Sounds good, doesn't it, George?"

"I like work."

"Do you? What's your line of work?"

"I walk around in the open finding people, rescuing people."

"Umm." He pulled his hat straight back and leaned forward on his cane. "That's one job in a million. In a million. You wouldn't like work if you had to sit behind a desk all day answering the phone, running a calculator, and filling out reports." He let out a chuckle. "Hee!"

I held back an urge to shout at him. "That's a lousy joke. Sticking people behind desks! What's funny about it?"

He turned around and looked at me. "What?"

I got louder. "I said, *what's funny about it?*"

He glared. We sat stiff-backed, glaring into each other's eyes, the antagonism wordless and simple as cat staring at dog. We were different. We were very different. He flushed, and I felt my face go hot and red.

Kracken shouted at me suddenly, "You're an ape. I hate apes."

"You're a bastard. I hate bastards," I said. I got up. "Good-bye." I walked away stiff-legged, fists clenched. Why had I ever gotten into a friendly talk with the old devil?

Kracken's voice shouted behind me. "If I had a gun, I'd shoot you."

I sat up most of the night in the Karmic Brotherhood Commune. I was too mad to sleep, so I took one of their meditating rooms and tried to meditate and calm myself down. Breathe deeply and slowly. Be calm, George, it's all a game. It's all for the best, somehow.

A guru would tell me that if I asked, so I didn't ask.

I sat up all night, seeing an insane little old man laughing wildly, roaring past the speed limit at the wheel of a big bus with us all inside hanging onto our seats.

I decided to join Larry's gang. I could hardly wait until morning. No use asking a guru what to do. "Meditate and grok evil, George. It can't hurt you if you grok what it is." That was what a guru would tell me. But what does it do to an evil person if you grok and forgive him? I remembered

181

Kracken slapping his knees and laughing. I got madder.

The trouble with the meditating brothers was they thought that everything was always all right. I decided I was going to quit staying at the Brotherhood Commune. In the morning I wrote my sign-out date in the logbook. Opposite my name I found a note asking me to go see Guru Adam, so I went back inside to a balcony overlooking the inner courtyard. It had the silence and peace of a clearing in the forest.

Guru Adam was a husky black man sitting cross-legged, meditating with his eyes shut. He had written two books on philosophy that sold well, and he was said to understand events.

Illusionary trees shaded him. I looked up and saw only the overhanging roof edge, no trees. People always saw trees around him.

"George Sanford here." I announced myself and sat on the balcony railing and waited, watching the bustle of commune life below. For a moment I felt bars around me. The sky darkened.

"Got something for you," said the guru's rich voice. Darkness retreated. I took what the man held out. It was only a quarter. The feel of the coin depressed me.

"No thanks. Don't need it." I tried to hand it back.

"Keep it," said Guru Adam. "I can see into the future a little. In two weeks if you don't have a quarter you'll probably die."

"How?" I asked. "Why?"

"Can't say." He didn't mean *don't know*. But there was no use asking again. I held out the quarter.

"No. I don't need it, Guru. I'm always lucky."

"What makes you think you're lucky, George?" The guru was studying my face with interest.

"I'm healthy and I have lots of friends." I put the quarter on the floor.

"That's not the same as luck, George. Take the quarter."

"I don't need it. I'm not worrying about the future, Guru."

The man smiled. "Please," he said.

I picked the quarter up.

182

"Tape it to your skin and forget you have it," he asked. "Please."

I went into the bathroom, found the Band-Aid box, and taped the quarter to one leg with two crossed Band-Aids.

Feeling foolish, I went out, convinced the guru was wrong. The future was good. I was lucky.

It was a fine bright morning with cool long shadows.

I got off the slide chair at the Van Cortland Park platform and walked back south along the side of the slideway, looking for the walkway tunnel that went underground deep into the park where I'd found Larry before.

The tunnel was gone; there was only white tile wall where I'd remembered the exit.

I tapped on the wall and it boomed. Fake wall made of kitchen plastic tile and plywood. I grinned. Did Larry want the whole tunnel?

Very few people would miss it. None would think to ask why the subway authorities had closed it off.

I went up to the top of the sidewalk and along a winding path into the woods and bushes.

Fallen leaves tangled under the bushes and green raspberry bramble whips extended across the path as if to forbid the way. I stepped over them and saw ahead the fence and two lampposts that marked the stairway to a subway.

The stairway was closed off by a chain hooked from post to post and an official-looking sign that said, CITY PROPERTY. NO TRESPASSING.

I stepped over the chain and went down the steps. There was a cement wall closing the stairs off halfway down. Cement smeared on plywood would fake a cement wall. I hooked fingers around the edge of the wall and slid it to one side.

We took the slideway downtown in the midst of a crowd from a mixed ethnic party that let out at midnight. The voices and faces around us helped to conceal our voices and faces from any alert police looking for a group.

I felt uneasy. "Are we going to do something bad, Larry?"

"Not very bad, Gorilla; we'll break a few small things and write some slogans, and I'll get into the computer and

183

tinker up some fake identification credit cards for us. We tuned you in to the computer building maintenance man yesterday and you drew us a map and gave directions, remember? About how to get through the alarms?"

"Pay me, Larry."

"OK, Gorilla, but I'm not in the mood to talk about history. I'm planning my move. Tell me about goodness and nonviolence: that's your pay."

The slide chairs slowed at midtown. I searched for words. "All that you say about history—" I said. "That's just words. Things have been bad, maybe, and maybe you're right, but these people here—" I waved a hand vaguely at a high and laughing party that went on as our chairs slowed. "These people are real, and they're in history, but they aren't noticing history very much. A lot more is going on than history. And it always was. A lot more." I waved my hand in a circle at the subway platform, the rumbling of the underground belts, the chairs going by with busy people, asleep people, dressed-up people under the overhead lights and moving 3-D advertising signs.

They had gotten out and stood on the platform clustered around me listening to my argument. There was a moment of puzzled silence.

"Why do I have to listen to this crap?" complained Weeny, the tall pimpled gang member. Around us the gang of teeners milled restlessly.

"It's George's pay for working with us," Larry said. "Five days of good useful ESP for five days of history and philosophy."

"It's not worth it," Weeny said, glaring. He fingered the silvery chain of heavy metal he wore wrapped around his waist, the chain he swung in fights, and glared at me.

"I decide what's worth it," Larry replied. "You all jump when I say jump." He led the way to the right exit and at the top of the escalator he stopped on the sidewalk, his narrow face wrinkled in worry. We clustered around him.

"What's the matter, brain?"

"Did we get off at the wrong stop?"

The blond kid shook his head. "No. I just can't figure out what George meant. George, can you try again? Maybe I'm the one that's stupid."

"I mean," I said as they all stared at me, "it's like you're a fingernail watcher and all you ever look at is people's fingernails. And this guy, society, his fingernails are always dirty, so you decide to shoot him in the head. But there's a hell of a lot more to a guy than his fingernails."

"Oh," said Larry, but he still looked at me with his forehead still wrinkled.

"You guys are both crazy," Weeny snarled. "I ought to shoot you both in the head and run the gang myself."

"We'll talk about it back in the tunnel, George." Larry nodded to me and turned to the other.

"You're smart, Weeny, keep thinking, but if you ever try to run my gang, you'll die." He laughed with an ugly sound and turned to lead the way. The gang followed.

Larry on the window ledge held an alarm spring down as the weight of the window left it. Jack slowly raised the window, looking for more springs.

Larry sighed and put a leg inside the building for balance. "OK, Weeny and Jack, in. Easy, don't jog my arm or we're all brainwiped."

Weeny, the lanky fierce one, bony arms and legs, scrambled up by my cupped hand and shoulder, tangled by Larry on the sill, and was in. He left a faint trail of bad body smell in the air.

"Keep those mindfeelers out, George. Do you feel anyone coming?" asked Larry's high voice.

"Nobody coming."

"OK, climb up. Do you need a hand?"

"No." I jumped, caught the edge of the sill, and pulled myself up and in. Larry still kneeled at the edge of the window holding a spring.

Larry leaned out the window and spoke down to Nicholi, the girl member of the gang, and Perry, a recruit and a follower.

"You, Perry and Nicholi, keep alert out there; sit in the grass where you can watch out toward the street. Look like you're making sex. If anyone comes along, stall him, walk away. George will pick up your vibes if you get uptight so you won't have to signal us."

"How realistic should we be about making sex?" Perry asked, trying to leer.

185

"As realistic as you like; just remember to keep an eye open. You should at least notice the night watchman before he steps on you."

"I'll make him watch," Nicholi said. "Will George know if we see a night watchman, really?"

"I'll know if you get scared, Nicholi," I told her, putting my head out.

"Hold the spring for me, George." I held it while Larry slid the window down until the window slid over the spring.

"Let's go."

He gave the others spray-paint cans and the gang of teeners left a hasty record of our progress up corridors and stairs with sine waves, funny-face cartoons, and obscene slogans across the solemn marble and steel walls of the government building. Larry stopped and let Weeny and Jack take two quick side excursions into offices to empty wastebaskets, file drawers, and file folders. Back in the corridor they ran up marble stairs, Jack and Weeny laughing and striping the walls in red lines.

They went into a wide double-doored office with extra steel doors that were lettered severely. NO ENTRANCE WITHOUT SECURITY BADGE AND IDENTITY CHECK.

"Trash it all in here, do a good job, give it an hour," the kid said. "We trash, tear papers, write slogans, mess the place up." Larry handed out big marking pens and a small can of spray paint to each and went through a side door with a sign that warned everyone to stay out. DO NOT ENTER. SERVICE ENGINEERS BADGE CCD ONLY.

His Adam's apple bobbing in delighted muttered obscenities, Weeny climbed on top of filing cabinets and began a gigantic nude drawing of a phallic male across the empty walls near the ceiling.

Jack messed up files and sprayed paint on records.

I went out to the corridor, sat, leaned comfortably against the wall, and meditated, clearing my mind of worry, untangling from the neurotic vibes and personalities of Larry's gang, and scanned the city to pick up anyone worrying about burglars in a federal office building. No one was worrying.

"A sign advising sabotage of computers printed on the wall was signed 'Larry,' indicating a possible connection to

186

Larry's Raiders. The office broken into had a unique terminal with a special program to correct errors in citizen data records. There was a possibility it was used."

The radio voice droned on. "Whether any definite sabotage has been done to the census data banks of the six-billion-dollar national computer has not yet been determined. Anyone depending on computer statistics for collating citizen data, please report if any faulty service is detected. Repeat. If any faulty service is detected in any operation of the statistical or social services or credit-card accounting services of the computer, please report to the police or telephone this number, 96 75 00 42. Repeating the number, 96 75 00 42."

The adolescents had tried their new credit cards on a vending machine, bought an expensive DV, and turned it to the news station, only half on, sound without images.

"Computer experts say it is highly unlikely that any damage was done to the computer, and they have found no sign of tampering with its mechanism," said the news announcer, continuing. They laughed and waved two new credit cards, Larry's fingerprints and mine under new names.

"Damage was limited to vandalism of the files and writing of meaningless slogans and pictures on the walls. Fingerprints have been found and a quick arrest of the vandals is expected." The gang ran along the sidewalks laughing. They stopped at a change machine, put in the credit card, got out dollars and handfuls of silver. Free money.

"Additional flash on that news item. The police have released three suspects' names already and declare that the vandalism of the computer building is potentially serious and part of the calculated program of citywide destruction of the Larry's Raiders gang." They sobered at the sound of their name, talked quietly, bought a takeout banquet and took it back to the subway tunnel, ate heavily, and slept late into the next day. When they got up, they were afraid to go out, afraid to turn on the news. The girl Nicholi turned it on. Three-dimensional images sprang into an appearance of reality in the air around her, and she groped through them to the sidelines.

The images were more than life-size, giants, but they

seemed familiar. "The most wanted suspects in the United States today are both young," said the voice of the announcer.

Focus cleared and the gang saw that the giants were Larry with his straw-colored hair and a fat, strong kid, bent over the task of assembling an engine in a speed test. He finished and looked up with a friendly smile on the round face. He made a V sign with his fingers. "410 sec." appeared printed above his head. I'd seen pictures of me before, but I never recognized them without being surprised. I'm not a fat kid now.

"That's you, George," said Perry excitedly. "That's you! You're on television!"

"I assembled it fast," I said. "But I couldn't read wiring schematics on tests so they didn't promote me." That was two years ago. I didn't get a degree in mechanics.

"When did you used to be fat?" Nicholi asked. "You're not fat now."

The tape of Larry showed him standing without expression, receiving an award. A class group showed dimly on either side of him. He accepted a rolled-up document and nodded. He was smaller than the students on either side of him. Thin face, big ears, straw-colored hair sticking out.

"Just like you, Larry. They'll nail you for sure if you go out," said Weeny. "I guess I'll have to lead the gang on raids instead of you."

The announcer's voice said, "Their names are George Sanford, twenty, and Larry Rubashov, fifteen. Larry Rubashov is wanted urgently for questioning in connection with the collapse of Brooklyn and New Jersey undersea domes, two small underwater city suburbs built on the continental shelf flanking the two sides of New York Harbor, East Coast, U.S.A." The TV showed air shots of Coast Guard rescue boats circling areas of floating debris on the ocean, then flicked to a close-up of a body being pulled into a boat. "Casualties were in the thousands," said the calm voice of the announcer.

"In a circular letter to the communes, villages, and incorporated subcities of the New York area, Larry Rubashov claimed responsibility for the disaster and advertised his advice to communes that wanted plans for attack or defense

188

against similar disasters in event of intercommune civil war. He asked a high price for his advice and called the disasters a sample."

The screen began to show quick shots of Larry and me taken separately at different times of our lives in different actions.

"I'm in trouble," I said. Images of myself were crowding the room. "Everybody that knows me. . . . People all over the city say hello. They'll all think I'm a killer."

Nicholi turned a dial and the sound went down. "I'm scared. I'm going to quit the gang," she said in a small frightened voice. She turned another dial and suddenly all the crowd of images left the center of the room and were flat images on a wall.

Larry came out of the subway men's room with his shirt off and his head and hair black. He held a spray can in one hand and stood blindly, his eyes squinted tightly shut.

"Nicholi, spray my head where I missed, will you?"

Obediently she took the bottle. "You're using hair paint." She read the label in surprise and then sprayed it into his pink ears, turning them black.

"Hair paint works fine." He stood making faces and expressions while it dried. The skin of his face crinkled and lined with each expression and remained crinkled as the expression passed, leaving lines of age. "Do my back and arms." He turned slowly, flexing his fingers as she sprayed his chest and arms and hands dark brown. His hair crinkled and frizzed as it dried. He ran his hands through it and it stood out in a startling bush of black frizzy hair.

They had all risen in fascination and stood in a circle watching the transformation. The fifteen-year-old skinny blond kid was gone and in his place was an old skinny black, perhaps a Bushman, stunted, as many adults were who had grown in areas of Africa blighted by famines.

"Your ears stick out. They'll know you by your ears," Weeny objected.

"Chewing gum," the small old black man said. "Anybody have chewing gum?"

Perry took some bubble gum from his mouth and they used it to fasten Larry's ears back tightly to his skull. His ears looked smaller when they fitted the shape of his head.

189

They admired the effect. The small brown gentleman no longer had any resemblance to a fifteen-year-old blond fugitive on the wanted list.

Nicholi clapped her hands and danced around them. "Let's go out. Let's go out and Larry can talk to policemen, ask them directions. They'll never know you, Larry."

Jack said, "Let's spray George black too."

"No. George can't be black like me." Larry pushed the spray can aside. "The police are looking for a pair, a big one and a little one. If they see a matched pair of blacks, a big one and a little one, they might think."

The TV went on, not listened to, as the four teeners tried to think up a disguise that would make me look different. I stared at the television trying to stop seeing those images of me shown as a criminal.

"A legal firm representing a tribe of Paiute Indians has obtained a last-minute injunction against the opening of the dikes in the Gulf of California that will let the sea in to finish the Salton Sea project. The water will run inland and downhill along its ancient prehistoric channels." It showed channels providing a water-power source at several new dams. "It will raise the water level of Laguna Salta, an inland lake, flood some of the Imperial Valley fruit-growing land, and raise the level of the Salton Sea from two hundred and sixty feet below sea level."

Larry came to me with a spray can of wax.

"Hold still, George; shut your eyes." I shut my eyes and stopped staring at the television.

"The whole world saw me on TV," I said. "They'll think I helped blow up Brooklyn Dome."

"It gave that impression, didn't it?" Larry said, spraying my face with a cool stiffening spray. "Make faces and suck in your cheeks. The wax will make lots of wrinkles."

We went out and walked the sidewalks without being stopped. The disguises worked.

I went down into the tunnel and heard hammering and shouted directions. Ahead, three gang members were trying to put a wall across the tunnel, dividing it into rooms. I dodged through the door opening, dodging epithets and faked friendly threats with hammers.

"Out of the way!"

190

"Wait, Gorilla, help us, we need more muscle."

"I have to do foam spraying at the other end." I put down the metal bottle of spray and followed directions, lifting and holding a twelve-foot heavy beam at exactly eight feet, arms up full stretch, standing on a brick, while Weeny, the pimply teener with the longest arms, reached up and sprayed Penetrating Instant Bond Foaming Action Glue into the crack between the butt end of the four-by-four and the slick tile wall.

"Hold steady, George!" Quickly Weeny went to the other end, readjusted the height of the beam against a crayon mark, and sprayed the other end.

I held the beam up while Weeny counted off. "Eighteen, nineteen, twenty. OK, George, you can let go."

I grimaced my doubt but let go of the weight and leaped away. Miraculously the beam did not fall, but clung to the wall, crossing the tunnel at eight feet high.

"Neat," said one of the gang members.

"It beats airplane glue," I said and picked up his metal foam bottle. "Gotta go."

The others picked up four-by-eight sheet wood and fitted it against the beam while Weeny readied the bottle of spray glue.

Nicholi, the girl-woman with curly black hair, put down her sheet-wood section and ran after me and touched my arm. "I'll go with you, George, and hold something up for you."

The others laughed. "That's Nicholi!"

"Hold up what?"

"Make it stand up by itself, Nicholi!"

We went around the bend of the corridor and away from the laughter.

"Where's Larry?" shouted the distant voices.

"He should be here, telling us if it's right."

Waking up in the late afternoon sitting on a hillside in the five-mile park, drinking coffee, I wondered if I was doing the right thing, peacefully sitting with Larry, giving him a chance to talk me into his view of history.

"Larry, what you did last week, selling Akbar Hisham to the Aztecs—why?"

191

"You have to admit it was funny, George." He lay down on his stomach, chewing grass and looking at a dragonfly. "Akbar Hisham met me at the Aztec Commune thinking I was selling him a way to get the Aztecs into trouble. He deserved what he got."

I smiled. "Maybe it's funny, but how did that help anybody or do anything for history?"

The kid rolled to his back on the grass and looked at the sky. "Gorilla, the state of the world is human boredom. People living peaceful lives are incredibly bored. The only excitement they get is from hating the job and the pains of the boredom. They think hobbies are to save you from boredom, not for fun. They think boredom is a part of civilization and there's no way to change it. They take tranquilizers. They deliberately make dangerous mistakes. They get sick and go to the hospital and get parts replaced. It's all boredom. They hope for earthquakes, they rush into fires like horses into a burning barn or into floods like lemmings. They stay on their rut like a train on rails when they see the rails run off a broken bridge just ahead. I'm just giving them a shoppers' choice of floods and fires and entertaining deaths and disasters. Escape is easy if they want to escape." He sat up and peeled the top off a can of instant hot breakfast.

"People wipe themselves out?" I asked. It was the weirdest idea yet!

"Take the people of the two undersea domes. It was supposed to be a big athletic thrill to live underwater, but they weren't doing any scuba, they were just living, like in a regular apartment. Any bunch of people who huddle under a balloon under the sea are waiting for an earthquake. They want to drown." He blew on the thick drink to cool it.

"You can't prove that, Larry."

"Maybe I can't, Gorilla, but it makes sense. Statistics of people who wipe out in big disasters, little accidents, and psychosomatic diseases fit the same life pattern as suicides."

"You mean people who die in accidents wanted to die?"

"The only people who survive the worst disasters are upbeat energetic people in a phase of spreading out, meeting new friends, making new plans." He moved to get away from a hot patch of sunlight.

192

"People not bored. People looking forward." I added it up and moved uneasily. "What are you trying to say, Larry, that all death is suicide?"

"Something like that."

"If I grabbed a gun and shot you, would it be suicide if you couldn't—" I hung up on words and put down the empty coffee cup in the grass.

"I wouldn't push you that far, Lead Head. I'm not in the mood for suicide today," Larry said cheerfully.

A blue jay flew across the grass, landed on a low branch, and screeched, blue and bright, the color of the sky.

Larry might be crazy after all. Kracken, the old economist, had been crazy, and he was the opposite of Larry, but, if Kracken was crazy it didn't prove the kid was sane.

I probed. Peaceful, a kind of loving seeking to free . . . to free someone . . . the big loving father from inside the machine . . . from inside the robot face the metal body that hid the loving, kind creative kin—a person who couldn't speak, who didn't know that rules, rules are a machine face over the human face . . . rules are an ax reaching out to shake hands where the warm fingers should be to touch. . . .

The layer was very deep; above it danced a devil's flicker of teasing and rapid thoughts of provoking others to violence, violence against Larry, violence against life, because violence was real, it touched with warm hot feelings. That thought was just like crazy little curly-headed Nicholi, a simple animal impulse. (Make 'em act like people, anger is natural, real, politeness is people hiding, not seen, not there.)

I could swing with *feelings*, but Nicholi was always starting fights among the others or trying to get herself raped. It didn't make sense in results. Larry was supposed to be smarter than that or anyhow not as childish, not as crazy. I moved uneasily, breaking the contact between my feelings and his. His knowledge of history was always surprising when he explained it. He never told his plans. I assumed his plans were as brilliant as his history lessons, but I couldn't be sure. His thinking was too fast and complicated for me to follow. I'd believed he had to be brilliant with brilliant plans for the future of the world. But. . . .

"Larry, what about the kids in those two domes? They

weren't in charge of where they were. Some of them died. Are you trying to say that they were suicides too?"

Something flickered in his mind. "I'm one of them," he said weirdly. "Dead a long time now." Larry got up, moving easily, with fake relaxation like a cat, talking fast in a practical tone as if he hadn't said that last remark at all.

"Sorry, George, we can't discuss kids and deaths. I'm not making any trouble this week. I don't want you at my throat from just talking."

"But what about the kids. . . ."

"Truce, George, truce for a week, remember? Let's go down inside."

A police copter hummed in the distance and we went down the steps fast and slid the fake wall shut behind us. I walked through the corridor until I could see a crowd of people dancing in the half darkness. Bouncy music.

Who? They came into focus. Show girls. The big stolen DV set was projecting illusions.

"Wow, what a view." Weeny rolled on the floor under the dimensional projections of dancing girls. The stolen holograph set was new and made big bright images. "Wow." Weeny clutched at legs. There was no stereo image from that direction unless the kids had stolen some porno tapes somehow.

Weeny clutched upward. The apparently solid dancing girls danced through him as if they were real and he was a ghost. He appeared and disappeared inside images. Dance music blared.

Jack and Perry walked through the crowd of images. "What's that on the floor?"

"Must be a DV." Perry stepped on Weeny's stomach and pretended not to notice and walked on.

"It's a pile of trash." Jack tried to step on him too, but Weeny rolled out of the way, snapped off the DV, and scrambled to a corner, cursing. He flopped down on his sleeping bag and stared out at the others, red-eyed like a cornered cat.

I remembered that ESP was powered by emotion. For practice I dipped into the mind of the pimply teener.

In his mind, Weeny had a frightened Jack and Perry at gun point and was forcing them to pee on each other. They begged for mercy or for a sense of humor, and he smiled and made them do it. I withdrew my mind from the imaginary scene, half amused, half sickened. Weeny was funny because he was not in power. If the skinny adolescent had command he would try to act out those scenes. And then he would not be funny!

Nicholi sat next to Jack and tickled his neck and played with his ears, casting meaningful smiles and glances at Perry.

Perry went over and sat on her other side and put an arm around her waist. "You love me better, don't you, Nicholi?"

"Sure I do." She transferred her attentions and tickles to Perry.

Red with pleasure, Perry looked at Jack. "See, I've got it all over you, Jack. I'm a real stud. You're just an imitation."

Jack got up and walked away without replying.

Nicholi smiled. I put myself in her place, sitting where she sat, smoothing her hair, smiling. Her vibes had no sex, only mischief, a kid's vibes of making trouble.

It all seemed useless, but they were busy and satisfied with their quarrels. I got up and wandered up and down restlessly. This wasn't work enough for me. It would be better to be out working for Rescue Squad.

The gang members stopped talking and watched me.

"Are you here, George, or are you tuning in someplace else?"

"Go up and kick him, Weeny. If he takes you apart, he's here."

Weeny did not move. He glared at me and imagined his chain wrapping around my neck. I glared back. Deliberately he began to imagine something worse. I held back an impulse to go over and step on him.

I explained why I was pacing. "It's just that I've got to have something to do. You guys aren't doing anything."

7

MEMORY gets scrambled. Days did not pass, but a week vanished, leaving no trace.

Suddenly I was sitting on the cement steps in the cage in Nicholi's room, a prisoner leaning back staring at the ceiling imagining stars. I was zonked out on some drug and stupid.

"Be a good buddy, George, shut your eyes and my voice will send you on a trip." In the darkness of shut eyes I heard Larry's clear, image-making words. "Your name is Carl Hodges. You're thinking about how calm the city people are all the time. How they don't know about all the things making the city run that could go wrong. You're thinking about how a little thing could go wrong and surprise them by making a lot of noise."

Half asleep, half in another body, standing in a place of switchboards and controls and unrolling graphs, I and the other body began to laugh.

"What's funny, Carl?" asked the clear voice.

"The old CD civil-defense warning system. It's still there, ready to howl. Everyone forgot it."

The police received a furious phone call from Carl Hodges, computer operator for prediction of breakdowns in city services, dispatcher for repair of wear and prevention of emergency in the overloaded services of the city.

"I'll try to connect you to the right department," said the switchboard girl, sounding confused. "It will take some time."

"I don't want to spare the time; I'm busy at my job. Just tape this and play the tape to whoever is in charge of George Sanbridge."

"Tape is operating, sir; all police calls are taped."

"Good. Tell them to get George Sanbridge the hell off my back. It was all right connecting with him for him to locate me, but now I keep getting nightmares of being kidnapped again by those crazy kids. And whenever I dream this junk

196

I'm dreaming I'm George Sandbag of the Rescue Squad. I know how it feels to be him, we stood back to back and fought off those kids for ten minutes, and he had a mind-lock on me so we were both coordinating the same person for the whole time. Being inside that guy is nothing like being me. I don't know what the hell's wrong with your methods over at that department, but either tell him to unhook from me and hang up the phone, or get him out of that cage and put him on a different assignment." The crash of a phone hanging up, the hum of a dial tone.

"We give thanks to the Spirit of Universal Life and the creative Spirit of the Universe that, nearing the end of another decade, we find ourselves still here and the Earth still here.

"No more species of animal have died out in the last five years, vegetation is making a comeback in the desert areas, and with the help of botanists, Earth is advancing its greenery to the very tops of mountains that used to be barren rock. As you all know, among the list of our blessings is that the oxygen percentage in the air has stopped falling and for the third straight year it has perceptibly increased. By next year's New Century Day, it will have reached nine point five."

A different voice cut in.

"You are listening to the President's State of the Union Message, delivered to the Environmental Party National Committee banquet, at the dedication of the newly con-structed dome city built at the edge of the expected new limits of the Salton Sea. The Salton Sea is now expanding with a slow inflow of sea water from the Gulf of California. The time is now three of five. We return you to the President's State of the Union Message."

I realized I was lying face down on something hard.

"We can take pride in our individual efforts. For the third year in a row we have reduced the gross national product by more than five percent. Everyone is trying hard to reduce consumption and learn repair skills. Gross National measures of Use Value have risen slightly or held their own. The quality of life is still improving. The previous administration policy of demanding a fifteen-year

197

guarantee on all manufactured goods at the time success-fully shut down more than fifteen thousand marginal producers."

I lay and listened to a radio broadcast of the President's State of the Union Message. The words were clear, but the meaning drifted away. "Reward the successful man-ufacturers of more durable goods by increase to a fifty-year guarantee. . . ."

As I slowly awoke, I realized that I was lying face down on my sleeping bag, with a hard pressure of a folded zipper against my face, as if I had fallen there. My back felt drafty and cool, and it hurt. I realized that I was lying down without a blanket or shirt, with my pants pulled down as far as my knees, binding my legs together. The skin of my back stung and itched and I ached like the aftermath of a tough fight. The itching of my back warned of trouble, the way a bad sunburn does before you touch it. Motion could hurt. I tried to remember what happened. Tuesday the gang was planning a raid I'd planned to talk Larry out of. Some joke on me they were snickering over. It seemed far away and vague. The radio faded in again. "You have been listening to the President's State of the Union Message.

"Yesterday the inhabitants of New York's boroughs of Manhattan and Brooklyn were startled when all the almost-forgotten air-raid warning sirens went off together. While this event was being investigated, all fire alarms went off, and one hour later burglar alarms in most of the major factories, warehouses, and department stores rang and half an hour later rang again.

"A message has been received by the radio and TV news stations, claiming that the ear-blasting din was started by Larry's Raiders, to demonstrate that they still have control of the city's services and can sell their powers of sabotage to the highest bidders. It was signed 'Larry.' However, Carl Hodges, the city services top computerman, said in an in-terview yesterday that his experience in being kidnapped by the juvenile gang and hypnotically questioned has been thoroughly reviewed by total recall therapy, and there are no further items of dangerous information that the juvenile gang members obtained from him that they have not already used. 'As far as I know,' Carl Hodges said, 'there

198

will be no new danger to the city services from Larry's Raiders.' "

"That's what they think!" said Larry's voice. The radio snapped off suddenly.

"You all right, George?"

The telephone rang. Telephone? I remembered Larry planned to run an extension receiver from the pay phone on the other side of the wall in the subway. I heard Larry answer in a disguised voice. I rolled my head and opened one eye and watched Larry talking through aluminum foil, avoiding the voice-detecting alarms the police had to monitor all calls. Larry hung up and came back. "You all right, George?"

"Uh." I sat up, waited through a roar of pain from my stiff-skinned back pain that was something a little worse than sunburn, and then stood up. Hastily I pulled up my pants and slid my shirt over my tender shoulders with slow care.

"Sure, I'm OK. I'm fine. What did I get into?"

"A kind of a fight with Weeny. You kind of lost because of bad luck, I guess. You kind of tripped and got messed up."

Partially lying, Larry looked away, not meeting my eyes, ashamed. "Sorry about that. I wasn't here to stop it." The kid was thinner, with face and hair looking dirty from dark brown dye half washed off in streaks. He gave out vibes of fear. "Put out your arm, George. Your back looks bad; you need an antibiotic shot."

I put an arm out through the bars and felt the needle go in. "What day is this, Larry? If it's Wednesday, I've got to clean up and report in to Rescue Squad." I felt a taste in my mouth, carried through the bloodstream, that was like the green tranquilizers. The room seemed bigger and warmer.

"It's not Wednesday." Larry was watching me, narrow green eyes very steady, holding very still with the hypo still dripping from his hand. "There isn't any Wednesday, just Tuesday and Thursday."

His voice had said that before, unremembered times. Wednesday vanished. It was funny. I began to laugh. As I laughed, Larry relaxed, moved, and smiled. He put away the hypo and came back with a quarter. "Take this to get out of the cage, George. We're going to do big things in the city

199

today. I'm not leaving you here alone again. From now on we'll be buddies. Everything I do, you'll be helping me."

George had been missing for ten days.

Ahmed finished a half day at the usual tasks of a Rescue Squad detective of anticipating and preventing trouble, then checked in at the police detection headquarters to add his formal assistance to the attempt to locate the Larry Rubashov gang. He had been loaned to the crime division, but he was not yet ready to really help. He was waiting for George to separate himself from the gang before he wanted the gang to be arrested.

But how long should he wait? The gang was too elusive, too lucky, too good at passing alarms. They had been stealing odd things, and Larry had left signs everywhere proclaiming that the communes should pay him blackmail and protection money against sabotage. The gang's luck was not possible unless George was helping them with ESP. Every day that passed made it more likely that Larry would bomb something or commit some major sabotage before he was stopped.

It was Ahmed's duty to help capture the gang, even if George got caught in the crunch. With his wide mouth compressed into a rigid line of indecision, Ahmed stood staring blindly at the bulletin board, his hands stiff at his sides.

The data coordinator for the Larry's Raiders case was on the phone, his desk stacked high with unproductive reports from searchers who had found nothing. He put a hand over the phone. "Ahmed, check through that box of incoming junk for me; see if there's anything hot."

Ahmed sat on the edge of the nearest desk, picked an envelope out of the input box, and opened it. He shook the envelope and a photo fell out of a tall aging stranger in a 1950-style charcoal suit, an upright, stiff-backed, distinguished man. There was something vaguely familiar about the shape of his shoulders. His hands hung at his sides slightly away from his body, slightly curved into cups, the hands of a person who thought during action, the hands of a person whose hands twitched when he thought. Like George.

Ahmed opened a folder and found a typed list of all the

equipment and goods taken during the second round of citywide clamor of burglar alarms. It was a long list, taken from twelve places, for possibly other thieves had realized their chance when thinking over the first uproar, that universal alarms were as good as no alarms, and made away with goods during the second din. Yet some of the items on the list had probably been carefully planned and collected by Larry and his gang members and would show the drift of his plans.

A photograph fell out of the folder, another one of the same tall man, standing at a slant, mouth open in a foolish drunken laugh that did not match the worry lines of the strong square face.

Ahmed held it up. "Who's this?"

The data man covered the phone with his hand. "Nobody in particular. Mechanics teacher on a weekend binge. His friend says it's psychotherapist's advice that he get drunk and have fun. The automatic identification service keeps sending in photos snapped from the automatic cameras of him drunk all over the city. He has high similarity to George Sanford in body proportions. You know, shoulder width, wrist width, ear shape, so the computer sorts them out and sends them through. But it's not him, less weight, more height, more age. A valid computer ID." He shrugged.

"File in the bottom drawer, 'Rejects, suspect photos.' "

Ahmed pulled open the file drawer, took out the "Reject" folder photos of blond skinny kids, short blond teeners, long skinny, pimply teeners with big Adam's apples, and big husky fullback types with round faces, all of them vaguely resembling either George, Larry, or members of Larry's gang. A sheaf of photographs of the mechanics teacher was clipped together separately.

Shoulders stiffly erect, like a man fighting the aches of age, not George's good-natured slouch, the aging face lean and worried, the neck thinner and wrinkled. What can a disguise do to thin and wrinkle your neck?

But the heavy bones, the thick wrists, and the shape of hands were George. Ahmed wanted to read the list but his hands lingered on the photos, shuffling them. He was looking for George and these pictures all shouted George at him, first glance.

It was remarkable how wrong the instinctive recognition

201

could be. Instinct had been wrong last week too when he mistook a small old black man for Larry.

Ahmed saw similarity after similarity as he shuffled through the photographs. Typical way of carrying a heavy bag. . . .

The data man hung up the phone and came over and bent over his shoulder. "See something?"

Ahmed held up a multishot and tilted it. In flickers of five still shots the big man with black hair lost his laugh and reached up with a hand toward his nose in an uncertain gesture. The sleeve slid back, showing the big corded wrist with reddish hair on the back of the arm.

Ahmed knew that gesture; George scratched the side of his nose with his thumb and looked at the ground when he wondered if he'd just made a mistake.

In the background Ahmed saw a small black man, the same one he had mistaken for Larry.

"What do you see?" asked the man behind him.

Ahmed handed him the sheaf of photographs. "Put them all on broadcast. That's George Sanford," he said.

"Don't be fooled by a point-eight resemblance. There are similar people, you know."

"George lost about eighty pounds in the last eight months," Ahmed said. "And he probably grew an inch. His official measurements are out of date. If he'd lost another ten pounds, fast, and somebody made him up and he sprained his back, he'd look like this. Use a magnifying glass. In the color shots the hair on the back of his arms is red. That makes the black hair on the head a fake."

The data correlation chief for the case grabbed the sheaf of photos and rushed to the switchboard.

"All points, pick up this man. Seen in Manhattan, Brooklyn, and at Coney Island. Warning, may be dangerous. All points. Urgent, priority five. He may be near the Larry Rubashov gang. Be alert for companions; prepare for resistance and or group scattering of five people. All cruisers slow and inspect pedestrian groups. This is George Sanford, top name on your wanted list. Memorize this disguise." He began to hold up photographs flat against the camera eye.

Ahmed approached and leaned over his shoulder. "Larry Rubashov is disguised as a small black man about

202

sixty years old in appearance with a bandaged or damaged right hand. Put that on the pickup call, too."

The data man's voice heightened in pitch with excitement as he relayed the information. He cut off and left the broadcast on repeating tape for the dispatcher to repeat. Ahmed's hand tightened a grip on the man's shoulder.

"Why did you say George was dangerous?"

"Don't freak out, Ahmed. We know he's your friend." He unplugged and replugged for a different call.

Ahmed's fingers tightened on his shoulder. "Why did you say he was dangerous? You know that gives permission for those trigger-happy patrolmen—"

"Anyone under Larry Rubashov's control is dangerous. That's the Commissioner's decision. But we're taking care of it." The data man spun his chair around and faced Ahmed's glare. "We've transferred you legally back to Rescue Squad. And Rescue Squad will have George listed as kidnapped. When they're located we'll try to stall in arresting the gang until you can get there and put the arm on George personally. So that when he's taken in it will classify as a rescue instead of an arrest. It will be your problem to keep him away from questioning."

Ahmed stopped packing his personal papers from his drawer into a briefcase, the gesture of a man quitting, and pushed the papers slowly back into the drawer, thinking. He said, "Thanks," and straightened with a smile of apology, a difficult effort on the long intense face, more an apologetic grimace than a smile.

"OK." The data man took a map and the stack of photos of George and started making red ink dots on the map of each place the photos were taken, writing in red ink the time of day the picture was snapped.

Ahmed looked at the list of items stolen, picking it up again from the data man's desk. "Twenty one-hour delay-action timers stolen from the scientific supply warehouse. That's enough for twenty time bombs."

"They're not timing hard boiled eggs," said the data man, quickly adding dots to the map. A red ink pattern of the gang's usual travels began to emerge on the map. "Keep thinking, Ahmed."

8

I woke up and found I was lying face down on my sleeping bag. Something had jolted me awake. My hands were tied behind my back. I heard the hiss of Weeny's chain and felt the slap and multiple bite of its small hooks. The chain was rippled and freed from digging into my skin and dragged back across the cement with a silvery ringing sound.

I heard him grunt with effort and I rolled up against the bars and heard the chain hit the bars above me and tangle in an ornamental knob. Leaning against the bars, I looked up at Weeny. All of his weakness was merely awkwardness and sudden new height. He was a man, with a man's savage intentness on purpose and need for conquest.

"Whatja hit me for?" I asked.

"You won't answer questions," Weeny snarled and shook his end of the chain, rippling it to get it loose from the bars.

"Try asking them when I'm awake, Maggot."

"You're awake, just drugged up. I owe you something for those bruises from last week. I don't forget."

I tested my bonds and twisted my head far enough to see that my hands were tied behind me. My hands and ankles were inexpertly tied by many turns of nylon cord. Nylon is the hardest kind of rope to untie. It has no give or stretch. It can't be forced. "You can't do this to a gang brother, Weeny. It's against the oath."

"You're no brother, sucker. That was only for three days, sucker. Our promises ran out."

"Then I can kill you when I get loose."

Weeny came close and contemptuously untangled the chain from the bars. "I can kill you before you get loose, sucker. I tied you up and beat on you before and you didn't get me then."

"You what? I don't remember." Weeny backed away along the line of the wall, coiling his chain. Something important in his words reached me. I'd lost seven days. The last clear day I remembered was Tuesday watching the gang quarrel while Larry was out disguised as a middle-aged black man. I groped in my mind for traces of a week of memory.

"Feel your back, sucker. I did that to you. Notice you've got a sore nose from landing on your face." Triumphantly Weeny stood dangling his chain in loops from his hand.

"I don't remember," I admitted. "Wednesday was six days ago? What am I still doing here?"

Weeny grinned with scraggle teeth. "Larry fooled you into this cage. Borrowed all your quarters and sent you inside to do some work. Sucker. We wouldn't give you anything to eat until Larry tricked you into drinking some Coke he drugged. You've been hypnotized and working for Larry ever since. But you won't answer questions when *I* ask. I'm just as much boss as Larry is. You'd better start answering *me,* or I'll beat you to a bloody pulp. He let you off the pills today, so you're not such a simple-minded robot tied to him. You can hear my voice too, now. You can be scared and you can remember. You're going to remember this beating. You'll never forget it."

He coiled the chain in his hand and lined his feet up to swing. He was eight feet away.

I heaved myself up to a kneeling position and leaned back till my hands touched my ankle cords and began to work on the knots. "Wait a minute; what do you want to know?"

Weeny was launching a blow with the chain. He twitched and hesitated and lost the rhythm of the back fling. He coiled the chain again in his hands slowly. "You're not scared. You're stalling." Suddenly the chain swung sideways on a rising sweep for the head. Years of make-believe play danger with my own kid gang under Ahmed's severe training made the scene familiar to me, the countermoves easy and familiar. I straightened more, making a tall target, and at the last second fell sideways. The chain passed above me and clanged into the bars. Weeny, cursing, pulled it back and as it jingled across the floor, I struggled back to a kneeling position and conspicuously worked my fingers against the knots at my ankles. Weeny was savage and energetic, but he was a beginner driven by dreams of glory rather than knowledge. Cursing, he aimed a hard downward blow at my busy hands.

I let go of the knots and pulled my hands back. The chain

caught me across the ankles and spent its blow on the floor. I leaned back and hunkered on the bright links of metal, catching the chain between my legs and thighs.

Weeny shouted an obscenity and pulled the chain. I grinned at him, hoping he would come within reach.

Weeny took out his switchblade knife and snapped the long blade open. My grin widened. In UN Brotherhood war games Ahmed had shown us this was easily countered by feet or hands.

I heard a voice from outside the bars. "Leave him alone, Weeny." Larry stood there, a kid ridiculously disguised in black streaks of a dye that was wearing off his face. "If you keep fooling with George you'll get killed," he said through the bars. He was carrying his air pistol. He pointed it at Weeny.

Weeny put his knife back in his pocket. "You mean, he'll get killed."

Larry turned to me. "George, tell him what you could do to him."

"I wasn't going to kill him. I was just gonna aim for his chest and not kick hard."

To Weeny, Larry said, "You were planning to get up close to George to get your chain, weren't you, Weeny?"

"Right. He's tied up. He can't get to me."

Larry said, "OK, George, show him."

I swung my weight backward, fell backward onto my shoulder blades and tied arms, straightened my legs, and shoved with my arms on the ground in a kick that reached up five feet and forward six feet. It went through air where a man's neck could be. I pulled my feet in and let the momentum of the kick roll me forward and standing, slightly off balance. I hopped sideways to regain balance and then hopped toward Weeny.

Startled, fumbling for his knife, Weeny backed into a corner. I stopped. "Just now I could have butted you into the wall, I guess. The tiles are pretty hard."

"The tiles would crush your skull, Weeny," Larry said through the bars seriously. "Tell it like it is, George; Weeny needs an education. If he'd been kicked in the neck he'd already be dead."

I turned and hopped away. Weeny moved to the turnstile, sidling sideways, holding his knife ready, slid a quarter into the slot, and pushed out of the cage away from me. He cursed at both of us like a cat spitting. "You think you're a couple of jokers," he concluded, his face white and his pimples and eyes red. "I'll remember it." He went out.

Larry did not look after him. "Sorry he bothered you. Need help to get untied, George?"

"No." I crouched. When I bent forward all the skin of my back pulled tight and hurt with the stiffness of half-healed damage. I looped my tied arms and worked them past my feet from back to front, then straightened with my wrists before my face and began untying the knots with my teeth. "I'm conscious, Larry."

"I notice. Something about being mad always wakes you up. You remember what day this is?"

"I don't remember anything since Tuesday night, but I'm conscious now."

"You aren't exactly unconscious when you're on pills, George, just sort of cooperative and obedient, and you laugh a lot. I took you off them this morning so you wouldn't get hooked. Four days is enough."

"What did you make me do?" The knots loosened. I sat down and used my half-freed hands to free my ankles.

"You've been a big help." Larry grinned.

I stood up. "What did I do? Did I hurt anybody?"

"Give up," Larry said and gestured with the muzzle of the gun. "Give up worrying about right and wrong. Join my gang and let me do the worrying."

I didn't answer. I felt outplayed and outmaneuvered and Larry was too smart. Larry stepped back from the bars, his voice raised nervously. "If you don't, I'll just keep you on drugs and keep you working for us anyhow."

I slowly chewed at the loose nylon knots. "Where are the others?" I asked.

"They're all still working on the explosives, connecting the timers." Watching my hands, Larry stepped back farther from the bars, out of arm's reach.

"What explosives?" The news was getting worse. I finished loosening the cords and slid one hand free.

"The explosives. The ones you told us how to get."

I slid the loops off my other hand and straightened the cord out, thinking about hanging myself.

Larry watched my face curiously. Larry couldn't pick up

207

my vibes. He could not read my expression. "You told us where they were stored and how to fake the invoice forms and you tuned in to an expert on making bombs and drew diagrams. You're getting better at— You don't remember any of it, do you?"

As a child joining the UN Brotherhood gang, I'd sworn to learn skills at fighting to save people from the enemies and killers. I had taken my oath seriously.

Suddenly the enemy and killer was me. I'd let myself be conned into giving bombs to mad children. I was sure now that Larry was mad. I had probed Larry for vibes of madness and had not found any, but I had looked for vibes of hatred, of a mad hatred. Larry never felt hate.

Ahmed had been right. Judge nuts by their actions. . . . What had the kid been doing with my help? Would there be another cataclysm of mass death like Jersey Dome? Would it be blamed on me? If another three thousand died, could I honestly say that it was not my fault?

I remembered a philosophy teacher who had said, "Nothing is an accident."

"You wanted to do it, George, or you wouldn't have done it; mistakes are no excuse," said the philosopher's voice in my mind. Had I wanted to put bombs into Larry's hands? And Weeny's hands and Nicholi's hands? Larry was a historian, a poet, and a leader, and insane. Weeny measured his own importance by how much he could destroy. Nicholi liked to stir up trouble and watch.

"Mistakes are no excuse," repeated the voice of my philosophy teacher. "You are what you have done, and you are what you do."

I stood dangling the cord, thinking of suicide, and put the cord in my pocket.

"Larry, I don't remember a thing since Tuesday. I don't remember about bombs. I wouldn't tell any punk gang about bombs. What are you feeding me?"

The kid took a bottle out of his pocket. "It's safe." He read the label aloud. " 'Pre-op. Adrenaline reduction and hypnotic euphoric. Makes the patient docile, compliant, and free from fear. Use for a maximum of eight hours before any major surgery or surgery in which the patient demonstrates deep anxiety. Lowers stress, makes preparation easier for the staff, and decreases postoperative shock. Warning. The patient will forget directions and instructions and will not recognize or adjust to any areas that the patient had not encountered the day before. Retrograde amnesia will block recall of events from four hours before the pill was taken to six hours after the pill was taken. One capsule per fifty kilos body weight every four hours. Critical ratio: twelve over one.' "

"That's bad," I said, thinking I could make Larry give me the bottle if I insulted his intelligence. "You didn't read the label first before you gave me the pills. You've trashed my brains. The label says amnesia, and I got amnesia, and it says eight hours, no more. How many hours in five days? A lot more than eight. You should have read the label. And critical ratio, that's the killing dose. It says twelve. How many pills have you given me? More than twelve, a lot more."

"Damn it, look for yourself, then." Larry clanged the bottle through the bars on the floor. "Here, read it. But don't trash it, George. I've got another bottle."

"I won't trash it." I held the label up and read it slowly, stepping away from the bars.

"See," Larry said, "you're getting it all backward. Critical ratio means how many times the effective dose is the killing dose. If two pills get you friendly and obedient, then it would take twelve times as many to kill you. That's twenty-four pills! All taken at once. You're not going to get poisoned just eating two at a time."

I read slowly. When it tilted, it showed different print, finer print with more medical details. I read aloud. " 'Overdose symptoms: nausea, failure of breathing reflex, blue skin, cold hands and feet, slow pulse, cardiac arrest.' What's that?"

"Heart stops."

I read the label again, then sighed and sat down on my sleeping bag and opened the top of the bottle and poured a handful of green capsules into my palm and counted them.

Larry went up to the bars and leaned on them. "What are you doing now?"

For a moment I looked through his eyes. He saw me as big, useful, and a good friend who just needed strong

209

persuasion and drugs to get him to help. I didn't answer. I started eating capsules.

"What are you doing?" Larry gripped the bars, stuck his face through between them, and shouted shrilly, "Stop! Quit doing that! George!" he screamed. "Quit it. Quit eating those pills!"

"Six," I said, taking two at a time. "Eight, twelve, fourteen. I don't think what you've been doing is right, Larry. You ought to stop. Sixteen, eighteen, twenty, twenty-two. They taste bad." I put my hand up flat to my mouth and chewed the remaining green capsules and swallowed. I grinned, watching Larry.

"God damn it," Larry said in terror. He clutched the bars, standing on tiptoe. "Stop doing that! Spit them out! What do you think you are doing?"

"Fixing it so I can't help you hurt people. Salt. My tongue is numb." I reached into my mouth with a finger and felt my tongue.

Larry felt through his pockets, muttering, "Don't want to hurt you, sucker." He found a small pillbox. "Here." Larry opened the box, took out a pink pill, and reached through the bars with it. "Here, take it."

"What is it?" I stood up, took the pill, and looked at it.

"A stimulant," Larry shrilled. "Take it quick, you stupid bastard. Chew it. It cancels the ones you just took. It's the strongest one I have."

Carefully I put the pink pill down on the cement and stepped on it.

Larry made animal groans and snarls, breathing through clenched teeth as he watched me grind the pill into pink powder. "Jesus, Jesus," he hissed in half prayer. "Hari Krishna. George, you're—you're very, very difficult."

I went over to the bars and handed Larry the bottle of green capsules, now only half full. I staggered and clutched the bars. "How's that for action? Shmarter than you are, Larry."

"Are you planning to die in there?" Larry backed off. "Die in that cage? You'd still be stuck in there forever. How would we— Shit, oh, shit, don't die in there." He fumbled in his pockets and wallet, letting out high-pitched whines of frustration. "Can't find it. Here. Found it!"

210

He produced a quarter and shoved it into my face. "Here, George, that's what you want, isn't it? A quarter to get out? You've won. Come out, for God's sake. Hurry up."

Larry started searching the piled side of the room, looking under piles of trash and supplies. "Oxygen tank. Where the hell is it?" He dashed into other rooms, crashing in sounds of search. "Where's the oxygen? The coffee maker is cold! Where's the extension plug?"

It took me three tries to get the quarter into the right slot. I pushed through the rotating bar door and fell down on my hands and knees. What I was doing wasn't interesting, because I didn't care. It was easier to notice what Larry was doing, because his excitement made a kind of sharp focus and bright light and excitement around him. He ran back in with an oxygen tank, opening it. It did not hiss. The handle had not been tightly closed. He cursed at the last person who used it. His excitement was funny; his words gave out red flashes of light. I laughed.

Larry pulled the extra bottle of green capsules out of his pocket and tilted it. Pages of print appeared and vanished and were replaced by other pages of print as he tilted it. I knew how it looked. I could see through his eyes. That was surprising. *Keep the patient moving in forced activity, active walking, coffee in large quantities, loud sound and activity, anger, fear, alternate hot and cold showers, and other natural stimulation until the ambulance arrives.*

"Oh, shit," Larry said. "Get up, you bastard; you gotta walk up and down." He helped me get to my feet and tried to start me walking, but I lurched and was too heavy. We both fell. Larry dashed through the other rooms. "Jack, Perry, Weeny! Where the hell is everybody? I need help here." The group working on making bomb timers blinked up at him, surprised.

"We've got to get all the bombs done in time for the raid tonight."

"The two biggest guys, Weeny and Perry. . . ." Larry took them back to the other end. Weeny looked at me trying to get up.

"Stand him up, take him out to the park, and walk him up and down," Larry said desperately.

Weeny laughed. "What's the matter? Is he sick?"

"He ate half a bottle of green pills. Hoist him up."

They hoisted, grunting. "Was he trying to kill himself?" the lanky, pimply teener asked, grinning. He got one shoulder under my shoulder and hooked my limp right arm around his neck like a handle.

"Yes."

"He's getting smarter. Hold up your side, Perry, ya bastid."

"Walk him in the park," Larry said. "George, stiffen up your legs. Walk. Keep walking. Before you go out, mindfeelers out, George. Any one thinking of this place?"

"No. But they know Naga Baku you." I got an image of police looking for the small black man that was Larry sprayed black. Larry's fake ID was no good now.

"Stiffen your legs, George. It's safe to take him out. Walk, George; keep walking." They half carried me out into the darkness of the park paths.

"Let's walk him over toward the cliff," Weeny said. "Keep walking, George." He cursed as my foot stepped on his foot. "Perry, what are we trying to wake him up for? If he woke up all the way, he'd cream us and go to the cops, wouldn't he? He'd break us into little bones."

"Probably," said the other voice in the dark. Perry, the follower, voiced few opinions of his own.

"Sure he would. Wouldn't you, George? Don't you want to go to the police and tell them what you've been doing?"

"M-make reports. Work for Rescue Squad. Rescue people." I said, "Sure, thanks."

"Sure," Weeny said.

We came to a sign: FORTY-FOOT DROP-OFF. STEEP SLOPE KEEP OFF. It guarded a low fence. "Step high over the fence, George." They helped me over the fence. On the other side the ground sloped, slippery with smooth grass. In the darkness I saw a dim bulk of trees and bushes at the edge. Weeny pushed Perry away and got behind me and grabbed both of my shoulders and pointed me down slope. "You're going to escape, George. Be ready to run. Rescue Squad is straight ahead down that hill. *Run.*" He pushed; I staggered ahead into the darkness downhill, going fast. I crashed into bush branches and fell, hitting things as I rolled. I grabbed bushes and stopped rolling at an edge. I was sleepy.

"What will we tell Larry?" Perry asked, his voice uphill and distant.

"Tell him George tried to get away to run back to Rescue Squad, and we lost sight of him in the dark and heard crashes and shit, we think he went over a cliff," Weeny said impatiently. "Don't worry."

"What if he didn't go over?" Perry asked. I decided to be Weeny, more awake.

"He'll probably die lying there without us walking him up and down. Stop asking stupid questions." Weeny stood nervously listening in the dark. Did he hear the faintest of creaks from the direction his enemy had fallen? "I'll make sure," he declared, fear rising in him. He felt his way down the steep dangerous slope until he was ten feet away from Perry, then, hidden by the dark, he took out his switchblade knife, opened it, and held it in his teeth while he used both hands to feel his way down the path of crushed bushes to the edge.

Near the edge of the cliff Weeny could see more clearly through the screen of trees and bushes into space. Miles away the lights of the city began again at the other side of the park.

Nearby he heard the heavy sound of breathing.

Logically it was only George Sanford, lying unconscious, poisoned by his overdose of hypnotic pills, stopped from rolling over the edge of the cliff only by some bush or stump, but darkness had its own threat. The deep sound raised his hair. Weeny gripped two small bushes together with one hand to keep from sliding over the sloping edge. He took his switchblade knife and felt forward with it in the dark, stretching his arm until the knife touched something that moved. He pulled back to a guard position, but nothing sudden came at him in the dark, and the slow sound of breathing continued.

Weeny remembered the big guy ignoring him, smiling at Weeny's threats. He remembered that Nicholi had liked George better. He remembered the confidence in those big crushing hands, and anger and fear drove him forward. He crawled forward into darkness again and touched the body. Everything he hated was in the touch of that thick calm flesh. Whispering a curse, Weeny thrust the long knife

213

deeply into something that gave, then scrambled away uphill, in a mixture of terror and satisfaction.

Behind him there was a startled grunt, a thrashing of arms, a crunching of bushes and a sliding sound, twigs cracking, and then after a pause, a crunch and a crash from below. Sanford had slid over the edge.

The makers of the label on the bottle of sedatives had recommended in the absence of a doctor or any stimulant drugs to try anger, fear, alternate hot and cold showers, activity, or other natural stimulation as a last-ditch postponement of death from overdose, to ward off the indifference and sleep that drifts downward to coma and death.

They would hardly have approved of the procedure of being jabbed in the trapezius muscle with a long sharp knife and pushed over the edge of a cliff as a form of natural stimulation but it worked. It woke me up and gave me things to do to keep me interested.

The cliff was an unstable dirt cliff, with trees and bushes at the edge slowly toppling over in the slow motion it takes centuries to see. I slid and fell from a curved overhang of roots, grabbing at things that pulled loose and fell with me. I found myself hanging free, holding a projecting tree root with one hand while slidings and crashes continued below me.

Things quieted again while a scattering of dislodged dirt pattered on my shoulders and head like hail. My hand slid down the root and then had an easy grip at the wide node where it forked. I dangled in the dark. My other arm hurt when I tried to move it, giving a grating pain in the back like a broken shoulder blade.

The night was dark and cloudy. I couldn't see much, but the lights of a small sidewalk with flights of stone steps slanting down the side of the cliff forty feet below me gave the impression that letting go would mean falling a distance to cement. I hung on.

As more of the pills dissolved in my stomach and entered my blood, my eyes tried to close. I tried to keep them open. I forgot why.

Somewhere else in the back of my head there were lights and people wide awake, talking about me. I tuned in, and it came in loud, with bright pictures and strong feelings. I was with the gang. But they didn't know I was there.

"George must have been unhappy if he killed himself," Nicholi said unhappily. "Did you do something to him, Weeny, again?"

"Sure he was unhappy. He was a cop," said Weeny. "He deserved to be unhappy. I hope he burns in hell."

"He wasn't a cop." Perry carefully finished positioning his bombs in the bottom of the bag where he could reach the timing knobs. "He was a rescue man."

Jack didn't say anything. He worked slowly and looked depressed.

Nicholi said, "But what will we do if we don't have George to tell us if it's safe?" She peeked into her shopping bag at her wrapped package of bombs.

"We'll take our chances," Weeny snarled. "Hurry up, I'm in charge when Larry is downtown."

"Without George how will we know if it's safe to come back? Maybe the police will find it and be waiting for us," Nicholi said and hesitated in a long silence of the others. She came to a decision. "I'm going to take all my jewelry and my good coat. I won't let them have it."

Jack and Perry were ready to go out, but they looked at each other and put down their shopping bags of bombs. "She's right."

"I'm going to bring my scuba breather. We might never come back to this place."

"I'm getting my stuff, too!"

"Forget that," Weeny yelled. "Larry says we have to be at the dikes a half hour before time to blow them up! Take your orders, you creeps. Forget about packing!" They ignored him and went back into the tunnel rooms to get their possessions. They didn't obey him the way they obeyed the kid. Furiously Weeny yelled after them as they scattered, "Forget it, I said! We've got to leave right now!"

Left alone, his orders ignored, Weeny stood shaking with rage, making up fantasies of revenge. He thought about resetting all the timers in the scattered shopping bags of explosives so the bags would blow up while the gang members still carried them, before they reached the X-marked places on the map and were left to blow holes in the walls that held back the sea.

There wasn't time to reset the timers before the others returned, so he decided not to try, but he knew they deserved it.

He was their gang king when Larry was not there. They should obey. He imagined them dying, apologizing that they had disobeyed him.

Like George Sanford died. Weeny sat down on a box and imagined himself sticking the knife into George again. "I bet you were enjoying drifting away on pills, George. I bet you didn't know anything was happening. When I stuck you, then you knew something was happening! I hope you know who stuck that knife into you. I hope you broke all your bones falling off that cliff and died slow and painful, thinking about me. If you're still dying, I hope you pick up what I'm thinking. You shouldn't have laughed at me. Nobody should laugh at me."

He imagined George Sanford crushed, regretting that he had laughed. Weeny smiled. "In a week nobody will know there ever was a George Sanford. They'll forget you. They'll know about me, William Weinard! They are all going to be scared of *me*."

In his mind an image of George Sanford laughed. "You did what? Stuck a knife in me? You think fierce thoughts, Maggot. Where are you?"

"Get out of my mind, George, you're dead," Weeny thought with sudden intense hatred. "Go flap around heaven in a bed sheet!"

He thought he heard George laughing somewhere far away, real laughter, like from outside the tunnel near that place on the cliff. Where George had gone over.

What if George was not dead? Weeny leaped to his feet and spun toward the closed door, and as he spun thought he saw George already inside the door, already only ten feet away, but he finished turning, and nobody was there. He stared at the space where he had thought a man would be, seeing the fading image of the hulking shoulders, the big fists, the round, expressionless blue eyes. . . .

"Why so scared?" asked the voice in his mind. "Jolt of scare really woke me up."

It would be reasonable for George to want to kill him,

Weeny knew. George already had owed him a lot of trouble before. That knife wound would cancel any good nature that had kept those big hands from his throat. Dead hands? What was waking up? Weeny realized he had been thinking as a telepath. *Stop thinking.* Can thinking wake the dead? Will your own thoughts get into them and—

"So I'm supposed to kill you, Weeny?"

"*Yes,*" Weeny's imagination screamed. "*You're a zombie. I've got a zombie after me!*" Again he imagined George strangling him. Hastily he grabbed his bag of explosives and yelled, "I'll meet you at the subway, guys," and ran out into the park. Dashing through that blind darkness, Weeny believed in a clear image of George alive, hanging by one hand from a branch at the edge of the cliff. It sustained his courage and gave him imagined time to run to the subway. But as he ran, a hulking shadowy shape of his imagination ran behind him, hands reaching. Weeny arrived at the lights of the slideway entrance, panting and sobbing with terror, and sat cowering on a bench, huddling his bag of explosives between his feet. Gradually the presence of bright lights and strangers began to seem a defense against ghosts.

George's voice sounded reasonable and farther away. "I'm supposed to strangle you. OK. If you think it's right. But, Weeny, how do I get off hanging from this root? How does the zombie climb up along a root to the edge of the cliff and come after you when he has only one good hand and he needs two things to hang on with?"

"*He'll use his teeth,*" Weeny thought, visualizing fangs, biting into the root, the zombie, blood-smeared, going rapidly hand and tooth almost swinging like Tarzan, up to the edge and back to ground, hulking to his feet in the darkness . . . following him . . . finding him at Coney Island alone, and then the big hands closing on his throat. . . .

"What's the matter?" said a voice near him.

Weeny leaped to his feet with a gasp, reaching for his knife. The knife was not in his pocket.

Again for a flash he saw the big form of George Sanford standing there, then his overactive, terrorized imagination let go of the image and he saw only his gang members grouped, looking at him.

"Yeah, what's the matter, Weeny? You're shaking."

Far away, he heard George laughing at him.

"Let's go," he said sullenly. They all chose slide chairs and loaded them with their shopping bags and slid with them out to the traffic lanes, headed downtown.

If George had just used teeth and one hand to climb back up to the edge of the cliff as he imagined him doing, then he'd be way behind. Besides, he couldn't get onto the subway. He didn't have a token. Even if he searched the tunnel rooms he wouldn't find the place under Weeny's sleeping bag where he had hidden his change.

"Try imagining me finding it, so I can follow you and strangle you," said George's voice in his mind. "I'm going in the door."

In a wave of panic, Weeny visualized George easily rolling back Weeny's sleeping bag, finding the change, and using it to get onto a slide chair and follow, a dark expressionless shape, smeared with red streaks of blood. A zombie from a horror movie.

Again he heard the laughing in the distance.

"You keep thinking about me so loud, Weeny, you're pulling me after you. I can't help it. I've got to do what you think. Because I'm kind of. . . ."

Weeny looked frantically from side to side, seeing only slide chairs and oblivious, confident adults sliding along downtown and uptown. His gang looked at him and away and at each other, bothered by his fear. He couldn't tell them about a ghost and voices in his head.

"It's no fun anymore," Nicholi said in a low voice. "I don't want to do it anymore." She suddenly placed her shopping bag in Jack's lap. "I'm getting off at Penn Station. I'm splitting." She unhooked her chair and turned it to slide into the slower grooves, slowing for the stop at midtown.

"Me too," said Jack. "I'm going to spend money and have fun. Tell Larry I quit." He turned his chair and slid away into the slower lanes, falling behind.

"Me too," said Perry and turned.

The gang was dissolved. The great schemes were over.

"Don't go away with the stuff!" Weeny half screamed. He realized he had to get to the Penn Station platform before he passed it and steered his chair from lane to lane in abrupt side slides and jerking slowdowns that forced sudden automatic safety-slowing of chairs in long lines upstream of

218

his crossing. He pulled the chair up to the far end of the Pennsy platform and ran after the cluster of teeners who had been his gang members, in a last effort to exert authority.

"Stop. Give me the bags."

They waited for him, and when he reached them, almost silently they piled the bags at his feet and walked away. As they passed store windows and displays, they began to joke with each other. Nicholi laughed at something Jack said.

Watching them go, Weeny imagined that they were telling jokes against him. "Blow the whole place up," he muttered. "Kill the bastards."

There was enough explosive in the four shopping bags to blow up the area. Weeny remembered a time they had tuned George to an engineer for the nuclear power plant, and he had drawn a map of the water-heat-cooling-fluid interchanges under the area that provided the evaporation heat for the free recycled hot water of the city. It was connected to the safety cooling system of the power plant somewhere and had some weak points.

Trying to remember the map, cursing under his breath as the four heavy bags banged his legs with each step, Weeny lugged the bags of explosives toward the entrances to the undertunnels.

He almost passed the entrance, a sort of giant garage door that was an unobtrusive part of the corridor wall. As George had predicted, the small door was there in the center. A simple combination number opened it, and on the other side Weeny found the place George had predicted, a wide tunnel, tilted downward, lined with pipes, conduits, and valves shuddering with the rumbling sound of water and circulating hot liquids. People on the other side of the walls were using the free hot shower, the free laundry, swimming in the hot swimming pools and relaxing in the sauna. The dirty water was distilled clean and recycled. People using the hot water did not ask where the free heat had come from but it was a by-product of the power production of the city, heat exchanged from the nuclear reactor's cooling system. The distilled water, being pure and without salts, carried no radiation back from the "hot" place it circulated through.

When George was tuned to a power-plant expert, he had

explained this to the gang. Weeny had suggested adding salt to the water and making the whole city radioactive wherever hot water was used. Larry had vetoed the idea and suggested a small charge of explosive to break the pipes and shut down the reactor from overheating when they wanted the city to suddenly lose all its power. He had not said what a large charge would do.

Weeny was prepared to find out. Humming, almost happy, Weeny found the dirty yellow coveralls on the floor near the laundry chute for workmen, where George had predicted them. He put on coveralls to look like a workman to the TV lenses, and humming, he carried the bags to a place where there was a wall of pipes. He was not sure what would happen when all these bombs went off but he planned to be twenty miles out of town and uphill when it happened. Whatever else it did, it would make a disaster that people would remember for years. If he ever found another gang like Larry's, he could join it and boast about being the man who started the New York Disaster of 1999. He was sure he would get admiration from the guys and all the bedmates he wanted from the chicks.

The feeling of George getting closer was still a bad feeling. Weeny whistled and tried harder to think of all the chicks he would get and how he would tell them. . . .

Would he tell them he had been followed by a zombie?

Was it real?

He imagined George out in the corridor, wondering where he had gone. He'd never remember the laundry chute with the yellow coveralls and the small door with the combination lock. George had been completely zonked out on pills when he had told them how to find those things.

"I don't feel wide awake now either," said a voice in his mind with the superior tones he disliked in George. George was not cleverly trying to put him down; George sincerely thought of Weeny as some sort of amusing bug that he might have to step on. "Yellow laundry chute?"

Imagination. . . . Don't freak out, Weeny, or you'll lose your great chance to blow the bastards up. Sucking his lower lip and making crying faces, Weeny started the careful, tedious process of setting all the bomb timers to go off in twenty minutes. He imagined George coming for him,

220

through the little door, down the sloping corridor, still out of sight around the corridor bend, closer and implacable and closer. . . .

"You keep thinking how I'm going to kill you. You keep thinking that it's right. And you're doing something wrong. I oughta make you stop doing it, Weeny. Dark whenever I stop moving. Gotta hurry."

"Shut up," Weeny muttered to the voice in his head and made crying squinty faces while setting the timers, imagining the feel of hands around his throat.

The place he stood in was a cul-de-sac, a side branch, dead end of the corridor, and the deep hum, rumble, and gurgle of the pipes in the wall deafened him to the sound of approaching footsteps. Was George coming?

Was George coming? I, George, bored with being Weeny, I went back to my own body. Vision was dark and blurry suddenly, skin numb. I was in a corridor.

I struggled to put on yellow coveralls and discovered the flat hilt of Weeny's knife projecting from my back, slanting almost under my arm. I pulled it out.

Now I moved the other arm without it hurting and slid it into the sleeve of the coverall. I zipped it up and went down the long slant of the corridor past the roar of washing machines on the other side of the wall and the hiss of showers. Annoying sticky trickles of blood ran down my sleeve and dripped off my fingers. It began to run blood-warm and sticky down my back and into my pants leg. Weeny was ahead of me thinking in bright confused images of anger and power of New York blowing up, and of the corridor blowing up, and of parts of people flying around, in a panic hurry to finish and get away before I caught him.

I stopped at the entrance to the side branch and watched Weeny frantically setting timers and muttering, "Go away, you're dead. Go away."

He looked up and saw me, exactly the monster figure he had imagined, big and expressionless, standing at a slight slant, red hands dangling, bright red blood on the yellow coveralls in streaks, a trail of red footsteps marked in the cement flooring behind me, a cartoon monster.

Weeny tried to make the whole scene unreal by unbelief, but nothing vanished. We were in a widened space. Weeny

221

thought of dodging by on the other side of three large pillars. I partially crouched and moved to the left, leaving red footprints.

Weeny looked for a way to dodge by on the right. Silently laughing, I moved to the right, as he had expected. Directed?

Don't think. Gibbering with terror, Weeny dashed straight down the center toward freedom and tried to dodge at the last moment. My fist caught him on the side of the head.

His moment of panic had been brief. The angular, pimply teener lay in a tangled heap, his pose still expressing terror in outline on the floor, but there were no more thoughts. Weeny's mind was dark inside.

I stepped across the prone body and tried to walk somewhere. Where? Waves of darkness rolled over me, darkening the scene around me. A strong chemical taste was in my mouth like bitter perfume, like those green pills. Why was I here? Where was I?

Was I here to rescue somebody? It was hard to stand up. Without the stimulation of being interested in Weeny's thoughts and fears, the overdose of sedatives was having its effect at last; *failure of breathing reflex, cardiac arrest.* . . . I felt cold and sleepy and wanted to lie down. The floor looked like a bed; a package on the floor looked like a pillow. I bent toward it and it shouted *Danger.* Danger from a package? Packages and shopping bags scattered around the room, leaning against big exposed pipes. I stared at them and they gave out the attached association of Weeny's memory. All the packages were explosives. Some were ticking.

Staggering, I went to an alarm box, broke the glass with my fist, and pulled the lever.

At a monitor watch station, floors above, an alarm bell began to ring with frenzied insistence. Two maintenance engineers looked up from a game. Screen 22 was blinking a red light. On screen they saw a workman in the standard yellow coveralls pulling the lever. Watching, they saw him fall.

9

THE rescue wagon floated up to the emergency gate at the hospital and slid out a rescue victim in a life-support stretcher. They took on a replacement life-support-system stretcher and went off on another call. The victim was brought into the resuscitation room with the balloon expansion vest forcing air out of the chest, the gas mask forcing air into the mouth, and an electric pacemaker forcing the heart to beat. The hospital technicians bandaged a bleeding wound, started a blood transfusion, took blood samples for analysis of the poison, and momentarily turned off the apparatus. No breathing, no heartbeat; they turned it back on and hooked in a blood pump and artificial kidney that circulated the blood briskly through the body and warmed and cleaned it as it went through the apparatus, removing strange salts of sedatives and replacing the normal salt, sugar, hormone, water balance. The stretcher, body, and equipment were rolled into a barrel-shaped container that pressured the breathing more deeply with sharp changes of air pressure in the barrel, and the entire barrel began a rocking and tilting that was intended to encourage circulation and would have made a conscious man acutely seasick.

When the heart started beating by itself, they took him out of the emergency equipment, subjected him to a stomach pump and flush, and put the semiconscious but healthy patient in a regular hospital bed.

A nurse changed the bandage on my back and a nurse's aide started scrubbing me.

"What's this for?" the nurse's aide asked brightly, not expecting much answer. I had been only partially awake when she started. Peroxide foamed in the warm sponge, getting off the long red-brown stripes of dried blood and leaving clean, tan skin.

"Over please." She nudged me. I rolled from my stomach

to my back and lay staring at the ceiling as she scrubbed at my legs.

"What's this for?" she asked again. "Can I take it off?"

I propped myself up on both elbows and looked. A quarter was taped to my thigh. I grinned. "Sure, kiddo, take it off."

"What's it for?"

I remembered the guru telling me that I would need a quarter to save my life. In a dim flickering of scrambled memory I remembered a miserable week in a cage that the quarter could have freed me from, and a time I wanted to die.

"A man gave it to me to keep me out of trouble. He was a guru. He could see the future, I think. Said it would save my life."

Briskly the pretty nurse's aide pulled at the tape, bringing off tape, quarter, and some of my leg hair. She sponged with her peroxide sponge, getting off some dried blood and leaving it clean and disinfected. "That's interesting. Did it work?"

I leaned back in the clean hospital bed and looked at the ceiling. I did not laugh. "No. I'm dead." Then I did laugh. "When he gave it to me he told me to forget I had it!"

A phone call to a hospital was taped and relayed to police Rescue Squad. They heard a voice that was muffled through cloth and rattled by foil, someone who was a fugitive, afraid of the voice-detector alarms the police had fastened to the phone switchboards. The voice said, "*A wanted man will be found unconscious in Van Cortlandt Park, at the foot of East Cliff between the stairs and sidewalk. If you delay he will die.*"

Muffled though it was, the high pitch of a child and the very intelligent precise use of words identified Larry Rubashov. Rescue Squad phoned Ahmed, waking him up, and he listened to the tape of the call. A police voice followed the tape and informed him that a police copter had cruised the cliff area with an infrascanner looking for warm bodies of human temperature and had registered nothing larger than squirrels and returned. They had decided the call was another trick by Larry.

224

Ahmed hung up the phone and thought. Larry had liked to talk to George. He would want him to live. Barbiturate coma is cold. If George had opposed the gang they might use sleeping pills to delay his action.

Ahmed took a police copter into the sky and, still partially awake, groped his way into the dark areas that a hand torch could not penetrate, scrabbling blindly up to his shoulders in a tangled, hazardous pile of fallen tree branches and growing vines. Dirt trickled down from the cliff above and pattered on his hair, proving something had fallen.

He bent to investigate a large smooth object, hit his face on a branch, felt a large smooth boulder under his hands, dropped his flashlight into a tangle of branches, and as he reached for it, his wrist radio started buzzing against his wrist.

With great difficulty he got his wrist to his ear without driving twigs into his eyes.

"Ahmed Kosvakatats," he muttered, acknowledging the call.

"Report from hospital admissions," said an impersonal voice cheerfully. "The general Statistics Computer hung up two hours on a double ID. It read out two names and histories on a DOA admitted to emergency at 165th Street General with Sanford's fingerprints. No pulse. He's in resuscitation."

A few frantic minutes later Ahmed brought the police copter in for a rough landing on the hospital roof landing platform. He asked directions of floor nurses, endured their surprise at his torn and dirty clothes, and arrived at the door of my hospital room.

I was inside, sitting up in bed, energetic, flushed, and healthy, holding hands with a pretty nurse, fussed over by two pretty nurse's aides and a girl medical student, asking them earnestly what they thought about right and wrong, and why it was important to figure it out, and telling them my adventures.

The nurses were between me and the door, blocking my view, but I gradually became aware of someone with a memory of frantic searching and a great fear, a male, feeling prickly, itchy, and tired, someone close by whose vibes of fear were changing to a warm flush of relief and

225

anger. Unseen and listening, Ahmed stood in the doorway and scowled, letting me finish my story, letting a nurse finish a sincere and stammering assurance to me that I had been a good person and no one blamed good people for trying to do what was right.

A girl kissed me on the forehead. Another patted my hand. I caught sight of Ahmed in a reflecting aluminum tray. Ahmed is usually a handsome fellow, but as the girls smiled at me, his scowl became something special. His smooth straight face darkened with a red flush; his mouth went out of sight behind thick black eyebrows and his mouth tightened to a white line.

The group of girls gradually caught sight of this un-friendly-looking visitor and turned to stare, and a girl stepped out of my line of sight.

"Uh, hello, Ahmed," I said uncertainly.

"Consider yourself rescued," Ahmed barked. He pulled a mess of folded paper out of his pocket and sorted out an official form.

"Sign here!" He handed the paper over. The girls passed it to me.

"Why rescued?" I took the paper and glanced around for a pen.

"I want you classified as rescued so you won't be classified as under arrest, you fool." Ahmed thrust a pen past a second nurse to me. "You have to be classified as *something*, you meathead, or you'll be wiped."

Meekly I signed.

Ahmed took the papers back. "You are now officially in protective custody as a material witness against Larry's Raiders and Larry Rubashov, who supposedly kidnapped you," he snapped. "Don't talk to members of the Police Department. If they try to arrest you, say you are already in custody and not allowed visitors and show them this." He tore off a carbon copy from behind the signed copy of the form and handed it to me. "Don't lose it, don't eat it, and don't wipe yourself with it. Just keep it!"

He stalked out. The hospital door whooshed vigorously, resisting his pull. If a hospital door could have slammed, its closing would have shaken the hospital.

"What was he mad at?" asked a pretty nurse's aide.

226

"I'd hate to tell you," I said, staring after him. "Sheesh, was he mad!"

The nurses had left and turned out the light, and I tried to sleep. The sun had not risen yet. I lay awake trying to remember where I had lost weight and what had happened in a whole week. I remembered the bars of the subway entrance like a cage, and the door that would not turn to let me out, because it was only an entrance door and turned only for a quarter.

I remembered that Larry had not given me a quarter. "Our vows have run out, George. Your time has run out. You're not a gang member anymore; you're just a strange cop stuck in there. We don't know you unless you join the gang."

There had been no food or water for days. On the other side of the bars Nicholi came into her bedroom at my end of the tunnel and undressed to get into her sleeping bag. She was little and cute with curly black hair, and before she left home her idea of fun had been to get her parents yelling and fighting each other. She liked excitement. She undressed slowly and did a dance of sex at me. She had a cute bouncy figure.

"Roar, George, roar. You're a tiger in a cage."

"Cut it out," I said.

The telephone rang loudly in my ear. I was in the hospital bed and Nicholi was probably already arrested, and Weeny had been arrested and brought to computer trial with evidence and lie detectors. The sun was still out of sight in the sky, but the sky was turning a pale, washed-out gray. The phone was still ringing. It was a pillow speaker; the ringing was under my ear. I reached out to the bedstand and got the blinking red light and brought the receiver to my ear. "Hello?"

Ahmed's voice barked. "What's the idea answering the phone? I told you not to speak to anybody. Where is Larry? Right now!"

"I—" I shut my eyes and pushed my hand against the side of my head, trying to remember the kid's voice, his eyes.... "Wait a minute. I'm trying to tune to him. Wait a minute. He's in a closed room, very safe, teaching his mother to talk.

227

I'm getting his feelings. That's crazy. I can't be getting it right."

"Try tuning again, George. It's important. Larry might be blowing up the city."

"He's very loving and crazy, Ahmed. I don't understand him. He thinks in strange fast pictures. His mother and father were both computer engineers. They tried to program him instead of talk to him and cracked him up."

"Tune to him, George. Talk to me about the philosophy you learned from him."

I opened my eyes and sat up straighter in the hospital bed. Two tough weeks in the kid gang would not be wasted if Ahmed really wanted to know Larry's ideas. I tried to pull it together.

"Larry thinks techs and computer people and research men are mostly autistics. It's put a drift to what they invent and how they build it. They're building their kind of world for their kind of people, not us. Autism is a kids' disease. Autistic kids feel deserted in a world of strange animals. They are afraid of people moving fast, laughing, or talking too loud around them. They sit quietly in one spot, play with construction sets, draw symbol pictures and invent codes, and talk to imaginary companions. The ones who aren't strange enough to be put separate from people grow up loners, live in places like monastaries, talk to imaginary companions, like saints, spirits, demons, gods, mumble chants and recite magic formulas, keep from being laughed at by persuading sane people that the magic is real, the spirits exist. Science gave autistics a job with a payoff—formulas and chants that work. They built technology for themselves. No stress, no fast action, no laughter. They got hold of the educational system, train kids to sit still and work symbols, not speak to each other, like autistics. No jobs left for healthy people now. You have to work with machines, sit quietly at a desk, don't talk with anyone except through a phone, talk with machines, go home alone, like an autistic, like them. Sit alone or with people, don't talk, turn on a machine, watch imaginary people. Join an anachron commune, live in an imaginary world. Crazy!"

"But that's civilization," Ahmed said. "I don't have to fight civilization, do I? Nobody needs to be rescued?"

"Nobody, everybody," I muttered.

"He didn't say the Objectivist Technocrat Party has a special plan to wipe out all us subhumans this week, did he?"

"No."

"Then there is no violent illegal plot to justify his countering with violent sabotage. If the autistics have sold us a mess of potage by making us lazy, it's our own business if we are suckers."

His tone sharpened. "What were Larry's plans?"

I was drifting into a mood of Larry's. He was trying to teach an unfeeling gagged person to talk, to feel, to understand feelings. "He didn't say what he was going to do, Ahmed. He said disasters are good; they shake people out of their grooves. People only die if they're dead already, too stiffened up to run. He's teaching someone poetry. I don't know where."

"I think I understand him better than you do, George. My bet is, he's planning to attack the central computer. I just told the Criminal Detection unit that guess. I made them believe I had inside information. Could he get into that building again?"

"Yes." A memory sprang clear. Me, drawing building plans with wiring for Larry and his gang. "Yes. He can get in."

"What is he planning to do?"

This time it was easy to tune in to Larry. I picked up that warm comfortable feeling. "He's in there already. You're right. He thinks it knows everything and can help him, like it's a person. The same way he felt about me. He thinks the techs have deliberately blocked it from talking like a person, so that they can talk to it in their crazy abstract language that has no emotions. He's cross-connecting its literary and translation services to its social science banks and he's asking it to explain in terms of evolution why he hates society and what he really wants and answer in poetry!"

"I'd expect it to blow! Is Larry armed? Does he have a gun?"

"He has a gun. And he can get the building to fight for him, Ahmed." Briefly I tuned to the mind of the designers of the building's safety systems to refresh my memory of what I had told Larry, and then explained to Ahmed that the building had safety doors and steel shutters against riots and bombs and citywide fires and internal doors and fire foam against inside fires. Ahmed questioned and I told him how to get past the defenses.

"Hold." Ahmed talked to one side and then came back on the phone. "They tried to get in to see if Larry was in there. The steel shutters closed over the windows and doors, and a team caught inside almost drowned in fire foam. They're trapped between two doors, breathing from an air hose the Rescue Squad slipped them through a water pipe."

"Cheers for Rescue Squad." I yawned. The sun was coming up and I had spent last night running around with a knife in me instead of sleeping. Ahmed's voice on the phone said, "Now they want me to try. They think I know how."

"You do." I yawned. "Go in sopping wet and cold and the sensors won't spray you with fire foam and drop fire doors around you. Larry reset the thermostat on the fire system is all."

"Right on." Ahmed hung up.

I turned the television on and napped. I half heard the announcer excitedly yapping about the police efforts and torchers trying to get into the main computer building. Gigantic crowds watched, applauding each try. I fell asleep into silence and woke sleepily at eight and saw a replay on the morning news of Ahmed emerging from the computer building with Larry at his side. The kid seemed smaller than usual and totally enraged, berating Ahmed in a shrill voice on a point of logic.

Ahmed took one of the waving arms and handcuffed it to his wrist. They stopped in full view of the camera and yelled at each other face to face, like two brothers arguing. Their voices were drowned by the crowd roaring enthusiasm and the excited explanations of the television commentator. The police surrounded the two and cut them off from view.

I turned off the TV and caught up on my sleep.

The vibes I picked up from the four million viewers of New York were so happy and entertained at the nine and ten A.M. news that I half woke, turned to a news channel, and left the TV on.

The social science computer, whose decisions guided
230

government and business, had ceased to answer in dull expressionless capitals resembling telegrams and printed its replies in normal print in witty, literate English, illustrating its meaning with jokes and proverbs, sometimes explaining the reason for a question in terms of human evolution from the ape, sometimes illustrating points with poetry in the style of Larry Rubashov. The announcer read some proverbs.

The computer programmers explained that this program could not be removed from the machine because it was a hookup of different fields to solve a specific question or problem concerned with human survival, a problem given it by Larry Rubashov. All its concern with human instinct and communication was on the order of subtotals to its problem. A problem could not be removed from the machine until solved. After that explanation the announcer came back on and read some particularly witty remarks from the computer about computer programmers, tracing their motives to job security and a desire to be mysterious.

The vibes of the New York listeners were scared but entertained.

The announcer said something dull. "The computerized swift processes of justice. . . ." I turned over, not listening. "Larry Rubashov has been declared guilty of extreme maladaptive behavior and sociopathological orientation and has been scheduled for the electroneural feedback treatment for personality correction popularly called 'wipe.' His attorney has filed no appeal for review by jury trial. This brilliant but warped genius—" I reached over and turned it off, remembering Larry. Some of the forgotten week came back to memory.

I half remembered and half dreamed that I was in the subway cage. I was hungry and thirsty and trying to work off the feeling of being trapped by practicing gymnastics on the iron bars that held me in.

Larry came into Nicholi's room and looked around. He drank from a bottle of Coke in one hand and looked at me. "How are you holding out, George?"

"Fine. I'm bored." I chinned myself. It was easier, because I weighed less. My hands shook in the same way they had when I was unemployed and broke and fat and

231

hungry. Being shaky had not been any big loss. I'd survived healthy.

Larry was trying to needle me into giving up. He took a theatrical swallow from the Coke bottle. "Do you think a lot about water? And Coke? And orange juice? Does your mouth taste it suddenly when you're trying to think of something else?"

"You've been there," I said, recognizing the accuracy of experience. Larry stared, caught in some ultimate fear. I caught a flash image of a small kid locked in a room without water. Horror in the kid's belief that they might never bring water unless he obeyed. Horror in the kid's belief that obedience was another kind of death. Only machines obeyed. Choose between two deaths.

"You must have had something weird for parents," I said.

The panic screamed and was hidden as Larry narrowed his eyes. "I can hold out against them," said the kid. "And I can hold out against you. Everybody tries to stop me. You're trying to stop me by being a good guy. But I'm still thinking. They haven't stopped me from thinking. You can't stop me either."

I was dreaming a memory, but suddenly there was a white flash. Lightning struck the kid. His shape turned white and blank like a light bulb. It said in a whisper, "*I can't obey. If I did exactly what you want, Mummydaddy, it wouldn't be me. You'd never get to know me.*" It was a whisper that was worse than a scream for help. There was a white flash in my mind. Larry vanished and had never been.

I awoke, holding very still, myself in danger too. Lightning waited to strike again.

I groped in my mind for what had happened, but could find nothing wrong, only a strange peaceful blankness in the area that had flashed. Something I wanted to know about life had been almost answered this week, and now I could not remember the question. The flash had done something to me. I could not explain the question I had been looking for in joining Larry's gang.

Larry had been wiped, and with him had gone all the questions I had given to him to answer.

I groped for Larry, reaching out across the city with ESP, and instead touched the lost peaceful blankness. Wipe was

232

usually rigged to remove all memory of authority connected with fear and hatred, all memories of punishments, all resolves for revenge. Larry's parents had tried to condition him since he was a baby. He'd had every free action of his life conditioned by fear, fear of punishment, fear of an imaginary authority. It had all burned. The treatment had removed his entire memory. The person that had been Larry Rubashov, poet, historian, and juvenile lunatic, had ceased to exist, leaving only a blank, living, fifteen-year-old body without a memory of self.

I got to my feet. There was still a directional feeling about the flash. Although I had been asleep, the fading echoes of it in my mind seemed to be close. What hospital was I in?

My room was empty. The bed graph stopped registering pulse, temperature, electrocardiograph, and electroencephalograph, and the wavery lines on the graphs changed to straight lines, but it would not signal to the central services that the patient was dead, because the weight register under the bedframe registered that I had taken my weight out of the bed. Trips to the bathroom were usual.

How do they tell if you are really in the bathroom—a weight meter on the toilet? I took a small square chest from beside the bed and put it on the toilet to register weight like a person.

I found my clothes on a hook in a narrow closet. They had been sticky with blood, but now they were clean and dry. I got dressed, hurrying to get to the source of that white flash, that death flash, and make the bureaucrats take it back, undo it somehow, put humpty-dumpty back together, give Larry back his brains and ask him again what he wanted, because there was something he wanted out of life that we should all want, something that life should have.

With hunch guiding me, I cut through back corridors, picked up a white coat in a closet, mumbled the right things to be mistaken for a doctor, and got from the wing I was in to the police psychiatric eighteenth floor. The elevator slowed, and flashed red letters: CRIMINAL JUSTICE POLICE PSYCHIATRIC.

I stepped out. There was a crowd of people in the hall. My mindfeelers were out, looking for Larry's vibes, ready for danger, and somehow each person registered separate-

233

ly; I knew who each one was and what he did, and I dismissed them from my mind, for none of them was Larry.

I stopped moving and rechecked the impression. *Had I really understood them all?* How much skill had I learned, fogged out on pills, trying to do impossible things hypnotized under Larry's commands? ESP is mostly an animal thing, and I'd only been an empath, picking up people's feelings, the same kind of feeling an animal picks up when he wants to know if you're a friend or enemy.

While I'd been hypnotized with Larry urging and coaxing, I'd learned to tune in on a professional's knowledge, tuning to pride of skill, pleasure at doing a good job, worry at having done a bad job. With it came all the expert knowledge, their memories like my own memories; I could borrow their education and be an expert in anything.

There were two detectives there and a police guard in uniform. *Satisfaction at a job completed and a criminal punished, wonder about the next assignment.* And hooked to it like a book half open was everything they knew about the cases they had been on. There was a psychiatric neurologist and a technician who had just set the dials and pulled the switch. *He peaked too fast. No time to back off the power.* They were all crowded into the hall looking after a stretcher being rolled into the down elevator. The door hissed shut and the kid on the stretcher was gone.

Beside me a lawyer said, "He had his thumb in his mouth!" *Did I do a good job? Did I protect his rights?* His mind reviewed the case at high speed. I learned some law. It had been a total wipe. Very unusual. The kid on the stretcher had been Larry; he wasn't Larry Rubashov anymore. They would educate him again and give him a different name. Was Larry Rubashov legally dead? *Does loss of identity constitute capital punishment?* worried the lawyer. *If so, did I properly protect my client against possible execution?*

Still looking blankly after the closed door, the guard put out a hand absently to me. "Pass, please."

I fumbled around in my pockets, got out the pass I'd used to visit the wing last month. It was folded and looked old.

The guard read it, puzzled. "This one is from last month. Where's today's, Doctor?" He took another look at the pass. "Ahm, Mr. Sanford."

234

"Sanford?" One of the detectives turned and looked at me with a jolt of alertness and a picture of photographs on the wanted list dancing before his eyes like sugarplums. "George Sanford?"

Ahmed had told me to stay in bed till he got me off the wanted list. I had not stayed in bed long enough. I'd gotten up too soon. I was still a wanted criminal.

They were very clever, very quick with their routine. I was arrested in quiet tones, they got a printout of all the evidence and fingerprints from the Larry's Raiders case, and they asked me if I minded telling my version of how it all happened while sitting in a lie-detector rig.

I sat in the lie-detector chair and told them my version of how it all happened. The lawyer asked to be my lawyer and toward the end of the story he asked me to go into more detail about why I had followed Weeny and stopped his bombs from blowing up the water system, but I had to explain that I was too zonked out on pills to know what I was doing or why. He looked disappointed. I didn't explain that I had suicided. That was personal.

The detectives had been making notes. They went back over every minor raid I'd gone on in exchange for arguing with Larry, and they asked what I had done. They went over every time I'd been asked how to get into places and asked what I had said. They took a tape of my answers and nodded a lot and smiled.

The psychiatric neurologist came back in and said, "Recommend clemency on grounds of curable antisocial neuropathology, if treatment is accepted." He left.

"Imprisonment or rehab?" asked my lawyer. "Take your pick. You've rung up a score of about a year's worth of prison. Rehab—you take your chances on losing a small or a large chunk of memory and forgetting who you're mad at, but if you can walk when it's over, you can walk right out."

"Rehab," I said. "I'm not mad at anybody." Why do people want to lock people in cages?

"Then we part ways; next you get a counselor, a legal adviser with the psychiatric side. Good luck," said my lawyer and meant it. *Most of them aren't hurt by it. It's better to be free,* he thought, and the thought carried through to me

235

on a wave of professional pride and concern for his clients, a strong feeling with good vibes.

I was led into a room by guards in white coats and sat on an old oak armchair before an oak desk. Behind the desk a fatherly-looking man in white hair with a trimmed white beard made a steeple of his hands and tapped his fingertips together and secretly gloated with feelings of power suitable to Hitler.

"George Sanford, you have some other things on your record that indicate some variation from the norm of the average healthy personality. This latest set of doubtful actions and possible responsibility for the criminal actions of others, others whom you did not stop, has added discredit points to your record and made the cumulative points of borderline antisocial actions well over twenty points. This makes you liable for personality correction. Bearing this consideration in mind, do you wish to alter your recent testimony or confession in any way?" He looked at me sadly over the steepled, praying hands, inwardly laughing.

He reminded me of what Ahmed had told me about sadists as personnel in mental hospitals. How can people like that get into places without being recognized?

"Do you mean, do I want to change what I told you people about working with Larry?"

"Approximately, yes." He cut out the praying pose and clasped his hands tightly together on the desk.

"No. I don't think I want to change it. May I hear what I said?"

He replayed the tape. It was only the questions about the raids I had helped.

"OK," I said. "That's what I did. I tried to tell Larry it was wrong, but he could always talk up a good argument. The tape's right."

"Will you sign this typewritten transcript of your tape, please?"

"What does it say?"

"It only says exactly what you said on the tape. Will you sign here, please?"

"OK." I signed.

He rang a bell. White-jacketed men came in and put me

into a white jacket with long trailing sleeves and wrapped the sleeves twice around my middle and tied the ends, leaving my arms wrapped in a loose but motionless folded position across my chest.

"What's this?"

"A straitjacket."

Six of them escorted me into the little white padded room and sat me down in a chair like an electric chair. No use fighting six.

I usually feel lucky but I usually stay out of trouble and don't fight the system. I was alert for a way out of this. I looked into their minds for when prisoners had escaped or when procedures had been called off. How?

They had no answer. They could not remember prisoners escaping or wipes being called off. They were convinced that what they were doing was good. They believed that after wipe and rehab, with parts of his personality missing, the freed prisoner would live a better and happier life.

They fastened some wires to the back of my neck. I began to get mad at being handled like an object. But I remembered that the purpose of the rough procedure was to get you hating authority. Whatever you were hot about, whatever you concentrated on with any feeling, the wires were going to wipe out with an overload of a white blast like sex or pain or a fuse blowing. If I let them get me mad they would wipe out my ability to get mad at the system. I would smile when people were pushed around by rules.

The straitjacket and straps seemed loose and comfortable, but I could not move. A doctor was taking a pulse from my neck artery. "Weight two hundred?" He set a hypo to a marker and injected the whole thing into my neck. The injection took hold with a tight feeling of all my muscles and a tight feeling in my chest and a feeling of fear that was chemical and not the way I usually felt.

The doctor stood back. We locked eyes and I tried to hook into him, to make him feel what I felt. It usually worked in an emergency. Teachers had filled out forms for me all my childhood. The Aztec priest had stopped the execution. If he recognized that he felt the way I felt, he would be afraid the wipe would also wipe him, and he'd sabotage it. But I couldn't tune to him. He was off on some line of thought and feeling that I couldn't locate and couldn't understand.

The doctor stared back into my face, trying to read it, as I was trying to read him. We both failed. Maybe he wondered why I didn't say anything.

Nothing I said would get me out.

The doctor and attendants went out and the door shut behind them with a soft deep thud, the sound of soundproofing. In the room it was very quiet and padded and I sat comfortably, unable to move, with wires fastened to my forehead and the back of my neck.

Did everyone always want to imprison others and gloat? I remembered the feeling of power and maturity Weeny had felt seeing me in the cage and himself free. Weeny had a lousy personality, but he was kind of basic and human in a lousy way. He was not strange, just mean and nasty and human. (Dig power, the feeling of power and control over others, the pleasure of POWER, the pleasure of being free. A tingle in my forehead and a white flash in my thought amplifying—ELECTRICITY.)

Electricity. Defend thyself, George. Defend against evil by understanding it. That was what the guru had advised. I have to grok the bastards and forgive them or die the way Larry had died. The doctor! I had resented the doctor. (Shock.) UNDERSTAND the doctor fast. I groped for him, found him in a room with the technician monitoring a set of dials. I became the doctor, looked out through his eyes.

The technician had his back turned. The room was painted light gray. The dials were set in a slanted console face with readout screens showing wavy lines of pulse and big red areas with large printed warnings and instructions under each dial. An idiot-proof console. I tried to read the warnings through the doctor's eyes.

The doctor realized that he was staring at the dials as if he had never seen them before. He tried to pull himself together. (Shock.) TRY to be self-doctor-self. His effort added to mine. (Shock.) DOCtor.

The technician said, not turning, "He's not into feedback yet. Input spike damps fast. Pulse steady at eight five. It's not contacting his neurosis. Maybe we didn't get him mad
238

enough, Doc. When we went out he was smiling. Maybe you should go in and make faces."

"Up the amps," the doctor said, angry at the technician. Electricity surged into my brain, ran along the channels of my attention and, strangely, it hit into the doctor's irritation at the technician and turned that irritation into hidden rage. The doctor's thoughts were burning now. "I'll tell you when to stop. Up slowly."

The technician advanced the dial slowly into the red striped area toward the solid red of danger. "Pulse ninety and steady. No feedback on the input; it still damps with one echo."

"But I'll bet he's not smiling," said the doctor and stoically endured the way the electricity coming through me amplified his pleasure into a painful blaze of FORCE POWER CONTROL PLEASURE REVENGE. He was used to hiding rages. The technician's voice snapped him out of it.

"He's in good shape; he's taking a lot," the technician said. "Breathing steady, pulse slowing again, eighty-nine, eighty-five, and leveling."

"Keep sliding it up until his pulse goes over a hundred." That was too much and he knew it.

"Why an overdose?" I asked in his mind. The electric boosting made my curiosity spread into his mind. He had to answer to satisfy his own question.

He answered, "Mild boosting is not designed to work unless there is obsessive feedback in the personality. Those quiet smiling types, like that big patient in there with the steady pulse, they don't have the circling hostility of the usual run of criminals. He'd go out smiling the way he came in if I don't . . . don't. . . ." He stopped nervously, wondering if the technician had really asked.

The boosting was forcing him to be interested, but he felt the shocks and was puzzled. It was a strange double sensation, being the doctor and being me.

The technician said, "You don't think that guy is sick or even a criminal type, is that what you mean?" He turned his head briefly for an unsmiling glance at the doctor's expression. "So you're giving him an overdose, right? So you'll look good, like you can get a big effect on every patient. Come in sick, leave well, come in well, leave sick! Big

239

doctor." He continued to inch the electric power dial up into the red.

"I'll get you fired," the doctor said in a strangled voice, holding back an impulse to get the man tangled in his wires and electrocuted.

"I'm obeying orders, Doc. I'm turning up the amps," the technician said. "You have no complaints about my job performance. Take up your complaints about free speech with the union."

The doctor decided to use the rules against him. Maybe get him wiped.

Wow, badness. Grok evil, George. How many people in places where people are restrained and forced are the bad kind who secretly enjoy making it worse? I remembered the "counselor," remembered secret laughter, remembered well, heard his fatherly voice, tuned in to him, and he began to burn. (Shock.) LAUGH. Burn. I scanned my mind around, tuned in their thought. "Power over Others is Revenge." The more, the better. Electricity was running shivers and trembles through my muscles. Send it out, send it through. Send it to others. Don't be me getting shocked; be them getting shocked.

Most of the ones I touched and tuned to began to blaze in positive feeds at mounting circles of pain-pleasure, hatred-power-pain. Very neurotic inflammable minds, many, I didn't count how many. Many blazing circling thoughts that were people. The next short eternity was very bad, like falling into the sun in the company of demons. I rode with it, being not me. Grok evil, George. If many people hold hands and one is given a shock, it is not diluted; all feel it equally and the heart-weak die.

The web of linked chains of similar minds with similar guilty thoughts flared to brightness and went out, like a chain of Christmas tree bulbs burning out from overload.

Silence. I was sitting, eyes closed and comfortable, in a quiet room.

Somewhere on a mountain it was cool and slightly foggy with the sun still in the east. The sea to the west was dark blue and cool-looking. A number of people were doing gardening chores and building a small house among some huts. They stopped working suddenly. I heard a voice very clearly from one with a hoe. "What was that?"

"Some kind of flash. Felt like an overload."

"But it was directed, controlled. Someone is using power."

"Suspend thought, everybody, and trace it."

"It feels like that man with the controller talent."

"Suspend thought."

They sat down on the ground in meditation postures and shut their eyes.

I lost sight of them. The eyes I was seeing through had closed. Someone else's eyes!

I opened my own eyes and tried to get up. I was in a little room, a little white room, and I was fastened to a chair. Wires dangled from my forehead, and a wire on the back of my neck gave a slight shock, but the shock felt quiet. Nothing for it to amplify, no thoughts.

I scanned my mind around. Everyone I'd been hooked into was missing, and it was quiet across the hall in the other room, where the technician sat staring blankly at the dials, slightly wiped, a little bad spot in his head burned out, slightly forgetting his job. Behind him the doctor was face down on the floor. Nobody else was conscious on this floor.

I (shock) wanted the technician to turn off the electricity.

I was stuck in this chair with the electricity turned up too high. I twisted my head, trying to knock the electrodes off on the back of the chair.

The voices began again, loud. The voices were familiar. The voices I usually heard in hallucinations. "Got it. It's George with the mind-control talent. He has just wiped a bunch of nit-picking bureaucrats by hooking into the nit-picker's sadism and pouring in feedback."

"Catch him when he's happy about it; maybe we can get a yes out of him this time."

(Shock.) That warning tingle at neck and forehead, the little white flash through my thoughts. Nobody else to lay it on now. Don't waste time listening to dream voices. (Shock.) Get out of here before the electricity turns on me and wipes me. In the next room across the hall the technician in charge of turning off the apparatus was sitting in his chair, staring at the control board, trying to put his understanding of it back together. I twisted my head, trying to scrape the electrodes off on the back of the chair.

Suddenly I reached through the mind of the technician

241

and moved his hand up to the right dial. It was a strange action that felt as if I were doing something childish and forbidden that I had not done in a long time.

"He's doing it. It's him and he's wide awake."

"George Sanford," said a voice in my head. "The controller. We've found you. See, it is good to control people. (Shock.) You are controlling someone for an honest need of some kind."

The voice said (shock), "I'm receiving an odd impression of electricity and danger. Where are you?" (Shock.)

I had the technician's hand up to the right dial and I commanded the hand to turn off the power. The hand twitched, but there was no habit left for that dial, a white blank; a burned-out white hole was where the knowledge had been. The dial was set into red. The technician knew that it meant danger, be careful, but the red area had been charged in his mind as a sinful weapon used against people, helpless people. Somehow his worry and guilt, a small unimportant part of him hidden by his professional pride, had nevertheless been caught in the backwash of the flare that burned out the doctor's concealed delights. The technician stared at the dials, trying to pull his scattered knowledge together into expert understanding.

The dream voices had started the usual dream argument. The shocks were tickling it up to a separate bright thread of my own voice talking in my head, arguing with them. (Shock.) The shocks began to bring out childish thoughts. BAD to control people. (Shock.) Controlled people drop the milk. The shocks hit the jackpot. Something caught fire. (SHOCK.) IT WAS ONLY PLAY. I DIDN'T MEAN TO KILL ANYONE. SILVER PLANE CRASHING. (SHOCK.) I COMMANDED I COMMANDED.

A five-year-old boy played airplane, buzzing and swooping with outstretched arms through an unfamiliar yard. His parents were inside the stranger's house. They had not brought his toy silver airplane for him to play with.

The child stopped buzzing and looked at a silver plane circling high in the sky. His mother had begged and coaxed him to stop telling people what to do. But she wanted him to play and be happy while they were inside. He would be happy if he had a silver plane to hold.

"Airplame," he said in his high, childish voice. "Airplame

come down." Then he ran and buzzed, imagining working the controls of the plane with his hands and feet, feeling real and grown up like the pilot. "The yard is *too small* for a landing field," said the real pilot up there, so the boy made believe it was big, saw it was big, like a landing field in a movie with the plane landing. The sound of the plane grew louder. "Airplame come down. Land here . . . here. . . ."

It was growing; it grew big, very big, too big, and still it grew. I held my hands out to push it away. Huge silver wings passed over me roaring, and there was a thundering screech and ripping sounds like a car accident. I felt my parents in the house were startled, then their warm thoughts suddenly went into silence, forever.

I ran toward the house, saw a sidewall tilt slowly outward and rain bricks; a tub tumbled slowly through the air, bending its pipes, and hit the yard. The ground thudded.

I stopped running and stood still. Not safe to run, not safe to do things. I made it happen. I could make it worse.

Sirens. People, shouts.

Big people bending down, big faces close. "What's your name, little boy?" "Did you live in that house?" "Where are your parents?"

"My parents were visiting. I don't live there. I have no name. Let me alone. I didn't do it. I'm not me."

"Of course you didn't do it. What's your name?"

I'm not me.

"What's your name?"

I'll never tell. I have no name.

Full name, please, last name first, middle initial. Years of forms to fill out.

Why do they keep asking? Why can't I answer?

(Shock.) SILVER WINGS BRIGHT AIRPLANE COME DOWN BRIGHT BRIGHT GONE, BRIGHT GONE NOTHING. Gone, nothing. I can answer. Who are you?

My name is Ralph George Ericson. My father's name is Ralphy and my mother calls me little George. I live at 1257 Altona Boulevard. That was before five. After five I lived in orphanages and foster homes in New York City. They called me George Sanford because I wouldn't tell them what my name was. I made them fill out the forms and write it down for me. But I never asked anybody to do anything else. I did what they wanted.

When I was five I could command people. order them around silently. I guess I still can.

Why haven't I been doing it all along? Some reason half forgotten. A silver airplane.

I tried to remember but the silver airplane buzzed in the sky of memory and nothing else happened. The memory was gone. I was sitting in the Criminal Justice wing of the hospital in a small room with a straitjacket holding my arms and a brainwipe rig fastened to my head and the electricity left turned on by mistake.

I reached my mind out to the corridor. Nobody conscious.

In the room across the hall the technician was kneeling by the doctor on the floor, taking his pulse. I commanded him and he came in and took the electrodes off my head and untied me from the straitjacket.

I stood up and stretched.

"You'll forget this," I told him.

He nodded.

Ahmed found me an hour later. I was asleep in my hospital bed, wearing my hospital nightgown. My clothes were hung back in the closet.

Ahmed shook my shoulder, talking almost hysterically.

"The mysterious attack of epilepsy makes circles around the wipe wing of Presbyterian. It hit when they were pulling the switch on you and it got the kind of bureaucrat you most dislike, the ones you'd blame for your troubles. You never liked pen pushers and people who asked you to fill out forms. Their symptoms resemble an overdose of wipe, electroshock therapy old style. I've only seen you get mad a few times in your life, George, but you did get violent. What do you have to say?"

"Say," I mumbled. "Say about what?"

"What makes you think you can get away with zapping all those people?"

I rolled over and opened gummy eyes. There was a bad taste in my mouth. I'd been enjoying deep quiet sleep with no coaxing voices from California and no nightmares from the past, just very warm good dreams, girls, love, leading armies. I pulled back to reality reluctantly. "Who knows I did anything?"

"The statistics computer. It ran the correlations and got a nice little correlation between the mysterious epilepsy attack and your punishment."

I shut my eyes for a while. The computer was a fink. "Ask the bastard what its excuse was for wiping Larry Rubashov."

Ahmed mumbled into his wrist radio and plugged one of the studs into his ear. "It says it never recommends wipe for that kind of thing, only for medical malfunctioning," he reported. "It's saying a lot about it."

I rolled on my face, burrowed my head against the pillow. "Tell me."

"Misfit social structure lacking adaptive activity outlets generates illness or apathy in the inferior and in the superior high-energy alpha it generates attack on social structures, or criminal violence. High-energy alpha misfits are necessary to progress, initiate the necessary social changes against the inertia of habit and the costs of change. Electronic wipe wipes the recorded pain behind social protest, thus partially heals the individual injury but leaves the general social malfunction. Wipe and other tranquilizers apply anesthesia to the spot where the shoe pinches and postpones the purchase of larger 'shoes' or updated social patterns. The wheel that squeaks gets the oil and should get oil, not soundproofing." Ahmed stopped talking abruptly and began to pace. I could hear him walking with abrupt impatient turns.

He said, "Since Larry got at the computer with his program for good English it talks too much. It searches literature for metaphors. No wonder people complain! It is now quoting the entire poem 'The Patriot' by Robert Browning. Do you want me to quote it?"

"No thanks. Ask what it thinks about me escaping from wipe?"

He muttered into the radio, then touched my shoulder and said in a low voice, "It says you did not escape from wipe. You have been subjected to voluntary personality restructuring and are now legally freed. You've been wiped." He was afraid his old friend George was gone, changed, missing.

That worried him but it did not worry me. I know where I'd been changed, and how. I opened my eyes and stared at

245

the sheet an inch from my nose. It was a felted fiber, like a big paper towel. "I'm not dead and neither are they. Ask it what would be the economic value of reporting to the police that I wiped all those people?"

Ahmed took a deep breath, standing over me. "Do you really want to ask that?"

"Yes."

He muttered into his wrist radio and waited. "It says that you can't be held legally responsible for doing something that's actually impossible."

I propped myself up on one elbow and looked at him. He was standing very stiffened up. He looked scared; he looked like a cop. He looked like a friend.

"I'm glad it said that," I said. "I've been pushed as far as I will push. If a regiment of cops came in here to arrest me I think I could tell them all to jump out of the window and they would all jump. I'm probably going to do a lot more impossible things."

Ahmed grew stiffer and more pale. "What part of you got wiped, George? Your conscience? Who are you planning to zap next?"

I sat up cross-legged in bed, feeling the draft from the back of the nightgown. Hospital nightgowns never reach all the way around the back. "Don't lean on me. Zapping those people was a mistake, an accident, an extra dividend. This is something better. Listen, Ahmed, it's something great. I've just discovered I can command people. It's a gift."

He looked over my head, his lips compressed, as if listening to a far sound. Ahmed has courage. He braced himself against death. I think he expected me to tell him to jump out the window. It's a high window. He looked back at me and sneered, disgusted. "A gift, sure, to a baby Hitler! Merry Christmas, George, Santa Claus just gave you a nice, shiny machine gun."

It hit. My guts hurt with loss. Christmas was taken back. Ahmed had done it. It hit. I yelled suddenly, "That's different! That's different! Shut up." I saw the fragments of the dreams as I denied them, pushed them away, tried to pretend I'd never wanted, never planned (not dreams, plans). Dreams of myself with a harem of the most likable girls in the world and I had commanded them all to be in love with me. I saw Ann's face, eyes wide and loving, and

246

her naked body as I pushed it away. Dreams of myself commanding armies, commanding the president of the UN, addressing vast obedient crowds. Power! Power dreams like the bastards I had wiped.

Ahmed had ruined all my dreams of power and glory. He was an alpha, a natural commander. He understood power. What's the difference if you order people around with telepathic hypnotism or with a machine gun? I saw the picture of the big bully twisting arms, making people obey. Me? Yes, me.

Ahmed was still more brilliant than I was. The flashlight of his mind shows up bugs in dark corners.

Ahmed was grinning with a kind of sympathy and gesturing messages silently in Indian sign language.

I remembered I had screamed at him. *"Shut up,"* I had screamed. He couldn't talk. He was not able to make a sound. It was frightening, as if I'd told my own brain to stop thinking.

"Go ahead and talk, Ahmed. Give me hell," I said. My guts were disappointed and hurting. Insides have greedy needs and dreams. He stopped gesturing weird Indian gestures and grinned.

I grinned back.

He said, "The definition of a reasonable man is someone who agrees with me. Have you had anything to eat recently?"

We ordered hospital room service and sat cross-legged one on each end of the bed and shared a big turkey dinner from the big snack tray between us. Turkey, cranberry, mashed potatoes. Thanksgiving.

"Why is a one-drawer bureau balanced on top of the toilet?" Ahmed asked. I looked into the bathroom. It was there. We both made an effort and didn't laugh.

He began to tell a joke. It was nice and quiet in the hospital room; the walls were a pinkish tan; but I remembered that I had forgotten to deal with that telepathy group on the mountain in California. Something had reminded me of them. Something odd.

Ahmed was still talking, but no sound was coming. Something was happening. A high-pitched whining noise rang in my head. Ahmed started to dissolve in spots of nothingness. He kept talking and gesturing silently. Patches of nothing-

247

ness appeared on the window and walls, growing bigger and merging into a blank world of spinning gray.

Slowly patches of something blue appeared spinning and expanding. Foggy blue sky and bright light. Pieces of people began to come together, sitting in a circle around me, men and women in long pastel robes, sitting on the grass. Off in the distance the sun sparkled low on the ocean through a golden haze of fog.

A pretty girl with red hair got up and came to me and hugged me.

"Welcome to California, George." The hug felt real. The wind was cool and damp and real. I looked around at these people sitting. Some were smiling at me, some serious. I liked them. They had been trying to get together with me all my life, and they had connected enough in my hallucinations so that I knew their faces. They had always been my friends.

But I knew what they wanted. They wanted to use my power of command. They wanted me to point my pretty new machine gun and pull the trigger.

They needed the same kind of kick in the pants Ahmed had given me. I straddled belligerently and frowned. "What the hell do you want?"

They stared. The meekest of them said, "You could help us end war. All you need to do is influence the leaders. We will put in a positive conditioning in their educational systems, make everybody want to obey laws, give them all a good feeling about right, eliminate all the differences of values they want to fight over."

"Peace is the cause of war," I said, just to be contrary. "People don't like peace." I was trying to think of a way to explain to them about power.

It hurts to have to give up power. They were offering me the world on a platter again, and I'd just already turned it down. Free power; everybody will love you, George, and you have the backing of the best planners. A whisper from memory said, *Get thee behind me, Shaitan.* Yes, behind me, where I couldn't see the goodies. I shouted, "What the hell gives you people the right to decide for the world?"

I like do-gooders. They are usually fine people with good vibes, but—*grok! Power over people;* they wanted it too. They began to get mad. The vibes made me feel madder and happier. The sorrow and temptation began to wash away in good red anger. They didn't understand what I was mad at, but they were feeling it back at me.

The redheaded girl touched my arm. "What happened to you? What's the matter? I know your soul. You have always been good, always obliging, nice, and kind."

The sea wind blew through my hospital nightgown across my bare back. What had happened to me? I usually would not have the guts to curse out a friendly meditating commune. I had changed. I was enjoying cursing them out. I was enjoying getting them mad.

I remembered Larry. Good thing that Larry had shown me how right someone can be when he is totally wrong. Good thing I met him first or I'd be picking the world like a juicy peach from a tree and thinking it was right. Good thing I'd met Weeny, that mangy cur dog, and seen how much he enjoyed being a cur. He was gone now, but he'd had his run. He'd lived his own way and paid a fair price. That flash that burned my brain had burned off the lid and let up everything I'd only half seen before. Grok evil, George. I had grokked. It was a game. Black chess pieces against white chess pieces.

"I got brainwiped today," I said. "They wiped Dr. Jekyll. I'm Mr. Hyde. What do you all want? Say it again."

They were getting to their feet, alerted and disturbed by the hassle. The oldest and most commanding said, "You know the answer, of course. We want you to help us." He had wavy hair and stood proudly like a king, like Akbar Hisham, king of hell.

"Say please," I said, and laughed.

They shuffled around in their pastel robes like a bunch of sulky angels or people in bathrobes after a shower. They couldn't say it. In spite of wanting to be humble, in spite of thinking of themselves as dedicated servants of the world good, they were not humble. Every one of them was an alpha, arrogant and bossy, and hiding it. They wanted to boss the world too. They wanted that harem I wanted. They had wanted a cat's-paw George, a respectful exploited George they could rescue and be nice and kind to. They wanted a good sweet guy who would pluck the world for them like their juicy peach and give it to them on a silver platter. I laughed at them.

"You want the world to do things the way you plan; you want the world on its knees. Say please, and get down on your knees, O designers of Utopia, O enlightened ones, O unascended masters of the secret of eternal goodness! If you kneel I might just do it for you." I waited.

They milled around, pushing each other forward and muttering to each other. No one kneeled. I laughed.

"You want to tell people what to do. If it's such a favor you're planning to do them, why don't you like taking orders?"

A moderate one in a pale green robe pushed forward from the crowd, his face wrinkled with the attempt to explain. "But we won't order them. We'll condition them to *want* to do it. They will think it is their *own* idea."

"They'll all have the *same* idea of right and wrong," said another, nodding.

"Harmony," said the leader. "It will be harmony and brotherhood."

"Twin brothers," I said. "Mass-produced people, all differences all covered up and hidden. No creation, no evolution. Evolution is, we're here to try our differences, enjoy our own thing, make it or fail our own way. The differences are what matters, but you won't let them have differences to argue over. Just mass-produced people with the same personality and philosophy. Your personality and philosophy. *Yours.*"

"It's a good personality and philosophy." The red-headed girl had retreated to the crowd of her friends, but she stepped forward defiantly. "My friends meditated on it. We've done research. We've contacted the greatest minds. We spent years. How many years have you spent thinking before you tell us we're wrong?"

"I went through hell to find out. I found out they have fun in hell. Maybe a person would be half happy living your way, doing your thing, for a lifetime, but he has only one lifetime and you want to make him live your lifetime instead of his own. You'd make them into saints. You'd take a man's chance to be himself. That's murder or robbery. You humble saints are trying to steal lives."

They glared back, good and angry, and their glares had power and wallop. They were masters or adepts or warlocks or something. Something with voltage.

250

I laughed. I wanted them angry. I could have commanded them to commit suicide and they would have done it. But I was not going to make them do anything. The sun was going down and reddening the sky above them. "I'm not the helper you want. The one you want is called Mr. Kracken. He lives in the 1949 Commune in New York City. You'll find him in the phone book. He's at least a century old and a master of good dirty politics. He'll tell you to go to hell. He'll tell you how to prevent a war between the Asteroid Belt and Earth by some great dirty trick. Kracken. Remember that name. It's spelled with a K. Where am I? What is this place?"

Most of them shut their mouths and glared. A fattish one answered in bored tones, "Monterey, California."

I said, "Send me back. Right now."

They didn't like being ordered. One of them raised an arm in a warlock's gesture to zap me with a bolt of lightning. I glared him down.

"I'm being polite," I said. "I'm not using my full powers to command you. I have more manners than you people do." I said, "You interrupted while I was listening to a friend tell a joke. I didn't hear the end of the joke. Send me back."

They looked at each other, feeling insulted, almost holding their breaths with rage, but I was no use to them standing on their mountain in the sunset cursing them. I was no use to their purposes. No one could think of a good reason to not send me back.

The older ones circulated among the group; they muttered comment; they shrugged; they nodded. They formed a circle, closed their eyes, and sent me back.

The procedure was interesting, involving a mixture of space, time, the fourth dimension, and sheer imagination.

I reappeared in New York standing on the hospital bed.

Ahmed was standing with his hand on the phone. I felt his shock. It shook the air. Careful not to disturb the rest of the turkey dinner on its tray, I climbed down to the floor and took my clothes from the closet. The air was hot. The walls were pink-tan and solid. Everything felt solid and good. New York. I was back in my city.

Ahmed said in a shaking voice, "I used the radio and asked the statistics computer where you were. It said you

251

were in the bathroom." He pointed to the bureau balanced on the toilet.

I stripped off the nightgown and got into my pants. "Ahmed, did I really vanish just then?"

Ahmed's shock was still ringing in the air like a deep silent gong, a vibration. "You ESP people are all freaks," he said, pale and swaying slightly like a tall post.

"How long was I in Monterey?" I pulled my shirt over my head.

"If I say I saw you vanish, I'd be crazy. And if I didn't see you vanish, you're crazy. Don't ask me what I saw, George," Ahmed said. He relaxed and palmed his eyes with both hands and began to breathe easily again. He tried to smile.

"Tell me the rest of that joke," I said, putting on my shoes.

Ahmed took the nightstand off the toilet and put it back in place. "What joke? You haven't done any work for Rescue Squad for three weeks. If you're all through appearing and disappearing, how about earning some money?" He was trying to get back on top, trying to be my boss again.

I stood up and looked at him eye to eye. I felt taller than Ahmed now, and somehow I wasn't mad at him anymore. Nothing he could say could put me down.

He scowled and backed off and bowed a great salaam. "O Commander of the Unfaithful, we have a job you can do. If you don't mind getting out of bed, my lord."

"What is it?"

Ahmed put his wrist radio back to his ear and asked and reported to me. "She's still alive. They have a teenager on a window ledge for four hours. She says she is going to kill herself. George, can you tell the little fool to come in off the window ledge and make her obey?"

"Yes."

"Come on, then."

Hurrying, we checked out of the hospital and went out into the hot, dry, crowded New York night. I love New York.

252